The Bondmaid

The Bondmaid

CATHERINE LIM

THE OVERLOOK PRESS
WOODSTOCK • NEW YORK

First published in the United States of America in 1997 by
The Overlook Press, Peter Mayer Publishers, Inc.
Lewis Hollow Road
Woodstock, New York 12498

Library of Congress Cataloging-in-Publication Data

Lim, Catherine.
  The bondmaid / Catherine Lim.
  p.   m.
  I. Title
PR9570.S53L473   1997   823—dc21   97-9908

Originally published in Singapore by Catherine Lim Publishing

BOOK DESIGN AND TYPE FORMATTING BY BERNARD SCHLEIFER

Manufactured in the United States of America
FIRST EDITION
9 8 7 6 5 4 3 2 1
ISBN 0-87951-790-5

To Jean and Peter

CONTENTS

PROLOGUE

IN THE LATER PART of 1992, the Singapore newspapers were full of reports of an old man who held a whole nation in thrall. He was the caretaker of a little dilapidated shrine on a small plot of land, fronting what is now the Kio San Thong Road, that stood in the way of a three-hundred-million dollar industrial development project: until he gave his signed permission, the bulldozers could not move in. It was reported that when the developers offered him compensation of several million dollars, he spat, cursed and chased them away.

The newspapers showed pictures of a tiny, wizened old man angrily shooing away the reporters and, on one occasion, using a long bamboo pole to hit a reporter taking pictures of the shrine and the small wooden hut adjoining it. There was a story, never properly pieced together, of a young woman who had died there under the most tragic circumstances, sometime in the middle 1950s, and was later seen in the vicinity by many people. They erected a shrine to her and, for some reason, called her "Goddess with Eyes and Ears." The old caretaker was said to be connected with her in some way—a brother? a friend? a lover?

One evening, the old man's hut caught fire. By the time he was pulled out, he was already dead.

The developers arranged for a team of monks to conduct elaborate ceremonies of appeasement at the shrine. Then the bulldozers moved in. Today, a huge petrochemical complex stands where once the strange goddess with eyes and ears dispensed miracles.

PART ONE

Child

I

THE CHILD HAN was about to be taken away.

Just now, in the darkness of dawn, she lay asleep with her five brothers and sisters on the large plank bed, in an enormous entanglement of arms, legs, pillows, bolsters and small possessions impossible to unclutch even in sleep—a bright pink plastic doll wedged between her left cheek and Oldest Brother's right buttock, a blue caterpillar that had wound its way to Little Sister's toes and stuck there, Little Sister's rubber teat, sucked thin, flat and dry, fallen from her mouth but not from its string around her neck.

But no matter; they slept soundly on. They had begun the night neatly enough. They had each lain down in their assigned places on the bed, taking care to curl up their legs and make the necessary adjustments in sleeping positions to fit into the curves of each other's bodies so that there would be place for all. Oldest Brother, ever the buffoon, had assumed a mien of severest censure and shrieked, "Remember, *phoo-oot* time's over!", meaning that they should all have done their farting for the night; the one whose face was farted into had right of reciprocal action.

They had, moreover, abided by the strict rules of the rotational sharing of the three pillows and two bolsters; that day being a Wednesday, it was the three oldest ones' turn. But in the course of sleep, they had all moved outside their allotted territory and had engaged in either defensive or attacking moves in relation to the much coveted pillows and bolsters, so that by morning all had come together in this untidy, indistinguishable heap. The child Han, the youngest, lay on top of the heap, victoriously clutching a blue bolster, one small fist thrust into the cheek of an older brother who, in turn, had a leg draped over a sister's shoulder.

The bed bore all the distressing signs of overpopulation. It creaked and sagged; its mattress, stuffed with coconut fibers, had burst under the continuous pressure of six pairs of stomping feet in play, releasing little tufts of stiff hairs that poked out and chafed young skins. The mother's mending needle had tried to poke them back in, but to no avail. Polluted beyond saving by its endless absorption of the night's detritus of urine, sweat, saliva and hot dreams, the mattress swelled with the growth of a whole parasitic colony, hidden deep in its many folds, invisible to the eye. In the dead of night, the bedbugs came out in hordes and attacked the sleeping children, twisting arms, legs and thighs in a convulsion of scratching. A thin child looked fat, a pale child rosy, from the bites.

Bedbugs never bit those from whose bodies they had spontaneously arisen. The children blamed their presence in the mattress on an old, obese, flatulent neighbor who lived next door and who slept peacefully every night of her life while her bugs, created to her corpulent image, marched outwards, like an invading army, and ravaged other bodies in the village.

Revenge was particularly sweet when, under the creative leadership of Oldest Brother, the children mounted a counterattack, digging the enemy out with their mother's hairpins and subjecting them to a slow death in a saucer filled with kerosene. Otherwise, death was by the simple process of squelching, the innumerable brown stains all over the mattress testifying to their rich squelchiness. Afterwards the children thrust victorious thumbs or forefingers under each other's noses and laughed to see the spluttering recoil from bug-smell.

They did it to their mother sometimes and laughed when she slapped down the offending finger. But not to the father. In his absence, his space beside their mother's on the other bed in the house, which had a cotton, not a coconut fiber, mattress, and a pillow of its own, ought to have been seized upon; indeed, on a few occasions, in the middle of the night, a child, tearful from too many bug bites or the feel of spreading wet underneath, had wandered into the parents' room and climbed up into that free space.

The mother had warned, "Make sure you don't kick me," by way of protecting the unborn child in her now fearfully swollen belly. Unborn children too jostled for bed-space, amniotically safe against the knocking and buffeting from unruly sibling limbs in sleep. But not always against the invasive fumes of raw opium or the spasms induced by young pineapple taken with beer, or the pummelings of determined fists. The mother had tried the entire despairing range and had come home in a trishaw, pale and beginning to bleed, from the abortionist's house at the far end of the village. Still the child would not be dislodged and continued its robust kicking. The abortionist said it had never happened before; mostly, the little things fell out after the first pellet of opium, without aid of pineapple or beer. Truly, this was Sky God's sign that the child should be allowed to live.

"Don't kick me," she warned the children. But they preferred to remain together on their own bed. They feared their father and, by extension, his bed. He came home seldom and went into a roaring temper if he prepared for sleep and suddenly caught the smell of dried urine in his nostrils which would twitch menacingly as he bent to sniff his mattress and then flare with vengeful anger as he rose and roared for the culprit.

Only two of the six children bed-wetted, but he punished all. He liked to punish his children in a group, his large knuckles descending ripplingly upon a sea of small heads, or his thick belt, ripped from his waist, lashing at a forest of skipping legs. But mostly he made them range themselves in order of age in a row before him, as he sat by the table, in his white singlet and pajama trousers, drinking his beer. The warmth of Guinness

Stout suffused his whole body, relaxed it and settled it lugubriously in the chair, draping his long arms over the sides. Deceptive warmth: without warning, it distilled itself into a tight knot of pure malignant energy in the man's right fist, making it shoot out suddenly, in a tremendous roar, pulling the rest of the body up bolt upright. The father was now wide awake once more. He glared at the row of small frightened faces in front of him and one by one, they moved up to meet his raised fist.

Not solidarity alone, but total dependence on each other for solace prevented each child, after the impact, from running away with the red cheek bruise and the hot tears; instead he or she stepped out and waited patiently by the side as the next, and the next moved up, until the row at last came to an end, and they could all come together and run in a body to their bed, scramble up, huddle together and set up the much delayed but perfectly harmonized howl of grievance and hurt.

The mother had, on one occasion, appeared later, after the father left the house, with a plate of bread sprinkled generously with sugar and a bottle of F & N Orange Crush, uncapped to yield exactly six equal portions, to comfort the children and unhuddle them.

In his time, the father too had stood, trembling, in punitive assembly with his siblings, and his father before him, in a long tradition of that cruelty, not just of parents, but of deities and gods themselves in their temples and river shrines, which sees fit to visit upon all the sins of one.

Once the child Han saved all of them. They were as usual ranged before the father sitting at the table, his beer before him. The mother stood at the kitchen doorway, looking on dully.

Oldest Brother stepped forward, his face in taut and quivering readiness to meet the impact of the strong hand always made stronger by drink, but the child Han struck first. She broke off from her position at the end of the row, ran to her father, stood before him, then began a comical little dance—a similar one had earned her two biscuits from a smiling neighbor only the week before.

She had picked it up from somewhere and knew its movements perfectly, swaying her hips, clapping her hands and providing her own accompaniment in a clear, shrill treble:

The bird looks
The bee cries
The ants yearn
For my little flower
My sweet little opening flower.

She finished with a bold rump waggle and a flawless imitation of the coquette's classic fluttering eyelash peep from behind a fan. The rest of the children tittered and glanced nervously at the father. The man whose stream of drunken energy had been stopped midway by the sudden approach of the child and had subsided into a vague, slurred murmuring for the entire duration of the dance, seemed not amused and stared at her.

"Eh?" he said as the child suddenly rushed forward, climbed up on his knee, kissed him wetly on the cheek and said, with the artfullest winsomeness of any four-year old, "You are my father and I love you very much."

The man said, "Eh?" again and gazed with frowning melancholy upon the little girl who kept her arms resolutely around his neck. He repeated, thickly and stupidly, her words of endearment, then his brutality collapsed inwards into a soft center and dissolved in a puddle of tears. The huge man blubbered about the sadness of his life and rubbed his eyes with a fist.

"Don't cry, Father," said the artful one, glowing in the triumph of the massive rescue.

The man was capable of much generosity to his wife and children. On those days when he came home in a good mood, with money in his pockets, he liked to enter the house roaring, pull out an impressive wad of notes, stuff it down his wife's blouse or collar and watch her pull it out and count it in tremulous joy. With the same buoyancy, he scooped coins out of his pockets and rained them upon his children's upturned palms, laughing to see them go down excitedly on all fours to retrieve missing coins from under cupboards and feet.

"Come get it." The perverse man had the idea to wedge a large coin between his buttocks; the jollity of drink and sudden fortune made him indulge in horseplay of the most childish kind, the idea being to let out a tremendous fart at the moment of the coin's retrieval.

His wife shook her head at the man's inanity.

"Siau, siau," she muttered but was thankful for that wad of notes that would enable her to go to the provisions shop to settle old debts, replenish her supply of Tiger Balm for rubbing on the constantly throbbing temples, and try her luck in the village lottery on numbers based on the date and time of her husband's largesse or on the number of times the child inside had kicked or turned.

The father had an enormous tattoo of a black-faced demon-warrior on his right arm. The tattoo maker had pricked in a grotesquerie of horns, fangs and coiled snakes which uncoiled and danced to the rhythm of moving muscles. The father liked to push up his sleeve, flex his arm and invite his children to come and watch, laughing in great merriment to see them break into a screaming, giggling run for their bed.

Sometimes he liked to gather his children around him to tell them stories.

Long, long ago, it was the men who bled every month, not the women. The men obviously could not use the cloth pads worn by the women but protected their penises with long bamboo shields. These proved very inconvenient in their work of ploughing, sowing and harvesting. So they begged Sky God to take away the inconvenience and give it to the women instead. Sky God pitied them and granted their request.

"Siau, siau," muttered his wife. "Telling such stories to children."

His wife cursed him, but never in his presence.

"Sky God, bless my husband with good health
Sky God, bless my husband with prosperity
Sky God, bless my husband with good behavior."

Every morning she lit a joss-stick to the great god who manifested himself in fiery rumbles of thunder and lightning across the skies, which children were taught to greet with soft reverential *'pup pup'* noises with their lips, to catch some of this sweeping divine energy. The energy was also in the god's huge staring eyes, the immense streams of black hair and beard, the sunburst of gleaming victorious spears on his back, and most of all, the mighty feet laid on a heap of crushed, yowling demons, as he sat, legs wide apart, on his golden throne and received the obeisance of a thousand worshippers.

The god might consider it presumptuous of her to hitch three major requests to one little joss-stick with its pathetic wisp of smoke when he was used to billowing clouds from a hundred golden temple urns. But he had only himself to blame for the continuing meagerness of her offerings: if he was omnipotent, why had he not changed her husband's fortunes or character?

"Sky God has no eyes nor ears."

Even gods had to be reminded of their remissness, in her case, of an unconscionably prolonged blindness and deafness to her pleas. From her marriage at sixteen, she had lit joss-sticks and never known a day of peace or happiness.

Oldest Brother was the one to peep through a narrow slit in the plank wall of their parents' bedroom and signal to the others, by a quick wave of the hand, to come and watch too.

They watched, six faces pressed against the slits in the planks. The child Han, not seeing anything and determined always to have her share of spoils, clamored to be held up and was clapped on the mouth by Oldest Brother.

Later they discussed what the heaving and thrusting movements meant. Oldest Brother who was nine said he knew what it was all about and duly demonstrated, guffawing, with a few thrusts of his own thin hips inside flapping khaki shorts. That was how babies were made, he said, and by way of further demonstration, he made a circle with the thumb and forefinger of his left hand and thrust the forefinger of his right through it repeatedly. The others followed and for some minutes there was a lively competition to see who could go fastest, until their mother, hearing their screaming laughter and rushing in to see a frenzy of finger pistons, descended upon them, yelling, "Don't ever let me catch you do that again!" But Oldest Brother, through the wisdom of his clowning, had enlightened the rest by drawing for them the indisputable link between their father's panting exertions each time he came home and the subsequent swelling of their mother's belly.

Indeed, the father's rare visits home and the mother's regular manifestations of those rare visits had combined to offer an example of unparalleled fecundity even in that village of fecund women, where every gathering, at the water pump, market stalls or provisions shop, invariably threw up a clutch of rounding bellies in varying stages of roundedness.

The mother's belly, large, smooth and firm as a melon, pulling up her cotton trousers from ankle to mid-calf, was the most familiar sight and drew light-hearted analogies.

"*Pok*," the neighbors teased. "Why, you go *pok* every year!", in perfect imitation of the sharp exploding sound of the ripened rubber seed-pod when it burst and scattered the hard, smooth brown seeds that children liked to pick up and play with. It was inappropriate to make comments to children about their mother's condition, but the loudest and idlest of the neighbors, chewing a piece of sugarcane and watching the children walk by on their way to the village shop, stopped them, crudely poked out her stomach and flung out playful arms to encircle a huge space of air in front. The children said nothing and walked on sullenly. The woman shouted, "Why are you always together? Can't you do anything separately? Why, you even shit together!" For the story, told by the mother herself in a rare mood of jocularity, was that all her children feared darkness and never ventured alone at night to the toilet outside the house. They woke each other up and went in a body, one lit candle among them. The small wooden outhouse on stilts proved too small for six jostling bodies; one fell into the bucket below and was hauled up screaming. The mother who was seldom in the mood for laughter had provoked gales of merriment describing how she depleted the village well cleaning up the little fool.

The neighbors joked about the pregnancies but never about the births which were squalid and pitiful, invariably taking place in the absence of the father who could never be found and brought home. Each baby, in its turn, had tumbled on to a heap of donated torn towels and sarongs and thereafter gone on to depend on donated milk powder and swaddling clothes which came in a steady stream of neighborly generosity.

The midwife who would have liked to give her services free but could not as her livelihood depended on them, was nevertheless kind enough to make the rounds of the neighborhood to secure the needed baby things. Even the rough sugarcane woman came with strips of a bedsheet and a bowl of nourishing herbal brew.

"They simply refuse to come out, not even with three pellets of opium," said the awe-stricken midwife who was also an abortionist. "So she will go on having babies. Who can go against Sky God's will?"

The mother, all the while, lay white and helpless, her eyes bright with unshed tears. Only one of the babies had been lucky: a computation based on the day and hour of the birth had provided a winning lottery number and brought in a small sum of money. She had had two more babies after the child Han, and she gave both away for adoption; they were girl babies, anyway.

This cold, dark morning, pregnant yet again, she lay on her bed, wide awake, staring into the darkness, while her children slept soundly in the next room in harmonious disorder of bodies.

Outside, the old bald village rooster began to crow. It crowed

its poor old heart out each dawn in its two-fold duty of banishing the night's ghosts and waking up the still living. A cemetery
lay outside the village. The rooster broke up trysting ghost lovers
and sent them back weeping into their tombs; it disrupted
seances at graves and left transactions uncompleted, for the
vaporous forms of the dead, pushing their way up through the
hollows of the bamboo stakes driven deep into their graves by
the hopeful living, had to stop halfway and go down again.

The night soil man saw a female ghost. Up long before anyone in the village, with his large collecting buckets strung at each
end of the long pole across his shoulder, he froze as the shape
loomed before him. He saw a woman in a long white dress,
swaying in front of him, an immense curtain of hair pulled over
her face, which she slowly parted with both hands as she came
closer to peer into his face. He shouted, ran and fell, dropping his
buckets which splashed over a wide area of ground so that for
days the village reeked of the evidence of the ghostly encounter.
Some said she was a young woman who had been raped and
killed by Japanese soldiers during the Occupation, some that she
was the crazy woman who had killed her child, then run screaming under a full moon to jump into a well. A little jar of joss-sticks
and a plate of oranges and flowers later appeared on the spot
where the night soil man had seen her.

Children passing the cemetery on their way to the town
quickly pressed their palms together and moved them rapidly
up and down in prayerful contrition and supplication. The contrition was for any inadvertent offense, for spirits were known to
reside in grassy mounds or tree trunks that children might heedlessly step or urinate on; the supplication was for fathers to make
money, for death conferred upon even the humblest man or
woman the power to give winning lottery numbers in dreams.
A servant boy, imbecile and mute, a grandson of the flatulent,
bedbug-generating old woman, was killed by a falling rubber
tree and thereafter dispensed wealth through such lucky dream
numbers. He asked in return for only a meal of suckling pig and

roast fowl, and was given all he could eat—for days his grave was suffused with the delicious aroma of a dozen sizzling meats. His grandmother, pleased beyond words, was given some of the food to take home. Parents also taught children not to say anything should they smell mysterious flower scents in the air. Tight-lipped, grave-faced, the children walked on, avoiding the sight of the rows of granite and marble slabs rising out of the tall stiff grass, with their remains of food, tea and joss-stick offerings rotting into the earth.

Only the rooster was unafraid; it cleared the way for the living each day by sternly dispatching the dead back to their abodes. Its call was a lonely, persistent one, always ending with a cry, very like a human sob that hung tremblingly for a long time upon the cold morning air. After the last ghost had fled and the first lights appeared in kitchens, the old faithful heart gave out, and the rooster keeled over and died. But it had already set in motion the reassuring sounds of life's continuity—the chopping of firewood in readiness for the day's meals, the barking of a dog, the fitful crying of a baby. Of life's endurance too: for somewhere, the wracked coughing of the consumptive widow determined to stay alive for her crippled son floated out to swell the dawn's affirmation of hope.

The children slept through the noise and death. The mother got up, pale and trembling, threw a towel around her shoulders and walked out of the house to where Sky God's urn stood on the ground. The remnants of joss-stick stood forlornly in the ash, sending no more smoke up to heaven. Beside it was a little saucer of decaying pink balsam petals.

Years ago, her widowed mother, who took in mountains of washing everyday to support eight children, so that the skin of her hands hardened, cracked and bled, had said, "Sky God has ears and eyes," not as a statement of truth but of hope. "Who will dare deny that Sky God has the largest ears, the brightest eyes?" Gods too were susceptible to flattery and lapped up praise like children.

23

The wretched woman had died in the full conviction that all those who had contributed to her sufferings, including an evil-hearted sister-in-law, would in due time receive divine retribution.

Her mother was a fool. She would not be like her mother.

With one deft toe, she tipped over the urn and spilled the joss-sticks and ash. She spat into the ash. Then she turned and walked back into the house, in final renunciation of a hopelessly inept god that women had cried to from time immemorial.

Now it was time for the child Han to be taken away.

The mother went to the children's room and made straight for the bed and the child. Extricating her from the heap, she pulled her up to a sitting position, bent down and whispered urgently, "Get up. We have to leave soon." The child, her eyes closed, swayed in the heaviness of sleep, then fell back and was once more absorbed into the warmly breathing heap, safe against the terrors of the coming day. The mother yanked her up by the armpits and lifted her off the bed and on to the floor. She stood unsteadily, then her legs gave way and she went noiselessly down on the floor where she would have continued sleeping if her mother had not hurriedly pulled her up and carried her out of the room, her head lolling, her legs astride the enormous melon of a belly. "I say get up; we've a lot of things to do," said the woman, keeping her voice low so as not to wake the others.

She set the child on her feet in the kitchen and dealt a few sharp taps on her cheeks to wake her up. The child murmured and opened her eyes sleepily.

"Take off your clothes," she ordered. She went outside, in the darkness, to the well, drew up a large bucket of water and returned to find the child still fully clothed and rubbing her eyes with her fists.

"Bad child, I told you to take off your clothes," muttered the woman. She squatted down and began to unbutton the blouse and loosen the strings of the trousers. The child, her eyes half-closed, her hands grasping her mother's shoulders, lifted one leg, then the other, to step out of the trousers. Her mother dipped a piece of cloth into the bucket of water and began to clean her face, neck, body, downwards to the small spaces between her toes. The touch of the wet rag woke up the child at last; she looked around in bewilderment, puckered her face and began to cry.

"Sssh, sssh," said the mother in a fierce whisper. She dried the child hurriedly with a small towel, then began to dress her. The clothes had been laid out on a chair the night before. They were new clothes, such as were given out only for wearing on the first day of the New Year. The child knew it was not the New Year, but the morning's confusion was too much for the asking of questions, so she was silent, obediently stretching out an arm to put into a sleeve or lifting a leg to put into the trousers, as her mother ordered. It was a bright red cotton suit with pretty yellow frog buttons, and it made the child, with her round, shiny, four-year-old face and large dark eyes, look like a doll.

The mother took a step backwards and surveyed her.

"They'll say you're too thin and pale," she muttered. She went to a small cupboard in a corner and brought out a quilted cotton jacket. It was several sizes too big for the child but it had the desired effect of adding some bulk to her small frame. "Wait," said the mother, still not satisfied, and she went to the ancestral altar at the other end of the room. No urn of regard and remembrance stood before the ancestor whose framed photograph hung overhead, draped with wisps of cobwebs. The woman wanted no more traffic with gods and ancestors; her business was with the living. She searched among the jumble of objects on the altar turned utility shelf, pushing aside combs, hairpins, powder boxes and buttons to pull out what she wanted—the bright red wrapping paper that the joss-sticks had come in, saved for an occasion such as this. She tore off a piece and moistened it on her tongue. Then she returned to her daughter and rubbed the moistened piece on the child's cheeks. Two spots of color appeared, making the child more doll-like than ever. The woman again stepped backwards for another quick look. Something else was missing—the child had no shoes.

She looked around for shoes. She found a pair but they were too small. Then she saw a pair of rubber slippers under a cupboard and dived for them. They were, like the quilted jacket, several sizes too big for the child but they would do. She found a piece of pink ribbon, worked it into a dainty butterfly and pinned it to the child's hair. The entire exercise was now completed. The child Han was ready. "You must eat something and then we should start out. We don't want to be late."

It was at this point that the child's sullen perplexity cleared for a look of understanding which lit up into pure joy. The transformation filled out her cheeks, brightened her eyes, irradiated her skin. She was a child of heartbreaking beauty. "Oh Mama, I want the Peanut Balls and the Sugar Man and the Rainbow Sticks and the Green Melon Monkey," she cried excitedly, in vivid recollection of the mother's promise the day before.

The mother's impatience gathered into a bursting knot of exasperation at so much nonsensical talk in the midst of such serious business, then checked itself. It subsided into the sheepishness that mothers need not feel if they were only tricking their children into going to school or the dentist. Years later, recounting the incident in the calm of a ravaged life coming to its close, the mother, by way of self reproach, spoke of the remorse that even a cow innocently following its keeper to the slaughterhouse might excite.

"But at that time I felt nothing," she said sorrowfully. "I had too many troubles and I felt nothing." Which was not exactly true, for as she adjusted the butterfly ribbon and quilted jacket, she was heavy with the deception and blinked back tears.

She fed the child a bowl of rice porridge with an egg inside. The child was not used to being given eggs; these were only for special occasions such as birthdays or the New Year or illness, but all questions were forgotten in the mounting excitement of the promised visit to the town's biggest sweet shop.

"I want Fat Man's Buttocks and Pig's Arse and—"

The names had been their own, spontaneously generated as they stood in a row gazing wistfully at the large glass jars of sweets in the village shop. Oldest Brother had pointed to a sweet of a strange pinkish color and crinkly appearance and immediately named it 'Pig's Arse', slapping his thighs in great enjoyment at his own joke. The scatological cue was quickly taken up by the others in a joyous wave of name-giving—'Old Woman's Shit', 'Dog's Penis', 'Monkey's Balls'. The sweet shop owner came out and shooed them off. The child Han, recollecting the provocative power of the finger-piston sign, aimed it at the man. He gave a loud yell and made a dash for her; they scampered off, out of his reach.   By themselves they laughed uproariously, the child basking in the warm glow of Oldest Brother's praise. The naming had tamed the yearning.

"Alright, alright," said the woman. "Don't talk so much. Eat."

When the child had swallowed the last spoonful, the mother wiped her mouth carefully and gave her some water to drink. "Now we must leave," she said. "We have a long walk."

She stood before the round mirror hanging on the kitchen wall and did a quick survey of her own appearance. Each pregnancy stripped her of more flesh, robbed her of more teeth. Only her two gold fixtures stood intact in a dereliction of rotting brown stumps. All her babies were born healthy and good-sized; only she wasted away.

I am not yet thirty and I look like an old woman, she thought.

Sixteen had marked the end of beauty and glow. She had been the most beautiful girl in her village. A man who owned a rubber plantation and was driven around in a car wanted her and asked her mother. She, fool that she was, ran away with another man, a wastrel who made her pregnant every year and left no money for the children's food or clothes. She later learnt that the rich man's concubine, a girl from the same village and without half her beauty, was installed in a house of her own and wore gold bangles that stacked right up to her elbows and gold chains thick as ropes.

She would have one more child after this one and learn the news, as she lay beside her swaddled newborn, that her husband, away in a town on a job that he never talked about, had been killed by a fellow worker over a woman. His body had been found in a remote coconut plantation, the face smashed in, all the features horribly erased. There was one more discovery: his genitals had been found some distance from the body, cut off in a brutal bunch and flung off, in a clear message that the man's punishment for messing around with other men's women was not for this world only, but also the next, where dismembered male ghosts forever howled out their solitude. His wife had wept, then risen and said, with the bitterest of laughs, "He does have eyes and ears!" referring not to the dead husband but the repudiated god. By that time, the child Han was lost to her forever. But she never minded. She knew what she was about.

That morning she took the child, pretty and dainty in the red suit and pink ribbon, and was about to lead her out of the house when the other children appeared, one by one, roused from sleep by all the talk and noise. In later years, they too would leave their home. The departure of the child Han and their mother's subsequent decline into hopeless addiction to the town's gambling parlors, brought a creeping fatalism so that some years after the father's death took place, the break-up was complete: Oldest Brother had run away to nobody knew where and the rest had been given away in adoption, gone into pitiful employment as servants or cleaners in eating houses or simply vanished.

But on that day, they were still together, and they gathered to watch their mother and sister leave the house. The older ones immediately spotted their appropriated possessions and raised a cry of protest.

"She's wearing my jacket!"

"Those are my slippers! Give me back my slippers!"

They made to retrieve their property and their mother silenced them by dealing cuffs and slaps all round.

The child Han who had been bursting to share the good news, now proclaimed with exuberant magnanimity, "Never mind, Oldest Brother, Older Sister. I will give you back your things when I come back. And I will share my sweets with you. You can have a Peanut Ball each—"

"Peanut Ball! My balls!" yelped Oldest Brother derisively. "What an idiot you are—."

"That's enough!" cried the woman sharply and she turned to the boy and slapped him across the mouth. "You mind your own business!"

To the others she said, with no softening in tone, "And the rest of you, behave. If you are good, I will buy you some noodles!" Undeterred, Oldest Brother began to act the buffoon, contorting his body, grimacing horribly and mouthing words silently. The child Han laughed in delight, clapping a hand to her mouth. The mother aimed another slap at the boy, missed and finally dragged the child out of the house.

She walked briskly, despite the huge belly; the child shuffled clumsily, impeded by the oversized slippers and the frequent need to turn around and look at her siblings clustered at the doorway, watching her departure.

"Whatever's the matter? Can't you walk faster? I told you we have a long way to go!" the woman cried with weary impatience.

The child suddenly stopped. She turned and faced the small crowd at the doorway, now separated from her by an immeasurable distance. Her little face was aglow with eager joy.

"Wait till I come back!" she shouted to them. "I'll bring back lots, I promise!"

She wanted to demonstrate the actual size of the promise, for which she would need both hands. So she pulled her hand out of her mother's, freeing it to join the other in describing an enormous, wondrous arc in the air.

"What are you doing?" cried the mother. She wanted the deed over and done with quickly and here was the child causing all the delays.

The child obediently put her hand back in her mother's and together they resumed their walking.

It was the mother's turn to stop. She looked at the child in sad contrition for what she was about to do.

"You were a special baby, you came out legs first," she said, touching the child's cheek sorrowfully. Babies who came out legs first, against the natural order, were either very bright or very stupid. "You will be clever enough to take care of yourself; Oldest Brother will be a useless duffer all his life." It was a sharing of confidences, not so much with the child who looked up at her in round eyed puzzlement, as with the myriad spirits in the air who supposedly loved and protected children, in the hope that they would understand and forgive.

There was a small stone shrine on a grassy verge by the road that she spotted and walked briskly to. The vengeful anger of some gods might be canceled out by the goodwill of others, and so the woman, bowing her head and pressing her palms together, made ready to secure the goodwill of the tiny deity inside before she realized, with a start, that it was a deity of another people, having an elephant's face and three pairs of purple arms. Nevertheless, she completed her prayer and returned to the child watching her from the road.

The child said "Mama" and pointed to her discomfort.

"I told you to do it at home," said the woman impatiently. She took the child to a spot as far away from the shrine as she could, out of respect, and afterwards cleaned her with some dried leaves.

In the later years, when she was a young woman, the memory of that day, her last with her family, would fill her most pensive moments. She could remember, in every vividness of detail, the yanking up from the warm bed, the splash of cold water, the brushing against her face and body of that round hard belly and those work-roughened hands. But she chose to cast all these aside. She invested the memory instead, with tender grace, festooning it with the specially cooked porridge-with-egg, the pretty new clothes, the siblings gathered to say goodbye, the golden arc of her promise.

II

THE CHILD HAN AND HER mother stood before the huge mansion, with its enormous green pillars, its curving red roof, its two ferocious stone lions guarding the entrance. The child had never seen anything so magnificent. Clutching her mother's hand tightly, she did a quick mental revision of the sweet shop, for later telling at home. She had thought it to be like the village shop, but ten times bigger. It was totally different and one hundred times bigger. The child carefully took in the details of the wondrous roof, like a temple's—her arms went up in anticipatory curves in the air—and the angry expression on the lions' faces—her face contorted in a fair imitation of the ferocity. Such a splendid exterior bespoke a magical interior, and the child tugged excitedly at her mother's hand and repeated, as she had done several times in the course of their walk, the names of her favorite sweets.

The mother looked down at her small upturned face and was suddenly galvanized into another bout of feverish activity to improve her appearance. She bent down and her hands flew to smooth and adjust hair, clothes, slippers. The butterfly ribbon had dropped off along the way; the coloring on the cheeks from the joss-stick paper had disappeared. The mother shook her head and made small vexed sounds. She laid a forefinger on her tongue, wetted it and applied it vigorously on the child's chin to remove a small smudge there. Remembering something, she squatted down and checked the child's trousers for smell or stain. The child was fine there, but the nose had begun to dribble, so she quickly pulled out a handkerchief and wiped it.

The mother's agitation grew. She said to the child with a

shrill intensity in her voice, "You must be very polite to the lady in the house. You must not touch anything. You must not behave badly."

The child was puzzled but said, "Yes, Mother."

"Be polite, say 'Good morning' to the lady," continued the mother. "Don't touch or break anything as the grand lady will be very angry."

"Yes, Mother. Mother, can I have the—"

"Remember what I told you. We'll go in now."

The child saw a small yellow horse on the ground, lying on its side and immediately darted forward to pick it up. Near it was another, a red one, and a little distance away, yet another, a blue. Some rich child in the mansion, replete with toys, had flung out a redundant rainbow stable.

The child Han fell upon them with delight.

"This one's for Older Brother, and this one—"

"What's that? Stop!" shrieked the mother. She made the child drop all the horses back to the ground.

"Do you want to be called a thief as well?"

The mother's peevishness that morning was now too much for the child. Her face reddened and two huge tears glistened in her eyes, then rolled silently down her cheeks. Slowly she turned and fixed her eyes, unblinkingly, reproachfully, on her mother's.

"Don't look at me like that!"

The child's silent reproach was worse than any screaming defiance.

"Don't look at me like that. I'm your mother."

The mother wanted her last act, before they finally entered the mansion, to be a kind one. She removed something from her wrist and put it round the child's. It was a bracelet of braided red thread, through which was threaded a solitary piece of jade. The piece was roughly carved to yield the features of Sky God. Sky God, omnipotent deity, could yet be enclosed in small pieces of protective jewelry for wearing on chests and wrists. It was her first and last gift to the child. She adjusted the size to fit the small wrist. The child looked on indifferently.

"Bad Mama. Your mother's bad, bad, yes?" said the woman. "Come, beat Mama. Here's Mama's hand, see? Come, beat."

The reversal of roles that would have children pounding away at their parents with their small fists and the parents breaking out in exaggerated cries of pain and shoots of tears was an unfailing grown-up ploy to restore goodwill. But the child Han turned her face away and the mother gave up.

III

THERE WAS INDEED A rich child in the mansion, but just now the richness was only in the multitude of toys and possessions around him from which, in a fit of piqued boredom, he had detached some colorful horses and flung them out of the window. He had moreover stomped on and dented the handsome painted horse carriage and decapitated a wooden goose. A round-bellied old man and his dancing monkey suffered a lesser fate, having been merely thrown into a corner and left in a heap there, and a row of red-cheeked, golden-haired miniature men and women in European folk-dress, standing on a high shelf, suffered not at all.

The show of temper over, the little boy flung himself upon his large bed with the silken hangings and went to sleep. Or pretended to. His delight was to close his eyelids tightly and freeze his limbs into perfect immobility for hours to frighten his bondmaid.

"Oh, whatever shall I do? Our little master Wu is dead! How can I tell his grandmother and grandfather? They will kill me with a sword!"

The bondmaid Lan whose sole duty in the huge house was to attend to the child had, for his amusement, killed herself off in the most horrendous way. She had so far been stabbed with

33

knives, hung by her hair from the ceiling, dunked into a cauldron of boiling oil, dunked into a barrel of pickled pig's entrails, thrown into a pit of red ants the size of rats, eaten alive by a wild man in a jungle. She would then watch the little boy's face for the reluctant smile to appear around the corners of the determinedly clamped mouth, and sigh when it came at last, signaling the end of a tantrum. That evening the mouth remained relentlessly rigid.

The bondmaid gave up and began to pick up the scattered toys on the floor and return them to their places on shelves inside glass cabinets. His grandparents and relatives brought toys that spilled into an adjoining room: it was remarkable how the little boy, while examining a gleaming motor-car or fire-engine or warrior-god whose enormous belly dispensed peanuts, could drop it and concentrate his attention on a blue-bottle on the wall or move to the window to watch the ragged village children below, kicking a coconut husk.

"I want Spitface."

It was part of the boy's perverseness to ask for Spitface at a time when the man was probably already asleep in the woodshed or wandering idiotically somewhere in the town. The bondmaid said, "Master Wu is such a good boy, Master Wu mustn't—"

She looked round the room for inspiration and saw on a shelf a row of jars of candied almonds, ginger and plums that had been brought as a gift by an effusive relative because the boy had happened to show a liking for them during a visit. The maid said, "Hey, look at these lovely candies! Why, you have a sweet-shop in your room! Now, which little boy in the whole of this town can say he has a sweet-shop in his room? Would you like an Almond Lady or a Ginger Dog?" Her voice rose in eager appeal.

"I want to see Spitface."

"Oh, our master Wu is such a good little boy. He mustn't—"

She saw the boy's face redden and expand in preparation for a mighty roar and fled to locate Spitface.

Fortunately, he was asleep in the woodshed, at the back of the house. The maid shook him violently to rouse him from his deep, snoring stupor. The man rose groggily from his sleeping mat and was dragged off to appear before the boy.

Thus named for the grotesqueness of his appearance which made dogs bark and children spit at him, he was part of the village debris that occasionally washed up on rich houses and stayed. He chopped firewood and ran errands for his meals and sleeping space in the woodshed, received new clothes and sandals during the New Year and made it possible for the bondmaids, if they silently cursed Sky God for their lowly positions, to reflect that there were others lowlier still.

In the boy's presence, Spitface shook off sleep and grinned. Falling into his role immediately, he fell to the floor on all fours, gesturing the offer of a ride on his back which he knew the boy enjoyed, his wild tufts of hair, ragged clothes and thick, knobby limbs giving him the aspect of some friendly beast of burden.

The boy, his command so quickly complied with, as quickly lost interest, turned his fine handsome young face away and indicated he wanted to sleep.

"I want *Chor Kong Kong*."

The bondmaid Lan let out a weary little sigh.

"Oh, master Wu is such a good boy. He would not want to disturb his dear great grandfather who is now sound asleep—"

"I want to see *Chor Kong Kong*! Take me to see *Chor Kong Kong*!"

The boy's perverseness was not at an end yet. It could only be met with compliance. "Alright," said the bondmaid and carried him up from his bed.

The Old One, eighty two years old, approaching senility, lived in a large room on the ground floor, at the far end of the mansion. He was beyond anything but food and sleep, and awaited his end quietly. The bondmaid Chu who was put in charge of him understood the nature of the late nocturnal visit. She rose from her chair in a corner of the room where she had been working on a patchwork blanket, scattering some small triangles of cloth on the floor. She indicated, by a finger to the lips, that the Old One was asleep and should not be disturbed.

"See, I told you Great Grandpa's asleep and mustn't be disturbed," whispered the bondmaid Lan and immediately regretted it, for the boy, his angry energies by no means dispersed, shot out a leg and kicked down an enamel basin from a table. The clanking sound woke up the old man. He stirred, then struggled to get up with little feeble cries of bewilderment. The bondmaid Chu rushed to calm him down. Still whimpering, he turned to look at his visitor. His sudden waking up coinciding with a flash of lucidity, he recognized the visitor and quavered excitedly, "My great grandson! My great grandson!"

The bondmaid Lan led the boy to him. The boy's visits had been few and far between, and always in the company of his grandmother or the male relatives on their obligatory filial calls; the novelty of this one, when he was close enough to study this great ancestor's sunken rheumy eyes that were purportedly growing blind, and the great long teeth that he had heard awful tales whispered about, caused the boy to sit attentively and make no more demands of his maid.

The old man seemed to be working himself into an excited state and talked about something in an incoherent jabber which became comprehensible only when he suddenly pointed a trembling finger in the direction of the far corner of the room. Here stood his coffin, and here was his lucidity at its best. While his memories of the past generally remained murky—even those of the cabaret girls who had so animated his youth and middle years—his recollection of why and how the coffin was brought into the house and remained to reside with him these twenty years was totally accurate and clear in every detail. The Old One was able to name dates, times, places which poured out in streams of recall. They washed over the little boy's head as so much incomprehensible talk of adults, but the child, studying intently those legendary frightful teeth gave the appearance of total attentiveness.

The old man eagerly told of how, when he reached the age of sixty five, the sons gave instructions for a coffin, the best, to be brought into the house for him, as an assurance against that most awful of men's fates, that is, dying at sea and never being found, or dying in a foreign country and not having a proper funeral. He did some traveling, for both business and pleasure, and so a coffinless death was a distinct worry. To allay his fears, his filial sons installed this coffin-in-waiting and thus pre-empted such a direful fate. He remembered the day the coffin was brought in by six strong men and put in the corner, a handsome structure of massive curving planes of the best teak. He and his coffin went on living happily for twenty more years and—here the old man's eyes lit up with a special sparkle and his voice broke into a gleeful cackle—there would be another twenty more years before both would call it a day and go into the ground together. There was a distinctly malicious quality in the glee, as if the Old One, secretly nursing a grievance, was anticipating its triumphant resolution.

"He's deep, that one. Both feet in the grave. But very deep, don't underestimate him," said his bondmaid Chu with a sharp laugh. Her small intense eyes, stark cheekbones and a habit of spitting energetically into the small spittoon kept beside her chair, had a simmering malice all their own.

The room of the oldest member in the House of Wu which should have been one of greatest repose, was charged with a sense of menace, felt even when the Old One was in deep tran-quil sleep and the bondmaid was quietly sitting in her chair, her head bent over her endless patchwork, or walking noiselessly about, putting things in order.

The boy looked with interest at the coffin; he remembered having heard some stories of coffins, but he was now feeling sleepy.

His great-grandfather, the bout of story-telling over, also began to nod. The coincidence of sleepiness was a relief to both maids who could now get ready to return their respective charges to their beds. They shared a larger relief: one taking care of the oldest, and the other the youngest male in the House of Wu, they were the only bondmaids in that great mansion who walked in and out of bedrooms unafraid.

The bondmaid Lan, once she made sure the boy was peacefully asleep, continued to pick up his toys and put them away. She gave out little sighs and clucking sounds of anxiety about the boy's recent tantrums which were sure to bring on bad dreams.

Tantrums and bad dreams came from the grassy mound behind the fruit trees at the back of the house. The boy had fallen and stubbed his toe against the mound, a small one only, of yellow earth and covered with tufts of dry grass. In the first place, he should not have been allowed to wander that far on his own. So the bondmaid came in for a double dose of his grandmother's anger. The mound was later found to contain a half-burnt candle and a scattering of coins, confirming the cause of the boy's subsequent feverishness.

Greatly alarmed, the matriarch, to prevent a further visitation of spirit wrath upon her son, had sent the *keo kia* woman to conduct the necessary propitiatory ceremonies. The *keo kia* woman was given the shirt that the boy had worn when he fell and disturbed the spirit abode. Old, almost blind and able to speak only in a thin quaver, she nevertheless mobilized her special gifts as mediator, to pull together the requisites of shirt, scissors, red candle, mirror and interminable chanting, into a flawless ritual of appeasement, after which the boy's fever left him. Thus had the *keo kia* woman, over five decades, stepped between offended gods and unruly children.

The grassy mound joined an old gnarled rambutan tree, a clump of bamboo and an ant-hill in an increasing number of favorite playing spots now rendered out-of-bounds to children by their surly residents who would punish a romping or urinating child with bad dreams, fevers and even hideously swollen testicles. One of the washerwomen in the mansion had a son thus afflicted; the matriarch was kind enough not only to lend the services of her *keo kia* woman but also to give the distraught woman some money for the temple medium's blessed water and holy oils to apply on the boy.

Bondmaids guilty of the transgression of letting precious sons or grandsons wander into tabooed territory, thus risking their well-being, were endangering their own. For the resulting punishment could wreck it permanently. It was told that, half a century before, the matriarch's grandmother put a cat inside an errant maid's trousers, made its escape impossible by tying up the trousers at the waist and leg ends and then repeatedly beat the creature into a tearing frenzy with a stout piece of firewood so that by the time it was released, it had shredded the errant flesh to ribbons.

The savagery of the dowager was transmitted down the female line but, happily, in steadily decreasing amounts. The matriarch's mother still punished ferociously; there was, moreover a ritualistic bias, for she always made sure that the punishment not only fitted the offense but took on its very character and applied precisely to that part of the body that had offended. Thus cups carelessly broken rebounded as punitive shards to cut the careless hand, lies flew back into the liar's mouth in the form of the most venomous red chili; defiant looks recoiled as so many pinches on the rebel's eyelids.

By the time the recriminatory stream flowed down to the matriarch, a calm gentle-mannered woman, it had dwindled into a trickle of a few perfunctory pinches on the offender's arms or thighs. The matriarch, as soon as she learnt of her grandson's fall on the grassy mound, sent for the bondmaid Chu and administered the due punishment, efficiently but without enthusiasm, as a matter of duty on behalf of the beloved grandson.

So when she appeared in the boy's room in the early morning, to look in on the sleeping boy, the maid sprang to nervous attention, her skin still tingling from the pinches.

The matriarch went to the bed, peered into the boy's face and laid a cool, dry hand on his brow. The very long, curling nail at the end of her little finger, a testimony to her exaltation above all female menial labor in the same way that her mother's and grandmother's bound feet had proclaimed their privileged status, did not get in the way of the affectionate pat.

The matriarch loved the child to distraction. He had every claim on her affection: he was the only grandson from an only son. Both his parents were dead, his mother from a bout of fever shortly after his birth and his father by his own hand, in a double tragedy that could only have been brought about by the most malignant of spirits. That was a terrible time for the House of Wu: two corpses lay in the house within two years. The misfortune was unspeakable; it was matter for awed gossip and speculation for months and it had to be prevented in the future by all the help that could be provided by fortune tellers, astrologers, geomancers. These were all consulted to assist in a massive exercise of appeasement and cleansing. From the White Light Temple came a troop of monks; for days, the villages around the great house heard the ringing of bells, the droning of prayers, saw the billows of smoke ascend in determined propitiation and the saffron-robed monks gliding in and out of the house and its grounds.

One of the monks had suddenly stopped chanting and stood petrified on a patch of waste ground some distance from the house. The evil came from there, he said; he could feel its emanations. A bondmaid had hanged herself there where a tree once stood, many years ago; her vicious, unhappy spirit roamed the place. It was duly placated by a sustained program of prayers, offerings and cleansing with holy water.

A fortune-teller, investigating independently, identified another source, and for a time a dark cloud of suspicion hovered over none other than the Old One himself, eighty years old and still with all his teeth intact, long sharp ones at that. An old man with sharp teeth had surely gained his longevity by eating up his progeny. A man should not live to bury his children and grandchildren; this old one had buried two within two years.

It was horrible; filial piety fought unfilial suspicion, filial piety won and was ashamed, but not before the Old One, wondering about certain insinuations and innuendoes, understood their cause and was deeply hurt.

"Coffin," he said, loudly addressing the object with its twenty-year-old layer of dust that nobody thought of wiping off, "some people would like to see you and me go off soon, but we'll show them!"

The White Light Temple monks completely discredited the fortune-teller, exonerated the Old One and concentrated their energies on appeasing the unhappy dead bondmaid, and the matter was never mentioned again. The spirit appeased and the fortunes of the House of Wu restored, the little master, nevertheless, had to be protected very carefully against its return.

The matriarch looked at the enamel chamberpot under the boy's bed and asked, "Have you eased him?" meaning that the maid should have gently awakened him, sometime during the night to help him urinate into the chamberpot so that he could continue to sleep peacefully; wet woke him up and made him fretful. The bondmaid slept in the same room for this purpose, also for telling him stories if he did not want to go to sleep and making sure he was properly covered with a warm blanket on stormy nights.

The matriarch delicately drew out the chamberpot from under the bed with her foot and checked its contents. The maid had done her duty. She then walked out of the room and from nowhere two bondmaids appeared to escort her to her room, one to do her hair and the other her eyebrows. The hair, still black, was smoothened with purest coconut oil, into a tight neat knot at the back and adorned with a row of jade pins. The eyebrows were plucked of every bit of extraneous hair that could have sprung up in the night, to maintain perfect, pencil arches; two taut threads, moving deftly against each other caught and twisted out the minutest of hairs.

The matriarch looked into the round mirror held up to her and pushed it down, to signify her satisfaction and readiness for the next activity of the morning's routine. She walked downstairs gracefully despite her bulk, with the two bondmaids in attendance. A third one appeared, with no apparent function but to swell the number of the serving in order to proclaim the importance of the served.

All wore the same austere hairstyle of hair pulled back into a tight, well-oiled back-knot, the same long-sleeved, long-trousered suit of equally austere grey or black. But while the dictates of womanly chastity and decorum made for dull homogeneity, those of status lifted the matriarch immeasurably above her serving maids; her clothes would always be of the finest silk, theirs of the plainest cotton, her ornaments always of jade and gold and diamonds, theirs of bone or silver at most. Above all, the power of which these appurtenances were only a small indicator, was written in every gesture of the soft, work-free hands with their delicately curling nails, in every haughty configuration of eyes, nose, mouth and plucked eyebrows.

The matriarch's features could light up in response to a ribald pleasantry or joke, her long-nailed hand could fly up to her mouth to cover a girlish giggle at the gossip of the washer-women. It was whispered that as a young woman, she was so enamored of the operas held in the market-place that she defied her father and slipped out, disguised as a peasant and accompanied by a loyal maid. She always sat in the front row and watched, enthralled, the actors in their rich glittering costumes glide and gesticulate lavishly in the heady din of drums, gongs, cymbals and flutes. In later years, she would smilingly refer to the escapade, but never in the hearing of the bondmaids in whose presence she always kept a dourly dignified demeanor.

She swept into the ancestral room: here the attending bondmaids fanned out in a brisk preparation for the next and last morning activity before breakfast. One brought her a bunch of lit joss-sticks, one a small golden prayer bell, the third a saucer of fragrant flower petals. The matriarch stood before the ancestral altar which was covered with heavy brocade and laden with a hundred golden urns, plaques, divine effigies, vases, bowls of fruit and flowers, porcelain cups of obeisant tea. With the joss sticks, she bowed reverentially and secured the blessings of gods and ancestors for the day.

Sometimes she swept in unannounced, went up to the altar, ran a finger along the side of a vase or urn, and coolly held up the incriminating dust to show the bondmaid in charge, reducing her to confused murmuring. On the Feast of the Hungry Ghosts, when an additional table was brought in to hold the immense plates of cooked meats and vegetables for the ghosts' banquet, the matriarch, perfectionist to the last, ran her expert eyes over the suckling pig, roast duck, braised goose and rested on the steamed chicken, to ascertain that it was virgin pullet, obtained at great cost and effort from the town market's only pullet stall, and not ordinary used hen not fit for offering to august ancestors and gods. Careless, lazy bondmaids might deceive the dead but not the living. The matriarch, detecting the deception, would call for a pair of chopsticks and a bin, and delicately poke out the unworthy offering, still glistening in its own oil.

"How do you expect the Reverend from the White Light Temple to make such as offering?" The Reverend who came for all important occasions was known to be fastidious.

The matriarch sat at table and waited for the patriarch to join her for breakfast. In her younger days, she ate alone; now age conferred upon her the privilege of eating with her husband. With the patriarch's appearance, more bondmaids materialized. Unseen presences in that huge mansion, they padded along corridors and in and out of rooms, carrying chamberpots, flasks of hot water and tea, hot towels, fans, their own firm young bodies, in response to a hundred needs and demands, as the doors in that huge mansion with its endless corridors, opened and closed, opened and closed, at all times of the day and night.

Now they brought in a multitude of dainty saucers and dishes containing every variety of salted vegetables, fermented soybean and pickled entrails, peasants' food that the patriarch, as a small boy, had enjoyed alongside the laborers on his grandfather's estate, squatting with them on long wooden benches while they shoveled into their mouths huge amounts of hot steaming rice with chopsticks that moved so fast they became a blur. Pig and fowl offal, fibrous vegetable stalks and fruit rinds, discarded from any cooking for the dead, reappeared as so many delicious dishes for the living, swimming in ingenious sauces.

The patriarch had come a long way from the peasant fare in the rough earthen bowls, but he never cared for the fine, rare meats and vegetables imported at great cost to grace rich tables. He kept his simple tastes, and his wife, herself from a wealthy family, balanced the simplicity with the opulence of ceramic and porcelain containers and ivory chopsticks.

The rice porridge that was the patriarch's unvarying staple for the entire duration of his life, was brought in last in an earthen pot that the heat might be kept in and the porridge ladled out piping hot, for the patriarch was known to leave the table, to the silent consternation of his wife and the bondmaids, if the first mouthful did not scald.

He and the matriarch sat opposite each other at the round table with its carved dragon legs, not talking or doing so in low murmurs, while their chopsticks deftly picked up tiny pieces of pickles. The matriarch spoke briefly about the grandson and the *keo kia* woman; the patriarch responded with just that degree of interest to establish, simultaneously, his concern for his grandson and his not wishing to be bothered about women's matters. After each meal, he retired to his rooms at the far end of the large mansion and busied himself with his calligraphy and business accounts books or went out to meet his friends, in his chauffeur-driven Ford, always impeccably dressed in his mandarin suit of a dark shade of grey or a light shade of cream. He wore a white topi against the sun and carried a walking stick, though he had need of none, possessing a ramrod posture that enhanced his patrician bearing. In an illustrious line that now sadly included a senile father, a dead son and a temperamental grandson, he did the proper thing by all: he ensured that the Old One lacked nothing and was prepared to bring in the region's finest physicians and stage the country's most lavish funeral when the time came; towards the tragic dead son, he could do nothing and left the womenfolk to the daily ritual of remembrance and regard at the young man's altar, and as for the grandson, there was nothing he would not do to secure the best education and best preparation to take over the fortunes of the House of Wu.

In one respect the patriarch was unlike other men of his exalted and privileged position—he had no concubines and no wish for any. It was a singularity that made him stand apart from his peers, and even become the target of much private ribaldry: what was wrong with the man that he had forsaken the divinely appointed practice whereby males kept a variety of women for the harvesting of their secret ying? His father surely knew better how to live; the Old One's escapades with dancing girls and even other men's mistresses came in for greater ribaldry. Did the old crafty one have recourse to the rejuvenating powers of snake blood, or, even more reliably, a young virgin's?

There was a bondmaid, many years ago, that the patriarch had summoned to his bed because she was exceptionally pretty, but she turned her out to be talkative and silly, and moreover smelt. He turned her out, with the same finickiness that he rejected spoons that were not scrupulously clean, and rice porridge that was not scaldingly hot.

He went back to his calligraphy and his business books, and left other men to their pursuits. To his large mansion had gravitated a continuing stream of wastrel cousins and half-brothers confident of living well on his largesse and the secret pleasures promised by those young, compliant bondmaids flitting in and out of rooms. The patriarch tolerated the raucousness of the cousins and half brothers provided they did not upset the even tenor of his life.

"Men—they are like the barnyard roosters ever in chase of hens and pullets," the matriarch had commented, referring not to her husband, but the male relatives and mostly, her father-in-law, the Old One with the long, sharp teeth of longevity and the long nose of ageless desire that could sniff out any accommodating young body. The Old One, until disease crippled him and confined him to his room, was said to have had his will of every single bondmaid that passed through the House of Wu.

The matriarch waited for the patriarch to leave the room, then she too rose to go, to the main hall where she was to receive a woman who had a child to sell. She sat in her chair with its back of magnificent inlaid mother of-pearl, flanked on each side by a bondmaid as was her wont when she received village women presenting themselves and offering for inspection their female children prior to an adoption or sale. From the chair of authority, she delivered judgments on the poor pathetic creatures, inspected the offspring to see if they had healthy scalps and teeth and completed the transactions with a sum of money in a sealed red envelop. She now owned them body and soul, for they had become her bondmaids.

From the time of her mother and her mother's mother, little girls had been thus brought into the house, to grow up and be bonded into any serving role, whether as menial servant or secondary concubine in that immense household.

The expert eyebrow-plucker, upon a signal from the matriarch, now doubled up as back-knocker. Her young hands, curled up into tight balled fists of pure energy, descended upon the matriarch's back in an exquisitely controlled pattern of rapid rhythmic knocks that swept across the entire expanse of back and shoulders, removing every ache, banishing every discomfort. Bondmaids knocked matriarchs' backs, matriarchs knocked patriarchs' backs in a simultaneous offering of obeisance and therapy.

The matriarch fell asleep briefly under the very soothing ministrations of the extremely capable bondmaid. When she opened her eyes again, they looked upon the child Han and her mother who had just come in and presented themselves. Both looked tired and dusty; the child clung to the mother and stared warily at everyone around her.

"She is very thin," the matriarch commented. The child had, in the heat of the long walk, wriggled out of the quilted jacket by which the mother had hoped to cover her thinness, and had refused to put it on again.

The matriarch turned for endorsement to the bondmaid standing on her right, who appeared superior to the other bond-maids by virtue of her age, her severe expression, her clothes which were definitely of finer cut and material, the jade bangle on her left wrist and, most of all, a certain hauteur of bearing successfully copied from the matriarch. Only she stood with her hands firmly crossed in front; the other bondmaids had theirs deferentially by their sides, the more ready to spring into obeisant action. Only she had her chin raised; the others lowered their heads slightly.

The mother, taking the cue, turned to face this intimidating personage with a timid smile. She waited anxiously for her response. Choyin—for that was her name—rose to the full height of her importance as head bondmaid in the house and said tersely, "Very thin. She is all skin and bone." She asked the mother, "Does your child have worms?" Thirty-five years ago, she herself had been brought in as an unkempt, pot-bellied child in much need of de-lousing and de-worming.

The mother replied with nervous effusiveness, "Oh no, the child is very healthy. No worms at all," adding, "she has never been ill. Only a running nose now and again." She was thankful that the nose had stopped dribbling.

"Very small for her age," said the matriarch and gestured for a closer look. She liked to lift up a child's thin arm and encircle it with forefinger and thumb to demonstrate the thinness.

But the child refused to move, clinging tightly to the mother.

"Scabs on her legs," said Choyin in continuing depreciation of the child's worth, to strengthen the buyer's position.

The mother was visibly upset. She was depending on a successful completion of the transaction; if it failed, she would be at her wits' end. So she began, once again, to reassure them of the child's good health and obedient behavior.

The matriarch's interest shifted from the child to the mother. She asked, "Did you walk all the way in your condition?" Herself cosseted and swaddled and fed the best ginseng and herbal brews each time she got pregnant, she could now, in old age, wonder with some pity and much curiosity about how the other side lived.

The woman was relieved by the change in tone. She began to thank the matriarch effusively for the honor and kindness shown in making an offer for her daughter, and to express every fervent hope that the child would grow up and serve her well. The matriarch once more turned to Choyin and said something. The head bondmaid went to a nearby table, picked up a red envelope and handed it to the mother. It was not the proper thing to do under the circumstances, but the mother, in her feverish haste to complete the business and leave these hateful people, actually opened the envelope right there and then and counted the money inside. The matriarch and Choyin exchanged arch glances.

"Thank you," she said to the matriarch with all the deference she could muster.

Now it was time to leave the child. The child had both hands tightly on her arm. She pulled away one hand, then the other. The child responded with hysterical energy. Her warning instincts had been alerted by the close inspection of her person and sharpened by the sight of the money changing hands. Now they mobilized all her energies for the ultimate move against a fleeing parent: she threw herself upon her mother and curled all four limbs around her mother's legs, immobilizing her. The mother let out a nervous laugh, by way of apologizing for the child's unreasonableness, since her price money had already been collected. She said to the child in a severe voice, "You are behaving very badly." She added, raising her voice for all to hear, to have done with the proprieties required of the occasion: "Be good. Be obedient. You are lucky to be in the House of Wu. Value your good fortune. Serve your mistress well." She tried to shake off, without success, the child who looked like a small tenacious tree creature that only death could force to uncurl and drop to the ground.

"Don't leave me! Mother, please don't leave me!" sobbed the child.

The mother made one last effort to deal with an increasingly awkward situation. "I'm not leaving you," she said soothingly. "I'll be gone only for a short while, and then I'll come back for you. Only a very short while!"

The shock of the first lie still vibrating through her little four-year-old frame, the child was not about to be taken in by a second. From her position on her mother's legs, she did a determined climb up into her mother's arms. She wriggled past the enormous belly and into the arms, compelling them to fold around her. Burrowing deep into the arms like a small terrified animal, she curled tightly inside the protective warmth. She closed her eyes and remained perfectly still, thinking that not seeing those strange people would make them disappear so that she and her mother could once again be by themselves and safe together. She wanted so much to go home, to be back with her brothers and sisters.

The mother sighed. Holding the child in her arms and rocking her gently to calm her trembling body, she pondered the next move.

"Mama, let's go home," sobbed the child. Her little four-year-old mind had enough astuteness to make her try a different tack. She said, "Mama, I won't ask for sweets again. I promise not to bite Oldest Brother. I promise not to steal Little Sister's rice. I promise not to wet my trousers." The litany elicited a small curl of a smile on the matriarch's impassive face. By way of supreme renunciation, the child brought out of her pocket the yellow horse and handed it to her mother.

The woman was all effusive apology. Told her not to take it. Lying on the ground as they came in. Made her put it back. Naughty child. Only naughty. No thief.

The matriarch made a small gesture, dismissing it all as of no consequence, and the mother, relieved, went on talking to the child. "You are a bad girl and I shall have to take you home to punish you. The cane. And no more sugar buns."

The child nodded. She would have nodded to the threat of the most fearful punishment she knew: being dragged to the well and forcibly held, by the arms, over its dark menacing depths, as she had seen her mother do to Oldest Brother on one occasion. A neighbor had rushed out to the screams of the kicking boy and rescued him. Afterwards the neighbors scolded the weeping mother. "*Siau, siau.* Are you mad? Have you lost your mind?"

The child nodded eagerly to the warning of the cane and the withdrawal of her favorite food.

"You have tired me and made me very thirsty. I need a drink of water," continued the mother. "Wait here. I'll get a drink of water and then we'll go home. Bad girl. Remember, the cane!"

She put the child back on the floor and disappeared.

The child stood waiting in tearful tremulousness, avoiding the faces looking down at her. She kept looking in the direction where her mother had disappeared, her eyes wide with mounting tension.

No mother appeared. Something had gone very wrong. Danger threatened, danger with an adult face which could, however, be averted if children were quick enough. Thus the child Han, her small body wound up to the point of a hurling explosion, managed, once more, the coquette's dance of appeasement, waggling her bottom even more convincingly. Her voice rose in a tearful treble:

The bird looks
The bee cries
The ants yearn
For my flower —

The matriarch looked up in surprise and gave a little giggle, the bondmaids followed and the room soon filled with women's amused laughter. The child stopped and stood surlily biting her lip, aware that nothing was being put right. Again she looked in the direction of the mother's disappearance, her face taut and white. It was only when the matriarch got up from her chair and said to Choyin, "See that she has a good bath. And give her something to eat," that the horrible truth dawned on her. She rushed to the door, screaming, "Mama! Mama!" and was pulled back by two pairs of hands. They were joined by a third, for the child had become a maniacal force, screaming, kicking, biting, spitting.

"A bad beginning, indeed," murmured the matriarch. She and her bondmaids looked at the child now writhing upon the floor in all the pain of abandonment and despair. They had never seen anything like it before.

A man entered from the passageway leading from the kitchen and joined the circle of spectators. Choyin said sharply, "Spitface, have you finished the firewood yet? You have no business to be here!"

Spitface pointed excitedly to the child still thrashing upon the floor and made little sharp grunting noises. Always reacting with child-like delight to any scene of noise and activity, he began to jump up and down, clapping and hooting. There was a lull in the screaming as the child turned to look at him, a wild man in the midst of neat women. Encouraged, he dug into the pockets of his khaki shorts and brought out an assortment of small objects which he spread in an extravagant display on the floor in front of the child.

He selected a sweet in a pretty silver wrapper and offered it to her, grinning. She promptly knocked it out of his hand, turned away and began screaming afresh. Spitface would not give up. He went down on the floor and crawled towards the child, offering a ride on his back. He stretched out a hand to touch her. She whirled upon him in a sudden surge of fury, grabbed the hand and bit it deeply. Retreating, he howled in pain, bent over, his mouth ridiculously rounded in a long sustained wail, the ultimate comic figure.

Here was diversion indeed and the bondmaids gathered closer to watch and giggle. They had appeared from various parts of the house, attracted by the noise. One held a half-ironed shirt in her hand, another carried an enormous hot-water flask, a third was wiping her hands on her apron.

"Don't frighten the child, Spitface. She's already in a bad state."

"You've come in again without washing your feet. Look at your toenails!"

"Go back to your firewood!"

The matriarch rose from her chair for the second time.

"The child is best left alone," she said. "Let her calm down. Then let her have a bath and some food. Also the kerosene for her hair. They all come with head-lice." She swept out of the room, followed by Choyin. The bondmaids duly dispersed. Spitface hovered by, eager to befriend the child. He made another attempt to touch her and withdrew with a little gasp of alarm as she made to bite him a second time. She then turned away from him and continued screaming. The screaming went on and on unabated; she was sure to be sick in a while.

"A four-year-old possessed by the very devil. We shall have to see," murmured the matriarch as she returned to her rooms.

In another room, not far from the matriarch's the young master Wu, submitting his hair to be combed before the morning visit to his grandfather and grandmother, said suddenly, "What's that? Who's crying?" He listened intently, then said determinedly, getting up, "I want to go and see."

His bondmaid Lan, terrified of a second blunder and a second visitation of the matriarchal wrath, resorted to a slew of imaginative ploys to hold the boy back. Only a cat. A cat stealing fish and being whacked by Choyin.

The boy said, "I want to see the cat."

A giant spider on the wall over there. Look. A big lizard about to do battle with it.

The boy disdained to look.

"I want to go and see."

Even stories were brushed aside. She had of necessity become a consummate story-teller, decking her tales with multi-headed monsters, black-tongued ghosts and warriors unscathed by sword, fire and ice-mountain. Even relentless potentates were disarmed by the magic of women's stories. Once upon a time. It was gratifying to watch the boy's eyes widen.

Once upon a time, there was a little prince whose father, a great emperor, would do anything for him. One day the boy fell ill. A magician said that the only cure was the fruit from a certain tree, one of its kind in the world. The fruit would appear only after the roots of the tree were nourished with the blood of one thousand virgins.

"What is one thousand virgins?" said the emperor whose huge palace and surrounding walls had been built on the bones and blood of ten thousand men. Accordingly, he sent his men to round up one thousand young girls who were then taken to the tree and beheaded there, so that their blood flowed deep into the earth around the tree. The fruit duly appeared and was plucked for the young prince; he ate it and was saved.

But no narrative could withstand the competition of a sudden wail from the strange peasant child, which came loud and clear, making the boy stand up suddenly. "I want to go and see," he repeated and walked to the door. He had wanted to ask, "What's a virgin?" but thought that could wait.

"Wait—"

The bondmaid Lan had only recently discovered the secret

power of her body. She was lying beside the boy on his bed telling him stories to put him to sleep—his nervous energy had reached a particularly high level after the excitement of the lavish birthday celebration dinner when his hand, wandering idly, strayed upon her left breast. It jumped, stayed still, then began a tentative exploration of the firm roundness. It moved in slow circles, luxuriously, sensuously. There was a sharp intake of breath by the maid, also by the boy in a simultaneous *frisson* of daring discovery. The maid lay silent and still; the boy's hand quickened to the novelty of the sensation and began to move more purposefully, testing the young firmness and smooth curvature, finally closing in upon the hard bud of the nipple.

There was no stopping him now. With the same aggressiveness that he always demanded to see things only hinted at or hidden from sight, he now demanded to see what he had so thrillingly touched. Not with words, for the palpability of the situation admitted of no verbal intrusions; the boy sat up and boldly, wordlessly, lifted the maid's blouse. She sat up, too, to allow for her breasts to pull into the full roundness and beauty lost in a lying position, pushing her blouse up to her chin and watched the boy's eyes enlarge in wonder at the sight. Small boy and naked maid sat facing each other on the bed, and then she pulled down her blouse, and it was over. It was too large an experience to be fully savored all at once, like a box of rich candies to be consumed in carefully staggered sittings, or an intriguing toy to be played with, then put away, then played with again, for a cumulative yielding of pleasure.

Both boy and maid understood.

The boy lay down, turned away from the maid and gave the appearance of sleep. He had entered a world of women's secrets that lay hidden under their clothes and the clothes under their clothes. The secrets had been undiscoverable too under the thick layers of women's hushed conversations as soon as they noticed his approach, in the forbidding enclosures of fingers put to lips as soon as they heard his footsteps. They whipped away secret garments from clotheslines, did frantic adjustments to the buttons of their blouses or the strings of their trousers when he burst into their rooms.

They were hiding their secret from him, and now he had discovered it.

The maid's own discovery too promised much: it was that of the ultimate ploy in the secret armory against recalcitrant young masters. More than sweets, more than thrilling tales, her body could be used to calm and tame the boy tyrant. It made her work easier. It was the maximum weapon, to be called into use only in extreme situations, such as when her arms or thighs were in danger of a second shower of vengeful pinches.

"Wait—"

She caught the boy by the arm and drew him up close to her. Then she lifted his hand, slowly, and put it inside her blouse, laying it on her right breast. In recollection of the first encounter, it immediately cupped to the pleasing contours. No more tantalizing wails, happily, came from below to compete for the boy's attention, and he was allowed to relive fully the vertiginous pleasure on the night of his fifth birthday.

Thus was the boy enticed to sit down and have his hair combed. The maid dipped a finger into a jar of Brylcreem and smeared it in the hair, to produce a neatness and gleam that his grandfather liked to see. She said, "There you are! You're ready!"

IV

As DARKNESS FELL, the child sat up on the floor, a solitary presence in a vast space carved out for her in that house to tame her into silence.

The insane storm of her rage had subsided into small gusts of choking despair, as she looked around her, unmindful of the wet in her trousers and the vomit on her blouse. Frenzied thrashing and screaming being now futile and in any case impossible in her exhausted state, she had recourse to the last remaining resource in a child's repertoire of rescue: she began to call her mother, in repetitive chant, as if its incantatory power could somehow pull out of the surrounding darkness the familiar sound of returning footsteps, the familiar sight of the comforting face.

"Ma-ma. Ma-ma. Ma-ma."

The child rocked herself backwards and forwards, in rhythm with the chanting; she might have been any temple worshipper in deep trance, awaiting a god's coming.

"Ma-ma. Ma-ma. Ma-ma."

The night sounds flowed and washed over her unheeded—someone coughing, a utensil clattering to the floor, a chair being moved, and from the streets outside, a dog's whine, the tock-tock of the food hawker's knocking sticks as he made the night rounds with his cart.

Her cries for that parent had never gone unheeded—as an infant, wet and hungry in the sarong cradle hanging from a ceiling beam, bawling for the proper cradle of the maternal arms, as a toddler lost in a forest of adult legs in the market-place, frantically looking up each pair to see if it was attached to the familiar face.

The mother had appeared each time, picked her up and soothed her. She had immediately quieted to the comfort of the rubber teat pushed into her mouth, the warmth of that space between neck and shoulder that she liked to wedge her small head in, to sniff at familiar smells, feel the familiar contours of bone and pulsating muscle.

The incantation might have lulled her into deep sleep and oblivion: at some point of returning consciousness, she did a mental rearrangement, changing the invoked name. Treacherous mother was replaced by beloved Oldest Brother and she began to call his name, at first slowly, then with increasing tempo and urgency, enlarging the invocation to a full demand: "I want Oldest Brother to take me home." The child's lips trembled in an ache of most desperate longing: more than anyone in the world, she wanted to see the brother whose memory she would carry, long after she had forgotten the others.

"I want Oldest Brother to take me home."

"What's she saying?"

The young master Wu, in the arms of his bondmaid, watching from behind an upstairs pillar, strained to have a closer look at the child below sitting on the floor and talking to herself. "Be careful," said the bondmaid, holding him tightly. Word of the attack on Spitface had spread; every one of the bondmaids except herself had had a look at the savage child. Now was her turn.

"What's she saying? Why's she sitting like that? Why does she have only one slipper?" The questions could not come fast enough but the little boy, proud to be part of an apparent adult conspiracy, kept his voice co-operatively low.

"Be careful, she's like a wild animal. She bit Spitface."

"What?"

Now there was no stopping the boy's fervid curiosity which burst forth in a crescendo of questions: why did she bite Spitface? Did she have sharp teeth like a monster? Did Spitface cry? Did Spitface bite her back?

In his uncontrollable desire to take a closer look at the astounding attacker, he kicked his feet against the bondmaid's side, beat at her encircling arms and wriggled his body downwards, until she had to put him down on the floor. He made to rush downstairs but she restrained him.

"You must let me hold your hand," she warned, "otherwise this little girl who is no little girl but a demon in disguise will open her mouth and swallow you up."

Purveyor of astonishing information, the bondmaid immediately gained new respect in the boy's eyes and he allowed her to hold his hand as together they walked down the stairs and approached the child Han sitting on the floor.

She had subsided into a barely audible whimpering, thin wisps of despair strung across the growing gloom.

57

The boy stopped in front of her. She looked up, startled.

They stared at each other.

The bondmaid quickly positioned herself very close to the boy, in readiness to defend him against any attack. But the wild child seemed wild no longer; she sat abjectly in her mess and stared silently at the boy. The little space between them belied the immeasurable distance that separated them and ever would: he, male, heir, scion of the House of Wu, clad in a suit of fine blue silk and embroidered dragon shoes; she, female, newly sold, in the one new dress in her life in honor of the sale, now dank and stained by the unutterable terror of her abandonment.

The boy was suddenly overcome by an impulse to give her something, and began searching in the pockets of his silk suit. He found a red envelope containing gift money; it was one of many that he had received from the relatives on his fifth birthday, which his grandmother had forgotten to remove to put in the large tortoise-shell money box in his room.

The boy's pockets were often filled with small coins for the dispensing of charity to the numerous beggars who came to the mansion, in a continuation of that magnanimity that had distinguished his forbears, builders of roads and bridges in poor villages, donors of huge sacks of rice to feed the poorest of the poor. Under the fond eyes of his grandmother, he had, from a very young age, toddled unsteadily to put a coin on a broken, wizened palm and toddled back for the smile and nod of approval. Now he wished it were something other than money. A sweet or biscuit. An Almond Lady. Or a toy. A red or blue horse. He was sure the little girl would have liked that. Nevertheless, he took the red envelope out of his pocket and stretched out his hand stiffly, shyly, to give it to the child. She remained motionless, staring at him. The bondmaid Lan gave a gasp of alarm, darted forward, retrieved the money, picked up the boy and hurriedly climbed up the stairs back to his room.

V

THE CHILD HAN LAY on a mattress on the floor. She had been carried up to a small upstairs room, cleaned of the urine and vomit and put into a fresh suit of clothes. Her body, weakened by crying and hunger over three days, lay on the mattress, a limp rag doll emptied of its insides. Beside her, incongruously, was a small, bright yellow rubber duck; Spitface had slipped into the room when no one was looking and placed it there. He had first put it in her hand and closed her fingers, one by one, around it, but they had loosened immediately and let drop the gift. With little grunts of sorrow, Spitface tried again, then gave up, and finally placed the duck carefully by her side.

The child lay perfectly still, her eyes half closed, her mouth open.

In the last attempt to make her eat, Choyin had forced her mouth open and tried to push in a spoonful of milk. Earlier, someone had tried to feed her rice porridge which she resolutely clamped her mouth against and caused to splatter down her chin and neck so that she had to be cleaned all over again. Under Choyin's efficient ministrations, each child who had been brought into the House of Wu, had been cleansed of the last louse and worm, the last squalid remnant of her previous existence, and emerged well-fed and ready for service. This child defied all attempts.

They gave up. They looked in now and then and waited for her to die. A few years back, a child bondmaid with a harelip had died, aged five, on the same mattress in the same room, but from illness, not disobedience. This child's death was going to be different, because it was self willed. A demon inhabited her body.

The matriarch now appeared. She was accompanied by Choyin. Together they looked down on the tiny figure curled up on the mattress and spoke in low, grave tones.

"Good money paid for a child who starves herself to death," said Choyin who knew the amount from the expert feel of her fingers on the envelope as it was passed on to the child's mother.

She had been authorized, after the first day of the child's incessant crying, to send a messenger to the mother to take her back. The messenger came back with distressing news. The woman had run to hide as soon as she saw him. Then when forced to come out, she had begun scolding him in a shrill voice. The child would be perfectly normal in a few days, she shouted. She had finally broken down weeping, sitting on the doorstep, her enormous belly heaving. The money from the sale of one child was to be used to prepare for the coming of another.

"More likely she's lost it all in the gambling parlors," said Choyin.

"Send for the Reverend," said the matriarch. "He will drive the demon out of the child."

Spitface was despatched to the White Light Temple for the Reverend. Spitface had one leg shorter than the other, but he was amazingly fleet of foot and in no time at all, the Reverend presented himself at the House of Wu, having in fact just left it that morning after the ritual prayers at the family's ancestral altar, so that the summons came as a surprise.

The Reverend moved through the rooms of the mansion with all the ease of a welcome guest who was, moreover, relied on to ascertain the purity of the offerings on the ancestral altar, so that he had, on occasion, to reject a contaminated fowl and demand its replacement with pristine pullet.

A small room adjoining the ancestral room was reserved for the Reverend's use; in it, after the morning prayers were finished, he sat at a table and was served breakfast by a bondmaid. The back-knocking bondmaid whose name was Popo had that morning brought in his hot tea and favorite steaming rice buns. "Reverend." Her greeting was calm, but the calmness hid a growing anxiety which rose in a warm stream and colored her neck and cheeks as soon as she stood by the table to pour out the tea, and the Reverend slowly turned in his seat to have full view of her.

That was the start of the monk's other morning pleasure. He stared at her unrelentingly, delighting to cover a maid with her own maidenly blushes. The soft dimpled rotundity of his bald pate, cheeks, chin and hands, giving him the aspect of an over-fed, languorously contented infant, comported oddly with the sensuality of his moist red mouth and the brutality of his intense, deep-set eyes permanently narrowed into a gaze of searing power directed at friend and foe alike. His monk's robe of ascetic grey, the prayer beads around his neck, the lit joss-sticks in his hands and other appurtenances of his holy calling did nothing to soften the overall impression of brute power; indeed they invested that power with divine sanction and made it absolute.

Bondmaids never dared to lift their eyes in his august presence.

"Come."

The bondmaid Popo put the tea-pot down and walked, slowly, nervously, to stand before him. His soft hand went up inside her blouse, not in the manner of the lover but the greedy, voracious male. The maid's blushes passed into a stricken pale-ness with the increasing gluttony of the caress seeking its fill, forcing itself under the tight cotton bodice, ripping through the constraining buttons. While his hand plundered, his eyes roved over her face with slow menace, and fixed on hers, compelling them to lift to him. She looked up briefly, then looked down again in confused distress. He smiled; it was part of the pleasure to see the pain.

The pleasure was not at an end; it moved to its next stage. The Reverend removed his hand from under the blouse, spread his legs wide and directed her hand, small and cold and trem-bling, to touch the large eruption of his hot lust under the grey robe. He lay slumped back, eyes closed, sighing deeply in the full satiety of the particular pleasure.

He stopped there. He always stopped there, the safe bound-ary of a carefully crafted desire. Beyond this boundary were all the risks and hassles of hysterical pregnancies, within it, all the safety of a discreet pleasure that left no incriminating evidence. It was a meticulously considered plan of action, to achieve a fine strategic balance between desire and holy calling. He had learnt to effect a smooth transition from one to the other, within seconds of the sound of approaching footsteps or an opening door, dropping the bondmaid's hand from his tumescence, and turning, with casual ease, to resume his tea-drinking or prayer-chanting at the ancestral altar. Forty years old, he laid claim to bodies as young as fourteen, of which there were plenty available in the large households where he was often summoned for his service as respected monk from the White Light Temple. He had been performing, by special request of the matriarch, the weekly rituals for the ancestors in the House of Wu for the last six weeks during which time, his hands, soft, almost like a woman's, had roamed over as many bondmaids' bodies.

The Reverend had, for his emulation, a long line of illustrious holy fathers. Truly ascetic, they had renounced every bodily pleasure, fasting and meditating all their days, their bodies mere shells awaiting discardment upon flight of their radiant souls. Sometimes these bodies remained incorruptible. There was an old monk who died at age ninety two and lay for months in the temple, fresh and tranquil as in sleep, to receive an endless stream of devotees from all over the region, who exclaimed over the miracle of the still growing hair and beard, fingernails and toenails. Someone reported the fragrance of jasmine emanating from the corpse; and the devotees touched it with white handkerchiefs to capture the odor of his sanctity. Another was cremated, and his little fragments of bones when cleaned of the ashes were found to contain glittering crystals which the devotees begged to be allowed to take away as keepsakes.

The illustrious line was besmirched somewhat by the lurking presence of a few rogues who ate beef, drank wine and got women with children. A holy mendicant turned out to be less than holy; his begging bowl and penitential garb hid a raging lust expended on village girls for miles around. Another took up with a nun and had to flee the country.

Through his ingenious strategy of limiting his secret exploits to bondmaids who would never tell or who would be slapped into retraction if they did, the Reverend had arrived at a successful policy of containment that allowed him to enjoy the respect given to the first group of progenitors and escape the disgrace of the second. He was a very contented man.

With the bell, joss-sticks and blessed water of exorcism, he looked at the sick child on the mattress, while the matriarch and Choyin stood beside him. Spitface hovered at the doorway, straining to look at the child and making anxious little noises, and was waved away by Choyin. The young bondmaid Popo stood some distance away, her eyes on the ground. The Reverend's presence sent little tremors through her body. He turned and looked at her severely and made a small impatient gesture to the matriarch. She understood and dismissed the girl from the room. The presence of unclean female blood wrecked any ritual of cleansing. No chances could be taken with young women who therefore had to leave immediately. A menstruating woman had once heedlessly gone into a temple for the feast of the Nine Emperor Gods and been struck down.

The bondmaid Popo left in a hurry, and the matriarch murmured an apology into her handkerchief. The Reverend looked sternly at her retreating figure. He took every opportunity to reinforce his strategy of safe private seduction by exhibiting the greatest public indifference to the seduced or even better, the strongest public censure of her. It gave him a deeply satisfying sense of power to see her so thoroughly confused. Moreover, it provided precisely the evidence for discrediting any accusation that might arise in the future.

Having disposed of the bondmaid, he turned his full attention to the healing of the child on the mattress. He gave instructions for the child to be held up to a sitting position and given a drink of the blessed water. The child's mouth was opened and the water poured down her throat. It went down in a spluttering stream, wetting the entire front of her blouse. She was then laid back upon the mattress and her blouse lifted for a lit joss-stick to be applied to her chest and stomach. The demon had taken residence in four different locations in her body, all of which had to be burnt out. Ringing the bell in one hand and holding aloft the lit joss-stick in the other, the monk prayed, then poked and prodded, expelling the demon. The expulsion was signaled by a piercing scream from the child. She went into a convulsion; there came a tremendous retching sound and the child shot up into a sitting position and vomited. It was interminable, wracked vomiting, watched silently by the others. Choyin later told the other bondmaids of the bizarre stream of most evil-looking matter that was spewed out all over the mattress and floor, signifying the particular malevolence of the inhabitant.

"I have never seen anything like it in all my life," she said. In the other instances she had witnessed, the demons had made their exits peacefully and clearly, leaving no foulness.

The matriarch spoke briefly about it to the patriarch and gave only essential information, in deference to his wish not to be bothered by women's matters in the house, but she too had been awed and said the same thing: "I have never seen anything like that before."

The Reverend got ready to go.

"The child will live," he said.

He then instructed them to leave the joss-sticks in her room and to give her one more drink of the blessed water before the next cockcrow. The next time he came for the ancestral ritual, he would find a grateful *ang pow* discreetly placed on the altar table. His severity of mien and demeanor proscribed the crudity of a direct handing over of the red paper packet of money; the matriarch always left it delicately under an urn or beside a flower vase or near his pot of tea.

She accompanied him out of the room, murmuring thanks.

"The child will not live," whispered the bondmaid Popo to

the bondmaid Chu. They both spoke about an owl's cry heard in the night, drawn out and mournful. The bondmaid Chu said that it was not for the Old One who had survived many owl laments in his time. The Old One had insisted he would listen to no summons, except that of his coffin. A few years back, they had heard the same cry and the next morning the five-year-old child with the harelip was found dead on her mattress. The wild child with the demon was lying on the same mattress and was moreover wearing the same clothes, for dead bondmaids' clothes, no matter how meager, were afterwards carefully laundered and kept for future use. The similarities piled: both were about the same age, both fell ill within days of their arrival. One child ghost was about to come for another. Choyin said that owls did not cry for children, adding, "If she must die, she must die. We have done everything in our power."

The room where the child Han lay on her mattress on the floor, was too far away from the young master Wu's, for him to hear any of the sounds of impending death. He was thinking of her and would not stop asking questions, as he sat on his rosewood stool with the carved dragon legs, facing the bondmaid Lan who was feeding him rice porridge from a bowl. She fed him thus every day, carefully spooning the food into his mouth, her sole anxiety at every meal being to ensure that the bowl or plate was cleared of the last spoonful, for his grandmother sometimes made an unannounced appearance and asked questions if she saw unfinished food, with the same severity that she inquired about a cut on his leg, or a mosquito bite on his arm. The bondmaid carried the boy up and down the numerous flights of stairs in the great house, repeating, whenever he protested, his grandmother's favorite story to him of the little prince whose feet never touched the ground until he was ten years old because there were one hundred servants to carry him around.

The boy, sitting on his stool, asked again about the little girl. The questions, coming in a stream, unclamped his mouth wonderfully and allowed her to spoon in the food uninterruptedly.

"Will she die?"

The boy's questions had taken a turn for the morbid; he pictured the little girl dead, like a huge insect he once saw, lying on its back, its legs sticking stiffly in the air.

"Maybe yes, maybe no. Open your mouth. Good, good boy! I will tell your grandmother what a good boy you've been!" The bondmaid festooned with rich praise every small act of co-operation from the boy, in deference to his position.

The boy's eyes were fixed, intense and bright, on something behind her. She turned sharply and saw, standing at the door, the child Han.

The child stood there unsteadily, in all the dereliction of the abandoned waif, a strange brightness lighting up her large dark eyes and thin pale face. Her hair was matted, her clothes dank, her limbs tiny sticks. The bondmaid quickly put the bowl of porridge on the floor to free her arms for encircling the boy against this strange presence. Not against any attack of teeth or limbs, for the child looked no more capable of that, but against the greater danger of the preternaturally glittering eyes fixed on the boy. But the boy rose and shook off the protection, moving for a full view of the visitor at the door. He stood facing her, returning her gaze. She began to walk towards him in small, tottering steps. Midway, she swayed in her weakness but managed to steady herself to resume walking.

She stopped in front of him. It was at this point that her legs gave way beneath her and she crumbled into a sitting position on the floor. The boy squatted down on the floor and faced her. They looked at each other. Neither moved nor made a sound. The bondmaid dived to pick up the bowl of porridge and quickly turned to continue feeding the boy, in an attempt to block out this strange intrusion with the resumption of normality.

The boy, still looking at the child Han, gestured for the bondmaid to give him the bowl. He held it in one hand and scooped out a spoonful of porridge with the other. He held out the spoon to the child. She stared at him; he moved the spoon closer to her mouth and it opened slowly, to receive the proffered sustenance. The boy waited for her to finish, then offered a second spoonful. Again, she opened her mouth to receive it. Spoonful by spoonful, he fed her, and she ate slowly, silently till the food was finished and he put the empty bowl back on the floor. All this while, their looks never left each other's faces.

They were unaware of the small group of adults that had gathered to watch, summoned by the bondmaid Lan who had gone running out of the room in fright. The women stood in a tight knot, watching.

"The child will live," said the matriarch.

VI

THE CHILDREN WANTED TO put ants in Spitface's trousers while he was sleeping. The idea had come to the child Han while Spitface was giving the young master Wu a ride on his back and she was awaiting her turn. He had earlier been commandeered to swing them from his arms, retrieve a kite from a tree branch, be the monster for them to put to death with a sword. An ant had entered Spitface's shirt. Routinely called upon to clean out cockroaches and dead rats, and kill intruding iguanas or snakes, the man screamed and writhed to one ant, perhaps for the benefit of the children. They laughed and he laughed with them, for his delight was to be in their presence and to amuse them, especially the little girl. Somewhere in the dimness of his mind was the memory of an exquisite fairy child who came into his existence and irradiated it. He would do anything for her.

The young master Wu was for the giant black ants found in abundance in the branches of the rambutan tree at the back, the child Han for the smaller but more vicious red ants found in equal abundance under the dank logs beside the woodshed.

They settled for the red.

It was a plan that called for much careful preparation and

skillful evasion of adult prying eyes. The trickiest part was to secure the red ants and store them in a matchbox. The child Han would handle the entire operation; the young master Wu would be responsible for getting the matchbox which had to be an extra large one, as stipulated by Han, for the accommodation of at least twenty selected warriors to do battle inside Spitface's trousers. The division of labor was necessary. It was based on a shrewd assessment of the potential risks of the undertaking; if the young master should get bitten by a red ant, the resulting furor from the bondmaid Lan and the matriarch would most certainly put an end to all joint undertakings in the future, whereas all the bites of all the ants in the world on the child Han would be of no consequence.

The same astuteness had governed the children's decisions regarding their respective roles in each of the games they played. It had the odd effect of making the little six-year-old girl, small for her age and dainty as a doll, climb trees, balance on log piles, trap frogs and spiders, sharpen metal pieces to use as knives, make fires and creep along deep drains, while the tall, robust-looking seven-year-old boy stood by and watched and clapped, mindful of his clean skin and shoes. Sometimes the yearning got too much for the boy, and he took the risks and came home from play with scratches and dirty, mud caked shoes, submitting himself to the tiresome process of being cleaned and washed and, on one occasion, fed with purifying herbal brews.

In the two years since the child Han's recovery, the awareness of adult reproof had been the only moderating influence on their intense inseparability. As soon as he awoke, the boy asked to be taken down to play with her; as soon as she finished the small chores she had been assigned, she darted out of the servant's part of the mansion and went in search of the boy.

They met in a paroxysm of pure joy, whooping, clapping their hands, and jumping up and down, their movements quickly synchronizing to form a dance of childhood's engaging primitivism.

Master and servant, princeling and beggar: childhood's insouciance sent the walls tumbling, to make them race towards each other and lock in dance. Walls upon walls: the boy broke through the bounds of a lonely swaddled childhood in a house of protective females, the girl through the barricades of a hundred raised voices and hands to remind her of who she was and to keep her in her place.

They rushed towards each other in joy.

There were still the dues to be paid to the adult world before the joy. The boy had still to be dressed, to have his hair combed and smoothened with Brylcreem, to do morning obeisance to ancestors both living and dead, to go through the lessons with the tutors; the girl had still to clean the prawns, to remove the skins from a bucketful of peanuts, to pinch off the roots from a mound of beansprouts, to take up the cleaned chamberpots to each of the bedrooms in readiness for the night. Right now, her small six-year-old hands could only manage empty chamberpots; in a few years, they could be entrusted to carry down the filled vessels, brimming with the night's steaming acridity of strong males.

The children's fascination with each other was exclusive. The boy showed no interest in the stream of little visitors, as impeccably dressed as himself, brought into the house in a twitter of delighted cries by their mothers and bondmaids. It startled the visitors to see him turn his taut, handsome young face, already stamped with the authority of privilege, towards the little bondmaid in the drab peasant clothes, and instantly unlock in amity. The girl showed no interest in the village children who sometimes came up with their mothers to help in the housework, and definite contempt for a fellow child bondmaid, the last to be brought in, a plain, sad little girl with a snotty nose. The poor thing, nicknamed Pork Bun, followed Han around like a devoted dog but was waved away, unless she carried a sweet or toy in her pocket that could be easily wheedled out.

Somewhere in the child Han's mind was a dim memory of

herself Lying sick on a wet mattress, in a room filled with angry adult faces rising from joss-fumes. The faces became open screaming mouths, attacking hands, kicking feet. Somebody held her down and somebody else forced a drink down her throat which came out again in a raging torrent, carrying out everything with it, so that she felt completely empty, like an egg sucked out of its insides. She remembered an excruciating hunger, and then everybody stopped shouting and turned to look at the young master Wu who had come into the room. He went straight to her and gave her something sweet and warm to eat. Her stomach filled, and feeling well and strong again, she rose from the mattress and followed him out of the room.

The child never spoke about the memory to anybody.

There was the other memory of a loved older brother who had carried her about on his shoulders and on his hips, making her laugh out loud in joy. Some vestige of the old adulation remaining in her small faithful breast, she resuscitated it and re-directed it towards the young master, nursing it to feverish flowering so that she was ready to risk ten times the knocks on her head from Choyin's hard knuckles and ten times the pinches on her thighs from the bondmaid Lan, to be with him.

It was not proper, it was not proper at all, said Choyin to the matriarch, for both of them to be playing like this. It had never happened before, and it had made the child arrogant and unmanageable. Choyin described the defiant child's large eyes that dared to fix themselves on an adult face. The child had a way of turning to face an adult, that was most disconcerting: she did it slowly, purposefully, and once her eyes latched on, they never blinked.

"Don't look at me like that! I will pluck out those eyes and swallow them down with my tea!"

Adults threatened to swallow staring eyes, tear out lying tongues, wash out foul speech with burning detergents. A stinging slap across the face only made the eyes stare more determinedly, challengingly. The bondmaid Lan complained of the humiliation of being shouted at by the boy in the presence of others. He had never done that before. It was the child's influence. She added, with a sob, that she had given him her everything, her time, her energy and, she might have added, her breasts. A child-servant grown defiant, a young master ungracious: the old order had been upset, charging the air with a sense of more frightful things to come.

"They are but children," murmured the matriarch, and went on to acknowledge the salutary influence of the little bondmaid in one respect: her grandson now had fewer tantrums and bad dreams and, moreover, talked to her more. She smiled in recollection of a small incident reflecting her grandson's new winsomeness. The little bondmaid Han had come up to her and asked if she wanted any back-knocking. Surprised and amused, she nodded and subjected her back to be knocked by a pair of determined but unpracticed fists. Then she felt another pair and turned to see her grandson in laughing competition with the little girl.

"Grandmother, I will get rid of all your aches and pains!"

She had laughed out loud in her pleasure and saved the loving proclamation for gentle re-telling to friends and relatives.

Thus the prerogative of childhood and the matriarchal approbation stayed the chastising hands and voices of the other bondmaids and made them sink into murmuring resentment: a pauper's child, less than they, saved from death two years ago, now immeasurably exalted above her kind.

It would not be for long. Childhood came to an end, and with it, its privileges. When the child reached eleven, twelve, thirteen, when the breasts sprouted and had to be kept in by the chaste tight bodice, when the first trickle announced the precise beginning of womanhood, she would have to return to the world of her kind, and never lift her eyes in the presence of the young master again.

The animosities washed harmlessly over the child as she moved about in the rooms and grounds of the large house, like a small nimble animal. Her world was a radiantly simple one because it was organized around the one single need to be with the young master. Everything else fell into place in relation to this centrality. Thus the grandfather and the grandmother were to be minded, because the boy minded them; the whole assemblage of bondmaids could be ignored, because the boy ignored them. In between were those who came in for a limited generosity or an active dislike from the boy; she shaped her behavior towards them in fine attunement to his. The boy sometimes liked to play with Spitface and give him unfinished slices of watermelon or pineapple or rice cakes, but he showed a keen dislike for the poor snotty-nosed Pork Bun who always hung around him shyly, rubbing one bare foot upon the other. The child Han duly included Spitface in her games and pushed Pork Bun away, making her cry.

The child had early grasped the truth of the inequality of their positions that was palpable not only in the attitudes of those around them but in every detail of difference in sleeping space, food, clothes. The boy's room was twice the size of that which the child shared with four other bondmaids; they all slept on the floor on mats rolled up and stacked against the wall during the day. The boy was known to be fastidious about his food, spitting out chicken and liver, festive fare on the bondmaids' table. His bondmaid Lan had the sleekest hair and shiniest skin, it was said, from the rich discarded remnants in the boy's bowl or plate. The child had a faint recollection of fragrant egg in steaming porridge, and sometimes stared at the mixing of not one but two, in the boy's morning meal of fine noodles. The buttons on the boy's clothes were always of ivory or bone or silk; those on the child's only cloth.

The awareness curbed the child's buoyancy: she never asked to taste the candies and pickles in the countless jars in the boy's room or to play with his expensive toys, and she always rose and ran out of his room when the grandfather appeared. "Here," said the old man in a kindly voice, handing her a slice of mooncake, but she hesitated, fidgeted with a corner of her blouse and turned to look at the matriarch standing nearby.

"Go on. Take it," she said but still the child hesitated.

To reinforce the ancient creed of division, the boy made no offer of the candies and toys of privilege, although a sudden impulse of generosity might make him drop a half-eaten cake in his pocket and later bring it out to put in the girl's hand.

Aware of his importance, he could demonstrate it forcefully. "I am the master, and you are only a servant. Do it."

She did it, her lips trembling in the hurt of his meanness. She cried from no one's reproach but his. The equilibrium was somewhat restored later when the boy feared to bring a frog out of a hole, and she coolly put her hand in and brought it out, or when he ran away from a drunk laborer staggering against the large iron gates, and she boldly went up and screamed at him to go away.

"Do it."

The girl's lips trembled again, but the boy stood before her in the regal hauteur copied from his grandmother sitting in her tall chair with the inlaid mother-of-pearl back, in judgment over a recalcitrant servant. The little girl lifted up her blouse and pulled down her trousers. The boy was disappointed. He had a recollection of firm, creamy mounds under tight underclothes, pleasant to the touch, but he was staring at nothing, mere flatnesses. The girl pushed down her blouse and pulled up her trousers again.

The boy had a last and final exposure to woman's breasts: one morning he ran into a room where the old *keo kia* woman was sitting, half naked, and ran out again, horrified by the sight of her hanging withered dugs. Between his remembered pleasure of the bondmaid Lan's breasts, his disappointment with the child Han's and his revulsion of the old *keo kia* woman's, he became thoroughly nonplused and was permanently cured of his curiosity about that part of the female anatomy.

But childhood's prurience found other channels of expression: he and the child plotted to plant at least twenty red ants inside Spitface's trousers to make him remove them and run about in screaming nakedness.

The child, breathless with excitement, showed him the six red ants she had already dug out and promised that as soon as she finished the beansprouts, she would go for the remaining number.

She sat on a small wooden stool in the kitchen, a bamboo basket of beansprouts between her legs, and applied herself diligently to pinching off the brown thread roots, one by one. The work always made her drowsy. She drooped over the large mound, then jerked awake in the exciting promise of the day's adventure. The size of the remaining mound dismayed her. Seeing no one around, she seized a fistful and stuffed it deep inside the already cleaned mound. She went on pinching off the horrid brown roots, hating them and thinking only of the red ants. Looking around and seeing no one still, she grabbed another fistful and stuffed it inside the garbage pail.

A man walked by the open kitchen window and looked in. Thinking he might have seen her, she decided it was best to pretend she had not seen him, and so carried on the pinching, calmly and conscientiously. He coughed, she looked up and said, in greeting, "Reverend" with the due deference insisted on by the matriarch.

The Reverend, on his way to the ancestral room, had caught a glimpse of the child in the kitchen, and came to have a closer look. Looking at her with the proprietory interest of the rescuer for the rescued, he decided she showed promise of beauty, though she was too thin and far too small for her age. There was something about the largeness and intensity of her eyes that was compelling. The Reverend's appetite was of that kind that saw its prey in advance, so that little bondmaids of seven, ten, twelve were ranged with those of fifteen, sixteen, twenty in an endless, self-replenishing continuum of pleasure. The child Han with her exquisite features promised much; the other child with the dribbling nose and flat, blunt features was dismissable.

The Reverend filed away one more mental image for future reference and passed on. The child sighed with relief; she did not like him.

Another man passed the window and looked in. This time the child was not one bit afraid. She said imperiously, "Go away!" Spitface, grinning broadly, stretched his arms towards her through the window and dangled a secret gift inside the cupped hands.

The child picked up her stool, put it by the window, stood on it and began pulling apart Spitface's hands for the gift inside. It was only a string of a few broken beads. The child wrinkled her nose in disgust. Every day Spitface searched the large rubbish dumps in the town and brought back a haul of small presents for the child—combs, pencils, mirrors, purses, colored string, cardboard boxes and once, an intact porcelain monkey. The child rejected most but still fell prey to the blandishment of the cupped hands.

The child said again, ungenerously, "Go away," climbed down from the stool and went back to the beansprouts.

He stared after her disconsolately, his mouth hanging open. A beast in search of the fragile beauty to invest all the love of his large, hungry heart, he had found her in this little willful girl who had bitten him at their first encounter.

He was about to leave when she had an idea and called to him.

"Spitface, wait!"

She gestured for him to come in.

With a whoop of delight, he hurried towards her. Each day of wandering in the hot sun among the town's dumps and market places made the wild tufts of hair on his head wilder, the horrifying skin even more horrifying. Left in a refuse heap as an infant, he had never left it, carrying around the utter dereliction of body and mind. His mother had been evil in a previous life, he had been evil in a previous life, his mother had slaughtered too many chickens when she was pregnant with him, and screamed to a goat's head, hanging on an iron hook in the butcher's stall and swinging to leer at her, which was why he had goat's eyes. Squalor, deprivation, hideousness—Sky God's rampage of fun did not end there. The god gave him a loving heart as well, which forever condemned him to loneliness for nobody would love him back.

"Spitface, come here!"

The child then said, "Do it," pointing to the mound of unpinched beansprouts. Spitface set about the task eagerly, looking to the child to elaborate it into a game of two which would make him exceedingly happy. But the child was already poised to make a disappearance. The sudden entrance of Choyin put an end to all hopes and she quietly took back the basket of sprouts from Spitface and sat down again.

"You are a sly one," said Choyin, remembering the numerous occasions when the child had tried to foist her work on the witless Spitface and the equally imbecile Pork Bun.

The child bent over her work, to shut out the carping voice and concentrate on the pleasure to come.

They were ready at last. Stopping some distance from their destination of the woodshed, Han slowly opened the matchbox which Wu had secretly removed from the room of one of the men upstairs. Wu wanted to see the ants before they were released to do their work. Han had managed with the aid of small twigs and leaves to get them out of their hiding places under the logs and into the matchbox. She had been bitten only three times and she proudly showed Wu the welts on her forearm and foot. She claimed she knew which were the culprits and offered to identify them.

"Hey, they're all trying to get out! Close the box."

"Did you see the huge ones? They were the ones that bit me!"

"I say close the box! They're trying to escape!"

"Alright. But did you see the big ones? Imagine twenty of them sticking to Spitface's bird!"

In their excitement, the children did their primitive hopping dance again. The box dropped to the ground and was quickly retrieved. Wu wanted to hold it for a while. He began to shake it close to his ear, listening for any sound from inside.

"Stop that! You'll make them giddy. They won't be able to bite Spitface!"

To their delight, Spitface was asleep. To their greater delight, he was sleeping in a sitting position against a side of the wood-shed, his legs co-operatively raised and bent at the knee so that the loose shorts fell away to allow for conveniently wide entrances. Spitface moreover wore no underwear, and one testicle was clearly visible. The child Han pointed it out to Wu; both clapped their hands over their mouths in an explosion of giggles.

Han had assumed that her work of securing the ants, the most risky part of the operation, entitled her to the most pleasurable, and was about to creep up to Spitface with the matchbox when Wu suddenly decided to stake his own claim of the pleasure. The children began arguing until they saw, to their alarm, Spitface beginning to stir, which brought on a hasty effort at accommodation and further division of labor. Wu would empty the box of ants into the opened shorts; Han would watch out for any that tried to escape and push them back, to ensure full mobilization of the task force.

The children, quivering with excitement, approached the sleeping Spitface. He had lowered one leg which now lay stretched out on the ground but the other was still obligingly raised. Wu crept up with elaborate secrecy, opened the matchbox and shook out its entire contents into the opened shorts. As expected, some ran outwards, but Han adroitly lifted up the edge of the shorts and shook them back in. Then she and Wu crept away, again with a great display of secrecy, putting their fingers to their lips, and hid behind a large disused oil drum to await the outcome.

Spitface slept on peacefully. He shifted a little once or twice and the children nudged each other hopefully. But nothing

77

happened. They were about to go away, concluding that the ants had managed to slip out, when Spitface sprang up with a loud roar. He looked around stupidly and clutched at various parts of his body to locate the source of the pain. His consciousness was then directed at a particular spot of his left buttock which he began to slap vigorously. He began slapping the right buttock as well, then had the idea to sit on the ground, grinding both in comical circular movements. There came another loud roar as Spitface's hand went to his genitals, indicating the enlargement of the ants' attack. By now, beginning to have a notion of the precise cause of his distress, he put his hand into his shorts, felt around and brought it out screaming as he stared at three savage giant ants clinging to it. Spitface started to hop about, alternately wringing his hands and using them to bear down with force upon his poor besieged member. Spitface's hopping was of that rare kind that would cause even the most solemn-faced child to laugh out loud with delight; it engaged every part of his body and every facial feature, throwing him into incredible contortions and convulsions that no war dance frenzy would rival. Han and Wu abandoned all attempt at secrecy, came out of their hiding place behind the oil drum and rolled on the ground in the fullness of their merriment.

Han wiped her eyes.

"Do you think he can still pee?" she asked.

VII

THE CHILDREN WANTED to test the power of the Old One's coffin.

They pretended to play by the carp pond, then, when no one was looking, they ran past some sheds to the far end of the mansion where the Old One's room was, huge and inhospitable, except to the coffin which had stood there undisturbed in a comer for more than twenty years.

The children peeped through a window and saw the bond-maid Chu trimming the Old One's beard. He sat obediently on his bed against a mound of pillows, a towel tied round his neck. She clipped expertly with a pair of scissors; when she finished, she picked up a smaller pair for the fingernails, and then worked on the toenails.

The Old One now and again looked at the bondmaid with a frowning effort at recollection. In the dimness of his memory some women, like flocks of colorful birds, stood out brilliantly and noisily, the loud cabaret girls in their bright sarongs, and one or two bondmaids with exceptional ability to please. The bondmaid Chu was elusive, yet a floating fragment of a face or voice remembered attached itself to her and made him frown quizzically.

"Why are you staring at me?" she demanded and the old man looked away, like a sheepish child.

The past authority of the former patriarch of the House of Wu, and the present helplessness of his dotage, the prescribed subservience of the bondmaid and the actual power of her position—all had come together in chaotic neutralization of each other, making Chu's position among the bondmaids a unique one, where a servant both served a master loyally and scolded him with impunity.

"Stop fidgeting."

"If you don't finish your porridge, I will beat you."

She took meticulous care of him, ensuring that he always looked neat and comfortable; his chamberpot was always properly emptied and cleaned, his clothes never showed any stain of food or urine, his nails never any dirt. He wandered when his mind did, always going to his coffin, laying upon it stories thick as the quilted red cloth pall on it, now faded with the years. Sometimes he wandered out of his room, as if in pursuit of some vaguely remembered pleasure, and was quickly pulled back by the bondmaid. He and the *keo kia* woman were the oldest in the mansion, but they never met; he remained confined to his room and she went about timidly in the part assigned to her, too old now to perform any rituals of appeasement on behalf of children, but allowed a bed and meals in that magnanimous house. On a full moon when the wails of demented women, children and dogs floated up into the skies, the Old One's low moans and the old *keo kia* woman's plaintive wails met somewhere in a commingling of sadness in the dark corridors of that large somber mansion.

The old woman would die soon, washed back into the debris of the little village she had come from, and the long stiff grasses would grow over her grave and erase forever all evidence of her existence on this earth. But the Old One would live some time yet and his funeral would be the biggest and grandest of the year, in which, in the midst of much pomp and ceremony, he would be at last laid in the ground in his coffin, and a marble tombstone erected which would bear his illustrious name and the dates of his birth and death. He would take his place with the other ancestors in the ancestral room and have his own altar with the plaques, joss-sticks, candles and flowers of filial regard and remembrance. On the Feast of the Hungry Ghosts, he would never be hungry, for his altar table would be loaded with the choicest meats and noodles and sweetmeats and wines, and he might, in a generosity magnified by his status as ghost-deity, tip the rich surfeit into the empty bowl of the *keo kia* woman who had nobody to remember her on feast days.

Meanwhile, he lay in his bed or pottered around his coffin, which had the power still of focusing his thoughts into a single intense point of joy or anger, depending on whether he remembered the filial concern behind its procurement, or the eagerness of the young to put him into it forever. The anger prevailed and linked with the moroseness of the maid, kept apart from the others but reputedly bribed with money and gold ornaments in exchange for total dedication, to charge the atmosphere in that room with a gloomy malevolence.

Life in the great house passed the Old One by; he was drawn

into it only twice a year—on his birthday, when progeny trooped in to pay respects, and on the first day of the New Year when, freshly bathed and dressed in a fine silk robe, he was led to the room of the ancestors for prayers and the ceremony of receiving cups of tea from offspring and relatives. He still kept his teeth; perhaps the fearful recollection of his possible responsibility for the deaths of the grandson and the grandson's wife, two young people in their prime, lingered to invest the long-toothed Old One's presence in the house with much foreboding.

After the trimming of the beard, fingernails and toenails, he was put to bed for his afternoon nap, and the bondmaid then sat in her chair and did her patchwork blanket. One lay folded up at the foot of the Old One's bed, one of many that had flowed from her hands in the interminable hours of watching and waiting. After a while, her head drooped over the needlework and the needle dropped from her hand as she fell into a gentle sleep.

"Let's do it now."

The children crept into the house, tiptoed to the coffin, lifted up the heavy red pall and were dismayed to find it closed tight. It would be impossible to move aside the heavy lid. Their idea had been to go into the coffin and lie inside. They had heard stories about the salutary effects of lying inside a coffin. The Old One had lain inside many times; it gave him longer life. They pondered about what next to do. Their interest turned to another aspect of coffin lore.

"You go and knock on it," said Han. "You do it like this." She clenched one hand and brought its knuckles vigorously down upon the other.

"No, you do it," said Wu.

"No, you."

"No, you."

"Alright, I'm not scared." And the child Han raised a fist. It came down on the coffin surface but without force for the child was beginning to lose her confidence.

"You're scared!"

The child pulled herself together and gave two sharp raps. Suddenly unnerved by the boldness of the act, the children turned and ran outside. They stood still for a while, panting, then peeped in again, to see its outcome.

"He's still alive," whispered Han, staring at the Old One sleeping on his bed.

"How do you know? He's not moving. Maybe he's already dead."

"He's snoring. Can't you hear? That shows he's not dead."

The children continued to stare intently at the Old One. A fly buzzed near his nose. He sighed softly and turned his head a little on the pillow. That put an end to all doubts about his condition.

The children were disappointed. Knocking sounds heard from the coffin were supposed to signal the end of its owner's life. The children concluded it was a false belief. They had been hoping to see the Old One writhing in dramatic death on his bed as they had once seen a huge rat come to its end on the kitchen floor. It was one of several that had been successfully poisoned by the kitchen bondmaids, and it had crawled out in great agony from its hiding place to die in full view of the children. Han had breathlessly run to fetch Wu and together they had watched the death throes in fascination.

Now nothing was happening. Perhaps the knocking on the coffin had not been hard enough for it to work. Perhaps they ought to try again.

"I'll do it this time," said Wu in a new surge of courage brought on by the disappointment.

"No, I'll do it."

"I can knock harder than you. My knuckles are bigger. Boys' knuckles are bigger than girls'. See?" Wu's clenched fist shot up in vivid illustration.

"I can knock harder. You'll see," said Han determinedly.

"I know! We'll knock together. When I say 'Begin!', we'll begin knocking together. Three times."

"No, six times. Six hard knocks."

"Okay."

The children stood side by side facing the coffin, their faces taut with expectation and excitement.

"Begin!"

They knocked enthusiastically and energetically. Their knuckles bounced off the hard wood and hurt but the hurting was part of the challenge. They went beyond the six agreed knocks, in dizzying competitive display of their powers, and only stopped when a ferocious presence descended upon them and angrily swept their fists off the coffin.

"What are you doing? Can't you see Great Grandfather is sleeping?" hissed Chu, while one hand flew to smack Han's head and the other kept a restraining hold on Wu.

"You mustn't do things like that," she said reproachfully to the boy. "If you do that once more, I shall have to tell your grand-mother."

The matriarch, despite her known indulgence of the boy, could be depended upon to rebuke him for such a serious trans-gression. The bondmaid turned round to smack Han again, but the child adroitly slipped her grasp and ran out of the room, fol-lowed by Wu.

Outside, in the safety of a hiding place carved out of an old store-room, the children sat on the ground and discussed the failed adventure.

"They were really good knocks. Chu spoilt it all," said Wu ruefully.

"Maybe the Old One has already died. That's why she's so angry," suggested Han. They discussed the feasibility of going back to do a check, but decided against it. They continued to express their puzzlement as to why, despite the indisputably unambiguous coffin knockings, the coffin owner remained alive "But somebody in the house will die," said Han knowledgeably. "All the stories say so."

And it was at this point that the boy Wu's eyes opened wide

83

and his mouth dropped in a manifestation of utmost shock and terror. He stood still for a moment, his handsome young face drained of color. Then he scrambled up in panic and tore out of the room. Han did exactly the same thing, her own expression having followed the changes in his, in an access of sympathy born of pure soul-mateship. Wu's terror, guided by some over-powering purpose, took him on a screaming navigation of the courtyard, the kitchen, two rooms, a flight of stairs and two long corridors before he finally rushed, breathless and red-faced, into the room of his grandfather.

"Waa-ah, Grandson! Be careful!" cried the patriarch in aston-ishment as the boy ran to him and wrapped both arms tightly round his waist, almost knocking over the brushes and dishes of inks on his table. He put a newly finished scroll out of the way and turned his attention to the boy. The child Han stood at his doorway, not daring to go in, but red-faced with anxious crying.

"What's the matter, Grandson?" said the patriarch, putting both hands on the boy's head. The boy's blubbering left spots of wet on his fine grey silk suit.

"You're . . . you're . . . not . . . dead!" blurted the boy, still clinging tightly to him.

"Of course I'm not dead," said the old man. He gently lifted up the boy's face. "Whatever gave you such a strange idea, Grandson?" The boy looked up at his grandfather with a tear-smeared face and whimpered, "I'll never knock on a coffin again, Grandfather! I promise!" and promptly set up a loud howl of remorse.

"Now, now, little Grandson, you're alright, you're alright," said the patriarch, holding the boy with much affection, while at the door, the child Han, watching the entire happening and still not daring to go in, also set up a howl in unison with the young master Wu.

VIII

THE BOY WU WAS BEING CANED. Not by his grandfather nor his grandmother who would rather turn any instrument of torture upon their own aging bodies than allow it to touch the precious boy. Certainly not by any of the bondmaids of whom any such extreme violation of ancient codes could only be explained as a sudden demonic possession as indeed, had been the case, years ago, when a servant, carrying his young master on his back, suddenly tipped him into the mud of a rice-field and was subsequently beaten to death by the boy's father and uncles.

But stick and rod were deferentially put into the hands of the boy's tutor. Before the *sinseh,* exemplar of wisdom, dispenser of knowledge, every parent, whether peasant or emperor stood in the humble position of ceded power: beat my son if necessary to make him learn. The boy's tutor exercised the privileges of his exalted position fully; he twisted the boy's ears or rapped his knuckles for minor mistakes, brought the cane down upon his palm for serious ones. He told endless stories of the young scholar who grudged himself sleep every night to pore over his books by the light of a single kerosene lamp, tying his hair to a ceiling beam so that each time he nodded, the pain would jerk him awake.

The boy was slow that morning. The tutor, face and voice dangerously tightening, told him to recite again the verse from the classics. The boy repeated it six times and each time he faltered. The tutor picked up the cane, a thin, supple bamboo, told the boy to stretch out his hand, and brought it down on the palm with all the force of the morning's annoyance. The boy winced, but imperceptibly.

"Now say it again."

The boy's eyes reddened and filled with angry tears but he kept his chin up, to contain them. They were threatening to overflow; the boy raised his chin higher. Into his blurred vision swam the apoplectically empurpled face of his tormentor; in his ears exploded a volley of barking commands.

"The other hand! Stand straight. Now!"

The cane swished again and came down in a frenzy of cross-cutting strokes on the other palm. The boy continued to hold up a trembling chin; hydrology at last defeating all efforts, the tears came down in a furious flow, splattering both cheeks. Still he kept his lips tightly compressed and would not make a sound.

"You will not be allowed to go, my boy, till you get every word right."

Always having his way with the bondmaids whom his little feet could kick into submission, he grew exceedingly resentful of the tutor who would not so much as let him scratch an armpit or shift position in a chair. The formidable personage sometimes looked up, startled, to see a little curl of a smile playing around the corners of the boy's mouth, and would not have guessed that the child had already committed him to a pit of savage red ants, hung him up by his testicles on the rambutan tree or decapitated him, then set his head on a dinner platter with a red turnip stuck in his mouth, exactly in the manner of the roasted suckling pig (the last method of disposal having been suggested by Han who got the idea from staring at such an ancestral offering on the Feast of the Hungry Ghosts).

The boy, without looking up from his books was aware of a movement behind the open window facing him. He looked up quickly to see the child Han waving to him with something in her hand. The tutor swung round sharply, but the child had already ducked out of sight. The boy went on with the recitation. Now and again, his eyes lifted longingly to the window; the little girl outside, with whatever she was holding in her hand and waving at him—a long-promised caterpillar, a toy given by Spitface represented a world of release and joy now immeasurably removed from him

A cry of pain came from outside the window, and an angry rasping voice. The tutor watched him but he tried not to give any sign of being distracted. There was another yelp of pain and then the sounds died away: the child had been discovered there by

Choyin and was now being ignominiously dragged back, by the ear or a pigtail, to the kitchen.

"Get back to your chamberpots."

"Get back to your books."

In a simultaneity of reproof, the tutor and the head bondmaid once more reminded the children of their separate destinies.

The child Han was not daunted; as soon as Choyin had left the kitchen, she slipped out and returned to the boy's study room, a miniature replica of the patriarch's immense chamber of erudition with its fine collection of books, scrolls, paintings and august portraits of the great sages of learning.

The boy was there alone, standing on the floor, sulking. He ignored the child's presence, still smarting with the humiliation of the caned hands and the biting taunt ringing in his ears: your grandfather is a fine scholar. You will be nowhere near him.

Seven years old, he felt the full force of the adult insult. His little body was infused with the heat of anger which soon passed into a cold weight of fear: suppose he disappointed his grandfather and made him sad the rest of his life? Suppose his grandfather died of a broken heart?

The boy's hand went up to wipe a tear.

"Don't cry."

The child Han had no recollection of the time her words of gentle concern disarmed a brutal parent and saved an entire family, but the adeptness at soothing away tears had remained and been nurtured into a skill exclusively used in the service of a beloved young master and playmate.

"Don't cry."

Impelled purely by love, it could not but succeed, and soon the boy, drying his tears and forgetting the hateful tutor, was showing interest in what she had been waving so tantalizingly at the window and which now lay concealed in a cigarette box in her pocket.

"Let's get out of here."

The room, still redolent of the tutor's scholarly presence, was not a fit setting for the sharing of secrets. They slipped out and went to their favorite hiding place in one of the storerooms.

It was neither caterpillar not toy, but a tiny baby mouse—no, two baby mice, curled around each other in a pink furless ball.

The child Han had found them in a nest in Spitface's woodshed; the mother mouse was nowhere to be seen and two other baby mice were dead and stiff and not worth taking away.

They peered at the two live ones still curled in a ball in Han's hands.

The plan was to persuade Spitface to swallow them. The children had heard of, but never witnessed, the swallowing of baby mice. Weak men grew strong, strong men stronger from having a nest of live baby mice inside their stomachs. The groceries man who came every week and sometimes stayed to gossip with the bondmaids, had once swallowed six.

He had popped them into his mouth, one after the other in rapid succession, swallowed without difficulty, then finished with a large cup of warm rice wine. He had never had a cold or a cough since. He even claimed half the pock marks on his face had cleared.

The children, sitting side by side on the floor, expressed regret at not having been present to witness the remarkable ingestion. Did the baby mice squeak on their way down? Did they wriggle inside the man's stomach? Did they escape in the man's shit when he went to the lavatory?

The idea of securing Spitface's co-operation to settle these questions became irresistible. They discussed ways of carrying it out. They could tell him that the baby mice were peanut candies or rice cakes. No, even Spitface could not be tricked this way. The baby mice would cure him of the ugly clusters on his cheek and neck. The mice would lengthen his bad leg so that he would not have to limp anymore. The mice—

Han gave a yelp of pain as her pigtails were yanked from behind, and she was pulled up into a standing position.

The cigarette box fell to the floor, spilling out its contents.

"How dare you—your work not finished—disturbing the young master—"

Choyin's accusations came out in sharp rasps. She gave a l ittle scream as her foot lifted just in time and remained trem- blingly suspended over the baby mice on the floor, now uncurled into two separate bodies.

"What's that? What sort of a child are you—"

Her attention turned to the young master.

"Master Wu, you must get ready for your visitor! She'll be here in half an hour! Your maid Lan's looking all over the place for you—"

Once again they were separated. They came together in joy, were separated and came together again. Not storm nor fire could keep them apart.

Choyin, spy of children's secret activities, discoverer of their secret hiding places, later went back for the two baby mice. They were stiff and dead, having been played with by a cat and then abandoned. Choyin picked them up with a rag and threw them into a rubbish-bin.

"What sort of child do we have on our hands—"

Choyin had wanted to adopt the child. The prospect of old age and solitude looming at forty, she wanted to lay claim to this child, to be assured, at least, of a proper funeral upon death and proper remembrance thereafter. She did not want the fate of the keo kia woman who would never have an altar raised to her memory, who would forever be both a hungry and a greedy ghost, depending on the superfluity from other ghosts' tables. The duty of filial piety befell adopted daughters too, by heavenly mandate, so she would be saved from the keo kia woman's sad fate.

Not only in the next world, but in this too.

Old bondmaids, no longer capable of any work, were given their own bondmaids to attend to them. Or they disappeared into homes for destitutes and died pitiful deaths. Unsure of the good fortune of the first, she was determined to avoid the tragedy of the second. The child Han, bright, crafty, winning in her ways, would be her very instrument.

She had indeed been observing the strange child with this purpose in mind. Disliking her for her artful alliance with the young master, and by extension, with the matriarch and patriarch, Choyin nevertheless saw in this artfulness the very quality needed for successfully dealing, on behalf of an aged, helpless parent, with the harshnesses of the world outside the safe House of Wu.

"The child is clever and thinks well for her age," she had said to the other bondmaids, narrowing her eyes and tapping her forehead with a forefinger. She went on to recount various instances of the child's cleverness and as many instances of the stupidity of the other child, Pork Bun. Once the child Han discovered that the rice dumpling she had been given had no meat filling, unlike the one Pork Bun had; it was a matter of seconds before the rice dumplings changed hands, and Pork Bun sat quietly eating the plain one, believing it to be the best.

Sold into the House of Wu at the age of three and slowly raised to the position of head bondmaid to which was attached a small monthly wage, Choyin now had the means to do her own buying. The bondmaid Han might even be enticed to remain unmarried and devote herself totally to the adopted mother upon whose death she would inherit a modest sum saved over the long years and a small store of jewelry besides, comprising a jade bangle, two gold rings, a pair of gold ear-studs and a silver belt.

The more she thought of the plan, sitting alone in the privacy of the small room allowed for her exclusive use as head bondmaid, the more was she convinced of its desirability.

She had approached the matriarch. The matriarch had no objection. But the child had. One of the bondmaids happened to say casually to her, "And how would you like being Choyin's daughter?" and the child, looking up from the tray of onions she was peeling, had said coolly and firmly, "I will never be Choyin's daughter. Choyin is not fit to be my mother."

Brought immediately to the ears of the head bondmaid, the words burned. A child's words were of no consequence and could be consigned to the rubbish heap of childhood's nonsensical prattle. But they had the power to hurt too, and as soon as the bondmaid Lan came into the ironing room to tell her what the child had said, Choyin stopped ironing, and became still, allowing the anger to sink in, then build up. It overflowed in a torrent of angry tears. She had been humiliated in front of the others by a mere child; the loss of face was irreparable. If the child had come up to her later and offered the cup of propitiatory tea— indeed the bondmaid Lan had quickly taken on the role of peacemaker and got the tea ready—the situation could still have been saved. But the child had a demon's perverseness. She pushed the cup of tea away.

From that moment the antagonism of the forty-year old woman towards the six-year-old child became an animating force in her tight, bleak life.

"You are not fit to be near them. So go away."

Choyin chased the child Han away from the doorway where she had been lingering to catch a glimpse of the young master's visitor.

"Go away !"

She pushed the child away and returned to the other little girl, also six years old, but as removed from the peasant child as gold from dust, diamond from mud.

Sitting on a chair facing the young master Wu, shyly clutching the hand of her bondmaid, Miss Li-Li from the House of Chang exuded wealth and privilege. On her small dainty person were expended the efforts of indulgent parents commandeering a team of serving maids, seamstresses, hairstylists and jewelers, to turn an ordinary little girl into a dazzling child-goddess. The bondmaids crowded round her, exclaiming their wonder in little twittering cries as their eyes ranged over the perfect side knots of hair, each ringed by an exquisite circlet of pink flowers, the perfect fringe combed to a fine silkiness, the richly embroidered pink silk suit with miniature phoenixes on the collar and sleeves, the miniature ear-rings, necklaces and rings, the anklet on the left foot, surely of solid gold.

The little girl, looking shyly at them and not letting go of her bondmaid's hand, elicited further exclamations of wonder at her maidenly modesty. Her bondmaid Pin, basking in reflected glory, gently urged her to go and play with the young master Wu, sitting stiffly in a chair opposite, and similarly nudged by his bondmaid Lan.

But the children refused to move and merely looked at each other with shy awkwardness.

Cakes, sweets, toys—these would soon do the unthawing, as they must, at all gatherings organized for children. Meanwhile, the bondmaids from the two illustrious houses, facing each other, could not resist the temptation of demonstrating their respective loyalties by some sly, delicate jousting. The bondmaid Lan suggested taking the children out to the carp pond to look at the new carp; the young master's grandfather had recently put in six new ones for him, she said, the very best, obtained from China itself. The bondmaid Pin took up the suggestion, but let drop the demure hint that Miss Li-Li's goldfish pond had very special goldfish brought in from Taiwan, beside which mere carp might not be exactly attractive.

The first shot was thus fired. Each side immediately took both defensive and offensive positions, and the wealth of both houses was unabashedly cast into the ring in glittering competitive cascades. Carp was pitted against goldfish, clothes made by the best tailors in Hong Kong against those made by tailors appointed by no other than the Sultan of Johore and his family, the finest ginseng against the purest birdsnest.

Not present wealth alone, but happiness well into the future, physiognomically promised by the gods: Miss Li Li's mole of fortune above the upper lip was matched against Master Wu's long, extended ear-lobes of longevity. Deriving no solace from their own pitiable backgrounds—Lan's mother had given her to an indigent relative who had in turn given her away to the House of Wu; Pin's origin was even more meager, she being one of three small ragged children abandoned near a temple—the bond-maids found rich compensation in their present illustrious connections, and could, in later years, if their husbands beat or bullied them, say with some disdain, "I once worked in the House of—. What about you?"

So the bondmaids, intoxicated by the dazzling rivalry, took each other higher and higher up on a spiral of competitive display. Their voices grew shriller, their expressions more animated.

Then, as suddenly, they stopped, ashamed of the impropriety of their behavior. Their masters and mistresses would have disapproved of such indelicacy. Boasting belonged to boors. Accordingly, they took each other down in equally extravagant leaps of self abnegation.

"My Miss Li-Li is not as bright as your master Wu—"

"No, no, she's so much brighter. My master Wu does not learn as easily as Miss Li-Li—"

"No, no—"

The equilibrium thus restored, the bondmaids once more turned to their little charges and asked them what they wanted to do.

Miss Li-Li had a bashful finger in her mouth; her large eyes, fixed on the boy, told of a longing to play with him, but her little body tightened in awkward shyness against any nudging. The young master was beginning to look extremely bored; he pulled at the collar of his new suit and shifted about in his seat. The bondmaid Pin made the supreme mistake of leading Miss Li-Li to him and making her stand before him. With finger still in mouth, she stood coyly and uncertainly in front of him, a pink confection; he swung around abruptly in his seat and with his back to her, concentrated his attention on a lizard chasing an insect on the wall. The little girl continued standing before him, her finger deeper in her mouth, her eyes fixed upon him. He swung round again; they followed the direction of his eyes and saw to their dismay, the child Han at the doorway. The boy's bored look vanished; his eyes shone.

The bondmaids looked to Choyin to deal with the intruder. She said sternly to the child, "Go and finish the onions." The child's fingers were dirty from peeling off the onion-skins; one piece was sticking to the wet under her nose where she must have drawn her hand across. In the presence of the two dazzling children, she was a beggar from the garbage-dumps; she had no business being there.

"I thought I told you not to come here."

The child Han, ignoring her, flashed something at the boy— two empty tin cans joined by a long piece of string. The promise of an exciting game after an intolerable morning with the tutor and later the visitor, made the boy scramble down from his chair and move quickly towards the child Han.

"I want to go out to play!" he announced with some hauteur, and thereby freed the visitor of her shyness so that she too burst forth and cried, in her first utterance since her arrival, "I want to play too!"

There was no stopping them. The child Han turned to go, followed by the young master, now increasing his pace, and the dainty visitor who abandoned all daintiness by roughly pushing away her maid's hands and pulling an ugly face at her.

The other bondmaids again looked anxiously to Choyin to handle the crisis.

"You can only play by the carp-pond," she said firmly, and signaled to the maids to go with the children and see that the troublesome one created no more trouble.

The cakes and candies were set up under a tree near the carp-pond; meant only for the visitor and the young master, they were actually at the disposal of the peasant child. So the bondmaid Lan said pointedly, "They are not for you," and was ignored by the child who began to show the other two the use of the tin-cans as telephones. They took turns putting the cans to their ears and bellowing into them.

So far, so good; the bondmaids continued watching for a while, then decided they too needed some tea and walked back into the house.

Miss Li-Li soon complained that the cans smelt and went to sit on a swing by herself, her dainty feet curled up to avoid contact with dirt. She surveyed Han dispassionately, wondering about the ugly clothes and remembering a little beggar child she had once seen, sleeping under a temple staircase with her mother. The child had scabs on her legs which attracted a small swarm of flies. She asked Han if she and her mother ever slept under a temple staircase. The child Han suddenly burst out with: "There's a nest of baby birds just over there," indicating with an arm, "and they are all white. When they turn black, the mother bird will eat them up."

The awesome information sank in slowly. Miss Li-Li's eyes grew larger; her little mouth opened.

She said, "I want to see! Take me to see!"

"We must be very careful. If the mother bird sees us, she'll fly away."

"I want to see!" The anticipatory gleam of sadistic pleasure was at odds with the exquisite doll's face and pert dimples so much exclaimed over. Miss Li-Li got down from the swing.

"The mother bird has teeth, very sharp teeth that can bite off the babies' heads." The young master Wu, entering into the conspiracy with Han, outdid her in ghoulish details. With gusto, he painted a picture of a monster about to cannibalize its young in the most savage way, first ripping off the heads, then tearing apart the bodies for the entrails to spill out, these being the tastiest part of the meal.

Miss Li-Li quivered in the thrilling prospect of such a spectacle.

"Let's go!" she screamed imperiously. They rushed off. They ran out through the back gate at the bottom of the garden, and out into a large stretch of waste ground. She ran after them, panting, her little feet in their velvet shoes navigating small puddles, mounds, tufts of dry grass.

"Wait for me! Wait for me!"

They ran on and on.

"Hurry! Hurry! Or we'll be too late!"

They yelled back.

She plodded on bravely. Her little face tightened with tearful anxiety.

"Wait for me! I don't like these rough stones—"

They led her into a large mud puddle. She slipped and fell. Screaming, she tried to get up and fell again. Giving up, she sat in the mud and screamed hysterically for her bondmaid.

They watched from behind some bushes and laughed. They mimicked her screams and laughed again. Then they ran off to play by themselves.

IX

THE BARRAGE OF KNUCKLE RAPS on her head, slaps across her cheeks, pinches all over her thighs and arms, did nothing to crumble the child Han. She stood immovable as a rock in the midst of the raging storm, and when it subsided, it was, oddly, the perpetrator who wept. Choyin began to weep noisily in a mixture of agitation and anger, shaking her head vigorously and saying that she must have done something evil in her earlier life for Sky God to punish her with such a vicious child in this.

The little visitor had been finally brought back to the house, screaming and covered with mud. It was Spitface who had found her, but his efforts to pick her up only increased her screaming, so he had run back and got help. Her bondmaid Pin became hysterical and had to rub Tiger Balm on her forehead and chest to keep steady. There was a flurry of activity to get the screaming child out of her wet muddy clothes, give her a warm bath, give her something soothing to drink, rub soothing oil on her chest. Her bondmaid Pin wept noisily, wringing her hands. It was shocking—a visitor from the House of Chang subjected to such indignity.

The House of Wu swung into a massive exercise of appeasement. The matriarch went personally several times to the House of Chang to express her sincere regrets, to bring rich gifts for the little girl and, most importantly, to assure her parents that the culprit had already been severely punished. The matriarch, wishing to emphasize that the happening was an extreme aberration as shocking to her household as to outsiders, confided the special information of the child Han's strange nature, possibly of demonic origin. She recounted in close detail the incident of the attack on Spitface and the subsequent illness and exorcism.

"Why do you still allow a demon child to be under your roof?" said Miss Li-Li's grandmother coldly.

The matriarch could not say that if she sent away the demon child, her little grandson would fall sick from pining, so attached were they to each other. So she merely sighed and said, "What can one do? Her mother would not take her back," and again gave the assurance that the child had been duly dealt with.

What she had done was to shake her head, heave a great sigh and say to Choyin, "You do what you think is suitable. That child tires me. I don't want to think of her."

And that had been enough for Choyin to unleash the full force of her fury upon the child, not just for the latest audacity but a whole accumulation of past grievances.

Of the boy Wu's part in the incident, nobody spoke a word.

The child Han, as soon as Choyin had left, still sniffling noisily and lamenting a burdened life, ran upstairs to the room which she shared with four other bondmaids, unrolled her sleeping mat and curled on it, burying her face in the pillow and sobbing her little heart out, not in the pain of the earlier punishment which was beginning to develop into a fever, but of the certainty that she would not be allowed to play with the young master Wu again. She cried for a long time, finally falling into an exhausted, fitful sleep.

It was true—the young master was being prevented from coming out to play with her. The hollow spaces of his absence reverberated with chilling echoes that struck terror in her heart: suppose when they met again, he would no longer remember her? Suppose—and here she felt a tight little knot of pain in her stomach—they had taken him away to stay with that hateful girl of the pink flowers and velvet shoes? The clue was provided by the absence of his bondmaid Lan—she too was nowhere to be seen.

On the fourth day, she saw a group of them—Miss Li-Li and her bondmaid Pin, the young master Wu and his bondmaid Lan, and a tall, fat boy of about eleven or twelve whom she had never seen before—walking together into the reception room and disappearing into the smaller room adjoining it. She was cleaning a vase for the ancestral room, and at sight of them, she started up and dropped the vase, luckily unbreakable brass. It clanged across the floor. She froze, listening. Good, nobody heard, or somebody, having heard, did not bother to come to investigate. So the child quickly picked it up, put it back on the table and ran, breathlessly, to catch a glimpse of the young master. But the door was closed. She tried to open it and somebody slapped down her hand.

"Any more nonsense from you and—" Choyin's warning was all the more severe for its being left unfinished; it encompassed everything from double the number of the previous slaps and pinches to being sent away to an orphanage where, she was told, young people had to empty the old people's chamberpots every day, full of shit and vomit and blood.

The child knew there was a window looking into the room from the outside. She ran outside, dragged two flower pots, to a spot below the window ledge, put one on top of the other and mounted them to have a peep inside.

Watched by the bondmaids, the three children in the room

were on the floor, playing with trains whose magnificent tracks stretched the whole length of the room. Han had never seen the toy before; it must have been bought specially for the occasion. Handsome toys, lavish food on the table—Han had never seen such a spread; lavish adulation from the bondmaids—the bondmaid Pin was fanning Miss Li-Li with a paper fan and the bondmaid Lan was now and again wiping off the perspiration on young Master Wu's forehead with a small white towel. The humiliation of the first visit was being successfully erased by the extravagant generosity of the second.

Miss Li-Li, clad in her finest, another shade of pink, was smiling and pointing excitedly to the moving trains while the tall fat boy who was probably a brother or cousin, explained to Wu, with much authoritative eloquence, the special features of the expensive toy. At one point, they got together in a small tight group to cheer two competing trains, and the child, looking at the laughing trio in the radiance of wealth and privilege, suffered a dull ache in her chest and never felt more isolated. She tried to catch the boy Wu's eyes, waving a large cigarette-box (there was nothing inside this time) and ducking each time anyone looked in her direction. Cigarette-box stood no chance against train; the boy's eyes were glued on the toy and never lifted.

There was hope yet. No toy, no matter how splendid, was guarantee against boredom. The boy's room overflowed with cars, carriages, wooden animals, rubber animals, soldiers, acrobats, fat men on chamberpots, fat clowns with monkeys; he had merely looked at them, tinkered with them briefly and then cast them aside.

The child Han was prepared to wait out the boy's present absorption and then call to him again.

She saw the bondmaids picking up the trains and tracks and putting them aside, clearing some space in the room, heard Miss Li-Li and the tall fat boy say something in excited whispers as if in anticipation of a second stage of the afternoon's entertainment. The door opened and—the child Han caught her breath—in walked a dark, bearded man with a silver turban, carrying several bird cages with colorful, twittering birds inside. It turned out that he was no more than a wandering entertainer, much seen in the neighborhood, who used his birds sometimes to tell fortunes to housewives and bondmaids and sometimes to perform tricks to make children laugh.

The value of any entertainment for the child Han being derived purely from the boy Wu's presence by her side, she now glanced indifferently at the bearded man fussing over his cages of birds and talking gibberish to amuse the children, and stared intently at the young master to watch for that moment when he would look in her direction and she could wave to him.

The bird man rambled on interminably and did a lot of nonsensical things with his birds to make the children laugh. He got the birds to tweak his nose and ears and pretended to scream in pain. He harassed a large black bird, put his face close to its behind, made a loud farting sound to suggest that it was the bird's annoyed response, and pretended to curse and splutter at the foul smell. The children roared their merriment. Then the bird man commanded his birds to play with the children, inviting each child to come up and offer an arm or shoulder for a bird to peck. Miss Li-Li squealed with delight as a yellow and green parakeet stood on her shoulder and nuzzled her ear; the tall fat boy proprietorially held two black birds with yellow crests on his arm, and the boy Wu put his face close to a green parrot's and began to whistle. It was a merry party, and it dismayed the child Han because the boy Wu was too preoccupied to look up at her.

He did at last; he was carrying the green parrot on his arm and taking a careful walk when he caught sight of her. Her heart beating wildly, she waved at him. He merely stared, as if unable to fit her presence into the present scheme of enjoyment. Frantically, she pulled out the cigarette box, mouthing something, to suggest the wondrousness of its contents. But he had already turned his back on her and gone back to his friends.

The child Han turned pale. It had never happened before, and happening for the first time, it convulsed her with shock. The dull pain flared into a bright flame of anger. For the first time, other sensations—jealousy, a sense of betrayal, a screaming sense of loss—combined with longing to form a single surge of furious energy that pitched the child forward and caused her to beat at the window, shouting and crying. She banged with both fists, screaming to be allowed in. Everyone in the room turned round. If the young master had turned round, had said something kind, that would have put an end to the tearing pain, and she would have been content to wait outside quietly for the visitors to leave and for him to come to her again. But he merely watched, like the other two, while the bondmaids surged forward as one vengeful body to scold, beat and put things right. Then the boy turned away, the other two, taking the cue, did likewise and the bird man continued his antics.

It was the ultimate rejection and it ripped out the raw insides of her rage. She screamed uncontrollably and fell from the flower pots to the ground, where she lay sprawled in a heap, subsiding into a whimper. Choyin pulled her up.

"You! You again! Let's see this time!"

She was dragged back to the kitchen, put in a chair and tied up with a number of towels.

"Stay here. You are not to move. I shall know how to deal with you when the visitors are gone."

The child sat still on the chair; she was too dispirited to want to struggle out of the towels. For a while it appeared the fighting spirit had been totally sapped, so that not one movement, not one sound came from her. Only two persons stopped by to look at her. The bondmaid Chu, coming into the kitchen with a flask to get hot water for the Old One, shook her head, said nothing and went away. Spitface hovered by, circling her idiotically, and making anxious little noises, not sure what he should do. The child pretended not to notice him. He moved to fix his devoted melancholy face on her, and she turned her head abruptly to one side. The poor man would persist in his desire of catching her eyes. She at last screamed, "Go away!" spat vehemently, and he withdrew.

It seemed a long time before Choyin made her appearance and when at last she did, she went straight up to the child, untied her and said, "You have not one, but several demons in you. How can you be doing things like that to us when we have fed and clothed you these years? I don't want to beat you again; it is no use beating you."

But her hand was still raised to descend on that defiant face. Which it did, as soon as the last towel was untied. The child made to run off, Choyin tried to hold her down, they struggled. The child finally broke free and ran out of the kitchen. Once out of the house, she appeared unsure about where to go; she began running round the courtyard in circles, like a demented little animal, then stopped under a tree, close to the gate facing the road.

"That's right! Stay there! Nobody wants you. Stay there all you want."

The child thought, I will stay here. I will not go back into the house. I will not eat any food or drink any water. I will die here. They will come and find me dead. That will teach them.

She stood with defiant erectness a long while, her face turned away from the house. If her body had remained completely unmoving under the rain of slaps and pinches, it could maintain its perfectly uncompromising rigidity against whatever threatened now. A leaf fell on her nose, an insect ran over her feet. Faint noises came to her from the house; a bursting balloon, a tiny shriek from Miss Li-Li, a clattering of pans. From the outside somewhere came a cat's yowl, a dog's bark, a trishaw man's bell.

The noises mixed and confused her; a voice detached itself and said "Han." She turned round sharply.

A woman, thin, pale, haggard, stood at the gate, both hands clutching the metal bars, forlornest of forlorn prisoners. She looked at the child, then stretched a hand inside and repeated, "Han, my little daughter."

Two years had almost erased the memory of that face; the remaining fragment, sometimes floating in the night's dreams, was of a hard woman with a huge hard belly scolding a crying child, casting her off and running away. It did not match the picture of the wispy, weepy woman at the gate. Yet the remembered voice had the same quality. The child Han became confused and looked at her in frowning sullenness.

"Han, my little daughter. Don't you remember me?"

The wretched woman began to cry. Then she stopped, struck by an idea. She pointed to a thread bracelet on her right wrist, with a little piece of jade, in the image of Sky God, and excitedly pointed to the one on Han's wrist, gesticulating the similarity, clear indisputable evidence of a previous bonding. The child looked at her bracelet, always a matter of indifference to her, and then at the woman's. While the discovery of proof had excited the mother, it had no effect on the child. Her one desire being to be with the young master Wu again, everything that did not conduce to that purpose was worthless, including any visit by any stranger regardless of what they claimed.

The sound of voices in happy laughter floated out to invest this purpose with an aching, despairing urgency, so that the intrusion of this stranger could only annoy and exasperate. Besides, the claim of maternity, coming after Choyin's, was doubly noxious so the child made a face and determinedly turned her back to the woman at the gate. The woman began to cry noisily.

"I only wanted to have a look at you. I don't wish to take you back. You are with far better people. Your mother's only a beggar—"

The wails died away. When she turned to look again, the woman had gone.

She felt very tired and squatted down. She saw ants coming out of a hole in the ground and played desultorily with them, scattering them with a leaf. She stole a glance in the direction of the house; nobody appeared at doorway or window to look at her. If Choyin was peeping from somewhere, she would see victory, not surrender; so the child stood up again and presented a straight back. But tiredness overcame her; she squatted down again, then curled herself on the ground and promptly went to sleep.

She must have slept a long time; when she awoke, she was aware of growing darkness and lights beginning to appear in the windows. She felt extremely tired and hungry. A cold wind was starting to blow.

"Get up now. Get back into the house."

It was Choyin.

It was not the young master Wu. The young master Wu would have made such a difference.

The child turned her face away.

"Get up, I say. Why are you like that? Don't you want something to eat? Everyone's eaten."

The child continued to ignore her.

"Do as you like. If you want to stay out here all night, nobody can stop you."

Choyin walked back to the house.

The child's steely resolve returned. She stood up, proud and erect. The wind blew her hair, loosened from the pigtails, about her face. A large drop of water fell on her nose, followed by several more. Then the rain came, fast and furious.

She thought, I will die in the rain. Let them come and find me dead in the rain. The water pelted her mercilessly; her wet clothes clung to her body and she began to shiver. She saw, with grim triumph, anxious figures clustering at the door, dark against the light.

"Come in! Get out of the rain!"

The shrill urgency of the voice contained the adult's terror at seeing a small child resolutely standing alone, out in the darkness, in screaming wind and rain.

There was some urgent bustling at the doorway; somebody said, "Take this" and she wondered who it was who came crashing through the sheets of water towards her with a very large black umbrella.

It was Spitface. He caught her arm; she pulled it away. He held the umbrella over her; she knocked it off. He circled her unhappily making queer little grunting noises and alternately stretching out a hand and letting it fall hopelessly to his side. He at last made an effort to grab her by the waist; she wheeled round and beat off his hand so ferociously that he fled back to the house, dropping the umbrella which fell to the ground and rolled away in the wind.

At the doorway, the cluster of heads thickened. The strange child was repeating the bizarre behavior two years back. How long would she stay out in the storm? What should they do now?

And then when they thought the child was ready to drop in defeat—no human nor dog could be out in that storm for long—they saw her rise, saw the strange, wild child rise from the sodden ground, her wet clothes and hair plastered to her body, in a recharging of energy, fling her arms out and spin her body against the beating water in a furious dance. The demon child was dancing in the storm and singing a song. They could not hear the words which were muffled by the roar of the wind, but the child, her throat bursting, out-roared the wind and her words came charging upon their ears in screaming challenge:

The bird looks
The bee cries
The ants yearn
For Choyin's flower
For Choyin's stinking flower—

There followed a full assault, as Choyin's stinking arse, breasts and cunt were unfurled in ignominious display and flapped about in the storm for all to see. The cluster of heads at the doorway moved closer together in a reaction of shock and dismay.

"Somebody stop her. Somebody stop her, I say—" but Choyin's protest was too weak to be sustained against the onslaught of a child's tormented soul:

Chu's smelly shit
Lan's rotting cunt—
Pin's cunt, worse than
Rotting salt-fish—

The child's vituperative vocabulary, built up through a steady and secret absorption of adult gossip and banter, was now fully emptied upon the broadcasting power of a storm. A lightning flash lit up that small dancing figure, stark, white, transfigured, and a crushing roar of thunder spun it higher up the vortex of its fury. A child cursing its elders, a peasant child cursing its superiors. Blasphemy upon blasphemy—surely Sky God whose thunder peals and lighting bolts lent his endorsing power to curses and withered the cursed one with fear was in no collusion with a beggar-child?

There was another bustle at the doorway, even more urgent, for someone screamed and bodies came together in a scuffle.

"Oh no! Stop him! Somebody stop him!"

But it was too late. The young master Wu had broken free of the restraining hands and was running, against heavy lashings of rain, to join the crazy child.

"Oh stop him! Quick!"

He ran on, unafraid, and stopped in front of the child Han. The rain ran in rivulets down his face but he made no attempt to wipe them off, as he stood before her, saying nothing. She had stopped her wild dancing and was standing still too, staring at him, her teeth violently chattering, her eyes bright with a preternatural glow.

He has come, he has come, they said and fixed upon him an intensity that said further: he has come and they will never separate us again. The happiness washed off the pain in her

little heart as surely as the rain had washed off every bit of
dust from the rooftops that evening.

Choyin's filthy arse
Lan's foul, smelly cunt —

The boy's shout was louder than the girl's. They held hands,
facing each other, and leaped up and down in pure joy, while the
fury of the storm around them continued unabated.

Sinseh's stinking balls
Sinseh's rotting penis
Sinseh's face, full of shit —

The cathartic bursts had shifted to a new subject, and a
higher level of fervor as the tutor next took his turn to have his
corruptions published upon the wind.

Sinseh's face, full of shit
Sinseh's mouth, foul as his shit —

The boy and girl, still facing each other and holding hands,
leaped about with no diminution of energy or ardor.

The girl thought, I'm so happy, as another burst of thunder
threw them together and they collapsed in a heap on the ground,
still shouting and laughing.

PART TWO

Woman

I

THE MAID HAN WOKE UP in the cold silent darkness before dawn and lay very still on her mattress on the floor, as was her wont, absorbing the small sounds around her.

From the outside came the solitary cry of a bird and the melancholy whimper of a dog in response; from the inside, the rhythmic breathing of the other bondmaids deep in sleep on their mattresses. A gurgle, as someone turned and flung out an arm, broke the still surface of the pool of slumber and set up an agitation of ripples: a groan, as of an overcharged heart, the rough grinding of teeth, a fragment of speech, angry but incoherent, flung abruptly upon the stillness and as abruptly swallowed back. Awake, she lay still as a corpse; deep in sleep, they tossed and turned like restive children, finally curling fetally into the warm darkness of blankets and breathing easily again in the precious moments of snatched sleep before the day's labors.

For her, the preciousness of this limbo between night and dawn lay in its exclusive appropriation by lovers. She could see them by the hundreds, not only in the cemetery where they had emerged from their graves for the trysting, but anywhere and everywhere—in houses, temples, by the roadside, by disused wells, beside abandoned ponds, under trees, in the very kitchens where the first lights would soon be switched on to begin the work of another day—as long as they could be reached by the rooster's cry summoning them back.

As a child, she had been terrified by stories of these ghost lovers, but now she thought of them unafraid and would look at them unafraid if one day she chanced to meet them.

Ghost lovers joined by death in Heaven or Hell but pining for much-loved spots of special remembrance on Earth were allowed back and thus met in tremulous joy on ground hallowed by a last presence or final covenant. Han loved best of all the story she had heard as a girl of a pair of young lovers who, forbidden by their parents to marry, committed suicide by wading into a deep pond, wrists tied tightly together, thereafter claiming the spot as their own and seen there by people not yet born when they died.

Ghosts from Heaven met ghosts from Hell once a year through a remarkable concession by an understanding Sky God who did not think that even separate destinies in eternity should stand in the way of true love. Ghosts from Heaven and Hell met their still living lovers on Earth the whole year round, sometimes begetting ghost children. There was the story of a young woman who gave birth to a child who was found to cast no shadow, and another story of another young woman whose child had a shadow but also ghost-feet that never touched the ground.

A woman whose daughter had died in infancy had a dream, sixteen years later, of the girl, now a beautiful ghost-woman who told her mother she was lonely and in need of a lover. The woman immediately went on a search on her behalf and found someone whose infant son had died at about the same time and would now be about nineteen or twenty years old. In a rare instance where the living played matchmakers for the dead, the two happy mothers got together and arranged a marriage by effigy for their offspring: two large paper figures, together with a generous stack of gift ghost money, were ceremonially burnt. Every year just before dawn on the anniversary of their marriage, the ghost couple appeared on the very spot of its consummation, to signal their joy and gratitude to their respective parents.

Heaven, Hell and Earth, then, poured out their lovers who

poured out their hearts in an urgent commingling of desire in the brief hours before cockcrow.

As soon as the cry came, strung upon the cold morning air in uncompromising authority, these ghost lovers groaned, wailed, beat their fists upon heads or chests, tore their hair, made promises, extracted promises and fled. One or two might foolishly defy the order and suffer the penalty of being banished from Earth for all eternity, but generally all heeded the rooster when it got up on its feet, raised its head to the heavens and poured out the heart-rending cry. Loved and hated alike by the ghost lovers, it stood in splendid isolation from the rest of the twelve animals in the zodiac entrusted with the lesser tasks of dispensing good fortune and male children.

Han remembered a time when the rooster's cry had sent tremors through her body so that she moved to Lan's or PoPo's sleeping mat, for the semblance of protectiveness afforded by the touch of a human body, even an inhospitable one. When forbidden to do that, she had clung to a rag doll that Spitface had picked up from somewhere for her, biting off an ear one night in a climax of terror induced by a very bad dream. And there was another time, so far back she could only recall it with difficulty when the same fearful cry of the rooster—or was it the owl?— had made her burrow deep into a heap of warm bodies on a huge wooden bed, and lie very still there.

The teeth-grinding bondmaid Pork Bun was seeking the same solace. In the darkness, Han saw the girl's sleeping form edging towards her and settling itself heavily against her back, like a nervous child quieted by warm contact with its mother. Pork Bun had never lost her childhood timidity. Indeed it had increased with the stories of ghosts so freely circulated by the bondmaids in that large house. Cooking, ironing, stoking the great cement stoves, cleaning chamberpots, plucking fowl, they had an endless supply of stories, some retold and some made up on the spot by fertile imaginations springing up like some strange garish bloom in the vast greyness of their lives.

Someone had reported seeing the ghost of the old *keo kia* woman. Pork Bun went pale with fright because she remembered the old woman who, shortly before her death, had started to wander on her own to those places where she had conducted the *keo kia* ceremonies for sick children, re-enacting the rituals of appeasement with imaginary scissors, candles and joss-sticks. She had wandered off in the rain once and stood upon a small grassy mound under a tree, until someone found her and brought her home, wet and shivering. That moment of final decline, just before her death, when her long white hair, loosened from its back knot, was wetly plastered on her small, wrinkled scalp and her face wore the quizzical, hurt expression of a child unfairly punished, became fixed in her eternity, for her ghost thereafter took that guise, down to the detail of rivulets of rainwater running down the old stricken face.

Pork Bun began seeking the comfort of touch in sleep. If Han moved on the mat, she moved also; it contented her to be allowed the mere contact of fingertips. Forced to be on her own, she curled tightly on her mattress, whimpering softly, and stopped her ears against the sound of rising wind and storm. The teeth-grinding was part of the poor girl's general nervousness; it filled the air and made even sound sleepers stir in their sleep and cry out impatiently, "Stop that!"

In the darkness, Han lay still as the girl pressed against her so trustingly. Both eighteen, they looked mere children curled together on a mattress on the floor. In childhood, Han had pushed and shouted at the dull, coarse girl with the snotty nose. Now antipathy gave way to tolerance which softened into pity for the poor creature whose childhood nickname of "Pork Bun" had mutated into the even more damaging one of "Wind-in-the-Head" in cruel announcement to the world of yet another deficiency, this time of brainlessness.

As suddenly as she had slipped back into deep sleep from the teeth-grinding, the girl woke up with a start, sitting up bolt upright. She panted and sucked in a stray thread of spittle.

There was just a moment of looking around and recollection of purpose; then she scrambled up, rolled her mattress, stacked it against the wall and hurried out of the room.

Bondmaids' work began at cockcrow; Wind-in-the-Head had been regularly getting up well before the first summoning cry and leaving the room to go somewhere. Hurrying through the darkness in the urgency of the last half hour before cockcrow, Wind-in-the-Head might have been on her way to meet a ghost-lover. Ghost-lovers were tender and inspired no fear; the girl's suppressed sob of terror spoke of an earthly lover ensconced in the solidity of bed and male purpose somewhere in the rooms along the long dark corridors of the great house, and impatient for the expression of that purpose. Why are you late again? Haven't I told you to get here before cockcrow? Do you want everybody to know?

But the brainlessness could be disregarded in the enjoyment of the compliant softness of an otherwise ill-favored body.

Han watched her disappearing form and thought: "I will never be like Wind-in-the-Head," turning the thought into an urgent prayer ahead of the day's first lighting of joss-sticks: "Sky God, bless me and spare me the fate of Wind-in-the-Head." She could not stop there; the prayer rolled on with a more positive entreaty: "Sky God, give me what my heart-desires."

She left unspecified the desire, in the belief that even an all-knowing deity could be tricked into answering an audacious request if the audacity lay hidden under a generality.

On the other hand, the god was known to be singularly obtuse, so that petitioning women had to peel open the divine eyelids and unwax the divine ears.

"Sky God, give me what my heart desires. Bring him back safely home."

She had heard of ships lost in storms, of travelers in ships who did not make it home even if their ships did, because they died of strange sicknesses and were buried at sea. She had had bad dreams of him struck down by a raging fever, dying in the midst of strangers, sewn up in a sack and tossed upon the desolate ocean, while the ship continued its way homewards.

The curse of a coffinless death, triumphantly staved off by the Old One, had rebounded upon the great grandson in his prime. Han had started up from the dream in a panting fright, her face wet with tears. She thought, Old One, if you do this to him, you will have my curse forever.

The dream had the fearful quality of an omen, and she went about in a daze for the rest of the day, thinking: "I will not live if he dies." She would hang herself from a tree, plunge into a well and then seek him out every day of eternity if necessary, with every hour granted before cockcrow.

Loving a man, a woman suffers both when he is with her and when he is away from her. Presence and absence link into an impossible whip-lash of pain upon her body.

Those years of idyllic play together were soon over.

She was one morning carrying a filled chamberpot down the stairs—she must have been about nine years old. The chamberpot had been collected from the room of a male cousin whom all the bondmaids addressed as "Fourth Older Brother" and whom she mentally called "Open Robe" by virtue of a calendar hanging over his bed that showed a woman in precisely that state of dishabille, one large white breast peeping out.

The chamberpot was filled almost to overflowing, which she hated, as it invariably meant that, in the descent down the stairs, the swirls of stirring male acridity would heave to her fingers clamped around the rim. She had to go down ever so slowly, step by careful step.

Halfway down she saw the boy. He was hurrying somewhere. It was unusual to see him in that part of the house so early in the morning.

She held her breath. Her heart jumped inside, like a little trapped bird. They lived under the same roof, she saw him several times a day, and each time, it convulsed her small person with an aching longing, because she knew he was going further and further away from her.

The chamberpot slipped from her fingers and clattered down the stairs, and then all was chaos as the girl gave a little scream, sat down in helplessness and cried, half-splashed with urine, having had first a glimpse of the boy turning round to look once, then hurrying away.

Choyin and two other bondmaids appeared in a whirlwind of alarm and vexation, for the stairs were now badly splattered and would have to be thoroughly cleaned.

"You! You!" screeched Choyin, and she bounded up the stairs, pulled up the trembling girl by the ear and dragged her down. She sent her away to wash herself and change her clothes and then personally did the cleaning with a bucket of water and rags.

"I don't know what to do with that child!" she spluttered.

She knew what to do with the child; she pinched her thighs, then slapped her face and when there were still no tears in those large obdurate eyes, she hit her on the head with the stove poker. The child cried at last, both from the pain and the shame that the boy had seen the urine ablution and might be repulsed forever.

Perhaps he had not witnessed the full shame, for shortly after that when he was riding his bicycle in the garden and she approached him with some pieces of red paper and bamboo slats for making a paper lantern together, he paused, got down from his bicycle and walked towards her. He had had enough of riding; a diversion was welcome.

They worked on the paper lantern. Once or twice she looked timidly at him, but he did not laugh at her or say, "You smell of urine."

He got bored after a while, abandoned the half-finished lantern and went back to his bicycle.

She finished the lantern on her own; it was supposed to be a rooster with a fine comb and tail. The reality trailed sadly behind the aim in a mess of red paper gummed on a rib-cage of bamboo, and with a snort of disgust, she threw it into the dustbin.

Spitface who was watching her had an idea of how his gift-giving, always repulsed by the little girl, might this time, achieve its wish. He went to a shop in the town where a myriad colorful lanterns, in preparation for the Lantern and Mooncake Festival, hung from the ceiling rafters, and pointed to the owner a particularly beautiful one, of a red-and-green dragon. Spitface who had no money to pay for food or toys he desired and pointed to, was sometimes waved away, but not too unkindly for a whole town had learnt to tolerate if not treat with kindness, the poor misshapen creature who moved in and out of shops and eating places with the complete ease of a trusting child. A recalcitrant dog or child might still give trouble and snap and spit at him but would be smacked into greater charity.

The lantern shop owner said, "You want to give it to somebody? Your girlfriend, eh?", got a pole and brought down the green and red dragon. Later he made Spitface chop a small stack of firewood for his stove.

Spitface brought the lantern to the girl Han in a whoop of joy. She received it eagerly, with the same energy she sometimes rejected his less acceptable gifts. She thought, trembling with joy, I will take it to him. He will like it because it is so beautiful.

Spitface waited hopefully, perhaps to be thanked, smiled at, even touched, but looked dejected when the girl seized the lantern and ran away excitedly to hide it somewhere until the time when she would see the young master again for the gift-giving. She did not see him again till the evening of the Lantern and Mooncake Festival but a phalanx of four visiting male cousins blocked her out. They were all gathered in the front garden of the house amidst a rustle of paper dragons, roosters and horses, strung on bamboo sticks. A persistent wind prevented the candles inside the lanterns from being lit, but this only added to the boys' excitement. They laughed, shouted and challenged each other, waved aside adults' offers of help, and yelled to the bondmaids for more matches. After the lanterns, they were to go into the house for a feast of mooncakes.

The girl Han appeared in the shadowed edges of the brightly lit circle of lantern celebrants, timidly carrying the dragon gift of Spitface, a gift twice over, if only the boy could look in her direction, walk to her and be coaxed to receive it.

He was in the act of stamping out a burning horse; the lit candle inside had fallen from its stand and set the flimsy structure ablaze. The boy stepped repeatedly on the blaze, imperiously gesturing away an anxious male servant who had come running up. Putting out burning lanterns was definitely more fun than carrying them about in silly procession, and the cousins joined in the stomping in an orgy of primitive enjoyment as they defied the little licks of fire with their feet.

One of them saw a small pale girl watching them. She was carrying a lantern, but she was only a bondmaid, so he ran to her, grabbed the lantern, put a burning candle to it, threw it on the ground and invited the rest to stomp on it. They rushed forward joyfully; they had only a second to connect the arrival of the new source of pleasure with the servant girl standing in the shadows, before throwing themselves wholeheartedly into the pleasure. In two minutes, the dragon was a heap of charred sticks.

The girl Han gasped in dismay, ran forward, then checked herself, beaten back by the laughter of power and triumph. The boy Wu saw her, saw her stricken face and felt sorry. His kind nature detached itself sufficiently from the collective brutality, for him to say to her, in all sincerity of intention, "Never mind, I'll give you another one afterwards!"

The offer of reparation, shouted across the darkness and carried upon the wind, touched the group with a deep sense of unease, putting an instant end to the laughter and talking.

"Why did you say that? She's only a bondmaid."

The lantern-snatcher, at thirteen the oldest and therefore the most accountable for safeguarding the sanctity of tradition, delivered his rebuke in the gravest of tones. The others shifted and looked at the boy Wu from the corners of their eyes.

Only a bondmaid. The femaleness and the servitude made

the boy Wu's act of expiation doubly demeaning and deeply displeasing to the young, conscientious keeper of male prerogative, who went on to say, with even more vehemence, "*Siau!*" in final discharge of his displeasure. The imprecation broke the silence. It was taken up by the other three cousins who began chanting "*Siau! Siau!*", since it could only be madness that made one of their kind concede so shamefully to one of hers. The four locked together in a tribunal of shrill voices and menacing waving lanterns, facing him.

The boy went white with rage and shame. He felt hot tears springing into his eyes, an intense heat suffusing his face and neck. Unable to direct his anger at his cousins who began to gather round him once more in an unbreakable solidarity of blood, wealth and power, he moved swiftly out of the circle, faced the small frightened girl still hovering in the dim fringes of their bright circle of light and screamed, "Go away!"

When she hesitated, he screamed even more loudly: "I told you to go away. You are only a bondmaid!" and returned to be once more absorbed into the circle, his image redeemed.

He never spoke to her again.

He avoided her assiduously. When any of the cousins came on a visit, she was totally invisible; they could have walked or cycled through her laughing.

She went on a rampage of reclamation. If she could not reclaim the warm bond of their childhood, she wanted to repossess at least that small acknowledgment of her existence when he had paused in his bicycle-riding to make a lantern with her. So she waited for him to wheel out his bicycle and spin round the courtyard as he was wont to do some evenings: she would hang around, hoping to catch his eye to show him something enticing in her hands. When they were small children, they had thrilled to the enticement of secret gifts in each other's hands. Now he turned away quickly at mere sight of her, swinging his bicycle round and pedaling away furiously, or he simply pretended not to see her and continued to do what he was doing. In the cousins' absence, he said no more unkind words to her; indeed, he could be kind, once leaving an uneaten cake precisely where she could find it, but she had thrown it away; gifts were futile in the vast wreckage of ruined feeling.

She was about eleven years old when she went into Spitface's woodshed one morning because she remembered he had a cage with a bird in it. The bird was still there, but dead, a small bedraggled ball with two stiff tiny legs sticking out. She took the cage and dead bird and stole out of the woodshed.

That evening, as the boy was reading his comic books on a bench near the old carp pond, he was aware of a presence behind him and immediately stiffened his back against its onslaught. The girl approached slowly, holding the bird cage. The gift-giver was increasingly more doubtful about her gifts: the cage was dirty and rusty and the bird was already dead. But she remembered a time in their childhood when they did nothing for days except examine dead insects, birds and animals, sometimes burying them, sometimes setting them on fire.

She thought, "If he would come now and talk to me and we could bury this bird together, how happy I would be!", at the same time recollecting, with a sinking heart, that since that happy time, there had not been one occasion when he accepted her gifts.

He fidgeted in his seat under the intensity of her yearning plea. She made it worse for herself by adopting that pose of girls he hated most of all when his grandmother took him visiting and little girls were brought to play with him: the step-by-small-step edging towards him with the shy forefinger stuck in the mouth. He had on each occasion wanted to pull out the offending forefinger and push the girl away. The girl Han, approaching him in precisely that manner, was relegated forever to the nuisance group from which he was always glad to be rescued by his male cousins.

"The bird's already dead. There are ants in its eyes."

Undaunted by his determined concentration on the comic

book, she sought to provoke curiosity; even a tiny flicker would be something to build her hopes on. But the boy went on reading, though a reddening of his ears showed a burning discomfort. She hung around miserably for a while; then the boy abruptly left the bench and ran away.

She threw away the bird and cage.

Something remaining of that pain when she clung to a fleeing mother and cried in the darkness for an adored brother combined with the present sense of loss, to make her cry herself to sleep at night or turn and toss on her mat in the wreckage of dreams at dawn.

She was now an invisible presence to him. Loving a man, a woman is most pained by her invisibility to him.

Is that servant girl bothering you?"

An observant uncle had once noticed the boy's sudden discomfiture, turned round to look and established the cause through a glimpse of disappearing pigtails.

"Why don't you just beat her up? She'll never bother you again!"

The boy had never shouted at her again, would much less beat her. The remembrance of childhood affinity would not warrant its continuation but could at least stay the brutal hand of adulthood. So when the uncle offered to chastise the troublesome bondmaid, the boy said no.

"Why do you keep bothering the young master when he does not want to play anymore with you?"

Childhood over, and with it, the special privilege of an alliance with the young master, she was now isolated by a massive conspiracy to avenge the insult of that alliance.

Young miss, you are now where you properly belong. Let's see how different you can be from your kind.

The taunt was written in every line on Choyin's pinched face each time it was turned upon the girl.

Choyin might have relented somewhat if the girl, upon the nudging of the others, had come up, asked to be adopted and thus expiated that sin—never forgotten, even if forgiven—when she had raised her clear, little girl's voice, to say, in the full hearing of all, "Choyin is not fit to be my mother." But the girl had done no such thing or ever would, maintaining an aloofness that was surely discordant with her position.

"Spitface, you must not bother Miss Han in this way. You should know Miss Han does not like it."

The screaming exasperation had taken on the silken tones of delicate sarcasm, which Choyin delivered daily, unable to pass up any chance of doing combat with this girl who had robbed her of all peace of mind. The original arsenal of slaps, pinches and knuckle knocks had been beaten into fine verbal barbs regularly let fly to wound this hard girl to tears.

For the victory was the head bondmaid's now. The girl stood rejected by the young master, as all could see, whereas she, as head bondmaid, was the only one among them that he sometimes chose to speak to. It gave her immense satisfaction to be able to come into the kitchen and announce to no one in particular, "Master Wu said to me—", "Master Wu told me—", in the manner of the arch concubine coyly flaunting her favored position.

She looked from the corner of her eye to see and be gratified by the wounding. But it was a futile volley, easily repulsed by the cool indifference, and dropping harmlessly to the ground in a banal heap. Choyin would not be satisfied with less than her full share of gratification, so she would goad the hard girl to a response. Master Wu told her such and such a thing. Was not that unusual? What did Han think?

And still no satisfaction was forthcoming, for the proud girl would merely look up, say quietly, "Is that so?" and continue her work of cutting the vegetables or washing the rice grains under the tap or cleaning the kitchen god's altar table of its coating of joss-ash.

When she was twelve years old, she woke up one dawn to a patch of wetness in her trousers. In the dimness, she saw blood.

The blood had seeped through her trousers and on to the mattress. She found a rag, wetted it and used it to wipe off the stain on the mattress. Then she went to a large cardboard box containing a pile of cloth torn into strips, for the common use of all the young bondmaids in the house.

"They are like farmyard fowls. They can smell first blood."

The matriarch's remark, casually and smilingly made in conversation with visitors, had remained with her and caused her, each time she brought up the chamberpot or the hot tea, to pull in the budding breasts in retreat from the searching male eyes. Now their long noses of desire would smell her first blood too. Fourth Older Brother with the calendar picture of the woman in an open robe above his bed was beginning to look more closely at her. She was determined to be even more nimble with the setting of the chamberpots on their squares of mat or the pouring of the tea, and flee in an instant. She would never flee from the boy; it was he who fled from her.

"Stay in the kitchen and finish the beansprouts."

The hateful beansprouts of childhood in their interminable mounds on trays or in baskets, were still there, added to other chores. But that morning, they were Choyin's ploy to deny her the chance of seeing the young master for the last time.

He was leaving her. He was going to a faraway country.

On that day of his leaving she thought she would die from the pain. She had had no idea of its coming. There had been an accumulation of small hints that she should have been alerted to—the getting ready of two enormous trunks, brought out from somewhere, cleaned of dust and left standing in the corridor outside his room, the mention by his grandfather to a visitor of a great institution of learning in a far-off country, the expressions of worry by his grandmother that he might not take the cold or the food there, Choyin's flustered and elaborate care over piles of new shirts, jackets and socks and the determined, spiteful silence each time she had timidly asked, "What's happening? Is young master going away?" She had turned to the others too—Chu,

124

ever sharp and observant, still minding the Old One, Lan who surely knew because she had special claim as the boy's bond-maid for many years—but they, taking the cue from Choyin, would not tell her.

"It's none of our business," they said and turned away.

"Where is young master going? Do you know?"

Desperation had driven her to ask Spitface. Even imbeciles might be privy to secret knowledge she was denied and in the one or two coherent words that sometimes came out tortuously from the poor constricted mouth, she might find a clue. But of course Spitface could not tell. Capable of understanding the most elaborate instructions for errands, he was incapable of answering a simple question. When he saw her coming, his face had lit up with joy; he had sprung up from his folding-bed in the woodshed and stood in taut expectation before her, in the excited manner of a small child about to be given a treat. His tufts of hair gone scanty and grey, he kept the trustful, wistful look of the child undiscouraged by rejection. He walked up to Han; she turned abruptly and walked away.

An impossible chain of yearning: beast reached for bondmaid who reached for prince who retreated, in fright, into his gilded chamber. The whimsy of Sky God might have stretched the chain further at both ends: mangy beast yearned for imbecile who kicked him out of the way, prince yearned for goddess who scolded him for his presumption and shut him out of heaven.

She had seen the two large suitcases, strapped and buckled, being carried to the front of the house, and a black car drive up slowly and park in readiness. The patriarch came down from his rooms, a rare event. The matriarch looked agitated and tearful. Everyone was agog with excitement and everyone seemed determined to keep her out.

She pushed the basket of beansprouts aside and stole out. Knowing that as soon as she was seen, she would be driven back to the kitchen, she determinedly stayed out of sight, hiding first

125

behind a pillar, then a line of flapping bedsheets, pretending to bend down and fiddle with her slippers.

He was not in his room. She had missed her last chance of seeing him. He would be gone for many years. He might not even come back; if he did, she might be dead and gone. Stricken into a ghostlike paleness, she felt a churning pain in her stomach. She walked slowly down the stairs. She walked slowly and heavily, weighed down by an unutterable sadness. Someone was running up. She stood still, petrified, for there was he, bounding up two steps at a time, to return to his room for something forgotten.

He passed her, then paused and turned to look at her. Something must have touched him, for he moved towards her; perhaps it was the tears filling her eyes.

Males sniffed with desire but could also look upon crying women with pity, if the tears were on their account. Even boys on the threshold of manhood, discomfited by girls' presence, could forget their discomfiture and be moved by girls' tears.

She looked at him and wished she had a farewell gift. But her hands were empty.

His recollection of his own giving, not once but on many occasions in the distant time of their being children together and of the bursting joy of the receiving, must have impelled him to wish a return of some of that joy upon the poor little stricken face before him. For the boy had a kind heart and a wish for sparing pain. He searched his pockets and found something. It was a small penknife. As irrelevant as the gift of money when she had sat in the wet abjectness of the loneliness and terror of being abandoned, it was still a gift. He held it out to her, stiffly, awkwardly, wanting, but unable to say: "Don't cry."

I am not invisible after all, she thought joyfully. It was a peculiar kind of joy, expressible only in a most alarming convulsion of sobs and flood of tears. Alarmed, the boy ran past her down the stairs and was gone.

As long as he had been there in that house, even as an

achingly remote presence, she had been contented. Now his leaving gouged out the entire substance of her existence, leaving a screaming emptiness. The pain made her ill; for a week after he was gone, she lay on her mattress, pale and choking with grief, ignoring the hot rice porridge brought up to her by an anxious Wind-in-the-Head, and on one occasion, a nourishing herbal brew by Chu, from a store reserved exclusively for the Old One.

Then she rose and went back to her assigned duties in the house, sustained by one thought: he will come back. No matter how long he is gone, he will come back one day.

Women wait for their men, till the hair turns white on their heads. A woman whose fiancé left to work in another country waited for thirty years, and he finally came back and, touched by the faithful loving, remained with her till she died.

Over the years, from overheard snatches of conversation, she knew he was happy and doing well in the foreign country, and that he wrote back regularly to his grandfather and occasionally sent back gifts to his grandmother. She would have liked to see the shawl that she had heard his grandmother proudly describing to her visitors: "Such bright colors, fit only for the young! My grandson remembers his old grandmother but forgets her age!" The matriarch, grown fat and slow, moving with difficulty, became animated when talking of her grandson.

In a dream, one of his letters was for her. Somebody put it into her hand, saying, "Here, this one's for you." Though she could not read, she knew the full meaning of the words he wrote. They said, in the exact tones of that loved voice: "Thank you for your gift of the lantern. I hope you liked my gift, too," and he was referring, not to the small penknife which she now wore on a string, close to her heart, but a beautiful silk shawl of bright colors that had come with the letter.

Her dreams always saddened her.

By pure chance, she came upon one of his letters when she was cleaning the patriarch's room. For a moment, she thought of stealing it, taking it away, getting somebody to read it for her so she would know, whether in the voluminous information of the eight pages, there was any reference—even if only so slight—to her, to be her very sustenance till his return. Of course there would be none, poor fool that she was for even thinking of the possibility. Did she expect him, scion of the House of Wu, to write in his letter to his grandfather the patriarch, "Tell her that I sometimes think of her?"

She left the letter where it was.

The anticipation of his return, the recollection of that one fleeting moment on the staircase, five years back, when he turned and looked at her and gave her the penknife—these fed her in his absence. She had continually to plunder both future and past to fill the emptiness of the present.

Sky God had a soft spot for lovers. He allowed another dimension of time and place for their meeting.

"Run," he said. "They're after you. There's not much I can do. Run."

They were in a vast wilderness, dark, interspersed with so many grassy mounds that she kept tripping and falling down.

"You shouldn't have worn those slippers," he said. "They're too big. They make you fall."

"They're my mother's," she said. "I've no other pair."

They were in a large cemetery. Sky God shook his head.

"I told you to run," he said. "I told you I can't promise to help you much."

They wanted to say something back to Sky God, but he stayed hidden behind an immense curtain of joss fumes; they caught only slight glimpses of his magnificent black beard and the golden sunburst of spears behind his back.

"That's my mother," she whispered to him.

They looked at a woman, thin and work-worn but with an enormous belly, prostrating herself before the god with a bunch of joss-sticks in both hands.

"I hope Sky God never answers her prayers," she added spitefully, "for she abandoned me. She sold me to the Reverend who raped me. He got me to go to his bed every morning before cockcrow, so nobody would know, and did unspeakable things to me."

The rain came down in angry torrents; all was darkness and she cried, "Where are you?" before she realized he was grappling with the Reverend ant pinning him to the ground. He was shouting, "I think I've got the wretch! I'm going to teach him a lesson!"

They looked upon the Reverend lying dead in his coffin. He was horribly bloated, twice his size, and certainly dead, for there were large black ants crawling in his eyes and mouth. He was no longer capable of harming anybody. But still Sky Got urged them to keep running.

"I like you better than her," he said, pulling her up through the open window where she had crouched, watching him and crying.

"Then tell them," she said. "I want you to tell them."

He held her hand and faced them all—Li-Li, the bearded bird man, Choyin, Chu, Lan, Pin and *Sinseh*.

"I like her best of all," he announced and was not afraid to hold her hand.

"I'll teach you!" cried *Sinseh*, purple with rage and moved towards them, his bamboo cane raised in his hand.

He snatched the cane from *Sinseh* and hit him across the face.

"You dare!" roared *Sinseh*, but they were unafraid. Like bold children, they stuck out their tongues and roared back: "Eat your own stinking shit. Swallow your own stinking balls."

"You mustn't be so disrespectful," said the old *keo kia* woman gently. She was as usual wet all through, the rainwater running in small streams down her face. "Sky God punishes those who are disrespectful to the old by hurling one thunderbolt after another upon their bodies."

She noticed that the old *keo kia* woman's feet never touched the ground. She was going to ask her to protect Wind-in-the-Head who seemed to be in much trouble but the old woman had already disappeared.

So had he; a screaming panic rose in her. She shouted to him in the darkness but there was no reply. She stumbled along, still screaming. Somebody pushed and slapped her; another hit her on the head. She could hear their voices but could not see them.

She shouted for him to come back to her but he was gone.

"Sky God, please make him come back," she pleaded, and she reverently touched his image on the piece of jade on her wrist, like a monk or nun touching their prayer beads.

"What will you give me in return?" asked Sky God.

"Anything. Anything you say. Only bring him back," she replied.

"I can't think of anything at the moment," said Sky God, "but alright, I'll bring him back."

They were in a little hut and could hear the rain roaring outside. Spitface beat upon the door, asking to be allowed in. There was a small window, too small for him to squeeze through. He looked in and his mouth opened and shut in the extremity of his terror.

"Not yet," she said waving him away with her hand. "Please go away now, and don't bother us," and turning to him whom she loved so much, she said, "You've come back."

"I was only gone to bring you this. You must be so hungry," he said. And he fed her a bowl of rice porridge that warmed her and gave her new strength.

She lay against him, comforted by his touch.

"When you went away," she said, "I was sick for days. I thought I would die."

"I told you I was coming back," he said. "I told you I like you better. She is rich and beautiful, but I like you better."

She pressed herself closer to him and knew she would never experience such a happiness again.

The old *keo kia* woman said, "Didn't you hear the rooster? You two, you must be off. The others have already left. Quick, be off."

"But he can't leave me. He has just come," she pleaded.

"Well, don't tell me I didn't warn you," said the old *keo kia* woman. "The rooster's not to be disobeyed, you know."

But still they did not want to go.

"The rooster's cry does not reach us here," he said smiling. "They put me in a sack and threw me into the sea. It was a terrible fever, and they had no medicine in the ship for me. But now I am with you and I am contented."

She felt the warmth and kindness of the sea-waves washing over them. Somewhere in the distance, a solitary sea-bird called. Strange, she thought. People say the sea is the cruelest place to die in, because there is no coffin. But I feel safe and loved.

The rooster's cry, ever persistent, pierced the depths and reached their ears at last, faint but determined.

"Perhaps I had better go," he said.

"Are you leaving me again?" she asked sorrowfully.

"Only for a little while," he said.

II

SPITFACE HAD BEEN ASKED to get one pig's tail from the market, which would have been given free of charge, but the pork-seller misunderstood and bundled several, wrapping them up in an old newspaper and thinking they were for soup.

So when he came back and presented the package, stained with blood, in the kitchen, Choyin exclaimed and laughed and called to the others to come and have a look.

"You choose your pig's tail," said Choyin to Han, for she was the one chosen for the small ceremony of healing. Han selected the longest from the cluster of the blood-stained appendages.

"The rest will go into a soup for Spitface," said Choyin generously. "He can have the benefit of his mistake."

The selected pigtail was secretly spirited into the common bedroom, and kept out of sight of Wind-in-the-Head, the subject of the healing. Han, in charge of the operation, kept awake, lying quietly on her mattress and waiting in the darkness for the start of the teeth-grinding. It soon came. It was a strange grating sound, difficult to describe and impossible for teeth-grinders to reproduce on request, for it belonged exclusively to sleep, and vanished upon the instant of waking. Wind-in-the-Head's teeth-grinding was of that kind that turned the air into wood and set a rough-toothed saw upon it, sending the harsh vibrations into the very marrows of bones. The more she was scolded, the worse she became, until it was decided that the only thing to do was to apply the pig's tail cure.

It was a simple procedure. Han and Lan who had obligingly awakened to be of assistance, watched for the jaws to be fully moving, then took turns to slap them a few times each with the pig's tail. Wind-in-the-Head woke up with a fright at the first whack, but was restrained for the completion of the operation, a total of six whacks, three on each jaw.

When she was seven, Wind-in-the-Head had been chased by a stray dog and developed a raging fever in her terror; she was cured by having a bit of the dog's fur put behind her ear, Spitface having been given the task to track down the playful animal and pluck a few hairs off its coat. When she was ten, she developed mumps. Her swollen jaws were painted with a thick coat of indigo mixed with vinegar, and then the washerwoman's husband who was born in the Year of the Tiger, was requested to write the character "Tiger" on the wet blue dye with his finger; the powerful beast, thus loosed upon the offending swelling, quickly destroyed it. There were two males in the house born in the Year of the Tiger but it would have been the height of presumption to get either to perform the healing on the little bondmaid. Spitface's zodiacal identity being unknown, the washerwoman's husband was the best choice. Wind-in-the-Head's dependence on the animal world to cure her of her various ailments seemed a predestined thing.

The next morning, and the next, Han and Lan and Popo,

whose mattresses were around hers, were able to report that she had stopped her teeth-grinding.

III

IT WAS ONLY HALF A BOWL of red bean soup, but it was special with lotus seeds and longan added. It was still steaming hot; Han covered the bowl with a plate, then hurried to give it to Chu.

Away at the far end of the house with the Old One, Chu had less chance to taste the good things that sometimes appeared in the kitchen. Out of the abundance of groceries that the matriarch insisted on having in the store-rooms against any emergency of war and a consequent drying up of supplies of her favorite delicacies, the bondmaids, upon a whim, opened packets of dried beans, seeds, preserved fruit and fragrant fungus and treated themselves to sumptuous desserts.

"That's kind of you."

Han had said that herself once, also upon receiving of thoughtful food. Sick with pain and loss and Lying upon her mattress, she had risen with weakly whispered gratitude to receive a bowl of nourishing herbal brew brought in by Chu.

Small acts, whether of kindness or cruelty, were remembered and reciprocated with quiet purpose and amazing generative power: gift food and barbed words flew about with equal regularity, creating a dense pattern of criss-crossing lines of unremitting alliance and opposition beneath the calm surface of daily co-operation and co-ordination of housework in that great mansion. Thus was Han, for as long as she could remember, allied with Chu and ranged against Choyin; thus was Choyin allied with Lan and Popo against her. Even after Lan left to get married, the antagonism remained, and on her visits back, she made little biting remarks on Choyin's behalf. The weak-minded stood in between and looked in wondering stupidity from one tight face to another: Wind-in-the-Head could only understand a little of what was going on and Spitface none at all.

Chu said "Thank you" again in that brusque, authoritative manner of hers which antagonized Choyin.

Who does she think she is—

In that great house, bondmaids watched to pull down those who would presume to rise above their kind.

But it was true: her work of caring for the Old One had gained for Chu an ascendancy over the head bondmaid herself. Even the matriarch adopted a deferential attitude for she had an abiding fear of Chu leaving the house and abandoning the Old One.

"She has been taking good care of him these twenty four years, and he is used to her. What can I do?"

Bondmaids could hold their rich mistresses to ransom if they held their old men and young children in thrall. There was a bitter story from the House of Chang: an ancient patriarch cried every night, like a broken-hearted child, for his bondmaid who had been allowed to get married and leave, until she was at last allowed to return by a shrewd husband who parlayed this little circumstance of an old man's need and a young woman's kindness into great gain for himself.

There was little kindness in Chu's meticulous care of the Old One, but much money, for the matriarch, Choyin found out, gave Chu the biggest *ang pow* each New Year.

"Why don't you buy some yourself? You can afford to stack both arms with them!" Choyin had smilingly remarked when Chu admired a gold bangle the washerwoman was wearing. Chu had smiled back and said nothing, quietly putting away the little piece of malice in memory's well-kept reciprocatory chamber, as she would put a handkerchief or a key into the pocket of her neat, well-starched blouse.

Chu wanted to give the Old One a full bath, not one of the usual wet towel body wipes, and she needed help. So Han's presence was welcome. But first the red bean soup had to be eaten, in proper acknowledgment of the kind act, and to allow time for some relaxed chat, as increasingly, the forty-eight-year-old woman, cynical, lonely, sharp-tongued, welcomed the company of the intense, eighteen-year-old girl with a beauty that the males in the house were already noticing. Besides, she liked to instigate the younger bondmaids to a greater defiance of the hated Choyin. She liked to remind Han of the time when as a small girl, she had turned down Choyin's offer of adoption and made her cry in angry humiliation.

"You really made her cry. I've never seen her cry like this before."

She had saved that incident, deliciously satisfying, and extracted from it at least a dozen helpings of gentle venom, carefully administered over an appropriate period, to maintain the feud with the head bondmaid.

"When you were a small girl, you were very naughty. One day I caught you and young master playing round the Old One's coffin and making a lot of noise, and I chased you away."

Han allowed for memory's editing out of the shoves and pinches. She understood that the past incident was being brought up to clear the ground of their new alliance, once and for all, of any remaining animosity. She, on her part, absolved the older woman of her active participation in a virtual campaign of cruelty, for a time, against a small child condemned as demon-possessed by a monk. So she said, with quiet deference, "I remember. I was a naughty child. You were good to me," and thus secured the friendship of this strange, powerful woman with the fearful tongue.

"The bean soup tastes very good."

Chu, never loquacious, always busy, became eager for idle talk, in the pleasant sensation induced by good food and company.

"Let me show you something," she said and went to a small table with a drawer. She pulled open the drawer and brought out a photograph. It showed two young girls wearing identical samfoos, standing close together.

"Guess which one is me," said Chu. The high, stark cheekbones would mark her at any stage of life.

"My sister Wan, two years older," said Chu. She held the photograph and looked at it. The sister who was shorter and had a calmer, prettier face, stared out upon the world with a look of gentle melancholy.

The hard outlines of Chu's face and voice softened in the mention of this much loved sister who had died many years ago.

"She suffered very much." Chu could not go on, and took out a handkerchief from her pocket to press to her mouth. As soon as she returned the photograph to the drawer, the face and voice took on their hard edges again. She shook her head vigorously, as if to shake off the discomfiture of a secret indiscreetly revealed, and said, in a totally changed tone of voice, "We'll talk a bit. The Old One can wait for his bath." The bit was a dozen lubricious stories she had heard about the old man's past escapades with women, in which the cabaret girls always featured large. Thai, Burmese, Indian, Malay—his lust cut a large ethnic swathe, for he always said women were like food, to be served up in abundance, variety and hot spices. Once he got drunk, fell into a drain and was pulled up by a bevy of laughing girls who managed to carry him back into the cabaret hall. On another occasion, he danced with four girls, weaving in and out of them and stuffing wads of money down their blouses and up their sarongs.

"Look at him now," said Chu. "Would you believe that this same old fool who can't wipe the shit off his own arse had done all those things?"

He lay on his bed, watching them, like a frightened child trapped with adult tormentors, in quivering anticipation of the next stage of the tormenting. An old man of ninety five who stayed resolutely alive beyond all expectations, solid like his waiting coffin, but in purpose only, not in physicality, for his body was a mere shell and his head a virtual skull on which waved a few cottony tufts. The infamous good teeth were almost all gone too; Chu said she had stopped brushing them long ago and only cleaned the remaining ones occasionally with a small wet towel.

He had deteriorated badly in the last year or so. Before that, he was still able to wander about and speak coherently. One night he got up from bed and stole out of the room. Like a truant child, he had waited for Chu to fall asleep before he slipped out. Fortunately, she happened to wake up shortly after, saw the empty bed and went in search. She checked those places which he seemed to have some attraction for, including a leafy spot near the old carp pond, where she once found him quietly sitting on a bench. But he was nowhere in the house or grounds. She went outside the gates to look. He was nowhere to be seen. Suppose he had fallen into a monsoon drain and got washed away? Or been knocked down by a bullock cart and ground under its huge wooden wheels? She refused to panic. She was sure he would be found alive, for his time had not come yet. Therefore she would wait, and not alert the matriarch.

True enough, as she was looking up and down the road, peering into the darkness, she saw a trishawman peddling up, stopping in front of the gate and helping the Old One out of his vehicle. Wandering about near the old Lok Kum Tong temple. Looking totally lost. No shoes. The trishawman had recognized him immediately and gone to his help. He had insisted on remaining where he was; he said he was going to meet someone called Ah Paik. Coaxed into the trishaw at last, he had begun to call for Ah Paik again and to cry like a child, lamenting that Ah Paik was sure to be very angry and never agree to see him again.

"Ah Paik", repeated the trishawman with a significant smile, for he too knew of the old man's philandering—who in the town didn't? He began to be talkative, awaiting a reward, and would have gone on to do some impertinent surmising about this Ah Paik, if Chu had not pressed some money in his hand and sent

137

him away. She had taken an instant dislike to him, convinced
that he would begin to hang around the mansion with his
trishaw, in hopes of making more money out of a demented old
man with a past.

She cleaned the Old One of the mud on his feet, gave him a
drink of warm water, rubbed some oil on his chest and put him
to sleep. He began to show signs of agitation again, muttering
the name, not of Ah Paik, but the old *keo kia* woman, so she
wondered whether he had seen her ghost and followed her out
of the house.

"You mustn't do such a thing again, do you hear? You
nearly got me into trouble."

She had in the room an old wooden ruler which she used
more for threatening them punishing, and she held it in her hand
and shook it before his eyes, to emphasize the seriousness of her
warning.

He never wandered out again.

Chu said that in his time the Old One went through more
women than any patriarch. Ah Paik was probably one of them,
remembered long after the others, because he connected her
with a special act of kindness: even rich, powerful men had soft
centers into which they tearfully crumbled in the comforting
presence of a mistress or a concubine.

Women had always been his weakness. He brought to his
bed the cabaret girls, dance hostesses and servant girls, and went
to the beds of other men's mistresses, until he was caught and
severely punished.

"Didn't you ever hear of it?" cried Chu. "Everybody knows
about it. The woman was the mistress of a very rich and powerful man. An extremely beautiful woman. She encouraged him,
he went to her room, and a servant saw them and reported to the
master. He was badly beaten up and forced to pay a very large
sum in compensation. Let me show you."

She went to stand before the old man, her hands on her hips,
in playful mockery. She said, "You know we're talking about

you, Old One? Why are you staring at me like this? I'm going to pluck out your eyes and swallow them!" She aimed a playful jab at his eyes, and he blinked. She laughed and said, "Don't worry, Old One. We know you want to live for a long time more. Your coffin won't call yet."

She signaled to Han to join her by the bed.

"Come, I've something to show you."

She turned the old man's head slightly on the pillow, held it down and pointed to a scar, a faint whitish line running from behind his right ear down to his upper neck.

"That was where they cut him," she said. "They caught him and slashed him there with a long knife and left him bleeding on the floor."

She removed her hand from his head and the old man looked up timidly at them.

"You were naughty, naughty," she scolded and he fixed his eyes on her, like a worried child. "You paid for your naughtiness. Alright, Old One, go back to sleep. We'll wake you up for your bath later. A real good bath."

Spitface provided another pair of helping hands. It turned out Spitface came to the room often, emptied chamberpots, re-arranged furniture, located dead rats and lizards and removed them and was always rewarded with something to eat or some coins to put in his pocket.

"Look at the poor wretch," said Chu, as she and Han watched Spitface help the Old One to a sitting position. She was in the mood for exultant judgment which passed easily from one poor wretch to another. "Did anybody ever tell you that his mother left him in the rubbish dump in a paper bag and the rubbish-collector heard his cries and picked him up?"

The unloading of secret histories—other people's only, for hers was kept intact in that tight compact chest under the neat starched blouse—exhilarated her, and she went on to furnish yet more horrifying details. The rubbish collector at first thought the baby was a monkey, not a human, so grotesque did it look, and was in time to save it from a marauding dog that kept snapping at the paper bag, smelling fresh blood.

Aware that he was the subject of the animated talk, Spitface nodded amiably and grinned. That part of his brain that enabled him to maintain contact with the world softened all received speech tones into one friendly overture, unless of course, the speech was accompanied by a blow or kick in which case his features would contort into a grimace of pleading as he shrank from fist or foot. So he grinned happily at Chu throughout the recital of his repugnant fate in this life and the sins he must have committed in a previous one. He was happy, being in the same room with Han.

We poor fools, we all, thought Han and a sadness descended heavily on her. Two bondmaids, one imbecile, one senile old man—all mutilated in their own ways.

Three bondmaids: for Popo swept in excitedly then, carrying her baby. But bondmaid no longer: she was a happy young mother, with hair boldly permed, and a baby fat and sleek from the happy mothering.

The gloom retreated to the invasion of so much brightness, and all attendance on the Old One was halted to attend to the visitors. Even the Old One watched with curious interest, his eyes following every movement of mother and child.

The back-knocking Popo, much to the matriarch's disappointment, had left to get married. One of the washerwomen had approached the matriarch on behalf of a friend who had approached her on behalf of an only son: would the matriarch give her permission? The matriarch did, as she had graciously done in the case of Lan, shortly before, and within a month, Popo moved into another household.

The matriarch's magnanimity had created an appalling gap in her own life of ease, which, however was quickly filled by the magnanimity of others, in a proliferation of that virtue: the House of Chang sent over their own bondmaid Peipei who happened to be Popo's younger sister. It was a friendly tradition among the great houses of helping each other out in times of need by lending servants for as long as was needed.

The matriarch was very pleased, but not for long, for Peipei lacked her sister's back-knocking skills and failed to ease that broad silken back of its daily aches. Within five minutes of her visit with her baby, Popo had been highly gratified to be told by the matriarch—and she repeated this now to Chu and Han with much enthusiasm—about how badly she was missed. It was double gratification, for the matriarch, in the middle of the complaint, had slipped an *ang pow* into the pocket of the baby's vest.

"My back aches more than ever now, and you are not here to relieve the pain!"

Popo had done the appropriate thing, which was to beg the matriarch to forgive her unworthy sister. The unworthy girl herself entering the room then, Popo launched into a lecture of loud admonition and advice to her, the burden of which was: you are fortunate to be in the House of Wu, and you must show yourself less undeserving of the good fortune. The poor girl looked down and blushed, in her confusion.

They had never seen Popo so happy. Her permed hair and bright clothes were her confident dissociation from her past. But the joy was centered in the healthy, beautiful baby boy in her arms. To this child, the mother owed all her prosperity and happiness: his birth had enabled his grandparents to hold in their arms at last a male grandchild, and had pushed into obscurity a whole covey of little unhappy female cousins. His mother benefited hugely from his importance for she was relieved of much housework and moreover enjoyed nourishing herbal brews made by the formidable mother-in-law herself, so that she would be in perfect condition to nourish the precious grandson. So much beneficence flowed from one baby boy: he was her safeguard against the future ignominy of a string of female children, and her vindication against the past failure of a wasted life.

Popo, the back-knocker whose body had regularly submitted

itself to the brutal, roaming hands of the Reverend, was mutilated no longer.

She sat plumply on a chair, lifted her blouse and presented a large rich breast to her baby who immediately began to tug greedily at it, while Chu and Han continued to exclaim over his fat, placid cheeks and touched the delightful solidity of his legs which he idly knocked against his mother as he fed, to test the sound of the tiny silver bells around his ankles.

The secret of the Reverend's regular plundering had been known and protected, in that conspiracy of bondmaids that said: In this way, we protect ourselves. For who was to know how the wrath of so great a personage would wreak itself, once provoked? Chu, whose tight, closed life fed on the dark secrets of other people's, wanted to know if the Reverend had gone beyond the roaming.

"Men are rampant and don't know where to stop," she said and might have described her own curiosity, on a rampage to extract secrets from one of her own kind, now immeasurably removed by the prosperity of a marriage and the blessing of a male child.

She waved a hand in the direction of the Old One Lying on his bed and Spitface sitting on a stool beside him and said, "You need not mind them. Neither can understand a word of what we're saying."

Spitface was staring, open-mouthed, at the white smoothness of breast visible above the baby's head.

"What are you staring at? Have you never seen a woman's breasts before?"

The Old One turned to look at her and instantly came within the orbit of her mocking raillery: "You too, Old One, have you never seen a naked woman before?"

Bondmaids in possession of a little power wielded it with ferocity against weakened men.

No, Popo confided. Beyond the touching the Reverend had never had his way with her.

"He was protecting you then," said Chu. "If your husband had found out on your marriage night, he would have—" She left the direful utterance unfinished. A husband could beat his wife and shame her to all the relatives if the white trousers of the marriage bed showed no stain by the morning light; at the least, he could send her back to her family in disgrace or despatch a rebuke to them in the form of a suckling pig with its snout violently hacked off. Popo was lucky; the Reverend allowed her to carry her virginity into her marriage.

First maligned as a lecher, then acknowledged as a protector, the monk swung wildly in the two women's judgment, and then both turned to look at Han, eighteen, beautiful and most likely next target: had she been asked to take his tea to him after the morning ancestral prayers?

They will never have me, she thought. Neither the Reverend nor Open Robe. I am not Wind-in-the-Head.

"Well, what about you? You say nothing. He must have started fondling you already!"

Chu, her secret festering life bursting open in a thick malodorous stream, took the afternoon's prurience to shocking heights. She wanted the younger women to describe their softness against the hardness under the holy robe. Astonishing recrudescence of nubility in a forty-five-year-old woman. Young bondmaids sometimes discussed among themselves, with much blushing and giggling, what men did to women, and asked the older, more knowledgeable ones who either said darkly, "You will know when your time comes," or who, if they tended towards levity, gave coarse descriptions to raise laughs.

There was a flavor of bitter comedy about Chu's inquisitiveness that could not raise a laugh. The two younger women threw quick, uneasy glances at each other, and broke the awful spell by a swift return to duties at hand, Popo shifting her baby to feed at the other breast, and Han getting up and saying, "The Old One's bath. We had better do it before it gets cold," referring to the hot water in the huge kettle that Spitface had brought in.

143

The Old One was helped into the bathroom, seated on a wooden stool, thoroughly doused with large buckets of warm water poured over his head, lathered with soap, and doused again. With a small piece of rag, Chu cleaned his ears, nose, toes, every fold and crevice of aged flesh. She lifted his testicles, soft helpless bags, in her hands and cleaned them, then his penis, softer, more helpless still, and cleaned it too.

Such a major cleansing bespoke some serious purpose. Chu spoke it at last, and Han allowed not a twitch of muscle or flicker of eyelash to betray her excitement.

"Old One, be still. Don't you want your great grandson to see you clean and nice and fresh when he comes home?"

The voice could be harsh or silken; now it was in the wheedling tones of an adult about to secure the full co-operation of a child.

Significant information in that house was always released in small, tantalizing doses, to reduce the hearer to a helpless state of dependence, like the puppy or kitten in crazed pursuit of a jiggling string. Chu jiggled further. "Your great grandson who has become such a scholar. So tall and handsome as to be unrecognizable. Coming home soon."

The old man fixed large sad eyes on her. Han remained obdurately quiet.

Popo asked "When?" and Chu smiled and said, "I don't know", while her smile said she did know but would not tell.

Information released or withheld conferred an intoxicating sense of power over friend and foe alike.

I would tell you if I could. The Old One's eyes, now turned to fix sadly on Han, as she helped to dress him, had this kind offer, and it touched her into gentle pity which flowed over to Spitface who was struggling to get an arm into a sleeve.

In that great house where her heart had opened to only one person and stayed resolutely shut against all the others, it could begin to unbolt and admit those she felt pity for. Besides, these two had a small claim on her regard, for their connections with the beloved, the old man for being the great grandfather, the imbecile for being the occasional childhood playmate. A small scar on his forehead, underneath a wild tuft of hair, bore permanent testimony to this role, and if asked about the scar, Spitface could re-enact the entire incident when he carried the boy on his back and ran against a tree branch.

Choyin said the next day, "What are you doing this afternoon?" by way of getting her help to clean and get ready the young master's rooms. The same sense of power felt by keepers of portentous knowledge kept Choyin tight-lipped as she supervised the cleaning of floors, dusting of furniture, wiping of pictures on walls, and watched, from the corner of her eye, for any signs of curiosity or interest in the girl, that she could spin into a greater demonstration of this power.

But Han did not ask.

So everybody knows except me, thought the girl, quietly going about her work. How can I sleep at night, not knowing the day of his coming home?

The matriarch was sitting alone in her room, fanning herself. Han, seeing no one about, slipped in.

"The weather's getting colder, your aches must be worse," she said quietly. "Please let me," and she proceeded to knock on her back. Taken by surprise, the matriarch was nevertheless not averse to the offer, turning her broad back to the readied fists which, though not as skillful as Popo's, were certainly better than Peipei's, so that in a short while, the matriarch closed her eyes in lugubrious content and surrendered herself fully to a pleasurable sensation not known for a long while.

Completely relaxed, the matriarch began to talk: an eased back did for her tongue what drink did for others, loosening it upon a flow of idle talk that covered everyone in the house, including the inept Peipei.

"You were a strange child. You gave a lot of trouble, especially to Choyin. But you have turned out well."

She turned round to survey the girl approvingly, and in the

short pause before the back-knocking resumed, added, "You are already eighteen, aren't you?" meaning that the time would come soon to decide her fate.

A clogs-maker who had a stall in the market-place had sent somebody to ask for Lan, failing which mission, he was prepared to settle for Wind-in-the-Head.

"You are not at all bad-looking," said the matriarch in a kindly voice, again looking at the girl, meaning that she could end up as concubine or secondary wife to some rich man. Her prattle flowed on. When it reached the subject of the Old One, Han knew she had not long to wait.

"How happy he will be to see his great grandson again. We thank Sky God for allowing him to live so long."

Again she listened without the slightest betrayal of excitement.

He would be home in just two days.

IV

UNABLE TO SLEEP, wandering about the long corridors in the cold darkness of the dawn, Han heard the heaving, panting sounds coming out of a room and paused to listen. The door was slightly ajar; she peeped in and saw the heaving, panting bulk of Fourth Older Brother, half-naked, working itself upon the full nakedness of Wind-in-the-Head Lying on the bed. Her clothes lay in a heap on the floor, with the belt-rope on top, in a snake-coil. Fourth Older Brother pushed and shoved and grunted, like a voracious boar, while the white body beneath moved in compliant rhythm with the pushing and shoving, and another white body in an open robe, infinitely more alluring and as infinitely unattainable, hovered above in sultry languor.

The man must have his fill: the bedside lamp picked out of the dawn dimness the grim determination on the florid, pock-marked face, to achieve a systematic, downward plundering of neck, breasts and the final pleasure of the softness between the legs that even the most ill-favored peasant's body could yield. The man had his fill: with a sigh of pleasure, he collapsed panting on the small plundered body which lay very still beneath him, then rolled off and lay very still himself, one arm laid across his eyes in the full satiety of his pleasure, and also in order not to look upon that unlovely girl who must be gone before the others started waking up. She began to dress. Han hurried away.

Perhaps Wind-in-the-Head had seen her hurrying away, for a short while later, as she was stoking the stove in the kitchen, the girl came to her in great agitation and signaled that she needed to talk. They moved to a corner of the kitchen hidden behind two large shelves. As gentle in her language as she was coarse in her appearance, Wind-in-the-Head could not bring herself to describe her condition; she merely cried, like a child, and nodded or shook her head to Han's questions. Bondmaid had confided to bondmaid down the years in that vast house, in a sisterly sharing of fear and shame. Wind-in-the-Head had been carrying the shame for three months; it would only be a little while more before her fearful secret would be out. In a village near the house was an elderly woman skilled in disposing of fearful secrets for a fee, though her skill had not prevented a bondmaid or two from succumbing to the shock and pain and dying from the bleeding. The matriarch arranged and paid for the disposals with the same matter-of-factness with which she regularly commented on the farmyard rampancy of males.

"Please don't tell anyone," pleaded the girl, anxious to avoid the immediate punishment of a severe rebuke from the matriarch or even a rush of pinches on her thighs which the old lady, when sufficiently roused, could still administer.

She began to choke and make retching sounds, running to a little side-drain in the kitchen, squatting down and bending over it. Han squatted down beside her, rubbing down her back. It was no use; the retching would not stop, convulsing face and throat in a rictus of agony. The girl whimpered and looked around fearfully to see if anyone had come into the kitchen. She was safe. Choyin who normally appeared at this time was nowhere to be seen.

The girl rested for a while, breathing heavily and still squatting beside the drain, and then the vomit came out in a gushing stream. Han continued to rub down her back. Much eased, the girl stood up, wiped her mouth with the back of her hand and said she felt much better. Han went to get a bucket of water to wash the vomit down the drain and out into the connecting gutter outside the house; Choyin could smell incriminating evidence a mile away. She gave Wind-in-the-Head a cup of hot water, and told her to go upstairs to their room for a rest. A while later, impelled by both pity and kindness, she went up to see how the girl was, saw her Lying very still on the mattress staring at the ceiling and offered to rub Tiger Balm on her temples and chest.

Pity and kindness had got in the way of her own need. The tears rushed into her eyes and she clenched her hands in deepest vexation when she found out later that the young master had already arrived home and was now in his room. She had missed him by a mere half hour. It was all Wind-in-the-Head's fault.

So tall. So handsome. Almost unrecognizable. Choyin prattled on, scoring yet one more triumph, because she was one of those to greet him on his arrival and he had greeted her back. He remembered her and told her so.

V

SHE KNEW SHE WAS in time.

The Old One was Lying on his bed, freshly shaved, the white tufts on his skull smoothed down neatly. He was wearing a new pair of pajamas. The room matched him in neatness and freshness. Even the coffin in the corner was wiped clean of any dust.

Chu was not in the room, probably gone to fetch some hot water.

She looked at the Old One, and he looked back, always with those large, wistful eyes. She saw a bowl of half finished porridge on the table, and thought to hide the particularity of this sudden visit by a demonstration of helpfulness: I thought you would be very busy this morning and I came along to help you feed the Old One.

The pretense would have no chance against Chu's cynical gaze, but she did not care, she was mad with desire to see him, and this was her only chance.

She picked up the bowl and dipped the spoon in it, scooping up a mouthful. She stopped suddenly. The spoon had stirred into sight what could only puzzle deeply, for it had no place in food, or anywhere near food. Filth. An insect's filth. She looked closely. Cockroach droppings. Of that she was sure. Hidden deep in pure white rice porridge with clear intent, not accidentally dropped on the surface by a scurrying insect. She put the bowl back on the table, and it led her to the other half of the terrible intent: a glass of water, half hidden behind a tall flask, in which floated a distinct blob of human spittle. From the malice of bowl and glass, she looked at its target, and the old man looked back at her, with the trusting eyes of a child.

She heard footsteps and within a second regained her composure, standing by the bed and saying in a quiet voice to Chu, "I thought you would be very busy this morning and I came along to see if you needed help."

True enough, the deceit withered quickly in the intensity of the woman's glittering eyes fixed unwaveringly on her. Chu smiled a small tight smile that said, "I know. Why do you pretend with me?" But she liked it each time the girl wandered into the orbit of her power and influence. She said, "They will be here in a short while," once again establishing the supremacy of her position: only she, among the bondmaids, had no need to fight to get first glimpse of the young returning master. Coolly, adroitly, she was converting the visit of the young master to his great grandfather into a personal triumph.

He was in the room now; he had come in accompanied by the patriarch and the matriarch. Standing by the table, elaborately cleaning an already sparingly clean water jar, she lifted her eyes only once, and in that one glance took in very detail of his appearance. It would only be later, in the privacy of her thoughts on the quiet of her mattress on the floor that the image of this much loved man would be brought out and carefully spread out, for a slow, loving contemplation of every part, from the hair to the eyes to the very turn of wrist or ankle, and then placed beside the remembered image of the much loved boy five years back, for an equally slow and loving comparison.

Now the tumult of her emotions allowed for no such leisurely contemplation; it merely allowed each quivering fiber of her being, as she stood outwardly calm and kept her eyes down, to strain and catch at every word, every uttered syllable or sound coming from him, down to the slightest shuffle of shifting feet on the floor.

He spoke little. He sat on a chair beside his great grandfather and held the old man's hand. She heard him say, *"Chor Kong Kong,* I've come back. I arrived this morning," in a low, quiet voice, heard the patriarch, then the matriarch say something, and then the verbal communication was over, for the old man was no longer capable of speech. Isolated by his silence, the Old One looked upon his visitors with gentle melancholy. He began to cough a little, Chu brought up a cup of hot water, and the young man took it from her and gently held it to his great grandfather's lips, in a gesture of filial tenderness agreeable to all.

Loving a man, a woman grows eyes on the back of her head so that in a crowded room, with her back turned to him, she sees his every movement. Wanting him, she sprouts extra ears to catch at his every word above the din of one hundred people. The man has no idea, when he finally leaves the room without once noticing her, of the fullness of her pain.

He just sat by his great grandfather's bed, facing the old man, and never once looked at her. Did she dare move out of the obscurity of her position and into the range of his vision, so that he could look up, look at her, and in that one look, she could determine whether he still remembered her?

Opportunity followed wish and she snatched eagerly at it: Chu was looking around for a spittoon and so she darted forward with one.

"Here," she said, reinforcing presence with voice.

He was saying something to the matriarch and did not turn around. Chu took the utensil from her and the opportunity was over. She stepped back into obscurity, miserably, herself a spittoon, a flask, a chair, a table, part of the furniture in that great house, with no more claim to attention than any of these.

After they had left, Chu said with deliberate slowness, "How tall and handsome he's grown. I could hardly recognize him. Did you notice?"

Perhaps wanting him to turn to look at her in the presence of others was too great a hope. She did some retrospective whittling down of hope: suppose, as she had come forward with the spittoon, his body had shifted ever so slightly on the chair, or a muscle on his face had twitched or his voice undergone a tiny modulation. She would have caught at the message with joy. It would have been a sufficient reaping of hope on the very first day of his return, a small but precious glimmer which she would hold like a treasure in cupped hands, against the darkness of the long waiting years.

But there was nothing. It was a bad sign. He had come home. They were under the same roof. Therein must lie all her hope. And so she beat down the pain but it would come, like the cruel stream of Wind-in-the-Head's secret shame that morning.

She heard a harsh sound: it was Chu energetically scraping the porridge out of the bowl into the spittoon, then emptying the glass of water into it.

VI

SKY GOD HIMSELF, it was said, was not malicious, but his deputies who had charge of the lesser punishments of mortals were, turning these punishments into spectacles of pure self-indulgence.

A man mad with thirst became madder still, each time the cup of sweet sparkling water brought to him was dashed to the ground at the moment of its touching his lips. Another man, dying of hunger, had a bowl of steaming hot rice placed before him; each time his chopsticks dug into the food, they picked up clumps of feces.

Every day for thirty years, a woman waited to see her ghost lover. He was allowed out only at the moment of cockcrow, so that as soon as she saw him and ran towards him, he was pulled away by the rooster's call, his mouth gaping wide in the agony of stopped utterance.

He was home once again, after the long years, no ghost, but a palpable princely presence in that great house, around which all other presences re-organized themselves in a touching tribute of loyalty and regard. She was the ghost, condemned to be forever invisible to him, seeing, never seen. His presence, like a visiting celestial spirit, touched into brightness and joy the tired, gray lives in that vast house: suddenly, everyone was noticing how different things were. The patriarch who seldom smiled never stopped smiling for he never stopped talking about his grandson. The matriarch's joy, like a river winding through parched land broke through in munificent flood, conferring benefits upon all and sundry, including an old folks' home maintained by the White Light Temple which now received four sacks of rice instead of the previous two, and careless bondmaids who received no scolding for their carelessness and certainly no more pinches on their thighs.

She watched him move about in the radiance of his world from the melancholy shadows of hers, and longed for just one glance, one turn of his head in her direction, to throw off the punishment of invisibility. Sometimes, hurrying along the upstairs corridors with flasks of hot morning tea, she saw him in the courtyard below, in the slow magisterial movements of *tai-chi*, a god in mortal garb, slashing the air with hands and feet. She would linger to watch and superimpose upon those fine manly movements, the remembered image of a young boy's energetic limbs in a determined conquest of the tallest mountain in the world or the systematic demolition of an enemy ship in an ocean or, best of all, a dance of joy with a small girl in pouring rain.

Pulled out of her reverie by the sound of an opening door and Fourth Older Brother's soft, brutal gurgle, she would hurry on with the flasks.

She watched him in the company of numerous young friends and relatives who came, ate, drank, laughed, then took him out on motoring or horse-riding jaunts.

The magnanimity of the matriarch's love spilled over to embrace all his friends. Cook, she commanded the bondmaids. Put on the tables the best food. Make sure that the abalone is the finest and the mushrooms the very rare kind that my grandson likes. Eat, she urged his guests. Eat. Please don't stand on ceremony.

She watched the matriarch in her new joy, watched all the guests. She recognized some of them as the cousins who had come for the lantern and mooncake festival that night of her pain, so many years ago.

She recognized too, one female presence, always in the company of a chaperon: the girl Li-Li, from the House of Chang, now grown tall and beautiful. Queenly in every detail of pink silk dress—she did not seem to want any other color—silk slippers, tiny fan, delicate jewelry, the carefully arranged curls on her forehead and most of all, the hauteur of the small uplifted nose and dainty mole over the right upper lip, she came on occasional visits and brought and received gifts. She was the only one in the happy, laughing group of young people who gave a quick glance, or actually turned around for a second confirming glance that said bondmaids were not invisible after all. But her look was not kind. It said, "You, you," meaning "I have not forgotten. You were the nasty child who led me into a muddy hole and laughed at me. You. You."

I see him every day. We live under the same roof.

Women taunt each other uselessly.

It was of course the most puerile of claims, as senseless as the tax-collector's boast of wealth because so much money passed through his hands.

She saw him every day, but they were snatched, stolen glimpses only, when he did his morning exercises in the courtyard, or left the house with his friends and cousins in laughing camaraderie, or took a solitary walk in the grounds at the back. Once she saw him sitting by the carp pond, reading a book, as she had seen him in that time before his going away, when she had timidly walked up to him with a gift.

If only, she thought in an ache of longing. If only she had been given the duty of taking up his morning tea or removing his chamberpot or cleaning his room. She would have been able to break out of the hateful invisibility; she could break a cup or spill a flask of hot water, and her little gasp or scream might make him turn round and notice her and by noticing, say with his eyes if not his mouth: I remember.

But Choyin had appropriated for herself from the very first day of his return, all the tasks requiring direct attendance upon his person. Like the bullying child who hogs the best toys and pushes other children away, she staked her territory in that house and made the greatest prize of all out of the reach of the other bondmaids.

"The young master Wu said to me, when I brought him his tea—"

A man's small polite gestures were turned into barbs to stick into another woman.

He sometimes had his meals in a special dining room with his grandfather and grandmother. If only. If only she could stand by while he ate, and be the first to refill his bowl, his rice-wine cup. But Choyin had appointed Peipei to be the serving maid.

Her ifs were so many hooks for the hanging of tattered wishes. She woke up each morning with feverish expectation of a better day and went to sleep each night with pitifully meager gleanings—of a sight of him here, a snatch of laughter there, and on certain days, not even these, so that she wondered, in a sudden spasm of cold terror, if he had gone away again.

She had to be content with the gleanings. Unable to attend upon him at meals, she attended with more care to the fowl she plucked for his dinner, the spices she ground between stones to give his food the taste his grandmother said he missed so badly when he was away in the foreign country.

A loving woman fills a man's absence with the objects of his erstwhile presence. She touched a chair he had just sat on, traced with her feet a short stretch of ground his own feet had trod. She looked at his shirt hanging on the clothesline, recognizing it as the one he wore when he went to see the Old One on his first day home. She had watched Choyin starch and iron it; Choyin's territory extended to shirts and undergarments.

The head bondmaid had screamed at Wind-in-the-Head for daring to hang her own trousers beside the shirt on the clothesline. The proximity would have been even less forgivable if it had been in the wash-tub itself: women's clothes, bearing women's smells, defiled men and brought them bad luck and so had to be washed separately. Wind in-the-Head, pale with fright, had pulled her trousers off the clothesline and apologized profusely.

Not just the sight or touch of these things that would be hallowed by his eating them or using them: the very sound of his name exploded in her body in little shoots of longing, reducing it to a quivering mass underneath the calm exterior of gentle mien, downcast eyes and quietly efficient hands as she poured tea for the patriarch's and matriarch's visitors and heard the name in every proud utterance. My grandson. My grandson, the scholar.

Incalculably removed from the substance of his self, she had to be content with its lingering shadows and scents. She saw him once talking to and smiling at Spitface. She would change places even with a humble plant if he watered it tenderly every day.

"Please don't disturb me. I'm busy."

As a child, she had always screamed at Spitface to go away, but now she spoke to him in a quiet voice and found it in her heart sometimes to feel sorry for him and even accept his gifts.

He was not disturbing her. He had a gift for her, cupped in both hands in exactly the same tantalizing manner of those childhood years. For he stayed a child in the manner of his gift-giving and gift-receiving, still coming to her with small presents salvaged from rubbish dumps, and jumping up and down for joy if she gave him a rice dumpling or handkerchief or box of matches. She was the goddess, he the faithful beast-servant to whom her very spittle would be gift. Every year, in the general cleaning up before the New Year, the goddess threw out a huge accumulation of useless earthly offerings, but not into Spitface's favorite rubbish dumps, to prevent their retrieval and re-presentation, in a new tedious cycle of giving, receiving and rejection.

"I'm very busy."

She pointed to the flasks of morning tea she was getting ready to take to the upstairs rooms. She could see Choyin crossing the courtyard to go up to the young master's room, with a tray holding a tall green flask, a mug and a folded face towel; these were immediately invested with a sanctifying grace, because they were about to touch his face, his lips. Spitface uncupped his hands and something jumped out amidst a tremendous flapping of wings, but was quickly re-caught and hand-imprisoned once more.

It was a small black bird which he must have just found or

caught. With a touching faith in the power of each gift to please, whether it was bird, insect, or child's lollipop, he looked into Han's face, nodded eagerly and made little excited noises.

"You mustn't do that again, Spitface. You frightened me," said Han severely.

The bird quietened inside the dark tomb of the hands.

"Spitface, go and show it to Choyin. Quick," said Han pointing.

She watched as Spitface, glad to obey any command, hurried out and ran after Choyin.

The result was as expected. The sudden uprush of frenziedly flapping wings caused Choyin to shriek and drop the tray to the ground.

"You! You!" she screamed, flailing at Spitface with both hands. The man stared at her stupidly and let go of the bird which dropped to the ground and dragged about on one outspread wing. Han came up, said quietly, "I'll take up Master's tea," and was gone in a second.

She was outside his room now with the morning tea. There was an open space with a small table where the flask, mug and towel were to be placed; some masters preferred this arrangement, to a direct contact with serving maid, to keep propriety's distance. They made sure they came out only after the maids had left.

But she would not leave. She lingered, knowing this was her only chance of seeing him face to face.

He came out and gave a little start. Clearly expecting to be alone, he was startled—and displeased—to see the serving maid still there. She was just that—a serving maid with the morning tea.

She expected him, in his displeasure, to walk back into his room. But he did not. He lingered. He made a movement that could have said, "I want my tea now. Get it ready, then leave."

If he did not remember her, surely he would remember his gift to her? The penknife hung conspicuously from her neck on a chain, both gift and burden, accreting around itself the fears of the long waiting years and the hopes begotten on a staircase that day from a single act of spontaneous kindness when a boy looked at a crying girl and was moved to give her something. Always secretly hidden under her blouse from prying eyes, the gift was, for this morning only, pulled out and laid upon her anxious chest.

She bent down to pour the tea into the mug, and the penknife struck the side of the flask. He did not see. Or seeing, did not remember. Or remembering, did not want to tell. He drank his tea quickly, then returned to his room.

She had failed.

That afternoon, she visited Spitface in his woodshed with a gift of contrition, a cluster of small rice dumplings. Unable to connect the offering with the earlier incident when he had suffered a beating from Choyin on her account, he was overwhelmed by the magnanimity of the goddess visiting her beast-servant in his humble abode with rich gifts, her presence the richest of all. Beast servant was ready to prostrate himself in breathless enchantment.

He did not want her to leave. He wanted to have her, all to himself, for as long as possible. Like a happy child, he threw open the doors of the little broken cupboard beside his folding canvas bed, to reveal to her his own treasure trove of offerings, and selected from it a pair of wooden clogs he must have picked up or stolen from somewhere. She shook her head. She left in the sad realization that gifts, whether of love or remorse, always went wrong. "There's a man who wants to see you."

The unreasonableness of hope that would clutch at the feeblest straw! Of course a call from him would never be conveyed in these words; of course the messenger would not be the washerwoman's child. The little boy had hurried after her as she was walking up the stairs. The child repeated, "There's a man who wants to see you. He's in the kitchen," and ran off.

So the man was waiting in the kitchen. The hope should

have vanished completely at this point, but it persisted, stupidly: suppose, by some quirk of authority, that was his choice of meeting place?

She hurried breathlessly to the kitchen, and a tall, thin man with bad teeth, whom she had never seen before, rose from a chair to greet her.

He said, "I'm Oldest Brother."

She stared at him, and said nothing. She stared at him to see if there was anything in appearance, voice or manner that would touch a responsive chord of memory.

He repeated, smiling awkwardly, "I'm Oldest Brother," but was not presumptuous enough to ask, "Do you remember?", for the many years that had rolled between would surely have erased all remembrance.

Rejecting the mother who had suddenly appeared at the gate one evening and called her, twelve years ago, she was much less averse to the appearance of the sibling she remembered loving most of all. They began to talk, slowly and carefully, and continued looking at each other intently. As memory, aided by goodwill, worked to tease out the familiarity of this or that feature, and this or that shared childhood experience, in shadowy outline, if not in detail, they began to relax and smile at each other, and reserve gave way to the genuine pleasure of discovery.

"Do you remember the old bed we all shared—"

"Do you remember the sweet shop—"

Memory avoided a brutal father, a suffering mother.

Oldest Brother saw again the favorite little sister, four years old, waving goodbye from a distance, in an oversized jacket, and she saw again the much loved oldest brother who carried her on his back and whose name, not her mother's, she had called in her moment of darkest dread.

He looked terrible, being thin and sallow with rotting stumps for teeth, and smelt terrible, of drink and squalor. A woman with thickly powdered white face and rouged cheeks waited outside the kitchen by a side-gate, fanning herself and

159

now and then looking in sulkily. Han asked him to ask her in, but he laughed away the need, and said he would not take long; he had come to see her about something special.

Their mother was dying and wanted to see her. He himself had seen her only the day before. She was in a bad state, living in a small dark room in a house for destitutes, and she specifically asked to see her.

Brother and sister stood silent in the contemplation of their wasted lives.

Strangers for years, they were being brought together as family for one closing hour around a death-bed. It was a last filial duty and had to be done.

Han had seldom ventured out of the great house. She had been to the White Light Temple once for a special festival, and the House of Chang once, when extra help was needed for an important celebration and the matriarch had kindly sent Choyin and herself over. The bondmaids got excited over the occasional open-air opera performances in the market place and were allowed to attend, but she was totally uninterested. Now, in the company of a brother she had not seen for fourteen years, she was in a strange part of the town where old, dilapidated houses leaned against each other and old men and women sat in the shadowed doorways and watched visitors with intense, glittering eyes. She and her brother ascended a flight of dark narrow stairs that creaked to their weight, and went into a room, dark except for a shaft of light coming from a broken shutter, and musty with age and death. Han saw a very old woman, mere skin and bones, lying on a foul mattress, in a corner of the room, whimpering softly, and made to go to her, but was led by Oldest Brother to another corner where on an old plank bed with a thin cotton mattress, lay another woman, less old but equally wasted. A bedside table was cluttered with old cups, saucers and bowls and, in their midst, a brand new flask, and an unopened bottle of Tiger Oil, testimony to the son's recent largesse.

Their mother was Lying very still, with her eyes closed, a

white folded towel across her forehead, bearing no resemblance to the mother of memory. Oldest Brother called her softly and shook her shoulder gently to wake her up. She opened her eyes at last and looked upon them, but uncomprehendingly.

"This is Han. She is here. You asked to see her."

The lucidity lasted only a few minutes and brought on a burst of contrite tears, for the dying woman remembered the heartless abandonment, fourteen years before, for money lost within days at the gambling table, the lies fed to a trusting child, the shaking off of the small, clinging body, as one would shake off a troublesome insect and stamp on it. She indicated that she wanted to hold her daughter's hand. Han sat down by the bed, duly laid her hand upon her mother's and allowed the tears to flow freely.

"Sky God has punished me ever since," said the unhappy woman, for her life, from that time, had been a desperate slide from the gambling dens to the final dereliction of the destitutes' home. She had, on one occasion, according to Oldest Brother who had heard about it from others, been savagely beaten up by the loan sharks. They had dragged her out from behind a cupboard, refused to listen to her promise of settling her debts within a week, and slapped and punched her into unconsciousness.

"Sky God, forgive me."

The prayer marked the end of the lucidity, and the next half-hour was a tiresome tirade against neighbors, a dead husband, Sky God himself. The demented woman veered from one past incident to another, separated by gaps of ten, twenty, thirty years.

"He would have given me a good life. I saw her, covered with jewelry, and she wasn't even half as beautiful as myself. It was my fate to marry the other—him! The rice-pot was always empty, but he would spend the last dollar on his beer or his women."

Life's closure ought to see some small remembered sweetnesses mixed into the bitterness: hers was all gall which threatened to invade the last breath. The bitterness caused her voice to rise in a thin shriek which was picked up by the other dying woman who raised herself on the foul mattress, waved a feeble arm and tried to say something, knocking over a small spittoon.

Ignoring her, Oldest Brother and Han said to their mother, "No more. No more. Now take a rest," and arranged a filial blanket over the wasted body, feeling nothing but pity for the wretched woman who was their mother.

Han saw that the thread bracelet with the small jade face of Sky God was no longer on her wrist: perhaps it had been sold for a meal or a last lottery ticket or been wrested off by the loan sharks. Hers was intact; she had been wearing it these many years, but it meant nothing, so she removed it from her wrist and tied it round her mother's.

There was a last request from the dying woman and it was, strangely, on behalf of the room-mate in the corner. It had something to do with the return of a small sum of money, and a gift of biscuits and an umbrella, probably in settlement of an old quarrel. The imperatives of the deathbed—forgiveness, reconciliation, regret, remorse, final admonition and request—had been covered in their full range in the one hour of the visit.

The death took place that evening and, as was provided by the terms of charity applying to every inmate in that house, there would be a coffin, actually four rough planks nailed together, to take the body away and consign it to a common grave.

The heavily powdered companion appeared suddenly to reclaim the brand new flask and Tiger oil, and, after some whispered words to Oldest Brother, the bracelet on the dead woman's wrist.

"I would give her a proper funeral if I could but as you can see, I am struggling to make a living," said Oldest Brother but he would not say what the living was, and his companion who had not exchanged two words with Han, made an impatient movement to indicate they ought to be going.

"I could not give her a funeral. I am only a bondmaid."

This was thought only, not said. It was sufficient for Oldest Brother, retaining the brotherly generosity she remembered, to ask, with some concern, "Are you well? You look thin and pale. Can I help?"

He was in no position to help, and if asked, was likely to retreat, with the clowning of childhood, into some elaborate excuse connected with his struggling life or his strange companion. But there was kindness and that was enough for her. The tears gathered again in her eyes, connected with that other pain she could never bring herself to tell him.

"Are they treating you well?" he asked sternly, with something of childhood's bravado in the defense of a little sister against any bullying neighbor.

She gave a short dismissive laugh, the companion pulled at his arm, and their meeting was over. He went back to wherever he had come from, with his woman, and she went back to the great House of Wu.

It was back to a larger, deeper pain.

"The master wants to see you."

Her heart pounded violently inside her and sent a roaring into her ears. This time there was surely no mistake. The messenger was Choyin herself. There was no small constricted smile of malice to hint of a cruel joke; instead the tautness about the eyes and mouth said, "Now why would the master want to see you?" and was the best proof of there being no mistake.

"Where?" she asked quietly.

"The visitors' reception room," said the other and left abruptly.

The master wished to see her. Wish implied remembrance. He remembered her after all. In that great house she had learnt to hide the greatest internal tumult under the quietest outward demeanor, so she walked with small unhurried steps and calm, downcast eyes and presented herself at the doorway of the large reception room, reserved for the most important visitors.

163

She was summoned in by a shrill, imperious female voice.

"What did I tell you? It's the same person, isn't it?" said Miss Li-Li appealing to the other two in the room, the young master Wu sitting on a chair at a table, and a fat young man whom she recognized to be her cousin, leaning against a sideboard and pulling at a cigar.

So it was not the master who had sent for her after all but Miss Li-Li.

She stood before them quietly, a short distance away, and waited to see Miss Li-Li's purpose.

"I remember the strange look in those eyes; how could I forget?" The young woman went on, standing tall in a long, graceful dress of the signature pink, a graceful hand on her hip. She might have been disparaging a person well out of sight and hearing, instead of being right there in the same room, facing her. "We were in the room enjoying the bird man's show—remember?—and I was playing with two pretty little yellow birds and you, Wu, with a large green one, when there came this terrible commotion and we all turned to see a strange child beating at the window with both fists and screaming at the top of her voice. Luckily Choyin was able to push her down and close the window." It was clear that the triumph of the bird man incident was being revived to wipe out the humiliation of the fall into the muddy hole. No bondmaid who had dared to insult anyone from the House of Chang should be free from a continuing censure of the past misconduct, right into the bondage of her old age, if necessary.

"Weren't you the child who behaved so strangely that day?" demanded Li-Li. Han said "Yes" and Li-Li looked at her searchingly and smiled, unloading upon her head the years' accumulation of venomous contempt, before turning to the other two and saying triumphantly, "What did I tell you? I never forget strange or comical incidents. This one was both! The child fell over some flower pots and cut her leg and Choyin dragged her up. Choyin later told me she had to tie her to a chair in the kitchen to prevent her coming again to disturb us!"

The calm face of the servant girl infuriated her, inviting a retrospective slap but she restrained herself.

Li-Li regularly and enthusiastically gave out gifts of rice and cloth and money to the poor in the temple, and with equal enthusiasm punished those who dared to rise from the squalor of their lives to deride their benefactors. This girl was worse than derisive, she was dangerous. For she had dared to ally herself with the young master Wu to lord it over the other bondmaids. Now the young master was home again and she was once more launched upon an audacious campaign to win him.

"She's a clever, cunning one," Choyin had said. "Never under-estimate her."

Such a breach of propriety was insufferable and if nobody in the House of Wu did anything about it, the House of Chang would have to do some necessary intervention. It would devolve upon her, Li-Li, to put errant bondmaids in their place once and for all. In the light of the likely future alliance of the two houses, the sheer brazenness of this bondmaid in setting herself up as a rival, was staggering.

Miss Li-Li's fine, carefully painted lips were rounded in the discharge of a string of vituperations.

"I heard she was possessed by a demon. She went round biting and kicking everybody. She caused injury to that poor, misshapen imbecile who lives in your woodshed. She was most disrespectful to Choyin."

She. She.

The girl stood there, the object of vilification, referred to in the third person, for her presence did not count.

The cousin, hoping to please, laughed, said he remembered very well indeed and contributed one or two of his own recollections: the child once spat on a monk from the White Light Temple, once rushed in upon a lantern party and destroyed the lanterns.

Miss Li-Li, intoxicated with a sense of final victory over this

165

recalcitrant servant girl whom she should not have had the indignity to deal with, in the first place, gave a sharp derisive laugh. The laugh also meant: Wait till I'm in charge. Then you'll see. The cousin joined in, and their laughter filled the room, while Han remained standing where she was, her body permeated with the slow heat of anger and loathing, not sure whether she ought to continue standing there or turn and leave. She became aware of a sudden lull, as the laughter subsided, overtaken by a voice, in so different a tone that the laughter was suddenly hushed into awkward silence.

For the young master Wu was telling them that he too remembered: he remembered a child who had been abandoned by her mother, and lost none of her zest and joy. She had done some naughty things, but then, were not all children naughty?

The defense was gentle, in deference to the guests, and the line taken could only be that of compassion, in keeping with a tradition of the House of Wu in relation to the poor and unfortunate. Compassion rescued the strange behavior of the child from the accusatory context of unnaturalness and put it in clear orientation with normality: which four-year-old, abandoned by a parent, and left among strangers, would not behave thus?

Somewhere in the telling, genuine pleasure took over from pity, and the young master told, with much warmth of tone, about the time he and the vibrant little girl put red ants in Spitface's trousers and knocked on the Old One's coffin to frighten Chu. He smiled in the telling, then realized he had gone out of line and checked himself immediately. Miss Li-Li looked up sharply and gave him a look of intense displeasure, and the cousin, knowing something had gone awry but unable to tell what, toyed with a vase, whistled a foolish tune and waited to pick up cues. The master said to Han, without looking at her: "You may go now."

She raised her head to look at him; the intensity compelled him to look at her too, and for the first time since his homecoming, he looked straight into her eyes. The look could have meant, "Go away now. I've saved you this time. But don't count on it a second time." Or it could have meant: "I remember, see? And you thought I didn't. I remember everything about us."

She could not tell, and it infuriated her.

The impact of that afternoon's happening could not be absorbed all at once. Like the image on his first day, it had to be broken up carefully and subjected to slow rumination, for a bit-by-bit integration into her thoughts and feelings. If the experiences since his homecoming had added up to no more than a handful of pitiful gleanings, that of this one afternoon was a virtual harvest, needing much time for the winnowing and sifting.

The part that could most easily be sifted away related to Li-Li's feelings about her. Li-Li's jealousy—for surely it was that, and nothing else—was much cause for gratification. It exhilarated her that the sharp-eyed, sharp tongued Miss Li-Li of the House of Chang hated and feared her: what had the young master Wu made known, consciously or unconsciously, about his feelings for her that could call forth so much bitterness?

Therefore, contrary to his outward behavior towards her, he loved her. Therefore, Miss Li-Li's vehemence, no matter how strongly it expressed itself during her visits or how faithfully it was replicated in the day-to-day behavior of Choyin, could only be cause for rejoicing.

The logic of the heart thrilled her. She savored the triumph, like the addict sucking at his pipe, like the small child clutching a toy retrieved from the bully.

And then the exhilaration gave way to sobering realization: it was kindness, not love. The man was incapable of a harsh word, of causing pain to anyone. The others beat her and left her to die; he fed her from his own food bowl. They left her out in the rain and storm, he ran to join her and showed them she was no scum. They laughed at her and mocked her and called her demon-possessed and he tried to mute their laughter with compassion for her.

But it was still only kindness. It was no different from the kindness he had shown Lan, the bondmaid who had taken care of him in childhood. Her marriage had turned out to be very bad from the start; her husband beat her and gave her no money. On a visit to the great house, she tearfully showed a scar covered by a fringe of hair, and a child whom she fed sugar water instead of milk. Her sad story must have reached him for on her next visit, she received a generous sum of money from him through Choyin.

Women ask men, "Why are you so unkind to me?" and say a man's kindness is all. It was not enough for her. He did not look at her the way he looked at Miss Li-Li, or stood so close. His behavior to her was not that of a man who loved and wanted a woman. If she could not feed on a man's love, what was the point of feeding on another woman's hatred?

The conflict raged in her heart and spilled into a dream.

She stepped into the visitors' reception room, then stepped back with a start, for she saw them on a couch, close together, and he had his hand on her thigh. Their faces were drawn close together for a kiss. Upon seeing her, they sprang apart. Li-Li rushed forward, screaming, "You again! Are we never to be free from you!"

The cousin appeared from nowhere and the three of them caught her, pushed her out of a window and shut the window tightly against her, laughing to see her fall backwards upon some flower pots and cutting her legs.

Someone pulled her up. It was not Choyin, for the touch was gentle and the words were kind.

"Why are you only kind to me when others are unkind?' she said.

"Let's run," he said, "before they get us. Sky God promises to send lightning bolts to stop them! They will be only small lightning bolts though, like New Year firecrackers exploding in their buttocks." He was in jovial mood.

They were in his room which was very white and clean. He poured her a cup of hot tea to calm her. He said smiling,

"I remember. I remember everything about us, you see."

She said, "Remembrance and kindness, I've got both now. But they are not enough. I want something else."

"That too," he said.

They were on his bed. He had his hand on her thigh, then her breast.

VII

THE WASHERWOMAN'S LITTLE BOY—it would appear he had appointed himself her messenger—came to her as she was sprinkling water on clothes preparatory to the ironing and said breathlessly, "They've tied him up." There were other details. Black ink on his face. The Monkey God on the table. Burning joss-sticks. A banana unkindly stuck into his mouth.

It took some time to piece the small boy's excited information into a coherent picture. The picture was a grim one: Spitface was in trouble somewhere with a group of hooligans who had tied him to a chair and were tormenting him.

The small boy had witnessed everything and run to get help. Choyin said, "Leave him alone. He gets into trouble all the time." The small boy protested that he was in real trouble this time and was in fact crying. He appealed to Han. Then having delivered his message, he stood waiting, rubbing one bare foot on the other, for the reward that carne with delivering messages. Han went to a large tin on a shelf, took out two biscuits and gave them to him. The boy pocketed the biscuits and waited again, this time to lead Han to the scene of Spitface's disgrace and watch his rescue.

Rolling down her sleeves and picking up a black umbrella, she left the house.

The place was just a street away from the house of destitutes from which she had watched her mother's coffin being taken out. It was the front part of an old shophouse, used as a storing place for miscellaneous merchandise: huge bales of rubber sheets lay stacked up to the roof in one corner, and bulging sacks of something, probably charcoal, in another. Giant packages of joss-sticks hung from the ceiling, next to rows of paper umbrellas.

In the midst of the clutter was a single table and chair. Spitface was sitting on the chair, and as the child had described, was ignominiously tied to it by two long dirty towels. The detail about the banana was correct too; it lay, a black sodden heap, on Spitface's lap. Spitface looked terrified and was whimpering like a frightened child. He was not alone in the room. Two young men—clearly the remaining hooligan perpetrators—stood by grinning and at the doorway, three urchins stood, also grinning and nudging each other.

Han walked in and, at sight of her, Spitface's face broke out of its misery, and he tried to break free of the dirty towels. Han untied the towels, aware of the curious, searching looks of the hooligans. In a quick sweep, her eyes had taken them in and connected them immediately with the objects lying on the table—an image of the Monkey God, a scattering of joss-sticks, a mess of torn up prayer paper and peanuts, prayer sticks, a glass of water, a candle. There had been a ceremony of conjuration of the Monkey God, which was successful, judging by the mess on the table and floor: the medium must have fully and convincingly taken on the character of the god, pranced and danced about with playful energy, scattering paper and peanuts. Whether the conjurers succeeded in getting winning lottery numbers from him was not certain; they probably had not and so turned ritual into horseplay, for which Spitface, ambling in at the right moment, slobbering and bestial, was the ideal target. They must have had considerable fun before deciding to end it, for on Spitface's face were crudely painted the simian features of the playful god.

Han said, "Let's go home now," and Spitface, still whimpering, followed. The hooligans were too absorbed in the amazing

spectacle of so much cool beauty in the company of gross bes-
tiality, to stop them and it was only after Han, Spitface and the
washerwoman's boy were well out of the house and walking up
the street that one of them put his fingers to his mouth, emitted
a piercing whistle and shouted, "Lady, does your Monkey God
fuck?"

Back home, Han washed the paint off the face and applied
some ointment on a small gash above the right eyebrow. She said
in a severe voice, "You are not to go there again, do you understand?"

Spitface nodded miserably, suddenly an old man, with
scanty white tufts of hair, a hard leathery skin, blood-shot eyes,
a look of utter defeat. The joy of the child had gone out of him
and even the gift of a new box of matches could not coax it back.

"You heard what I said? You are not to go there again. They
are bad people and will harm you." Severity shaded into gentle
pity and she put her hand on the poor man's shoulder, in a reversal of the child's stance, so many years ago, when even a gift was
met with recoil.   She took away his blanket, torn and smelly, and
replaced it with a new one, then placed a small jar of Tiger Balm
for his use, on the top of his bedside cupboard, before leaving the
woodshed.

I have my troubles. I don't wish to be burdened with other
people's.

Other people would keep intruding. She was passing the
bathroom and heard a groan inside. She paused and went to put
her ear against the wooden door. The groaning subsided. There
was the sound of water being scooped up from the large cement
water tank and splashed forcefully on the floor. It flowed out, red
and menacing, from under the door and into the open area leading to a side-drain which led to the gutter outside. It was rich,
relentless woman's blood, frightening to look at, even to women.
There was repeated scooping and splashing; the sufferer was
frantic to wash away all evidence. Then it stopped and the
groaning started again.

"Are you all right?" whispered Han, and from behind the door, Wind-in-the-Head said weakly, "Yes."

"Open the door, let me help you," said Han, for she knew that was not the end of the bleeding.

The girl had tried everything, including one whole unripe pineapple and two bottles of beer. But the shame remained lodged. Then in desperation she went secretly by trishaw to the abortionist who was said never to have experienced a single failure. The abortionist gave her a bottle of something to drink. It was so very bitter, said Wind-in-the-Head, that she thought she could never finish the whole bottle, which was the abortionist's stern instruction.

But she managed to drink to the last bitter drop and an hour later had begun to bleed profusely.

"It's gone now and I'm all right," said the girl and promptly collapsed in a faint.

VIII

HOW PEACEFUL IT ALL IS, she thought, and she drank in deeply the peace of the tall, silent trees around her, the sleepy chirping insects hidden in the bushes, a wild pigeon or two circling the bit of blue sky not blocked out by the green canopy, the calm shimmer on the surface of the pond beside her, broken only by the soft plop of a wind-dropped seed.

Her spirits, lately weighed down by the troubles of poor Spitface and Wind-in-the-Head, took wing and soared in the wide expanses of this wonderful secret world which she claimed as her own, having discovered it years ago.

Places recommended themselves to her if they were connected with him. This special enclave of dear pond and leafy surroundings had not actually borne his presence; it had been too far for them, even at their boldest in those adventurous childhood years, to venture into, without incurring adult wrath. Some time after he had gone away, she discovered it on her own and loved it, a little haven of repose in the tumult of her life in that great house.

She would sit on an outcrop of hard earth beneath a large tree facing the pond, and say to herself, If, If, meaning "If he appeared now and sat beside me on this seat and talked to me, I would have no more wishes to bring before Sky God for the rest of my life."

But she remained a solitary occupant on the earth-seat, and in solitude listened to the soft sounds in the trees and upon the waters of the pond.

Sky God listened to prayers, but imperfectly. He had eyes and ears, but they were only half-opened. For Sky God had brought him back safely to her but put between them fearful walls. Sky God, playful in the monkey disguise, teased and tantalized, prancing about and kicking holes in the walls with his monkey feet, only to close them up again if she peeped and tried to reach for him.

She was once more behind the wall of his immense indifference. He had broken through the wall once, in answer to Sky God's command which had, in turn, been in answer to her prayer, and had duly defended her against unkindness with his kindness. The duty done, he had withdrawn into his own world again, saying, "You in your place, me in mine."

After that afternoon in the visitors' reception room, he had gone back to the happy, laughing world of his friends and cousins. Li-Li's laughter was brighter and shriller, for it would not be long before they became engaged, and in the haughty looks she threw in her direction each time she came on a visit were victory and warning and contempt: He's mine. Stay out. Who do you think you. Don't forget you are a—.

The triumph of Miss Li-Li was complete and it flowed into the ready receptacle of Choyin's eager loyalty, so that these two, in her mind's eyes, always stood as a pair, facing her and flapping their arms against their sides, in the crude manner of

She did not try to get his attention now, as she had so desperately done in the past. That part of the strategy of reclamation was over. She had entered a period of calm evaluation and stocktaking, like a merchant withdrawing temporarily from his frenzied ventures, to examine what he has at hand, to preserve it and build further on it, rather than risk its loss by further, unwise ventures.

Her gains were considerable: wanting only to be assured that he remembered her, she was given rich proof not only of remembrance but kind regard. No loving woman inhabits second place in a man's heart gladly; she must also have proof of his love for her, and ascendancy of that love over every other. A loving woman wants all.

That love would be secured by wary watching and patient waiting. It should never be jeopardized by impetuosity and folly; therefore she would not cause him any more discomfiture, would never again be the cause of the slightest embarrassment or unease in the presence of others. A man who suffers a public discomfiture on a woman's account loves her that much less.

The most beautiful ring in the world. The largest jade pendant. An anklet of solid gold. A belt of interwoven gold and silver ropes.

In her hearing, Choyin had breathlessly described the treasure trove that would be Li-Li's upon her marriage into the House of Wu. It had passed down the generations, and the matriarch, with more jewelry than she could wear in a lifetime, would be handing it all to the grand daughter-in-law in glittering demonstration of the legendary largesse of the House of Wu.

What do you think of Miss Li-Li's new jade pendant and ear-rings?

The malice narrowed into a question, specifically addressed, to force an answer for the spinning out of longer threads of venom. And as in the past, the girl Han lifted quiet and unconcerned eyes which said, "Really? I didn't know they were new, because I hadn't noticed the old."

She had reached a stage when the venom of Miss Li-Li and Choyin washed futilely over her, but not the stage when his indifference ceased to cause pain. Against the pain of being totally ignored when she accidentally met him along a corridor or almost collided with him at a doorway she brought the salve of that wondrous day of kindness and remembrance when he had risen in her defense against his own glittering world.

Each childhood incident that he had referred to now stood permanently lodged in her mind in bright ascendancy over all other incidents. The fullness of her gratification flowed retro-spectively to wash away the earlier hurt of his cold reserve when she had tried to get his attention in the Old One's room on his first morning home and later when she had brought up his morning tea. It flowed even further back to erase forever the hurt of those years before his going away when he had refused her gifts and turned his back on her.

Guarding jealousy her new gains and turning them over and over in her mind in slow, loving rumination, like a miser running loving fingers through his silver, she was much more at ease than she had ever been. She would not risk losing her precious hoard by any more impatient prayer to Sky God, in case the god turned peevish and said, "Whatever you have now, I shall take away. That will serve you right for hurrying me."

She would wait upon any divine whim.

Gods should not be by-passed for goddesses but might feel no slight if occasionally prayers were re-directed to their female counterparts, understandably occupying smaller temples or shrines. Beside the pond, under an old gnarled tree, stood a little stone shrine housing a little goddess, but so long abandoned that both shrine and goddess were in a sad state of decay. The shrine was a mere cluster of worn bricks and the goddess a shapeless block of stone with eyes and ears completely erased. There was only a patch of faint red paint where her robe must have been and a graceful curve of stone where her breasts must have been.

The abandonment, it was said, was the fault of the goddess herself. She was a forgetful goddess, always falling asleep so that prayers were unanswered and even her most loyal devotees left, after a while, in disgust. Perhaps one had even, in a fit of anger, smashed the statue against a rock face and blunted the divine features. No rusting urn for joss-sticks or blackened candle stump remained to tell that she was once loved and worshipped. She woke up from her sleep one day, remembered the prayer of a young lovesick maid and granted it, but by that time it was too late.

An abandoned goddess, anxious to reclaim her power, would prove a most valuable ally, far more than a god replete with obeisant regard. So Han untied the bundle she had brought with her, took out a cluster of joss-sticks, a small earthen jar, a box of matches and a handful of flower petals, to initiate this process of reclamation.

She lit the joss-sticks, stuck them in the jar and placed them reverently in front of the broken statue, then, as reverently, scattered the petals on the broken head. She cast down her eyes, put her palms together and moved them up and down, in graceful and ardent supplication.

"Forgetful Goddess, be forgetful no more."

She did not feel the need to tell the deity precisely what she was not supposed to forget, convinced that she would know anyway. It was an exclusive prayer, for him and herself alone. For us to be together. For us never to be separated again.

Others clamored for their needs to be included too, but she pushed them aside: Oldest Brother, tossed upon his raucous world of the rough appetites of fellow males that he must needs serve to make a living by bringing to them young frightened girls; her dead mother, perhaps confined behind hell's gates for her sins and not allowed out even for the Feast of the Hungry Ghosts; Wind-in the-Head, her body a wreck since that day of the bleeding in the bathroom and her mind a greater wreck with a hundred unceasing terrors; Spitface, lowest of the low, beyond a god's help, but perhaps not the gentle grace of a goddess who had herself experienced abandonment and despair.

These crowded upon her and cried out their needs: Pray for us, we too need help.

She was adamant; her prayers to the Forgetful Goddess would be for herself and him only, to ease the divine task. The goddess should not be made to feel confused and to complain: "So many of you, only one of me."

A bird flew in a graceful arc above her. No owl or black bird of bad omen, but a bright white pigeon, dropping a small feather which she picked up and examined in easeful contentment.

When they were children, they sometimes went to watch the large flock that came to sit on the rooftop at the back of the house, or on the clotheslines, and dropped food for the birds, or threw pebbles at them, depending on their mood. Flocks of pigeons continued to haunt that part of the house, and were thought to bring luck, so they were never chased away.

Chu was gazing at a number wheeling above the low wall surrounding the kitchen garden. Her taut back, even from a distance, told of some purpose, and not mere idle watching of lucky birds. A covered basket she carried on one arm, pressed close to her side, reinforced the impression of intent. Han watched her watch the pigeons, saw her observe closely one that had detached itself from the others, flown down and was now standing upon the low wall.

The purpose became clear when, after a few seconds of waiting, she waved away the pigeon and swooped upon what it left behind. Hurriedly taking a spoon out of the covered basket, Chu as hurriedly scooped up the moist, warm, freshly deposited blob and plunged the spoon into something in the basket. Han could almost see the bird's waste sinking into the pure whiteness of freshly boiled rice porridge. Cockroach dirt, pigeon dirt: was there a horrifying progression to finally choke the old man on his own dirt?

Han must have made some involuntary movement for Chu spun round then, saw her and went pale.

The paleness of guilt was for an instant only; it changed into a greater paleness of anger and the need to express the anger. Chu shouted, "Come here! I want to tell you something. Don't go away!" for Han made to run off, her whole taut body proclaiming, "I saw nothing. This is none of my business. I have no wish to be involved in other people's business."

Chu moved forward swiftly, grabbed the girl by the arm and screamed, "You have to listen to me. Come!"

Back in the Old One's room, abandoning the basket of evil intent, Chu told her tale.

At first it was a lunatic's outpouring, lacking any sense, and made worse by her constantly jumping up from her seat to stand before the Old One, in direct accusation, one hand on hip, the other making repeated thrusts at his face, while he cringed before her and gazed at her with the terrified look of a child.

Sister. Unspeakable things on a bed. Ten years. Twenty years. The greatest cruelty in the world. Sky God totally blind and deaf.

The incoherent rantings subsided into a coherent tale as Chu herself, her body shaking uncontrollably, subsided into a chair and sipped a cup of hot water Han brought to her.

It was a tale no different from the many that must have been told and re-told by bondmaids in the sad twilight of their years: a young innocent girl forced upon the bed of an old lecher who made her do what he could not or would not ask his wives and concubines to do, and, when she was of no more use to him, cast off on her own in an inhospitable world.

But this tale was different because the cruelty was much, much greater.

At the age of fifteen, Chu had been brought into the house to service the Old One, at that time called the Rampant One, for his sustained rampage through a long line of young virginal bodies from which he always arose, he boasted, much re-vitalized.

She was brought in to replace her sister—the beloved sister

never spoken about but enshrined in memory forever in that faded photograph in her drawer. The sister had also been brought in at fifteen. Discarded at twenty, she went home to die, her young body riddled with disease.

"He kept healthy, but he destroyed the bodies of young girls," wept Chu.

She nursed the sick sister who died shortly, and the parents, in thrall to the rich powerful man who gave them money to support their opium habit, handed him their younger daughter. Chu had never mentioned her parents; the first time she did, she salted their names with bitter tears.

"They were no parents. They gladly gave my sister and me to the man whose servants brought round both money and opium."

For ten years she was a slave on his bed.

"You would not believe what he did to me for his pleasure. In the hours before sleep, or in between sleep, his lust savaged my young body. He liked to see me tremble and cry. Sometimes he brought his cabaret girls to see me and laugh at me. Once they got drunk together and competed to see who could make me scream loudest. I fell ill about a year later and was sent home. My mother took me to a physician who said my body was ruined beyond any capacity for child-bearing. When I recovered, my mother sent me back. One day I could not take it any longer. I was about twenty years old. I ran home. My mother forced me to go back. My father was too weak to protect me. To punish me for running away, the Old One tormented me even more. I had lost all spirit by then. I stayed five more years, and then one day, the Old One found another young girl whom he became totally obsessed with, and decided to send me home. Both parents had already died by then and I went to stay with an aunt."

The narration of so much cruelty had to be punctuated by bouts of abuse against the perpetrator himself. Again and again, Chu rose from her chair and stood before the Old One, screaming so loudly, the veins throbbed dangerously on her throat:

179

"You had your fill of us, and you spat us out, like so much dirt."

His last mocking words, saved in the deep pools of tortured memory, were now dredged out and flung back at him.

"You called me worthless and useless and said I was fit for the rubbish dump only. You were seventy years old, a grandfather with white hair, and I was twenty, a young girl alone in the world, and you kicked me out exactly as you had done to my sister, ten years before! May you die the cruelest death of all!" She meant, "May you be struck dead by Sky God's lightning bolt and die biting your tongue," a death more fearsome than one without a coffin.

The Old One stared unblinkingly at her through all the tirade, and perhaps the extreme forcefulness of her delivery had succeeded in penetrating the dark depths of his memory and extracting a remorseful thought or two, for he began to blink and a small tear formed in the corner of one eye.

"For five years I lived with the aunt who added to my pain because she said women like myself, born in the Year of the Tiger and bearing teardrop moles, were fated for misery in this world. Then one day, somebody was sent from the House of Wu to ask me if I would return to take care of the Old One; he had had a stroke and required full-time care. They offered much money because he was a very difficult patient and was giving everybody a hard time. Somebody must have remembered me and, finding out about my wretched life with my aunt, must have thought they could tempt me to go back. They were right, but not about the money. I could throw the money back into their faces, because I no longer wanted it. I wanted something else. When they said, 'Will you come back and take care of the Old One,' I said, 'Gladly,' because I knew the time of revenge had come. This man was going to be in my hands twenty four hours of the day, and I wanted him to go on living for at least twenty four more years, so that I could wreak the fullness of my anger on him for all that he had done to me and my sister."

Cockroach, lizard and pigeon droppings, human feces did

not kill but dragged the tormentor down to a level lower than the beast, for even a starving cur would turn away from excrement. She had it in her power to make him lower than beast. She rejoiced in that power and got ready each bowl of porridge, each glass of water with alacrity.

With trembling hands, she opened the drawer and brought out her sister's photograph. Sobbing over it, she said, "Today I am happy. I am going afterwards to light a joss-stick to my sister and tonight, for the first time when she comes to me in my dreams, she will smile."

There was something else she pulled out of the drawer. It was securely tied up in a piece of cloth.

"Let me show you," said Chu.

Let me show you. The tight, closed life now yawned open, a malevolent cave, yielding dark secrets. She placed the cloth bundle on the table and untied it. It contained small stacks of money, tied neatly with rubber-bands.

"For taking care of the old fool," she said with a laugh. "I have more money than Choyin will ever have."

Han, unsure about what she should say, knew what she should do. She took the bowl of porridge out of the basket and scraped the stuff out into a spittoon.

IX

"MISS LI-LI WANTS to see you."

To be able to say, "The mistress wants to see you" would have been more gratifying to Choyin because more mortifying to that hard, insolent girl. But Choyin could wait for the marriage to savor in full the triumph over the girl who dared to aspire to the young master. Meanwhile, "Miss Li-Li" itself carried the full prestige of the House of Chang, against which no bondmaid, no matter how ingenious her schemes, could stand a chance.

Choyin walked briskly ahead of Han to the place of meeting, a smaller, more private room adjoining the visitors' reception room and immediately stationed herself beside the chair of the awesome young lady, in pink silk and abundance of fine jewels which now included the engagement ring, elegantly displayed on a dainty, fair hand placed on one knee.

They both faced the girl and, thinking to awe her into timidity by the combined impact of seniority and wealth, were vexed to find her more defiant than ever, her eyes not downcast but coolly looking into theirs.

How long have you been in the House of Wu? How old are you now? Do you have plans for the-future?

The rehearsed preamble served no purpose and was quickly abandoned. The girl, still looking straight at them, gave no reply or non-committal ones and Li-Li and Choyin glanced at each other in quick, silent consultation as to the next move. Dropping the pretext, Li-Li launched straight into the heart of the problem, for problem it was, such as no great house had ever had the indignity of encountering.

She had planned on a number of forceful persuasions to make the servant girl see the lunacy of her ambition and had even contrived an offer of money to her and that rogue of a brother, to leave the town forever and find useful employment elsewhere. But the girl's fractiousness, reflected in the hard glitter of her eyes and the tight lines around her mouth, made her abandon all cajoling for a matching hardness, so she heard her voice getting shriller, and felt her face getting hotter, as, with mounting fury, she called the girl a beggar, a liar, a cheat, a schemer.

"What are you trying to do to me? Don't think I don't know what your plans are. But you mustn't forget you're a bondmaid, a mere servant girl. How can you have such audacity? The young master of the House of Wu will never stoop so low as to look at a bondmaid!"

Women, angry at each other over men, can trap themselves fearfully by their angry outbursts.

"If that is so, then you have nothing to worry about."

The classic reply of one woman to expose the fears of another.

Exposed, Li-Li fell into a screaming rage. Angry with the fiancé for being responsible, in the first place, for this deplorable situation but unable to publicly blame him, she unleashed the full force of her fury upon the bondmaid. Scum. Filth. Garbage dump. Beggar. Worse than a beggar.

Choyin watched in grim approval. Also a bondmaid, also sold like a slave as a child, she was nevertheless removed from taint by her unquestioned loyalty.

"A prostitute. You are no better than one. Your brother is a pimp, your mother died in a gambling den. Don't think I don't know."

From screaming abuse to bodily assault was a natural step with recalcitrant servants, but the small dainty fists were stayed, and remained quivering in her lap.

Han thought, "It is fear of him," and was much comforted. His feeling for her might not yet amount to love, but it was sufficient to save her from attack by another woman.

She stayed where she was, silent, protected, while the whiplashes of anger flashed around her. They ended, most unexpectedly, in a burst of tears from the perpetrator, for the tumultuousness of the confrontation proved too much for the elegant young lady and she ran out-of the room, with her handkerchief pressed to her mouth, followed by Choyin.

Han felt no triumph, only a great weariness. She was feeling very tired. Even a loving woman is sometimes tempted to give up the fight and say, "The cost is too much. It is not worth it." But she deceives herself. Of course it is worth it, and she willingly takes up arms again on his account.

She took up arms of sorts against Fourth Older Brother who always recognized her footsteps along the corridor and immediately opened his door to look at her and speak to her in his suggestive low gurgle. Once she fended off the brutal piercing look by raising her tray of flasks to cover her face, and on another occasion, she actually swung a wooden clothes hanger against the arm that boldly stretched out to grab her. The defensive gestures, far from discouraging the hunter, added to the allurement of the prey and the excitement of the hunt. Fourth Older Brother had never been so titillated in his life. The compliance of that other bondmaid, the empty-headed one who came dutifully to his bed each dawn, was pleasing but he was not sorry when it ended with her sickness; indeed, during the last few times when she appeared slovenly and had begun to smell a little, he thought to put an end to the visits. This bondmaid was infinitely more beautiful and exciting. Her spiritedness raised her value to that of the sultry beauty in the open robe above his bed and made her a most desirable object of pursuit. Fourth Older Brother, ensconced in indolent contentment in the great house these many years, was ready to rouse himself in a systematic, all-absorbing chase.

He watched the girl bringing up the flasks of hot tea in the morning, and wondered whether to make a specific request for her service. He watched her sweeping the corridors and drank in, greedily, eagerly, every detail of her beauty, in particular the beauty that showed through the ugly cotton peasant blouse. He liked to watch the movement of her legs, and to anticipate the soft beauty in between. If that other bondmaid with the blunt features and squat body had given him pleasure, this one would transport him to paradise. Fourth Older Brother thought with satisfaction of the time when the patriarch might be prevailed upon to find him a suitable wife from a good family, and he could on his own make this bondmaid a secondary wife or concubine. The more he watched her, the more he wanted to bring her into his scheme of a pleasurable and easeful life.

Even with bondmaids there had to be the preliminaries of courtesy. With Wind-in-the-Head, he had begun with amiable inquiries about a cough he had noticed, then gone on to a few more friendly overtures before dispensing with niceties altogether and dragging the girl by the hand to his bed, ordering her to undress, and systematically going about his business. With this one, intelligent-looking, beautiful, intense, the preliminaries might have to be stretched to include compliments, persuasion, gifts.

Han was sweeping a corridor when she felt a presence behind her, stiffened, and turned to see Fourth Older Brother, still in his pajamas, leaning against the corridor railings and smiling at her. His opening remark was about her being earlier than expected that morning, and his disappointment at not having seen her the day before. She ignored-him and went on sweeping. He continued to look at her smiling, and made a remark about her beautiful dimples. There was a picture of a lovely lady in his room, also with beautiful dimples: would she want to have a look? She shook her head, said "No," swept up the last bit of dust and left.

He watched her, still smiling.

The next day, he shouted at her across a whole length of corridor: "I've spilt some tea on the floor. Would you come and clean up?" She had a picture of him slowly emptying his mug of half finished tea upon the floor, then bending to place the mug on its side in the puddle. She said "Yes" but went on with her work. She waited for that precise moment when he had to leave the room for some purpose, dashed in with a piece of rag, and was out before he returned.

When he saw her next, he stretched out a pa}m full of roasted chestnuts and said, "Would you like to try some? They're the best," and again smiled when she looked down, said "No, thank you" and left. He cracked a chestnut between his teeth, popped the rich flesh into his mouth, chewed slowly and watched the retreating figure.

The hunter was in a frenzy of eager anticipation.

Two hunters in pursuit of the same prey watched each other. The Reverend, going about his appointed duties in the great house, as he had been doing these many years, needed only to see once, through the corner of his eye, while chanting prayers at the ancestral altar, the shifting of Fourth Older Brother's body upon the entrance of the bondmaid Han into the room, to know what was going on.

One man's desire for a woman can sharpen another's for her, in energetic male rivalry. The Reverend wondered why that bondmaid with the large intense eyes and the pale beautiful face was the only one among the bondmaids who had not served him his morning tea and rice buns, after the ancestral prayers. In more than ten years of the unvarying routine, he had watched and touched and thrilled to the touch of uncountable bondmaids, but this one, the most desirable of all, lay outside his reach.

The Reverend had his wish, for shortly after that, in a re-assignment of duties arranged by Choyin, the bondmaid Han had charge of the monk's morning breakfast in the room adjoining the ancestral room. She came in with the tray of tea and his favorite rice buns, and he was content to keep his hands to himself and let his eyes do the roaming instead. They traveled all over the girl's face, her fine eyes, nose, mouth, chin and settled on her breasts, hidden behind the blouse and the bodice but unquestionably firm, rounded, beautiful. The years had deepened the pits and crevices in the soft fleshiness of pate, cheeks and neck, and narrowed the eyes to small slits of intensity between enormous cushions of fat, giving the Reverend the aspect of an overfed boar in torpid heat.

He had learnt to smile more at women and even deliver the occasional compliment where he felt it was deserved. He now looked with genuine pleasure upon this lovely girl whom, fourteen years ago, he had exorcised of a demon while she lay dying on a mattress. The reference to this significant event would be a fitting start of a conversation, and so he said, while he watched her pouring out the tea, "You have indeed grown. One would not have thought that possible, you know," and watched for an upward glance of curiosity. She said nothing, her eyes still downcast, and began arranging the buns on a plate, after which her duties would be over. He did not want her to leave yet and asked, "Do you remember that fourteen years ago, you were dying and I drove a devil out of your body?"

She said "Yes" and although she stood there a little longer, the terseness of her monosyllabic responses against the amiable abundance of his inquiries and comments was a little disconcerting to the monk grown vain about his power over women. Wondering what else he should say, he said nothing more and the girl left the room. Like Fourth Older Brother, he was not daunted, even thinking how a woman's reticence heightened her charms. Biting deeply into the rice buns, his mind roamed with lugubrious sensuousness and stripped the girl of her blouse and undergarment so that she stood before him with her firm white breasts which first his hands and then his mouth explored, in a maximization of the pleasure.

Hounded by woman's spite and man's lust, the bondmaid Han redoubled her prayers, no longer to Sky God, but to the Forgetful Goddess with no eyes or ears, in a change of allegiance as bold as it was risky, for Sky God, once renounced, never forgave. But she would, through sheer faith and perseverance, wake up the goddess to a realization of her former power. She visited the secret place with more joss-sticks and another saucerful of flower petals.

The Forgetful Goddess would surely wake up soon to help her.

Why did Fourth Older Brother and the Reverend, powerful as they were, fear to force their power on her? There was none of the fear with the other bondmaids. She asked the question for the solace of the answer: fear of the young master. His special feeling for her must have communicated itself to them, as it had to Miss Li-Li, and stayed their destructive hand, in the same way that it had thrown a protective cordon around her in childhood. He ignored and avoided her, giving her deep pain, but all the time, he was protecting her.

Tears came into her eyes. She prayed to the Forgetful Goddess: "Please bring us together. Never allow us to be separated again," not daring to think of his approaching marriage which would necessarily separate them. She was sure the Forgetful Goddess would help her, for had she not appeared in a dream, with perfect eyes and ears, and told her not to be afraid?

Meanwhile, she had to seek the help of human powers.

Entering the matriarch's room after ascertaining that she was alone, she once again offered her useful, back knocking fists. Peipei had improved somewhat, after the severe scolding from her sister Popo, but not nearly enough, and on cold days, was utterly useless. The matriarch rambled on in her jeremiad against inept back-knockers, and expressed her pleased surprise that Han, having little practice, could be so much more skillful. She had a mind, she said, to ask Choyin to re-organize work schedules to enable Han to attend regularly to her, but then Peipei was quite useless in housework, and it would not be a gracious thing to send her back to the House of Chang after they had shown so much kindness. The matriarch's garrulity increased with the increasingly pleasurable sensation of the back-knocking and reached such a high level of amiability that she was prepared to divulge to a bondmaid a secret of the House of Chang: could Han guess how many pieces of jewelry Li-Li's mother was giving her upon her marriage, to prevent a loss of face against the magnitude of the gift from the House of Wu? The matriarch gave a delighted little chuckle. The topic of marriage and gifts made her light-headed, almost skittish, and she turned round to face Han and say laughingly: "You too had an offer of marriage, you know!"

This intriguing bit of information could not go unelaborated and so Han asked with a smile: "An offer of marriage for me? From whom?"

It was Old Bao. Old Bao who had three wives and was looking for a fourth.

"He's not bad at all, you know," said the matriarch. "He has money and he treats all his wives well."

Han said, "I did not know anything of this offer," and the matriarch went on to say, "I was going to tell you. But then there was no need to. My grandson told me to turn down Old Bao's offer."

It was the prerogative of young masters to refuse to give away their serving maids in marriage for whatever reason. She had to know the reason; as always happened during moments of overwhelming excitement, her heart pounded wildly and the roaring sound started in her ears. She felt a draining of color from her lips and cheeks as she asked, in as calm a voice as she could, "Why?"

The matriarch said, "I don't know. He just told me to say no to Old Bao," showing no curiosity about her grandson's motives, his wish being her command. Thereafter she got distracted by the discovery of a broken finger-nail and the further discovery of a bent claw in her crab hairpin, and gave no more useful information.

Her heart leapt with awakened hope. He could not bear her to leave him. That was why. He was going to get married shortly, but he wanted her to continue to be in the same house with him.

In the tremulousness of her secret joy, she spun the scanty information offered by the matriarch into a resounding victory. She savored its various stages, smiling to herself: the conspiratorial whispers of Choyin and Li-Li, the offer to Old Bao and his eager response, the application to the matriarch for her permission, the matriarch's divulgence to the young master, the master's routing of the plotters.

The master had said, by his intervention if not by his words: I want her to stay. I cannot bear her to leave me. I may love her after all—who knows?

Miss Li-Li's screaming exasperation at their last meeting was now explained.

X

LI-LI SAT ON A CHAIR, hands laid demurely on her knees, Wu stood close to her, hands behind his back, and they looked out upon the world from the ornate gold frame of their engagement photograph with half smiles that were meant to be a compromise between the urge for joyful expression upon a betrothal and the need for public propriety.

She was dressed in her finest, and if it was not in the power of the camera to capture the auspicious pink of her dress, it at least conveyed the shimmer of most expensive silk and the glitter of jewels on earlobes, neck, chest, wrists, fingers and ankles. The slight incline of her head towards the man by her side, claiming full possession of him, seemed to be for the benefit of the bondmaid who, in her work of cleaning and dusting the visitors' reception room, was sure to come upon the photograph and examine it carefully.

Han did examine it; indeed, she forgot her work of cleaning altogether, abandoned broom and rag and stared at the photograph, holding the heavy frame in both hands. Wind-in-the-Head who had recovered from her recent illness and was working at the other end of the room watched her.

Eat your heart out, said the beautiful woman in the photograph, and smiled. Han spat her heart out; the bitter, anguished spittle landed, with perfect accuracy, on the woman's face, blocking it out, while the man by her side was spared. It flowed down slowly and Han put the photograph back on the table and watched her rich expectoration course slowly down from face to chest to hands, defiling dress and jewelry.

Wind-in-the-Head let out a small gasp. Pale from the recent devastation of her body, she looked paler still as she moved forward swiftly with a wet rag and wiped off the mess in an instinctive rush of friendly protectiveness, for who was to know what would happen if Choyin entered then, saw and went to inform the matriarch or the master?

Han unconcernedly picked up her own cleaning rag and began to wipe the dust off a large ceramic horse. The inner tumult was betrayed only by a tiny frown on her brow and a small tightening of the corners of her mouth. Every detail of the hateful photograph was imprinted in her mind; she wanted only to select out the beloved face, but it always slid behind the hateful woman's. The gentle incline of his body towards hers, even if it had been only compliance with the photographer's instructions in the studio, gave pain. The closeness of the engagement pose presaged the greater closeness of the marriage bed, which would give greater pain, as every woman must know who has lost her man to another woman and herself magnifies the loss by becoming compulsive peeper at their keyhole, watching the climax of love which could have been hers.

The solace of being under the same roof as him was receding very quickly in the expectation, daily spoken about by Choyin, that the couple would live in the bride's home after marriage. The greater wealth and prestige of the Changs warranted the arrangement. Choyin whispered a small problem related to the matter: the patriarch was reluctant to let his beloved grandson vacate his roof but was likely to concede to the claims of a greater house.

Abandoning the whisper for loud eager prattle, Choyin spoke about the plans for the wedding celebrations which would be on a scale never before seen. A team of seamstresses from Shanghai was already being assembled, the country's best jewelers were already being commissioned.

The details of the coming great event, endlessly described to the other bondmaids by Choyin in her new importance as the bride-to-be's confidante, came together in a phalanx of mockery of love's last hope. Yet hope held. For what master would have gone out of his way to prevent a bondmaid from being taken away unless he secretly loved her and wanted her for himself? Old Bao had been sent away empty-handed.

Hope expanded into dream. He would have his wife beside

him for the receiving of visitors and the taking of photographs and the having of heirs, but she herself would be assigned a special place in his secret life. Banished from the marriage bed, she would yet be ensconced in the most private chamber of his heart for the expression of the most ardent feelings from hers because, from the time of childhood, they had never stopped loving each other.

It was her turn to claim full possession, and looking again at the photograph of the man engaged to be married to another, she coolly blocked out the other, no more by spittle but by a piece of wet rag draped over.

A piercing scream tore the silence and made her pull away the rag guiltily. She and Wind-in-the-Head rushed out of the room to see Chu tearing down the passage way and screaming, as if demon-possessed. Halfway Chu stopped, turned, saw the two girls running towards her and began saying something to them in a voice made incoherent by terror. Choking, she gestured to them to follow her back to the Old One's room.

The cause of the screaming terror was a picture of perfect composure. The Old One lay peacefully on his bed, his eyes closed, his hands folded on his chest in calm repose. He had clearly been dead for several hours, without anyone's knowledge. Chu had thought he was asleep, and when she went to wake him up for his meal, found him cold and still.

"How could I have not known? I was in the room all the time; I only left for a very short while to go to the bathroom."

Chu went on lamenting tediously, wringing her hands, blowing into her handkerchief. "I did not know. How could I not know?"

Having power over the old man these many years, she felt cheated of the final power of superintending his exit: the Old One had chosen, at precisely the moment she left the room to go to the kitchen, to slip away.

Elevated as a ghost, he now had his own power, and in acknowledgment of it, the bondmaid, putting her handkerchief back into her blouse pocket, composed herself, knelt down before the pale, stiff corpse and said humbly, "I had to do what I did. You are gone now. Everything's over," while Han and Wind-in-the-Head ran to tell the matriarch and alert the rest of the bondmaids.

XI

THE DEATH OF THE SON by his own hand, twenty years ago, had been an unbelievable horror, striking everyone who looked upon the tragic young face in the coffin with a deep sense of something gone very wrong in the universe.

The death of the Old One was different. It was in the order of things, was indeed more an occasion of quiet celebration than mourning: an old man had lived to be ninety five and left behind a long line of progeny, including a great-grandson who had returned from abroad as an illustrious scholar, in time to give the old man his share of the pride and joy. Wealth, prestige happiness, successful offspring, a peaceful death in the bosom of his family—the Old One surely had the greatest share of the largesse from Sky God's store.

So it was that every one of the numerous visitors who came from all over the country to pay their respects congratulated rather than condoled, remarking, with the appropriate degree of warmth: "Such a blessed life. A great grandson. How many can claim such a blessing?"

The matriarch responded with much warmth on her side, thanking everyone profusely and privately regretting the necessity of postponing the favorite grandson's marriage till after the mourning period, a regret only less than that of having to abandon the favorite diamond, gold and jade hairpins for the plain silver ones of mourning. Her immediate concern was to make sure that the old dead one wanted for nothing. The same filial piety that had governed their provision for his every comfort during life should ensure a most magnificent wake and funeral in death, so that no relative or neighbor would have occasion to whisper: "Ah, I remember the funeral of the Old One's father. It was on a much bigger scale," or "He was once a patriarch of the House of Wu. They seem to have forgotten that."

Accordingly, into the mansion came teams of monks from the White Light Temple and nuns from an equally respected nunnery for prayers and ceremonies around the clock. Tradesmen came on their bicycles and carts with enormous stacks of joss-sticks, candles, prayer paper, paper flowers, fresh flowers and ritual pomelos and oranges, while from the House of Chang came a retinue of cooks and maids, to provide the needed help for feeding and serving the endless streams of visitors. Little children from the villages around came to gape and gawk, and take back stories of the magnificence they had witnessed, and good things as well, salvaged from the mounds of stuff thrown upon the rubbish dumps, such as still edible pomelos or still usable candles.

In the midst of the pomp lay the old man, reunited with his coffin at last, and looking so small and shrunken that he might have been mistaken for one of the paper or waxen effigies in the ancestral room that his portrait was soon to grace.

The emotions that swirled around him as he lay in the coffin in the visitors' reception room in that vast mansion had nothing to do with him or were only remotely connected with him: he had lived too long for progeny to feel anything but relief.

Thus the patriarch, wearing the filial gunny cowl and following the Reverend ringing a small mournful bell in a slow perambulation of the coffin, found himself thinking with a start, not of his dead father, but of the dead son, twenty years ago, whose allotment of years had been appropriated by a willful ancestor with unseemly long, sharp teeth. Thus, too, the great grandson, as he walked behind the patriarch, wearing the same cowl of deepest mourning, thought of his coming marriage and the great change it would make to his life, with something like regret, because he would be leaving the house of the grandfather he loved so dearly.

The matriarch, sitting quietly on a stool and watching the ceremony, worried that her back was going to give her more trouble than ever. Then she worried about whether the ang *pow* she was giving the Reverend for his services was commensurate with the extra trouble he was taking with the rituals. She mentally went over the acts of charity that should immediately follow the funeral—a large donation to the White Light Temple, free meals for the temple beggars, sacks of rice to a home of destitutes.

The mourning guests, not having to worry about the cost of a funeral, ate and drank freely and marveled at the munificence of the House of Wu. Further down the line, the servants and bondmaids went about their duties with quiet efficiency, not minding the extra work because there would be a generous ang *pow* attached to it. And further down still, Spitface, recovering something of the old cheerfulness after the mistreatment as the Monkey God, reveled in the new black shirt and pants he had been given to wear, and, together with an old beggar and a crazy deaf-mute who gravitated towards him in a natural grouping of the town's poor fools, moved excitedly among the guests and pointed with awe at the giant billows of smoke from huge joss-sticks and swinging censers.

Assembled in reverential mourning black for the dead old man, the mourners had entirely forgotten about him.

Only one sobbed continuously and uncontrollably and had to be led away since she was only a bondmaid, and her grief, outdoing that of family, might cause observing visitors to put an improper construction on the matter. The matriarch signaled to Han, with a small impatient gesture of her hand, to get Chu out of sight. Han led the woman, gaunt and pale, back to her room. Chu sat on a chair, a terrible sight, her face a raw red mass, her cheekbones sticking out, stark and white. She could not stop crying and waved away a cup of hot water that Han brought.

The old man having been the single cause for the exercise of all her energies and vital instincts, his death now created an appalling emptiness which completely disoriented her. She moved around, dazed, wild-eyed, unable to sleep. In her calmer moments, she said she had already made plans for her future: she would no longer remain in the House of Wu; after the funeral, she would go and live with a foster-sister in another town.

A house of death necessarily bred thoughts of gloom and foreboding. Also, by contrast, of eager life, a gesture of defiance against the looming mortality.

The Reverend, coming daily for the prayers and ceremonies, welcomed the opportunity to see the beautiful bondmaid Han more often than he normally would. The girl's youthful beauty and spiritedness made her a compelling antithesis to the bleak spirituality, which the Reverend, despite his calling, was rather averse to. In her bright eyes, glossy hair and firm flesh was all the promise of life and pleasure. He watched her move about in the performance of her various duties, and, as on previous occasions, disrobed her and coaxed her into full submission, so that nobody watching the monk swinging a censer and sending clouds of fragrant smoke up to heaven, or intoning a prayer for the dead from a sacred text, would have guessed that in his mind, he had already had his full pleasure of a beautiful young woman.

The watcher was watched in his turn. Fourth Older Brother, descending from the indolent ease of his secret room to take part in the various ceremonies, followed with a keen eye the monk's secretive movements and saw, on one occasion, his taking over some prayer candles from the girl in a slow, drawn out manner that allowed him to look into her face and touch the tips of her fingers. In the privacy of his room, Fourth Older Brother thumped a fist on the table and growled, "The bastard! He means to have her. We shall see."

The bondmaid's avoidance of him which had had an element

of pleasing coyness was now becoming irksome: he could not spend all his days pursuing a servant girl. He suspected that her cool insouciance was derived from a confidence connected in some way with the young master Wu, from something that the garrulous Choyin had once said in his presence. He growled again, this time against the bondmaid who certainly thought too highly of herself and had to be put in her place.

The watcher became the watched who turned round and became, by turn, the watcher, in a dizzying progression of swift role interchanging that took both men up a fevered race. In seven consecutive days of prayers and rituals in the house, the sharp-eyed, sharp-eared monk did not miss a single instance of Fourth Older Brother's efforts to secure the bond-maid's attention, whether subtle or crude, as when, in front of a large group of visitors, he ordered the maid to clean the table he was sitting at, and stared hard at her for the entire duration of the cleaning. The monk did not thump angry fists against the rival, but merely narrowed his eyes, smiled and thought, "We shall see."

The seeing had to wait out a proper period of time in a house of mourning. The old man's immense coffin, richly palled, was carried out at last by eight able-bodied men, in a long procession, to the accompaniment of gongs, drums and cymbals and the wails of a hundred hired mourners, to reinforce those of the bereaved, following the coffin in their mourning cowls. Amidst the intoning of a myriad monks, the coffin was lowered into the ground of that part of the cemetery reserved for the wealthy. Soon a magnificent tombstone, flanked by two stone lions, would be erected, with a fitting epitaph for an old man who could claim, in the magnitude of his worldly blessings, to be a special favorite of Sky God.

A no less privileged existence was ensured for him beyond the grave: a huge paper house replete with paper servants, carriages, furniture and fine clothes, was set on fire, and thus transported to the other world for his use, together with a substantial stack of ghost money that he would need to maintain a lifestyle in death that he had been used to in life. On the fortieth day, he was welcomed back. His room was arranged in exactly the way he had known it. That he did come back was certain, for not only was there a hollow in the pillow where his head must have lain, but also distinct footprints in the ash that had been strewn on the floor. The matriarch examined the cup of tea that had been placed beside the bed, and noticed at least half of it had been drunk, further proof of the Old One's return.

So he was not only happily resettled in the other world but was also in loving communication with still living progeny in this. He would never be forgotten. Filial piety would remember him every day in prayers at the ancestral altar and put out his favorite food in great abundance upon his grave every year during the Feast of the Hungry Ghosts. The tombstone would ever be free of unsightly weeds.

When the last bit of ash from the paper money had been blown away by the wind, when the last curl of joss-smoke had disappeared in the sky, and life in that great house resumed its course, the Reverend and Fourth Older Brother resumed their chase of the bondmaid.

The monk's strategy with serving maids had remained unchanged over twenty years. Indeed, it had little need for change, being the best possible accommodation of the various demands of his holy calling, on the one hand, and those of his natural appetite, on the other. Its enormous success with a long line of young maids had given him a sense of infallible power. Now this girl, whom he had rescued from the demons was challenging the power, was indeed seizing it to use against him. He could not allow a female, no matter how beautiful and desirable, to discomfit him and laugh secretly at him. The monk pondered a possible change in tactics, and came to the conclusion that he had been too liberal with his compliments and smiles; he would now assert his authority more and bring this hard girl to heel. Besides, he had heard about some offer of marriage being made to the girl by Old Bao and he hated the thought of the girl slipping his grasp forever.

Thus when she came in with his morning tea and buns, he instantly swung round in his chair to face her and swung open his legs, staring intently at her at the same time, in an unequivocal signaling of male intention. She arranged the cups and plates on the tables and poured out his tea, her eyes resolutely lowered. He stretched out a hand and began playing with a corner of her sleeve, still looking intently into her face, a small brutal smile hovering about his mouth. She went on with her work unconcernedly and then he grabbed her hand and pulled her to stand before him. The corpulent monk, holding her arms down firmly with both hands, stood her between his legs, grinning in the sheer delight of a novel position which he realized, with some amusement, he liked very much and would most certainly try again.

The massive legs under the grey silk robe would have closed up on the girl and effected a most delicious proximity, if she had not suddenly broken free of his grasp, reached for the teapot on the table and swept it down upon him. The lid fell off clattering to the floor and the hot tea flowed over one thigh. The Reverend jumped up with a gasp, and stared at the girl.

She said, "I'm sorry, that was careless of me. I'll go and get more tea," and he knew she had won. She would get someone else—probably the old Choyin or the ill favored one called Wind-in-the-Head—to bring a fresh pot of tea and a cleaning rag and would herself make all sorts of excuses never to do the morning duty again.

The scalding had done away with the desire for the time being, and brought into awareness a new feeling, one so strong that it would have to vent itself somehow. The Reverend had never been so humiliated in his life. A serving girl had abused him. He would have liked to catch hold of her, push her to a kneeling position and hit her repeatedly, but his instincts told him that would be an extreme folly and endanger his respected position as holy monk.

199

To his surprise, it was the bondmaid herself who came in with the second pot of tea, her quiet demeanor announcing a new strength, daring him to try to touch her again. He stared at her.

The quality of the staring had changed, being charged with menace. He said slowly, "You think you are very clever, Miss. But you have demons inside you. I thought I had driven them away but I can see that your body is filled with them." The girl left, without saying a word, her eyes still downcast.

On her mattress that evening, she prayed to the Forgetful Goddess, rubbing, between reverent fingers, not holy beads but the remains of the flower petals blessed by her at her shrine. The prayers were both thanksgiving and entreaty: she thanked the goddess for the victory over the monk and entreated her help for the next onslaught which she knew was coming soon, for only that evening Fourth Older Brother, on pretext of coming into the kitchen for something, had found her alone and come up very close, until he heard approaching footsteps and walked away.

She did not see him the next day and the next and then one morning, as she was sweeping the corridors, his door opened as usual and he came out.

"Your Oldest Brother left something for you, come and get it. I think he's in trouble," he said matter-of-factly and returned to his room, leaving the door ajar.

She looked up, a frightened look in her eyes, and he knew he had succeeded. She walked up to his room and hovered uneasily at the doorway.

"Come in," he said casually. "I don't know what it is. I can't make it out, but he said to give to you without delay. Here it is." He held out a small package in his hand, wrapped in red paper.

She had learnt, in that vast house of intrigues, to think quickly and act quickly. She could immediately connect Fourth Older Brother, with his insatiable appetites, with her brother's new business, could see both men in protracted negotiations while a frightened young girl waited in the background. But the connection ended there; it could not be extended to account for the mysterious package

She stretched out a hand for it and Fourth Older Brother, with the pleased look of someone in control once again, gently held it out of her reach and said, still more provocatively, "I didn't know you had a brother. You didn't tell me. Why don't you tell me? He's in trouble. I think I can help."

He waved Han to a chair beside his bed at the same time closing the door with his leg. She sat down nervously, holding the sides of the chair.

"What trouble is he in? Please tell me."

The girl's entreaty, the first she had ever made of him, called forth an even more expansive smile of self congratulatory pleasure, as he moved rapidly towards the successful completion of his scheme.

"Ah, you do want to know, don't he?" he said, in a deliciously satisfying delaying tactic that had the girl looking up in wondering anxiety at him. He saw how truly beautiful this young bondmaid was, and noticed once again, the wondrous curve of her breasts.

"Please tell me," said Han, and then realizing that the man could give no information because there was none, rose to go.

"Let's see what is inside this package," said Fourth Older Brother, handing it to her.

"Come on, open it."

She went up quickly, took the package and unwrapped it. Inside was the thread bracelet with Sky God's image on the piece of jade. A last gift to a dead woman, wrested from her wrist by a stranger, handed back to her son, passed on to her daughter's brutal tormentor who passed it to the daughter. The gift had come full circle, but she could not make out the dark forces underlying its journey.

"You are surprised," said Fourth Older Brother. "Please tell me all about this bracelet."

The girl made a movement to leave and Fourth Older

Brother, giving up all pretext, drew her to him by the hand.

"Come," he said. "Come, let's not play games with each other anymore. I want you. I dream of you every night. Come."

He saw a contortion of that beautiful, young face into something so hideously savage that he actually retreated a step in shock, saw a further contortion for the expulsion of a huge blob of spittle that flew and hit him in one eye.

"What—how dare you—," he spluttered, but the girl was already opening the door and running away.

XII

TOGETHER WITH THE JOSS-STICKS and two gift oranges, Han brought out a cleaning rag, for sometimes small jungle creatures ran over the goddess and dropped their dirt on her. She went to the edge of the pond, wetted the rag and came back for a thorough cleaning of the small stone statue; there was indeed a streak of something black across part of her face.

Then it was time to paint in the eyes and ears, so long absent from the divine face. Heavenly dragons were brought to life by potentates dotting their eyes with a brush; this sleepy goddess might be roused by freshly painted eyes and ears. With extreme care, she stood the statue on the hard earth-seat and, with a small brush dipped in black ink, she painted in, first the left eye, then the right, two almonds, irregularly shaped, with large dark pupils. She then did the ears, crude teapot handles, no better than a small child's efforts. She wished she had red paint, to give a pretty mouth.

The goddess was returned to her place in the shrine, now seeing, hearing. The act of revitalizing a deity was itself revitalizing. She felt an uplifting of spirits and was in the mood for chatter, so she sat down and chatted with the goddess, as with an understanding mother or an affectionate sister.

"Listen, Goddess. Two men want me and call for me incessantly. I want one man who never calls for me at all. Now that you have eyes to see and ears to hear, why don't you put things right? Why don't you put it in his mind to send for me and say, 'I have sent for you, I and no other, because I want and love you? Come.'"

It is a sad day when gods and goddesses are grown so careless and unheeding that the very words for the granting of favors have to be put into their mouths. But it had to be done.

XIII

OLDEST BROTHER WHOM SHE HAD not included in her prayers to the Forgetful Goddess bore all the signs of a newly favored son. For he not only looked in good health but wore new expensive-looking clothes and two massive gold rings.

This time he waited for her, not in the kitchen but outside, by a side-gate. His face lit up when he saw her and he came forward quickly with a gift box of cakes. He was alone; the heavily powdered woman companion was nowhere to be seen.

His last visit had to do with death; this one brimmed with life and hope, for he had come to persuade her to join him in a life where there was good money to be made. The expensive clothes, rings, cakes were ranged as proof: he told her that only a short while ago, he was so poor he did not have money for food. Their dying mother's request for a new flask and a bottle of Tiger Oil had left him nonplused and he had to pawn his watch for the money. He made a joke about pawning gold teeth in the future, for he had plans to have all his bad teeth removed and replaced with solid gold. As indisputable proof of his new wealth, he brought out a wad of notes from his shirt pocket and tried to push it into her hand.

Not money, but truth: she pointed to the thread bracelet on her wrist and wanted to know how Fourth Older Brother had managed to get hold of it. How did he know she was the sister anyway? How long had they known each other? What had he said about her? etc.

"Tell me," she said, "I want to know."

Here Oldest Brother lost some of his flamboyance, fidgeted, touched the back of his head and muttered something about Fourth Older Brother being one of their best clients. With this, he dismissed the matter as of no consequence, and returned to the purpose of his visit with renewed fervor.

Oldest Brother wanted his sister to leave her life as a bond-maid and live with him. He described his new life enthusiastically, pushing into the background all details even remotely hinting of the stigma and focusing only on the good money to be made. The vivid life of the establishment he was helping to run, called the House of Flowers, was carefully bleached of all its garish colors, for the benefit of the quiet, gentle sister, so that not a single mention was made of the girls, as young as fifteen who had drifted in from the villages or been placed there by their own desperate mothers, the men who quarreled over them, or slapped them, or vomited on them in drunken stupor, or stuffed money down their blouses and into their knickers, and the long retinue of go-betweens, including tattooed hooligans who demanded cuts and commissions. Oldest Brother pushed this raucous world out of the way as of no relevance and presented to his sister one of security and well-being. For, he said, he could make a special arrangement for her by which she could live apart from them, in her own room, with a client of her choice. Such arrangements had been made before and had proved quite successful. The client was likely to be wealthy and generous and after a time, might even consider taking her back to his home as secondary wife. He whispered the example of a woman, twenty years old, who had precisely this good fortune and was now the third wife of a rubber magnate, with ascendancy over the first and second wives.

From the bright promises of the House of Flowers, Oldest

Brother swung to the bleak prospects of the House of Wu: could she tell him how many of the bondmaids there had such a good future? He knew they were married off to vegetable-sellers and fishermen and shop attendants who beat them, or became the concubines of wastrel masters who ill-treated them, or never married and died in homes for the destitute.

Oldest Brother's eager volubility flowed on, before coming up against the obvious indifference of his sister who all the while looked at him listlessly or toyed with the strings on the gift box of cakes. He asked her, "Do you want to come with me or not?" and saw in the continuing silence that the proposition provoked so little interest as not to merit any answer.

Oldest Brother whose good nature in dealing with intractable girls and unreasonable clients was a great asset in the House of Flowers lost a little of it now and grew red-faced with impatience. He said, "Don't say I didn't try to help." He turned away sulkily. But he could not leave on such a harsh note. There was the lingering bond of childhood that made him say to himself: she is the only one I have. All the rest are gone. Therefore it was his duty to watch over her and protect her. So he pushed the wad of money into her pocket, told her to let him know if she needed more and was gone.

His direful prediction of bondmaids' fates was not likely to apply in the case of one bondmaid: although she was going to marry a clogs-maker twenty years older, she was happy and talked about her leaving the House of Wu with much eagerness. Wind-in-the-Head who was putting on weight and looking much better after her ordeal came to Han to give her the good news. She said the clogs maker had been very kind to her, sending over packets of nourishing herbs. Han had seen the man only once, a thin, wizened fellow who came with a gift for the matriarch and who smiled often, revealing a mouthful of gold teeth; on that basis, he could claim to already possess the wealth that Oldest Brother, for all his flaunting of his new prosperity, was only aspiring to.

Something like a blush passed over Wind-in-the-Head's features, actually rescuing them from-their plainness, as she said, "He calls me by my real name. He says that after our marriage, he wants everyone to call me by my real name."

Golden Fern. The name, the only thing of worth that her parents had given her, had been taken away by her heartless new owners and replaced with contemptible labels. Now a kind, loving man had reclaimed it on her behalf, and by his kindness and love would ensure that she would never lose it again. She would never grind her teeth in her sleep again.

Wind-in-the Head said that in a week she would leave the House of Wu forever. The prospect of her departure and Chu's filled Han with a sense of loss and deepened her fears about her own fate: what was going to happen to her now?

In the heaviness of sleep, she felt someone shake her shoulder.

"Wake up," a voice said. "There's something that I want to tell you."

"What is it?" she asked. The hand remained firmly laid on her shoulder. She struggled to open her eyes to see who it was.

"Oh no," she thought. "How could he have come into the room?" For Fourth Older Brother's face loomed before her.

He said, "Don't think you'll get away, Miss. You won't get away."

"Of course not," said another voice, and even before the face appeared, she knew it was the Reverend. "She scalded us and spat on us. She has six demons in her body. We'll have to get them out."

"Take the money," said someone and she felt her shoulder being shaken again. "I want you to have the money."

"Stuff it into her pocket," said Oldest Brother whose voice she heard, though she could not see him. "She is only pretending; she wants the money. She has no money of her own, you see, being only a bondmaid."

"Will you sleep with me if I give you money?" said Fourth

Older Brother. "I want you so much. You must come to my bed before cockcrow."

"I want you too," said the Reverend greedily. "I want first turn."

"No, me. She comes to my bed first."

"What! You think my sister's a prostitute? I'm taking her away!"

"So the brother wants first turn? Ha! Ha!"

There came the sound of shouting and cursing. The three men, moving shadows, now distinct, now coalescing into one giant shadow, pressed upon her. Above the din, the voice persisted, and the impatient shaking of her shoulder: "Get up! Here's the money. Take it."

With a tremendous effort, she opened her eyes and saw, in the dawn dimness, Chu bent over her on the mattress and shaking her with both hands. She struggled up, groggy, uncomprehending, trying to shake off the sleep in her eyes, as she had tried to shake off the dark shadows crowding upon her.

Chu pressed something into her hand. The heaviness in her mind cleared enough for her to recognize the bundle of money brought out from a drawer for showing together with the sister's photographs that terrible afternoon.

"I want you to have it," said Chu, then got up and left the room.

"Wait—", she said, but Chu was gone.

Sheer tiredness made her fall back on her mattress and in a moment the troubling shadows were back. They crowded upon her again, shouting, talking, whispering into her ears.

"Please leave her alone."

She recognized the old *keo kia* woman whose ghost had been roaming the house and grounds these many years. It was still a watery ghost: the rainwater was part of her eternity. At sight of her, the giant shadow shifted, then disappeared.

"Come with me," said the old *keo kia* woman. "She's in trouble and we have to help her."

"Who?" asked Han and she forced herself up. She was aware of detaching herself from the mattress, the blanket, the dropped bundle of money.

"Please hurry, we may be too late," said the *keo kia* woman.

Han followed her through a long dark corridor that led to the Old One's room. She heard the distant barking of a dog, the hoot of an owl, and saw the old *keo kia* woman disappear around a corner.

"Wait—," she said and thought, "It's strange. People are always pressing upon me or running away from me."

She went to look for her but the old woman was nowhere to be seen. Seeing a light in the Old One's room, she quickly walked towards it. She paused by the door and thought, "It's Chu", looking sadly upon the body hanging by a rope from the ceiling, swaying a little and casting a long shadow on the wall. She moved towards it, stood under it and gently touched the bare feet which were pointing downwards. She had never seen Chu without slippers or shoes on her feet.

Looking up, she saw the face looking down, oddly peaceful, despite the tongue hanging out. There was a definite comicality about Chu in death that was never present in life: head tilted to one side, hands loosely dangling, she had the posture of the clown.

"The old *keo kia* woman is supposed to be here with me, but she's disappeared," she said to the corpse. It was only when she heard a piercing scream, turned round to see Peipei wide-eyed with terror, heard the crash of a dropped flask, turned back to look at the corpse and felt the solidity of its feet swing against her face that she realized that this was no dream. Chu's body, hanging from the ceiling, in the darkness of dawn, was as real as the money in the cloth bundle she had left on her mattress, only a short while ago, as her last gift. She heard herself say weakly "Chu" and then all was darkness.

XIV

"HERE, TAKE THIS, it's yours."

Even Spitface could see there was something unusual about the gift-giving. Not only had the giver come in the middle of the night and roused him up by a violent shaking, but also that she looked pale as a ghost and had been crying.

"Take it, I say. It's yours," said Han, pushing the cloth bundle into Spitface's hands. The knot of the cloth loosened and some of the money dropped out, neat wads of notes tied up with rubber-bands. Han scooped them up and put them back into the bundle which she retied securely.

"Buy whatever you like to eat," she said to him, thinking of the times when he had stood outside the food shops, looking in wistfully upon steamed chicken and waxed duck and glistening noodles.

She took the bundle, walked to the small wooden cupboard beside his bed, opened it and hid the money in a deep corner, covering it with the objects she found strewn in the cupboard— cigarette tins, empty boxes, paper bags, combs, mirrors, joss-sticks.

"See?" she said. "Nobody must know where your money is. You take out a little bit at a time and you buy whatever good things you want to eat. Do you understand?"

Spitface looked at her and nodded eagerly. She left quickly.

XV

FOURTH OLDER BROTHER WAS avoiding her assiduously; of that she was glad, for otherwise he would have surely made use of Chu's suicide as the excuse to engage her in talk. Totally indifferent about whether bondmaids lived or died, he would yet have feigned a great interest or even concern, to derive from that poor woman's tragic death, at least half a dozen opportunities to serve his own secret wishes.

"So you saw the body, tell me about it," he would have grinned, while his eyes roamed over hers.

He had been avoiding her since the day she spat at him and she must welcome any development that put an end to the necessity of going to his room. Fleeing one man, she ran towards another who fled from her. The pursuer and the pursued linked in a pair, in a sudden reconfiguration of male affinities in that large house, and puzzled her greatly. For lately, Fourth Older Brother had attached himself to the young master She had never seen them talking to each other but now they seemed inseparable, the young, handsome twenty-year-old with the scholarly bearing, and the gross, pock-marked forty year-old exuding sweat and secret desire, a visually discordant pair.

Sometimes the master's young friends came to join them, forming the large, cheerful groups that had been such a happy part of his homecoming. He had lost much of the brightness and was inclined to be morose—all the bondmaids noticed it and whispered among themselves. The playful friends fled, leaving him to the company of the gross cousin who always stayed close to him, but reappeared for the abundance of good food and drink, upon any sign of the moroseness lifting.

She wanted to catch sight of him alone. It was difficult to extract the well-loved face from a mesh of others, to pull out the well-loved voice from a mixed babble. She thought that the face and voice were determinedly staying meshed, to hide themselves from the searching intensity of her love, as if they feared to betray themselves into giving more proof of remembrance and regard to one woman when they already belonged to another. On the few occasions when he had-seen her coming from the opposite direction, he had turned and gone another way, looking troubled.

A woman fears a man's indifference, but sees hope in his trepidation, since this could still resolve into a joyful outcome for her; she awaited this outcome with her own trepidation of hope.

She was sweeping outside the visitors' room when she paused to catch snatches of the conversation going on inside. She knew of the protracted negotiations related to the demands of the bride-to-be's parents for the marital home to be set up on their territory. She thought she knew the reason which had nothing to do with the greater claims of the wealthier, more prestigious House of Chang; its confirmation was in the angry looks Li-Li unfailingly threw at her, on each of her visits, and the unguarded admissions of Choyin, in a tone of intense irritation, that some beggars actually had it in their power to thwart the wishes of kings.

The voices of negotiation that morning were more animated than usual. She could hear the patriarch Wu's voice raised against the patriarch Chang's, followed by a fit of coughing, a sure sign of the old man's agitation. The young master Wu said something but she could not catch it, and would have gone nearer, would have even boldly put her ear to the door, if she had not heard the sound of approaching footsteps and quickly moved away.

That night, the young master went to Fourth Older Brother's room for some consolatory drinking. In the morning, Choyin cleared the room of ten empty beer bottles and a wine jar.

Fourth Older Brother consoled with more than drink.

Hiding behind a screen in his room, the young master Wu sat on a chair and peeped through a small slit. In the darkness, he saw Fourth Older Brother coming in with a young girl, and closing the door. There was a lamp on the bedside table, entirely for his benefit, for no demonstration by a mentor for the enlightenment of his pupil could be allowed to be only imperfectly witnessed. Accordingly, Fourth Older Brother conducted his seduction of the girl—very young-looking, heavily painted, probably lent by the House of Flowers—in a meticulous, step-by-step process by which the benefit to the observer should have precedence over the wishes of the seducer himself.

Fourth Older Brother arranged the girl's position on the bed in order to place her body in full view of the peeper behind the screen. The girl giggled shyly and was totally co-operative. Then Fourth Older Brother began systematically to work out his desire downwards, beginning from her ear-lobes and neck and nuzzling her into wriggling, giggling titillation.

"Stop it," said the girl with the learnt coy petulance that meant the opposite and drove the man to a higher frenzy of desire. He unbuttoned her blouse, pulled off her bodice and turned the light of the lamp upon the full beauty of her breasts, for though very young, she had the voluptuousness of a mature woman and had probably, on that basis, been placed in the category reserved for the special clients of the House of Flowers. Fourth Older Brother did a lingering exploration of the breasts, with one hand, then both hands, then his mouth, wetly slavering the rich smooth curves, tweaking, pinching, biting to raise gasps and little screams from the girl that would surely add to the pleasure of the watcher behind the screen. The girl was set against a mound of pillows on the bed, and in her half naked state and practiced coyness looked not unlike the bewitching siren in the calendar picture on the wall above.

Fourth Older Brother, still guided by the mentor's concern about a consummate demonstration, now removed her silk trousers, pulling them off with a loud laugh, and delighting in the girl's full eager compliance. She watched him closely to respond to the smallest quirk of desire, such being the instructions of the House of Flowers; he had removed her trousers but clearly preferred to watch her peeling off the last undergarment herself. So she removed it slowly, watching him, and tossed it aside provocatively. Fourth Older Brother let out a guffaw of delight, which the girl echoed with her own nervous giggle.

This was the crowning moment. Fourth Older Brother had no idea whether his young cousin, living for years in a foreign country and now engaged to be married, had ever had sight of a woman's nakedness. So he shifted the lamp to focus its light upon that part of her beauty, and took a special pleasure in the thought that by now, the desire of the young man watching from behind the screen must have worked itself up to a most agreeable pitch. His own desire reaching bursting point, he pulled off his trousers, then his undergarment, with frenzied impatience, and stood facing the girl on the bed in the full display of indisputable male power. Gurgling, he clambered upon the bed, threw himself upon her and plunged into her with all the energy of untamable desire. He pushed and shoved and panted, not thinking anymore of the protégé behind the screen, but his own pleasure which he must needs maximize, thus requiring the girl, at intervals, to sit up or lie on her side or lift up both legs or get down on the floor, finally returning her to the position of submission on her back before working out on her, with an enormous grunt, the last ounce of male appetite. He collapsed on her, panting heavily. All the while she stayed with wide-eyed vigilance underneath him, awaiting his next pleasure. No more was asked; he hurriedly got up, ordered her to dress, gave her some money and sent her out of the room.

Now was the time to verify the results of his little experiment. The young master Wu came out from behind the screen, looking pale and tense with desire. Fourth Older Brother, clapping him on the shoulder, laughed and said, "You will have one, too, young cousin. Go to your room now. But wait, let's have some wine first."

The bondmaid Han was surprised to be awakened from sleep by Choyin and told that the young master wanted to see her. At sound of his name, the girl sprang up.

Where?" she asked.

"His room," said Choyin, and once again her surliness attested to her displeasure about a scheme she had no understanding of. The girl washed her face hurriedly, combed her hair, put on a fresh suit of clothes. Her heart went mad with hope inside her, knocking against her so violently that she thought she would never be able to make the distance to his room. He wanted her, he loved her. Tonight would bear the stamp of the decision he must have made at last with regard to themselves, prior to his marriage, and she would wake up the next morning and be able to say to all, "He has made me his. He can't bear to be separated from me, you see."

His door was open. She stood at the doorway, trembling. She saw him sitting on his bed, disheveled, pale, wild-eyed.

"You have called, and I have come." The rehearsed words were locked inside her throat. Instead she found herself saying, "Are you ill?"

He said, "Come in," and stood up, facing her. With some surprise, he recognized her as the bondmaid Han, and for a while the image of the girl he had expected—young, painted, voluptuous—superimposed itself upon the girl he now saw before him. He shook off the confusion, as if he were shaking water from his eyes, and looked at her again. Now the fumes of drink cleared sufficiently for him to remember her as the childhood playmate, as indeed, the girl he had felt sorry for, and risen to protect against the unkindness of his own people. He also saw that she was extremely beautiful, and the awareness combined with a strong surge of desire for her so that he moved quickly towards her. He lurched forward and tore at her blouse.

Finding it resistant, he lifted it and put in a clumsy hand to begin the exploration of her body. His fingers touched the curves of one breast and stirred the rest of his body into feverish activity: suddenly he was all over her, groping, pushing, gasping. He was no young well-loved master; he was the hated cousin, he was the abhorred monk. She struck at his hand and said in a tense, hoarse whisper, "What are you doing?" but that only served to excite his passion more and produce a fresh spurt of energy that enabled his arms to encircle her and push her against a wall and his mouth to still try to get at the beauty of her breasts. She struggled, he grew stronger and more excited, panting heavily. Impatient for the final prize, he struggled with the strings of her trousers and was ready to rip them off, the last obstacle in the path of his rampaging desire.

She cried out weakly, "Please," they continued to grapple with each other, and then he gave a little yelp of pain, staggered backwards, sat upon his bed and looked with horror upon a small red gash on his left arm, from which a few drops of blood were beginning to trickle. She faced him, a look of equal horror on her face, holding tightly in her hand the little gift pen-knife, opened to reveal its sharp blade. They stared at each other, wild-eyed, speechless, unable as yet to absorb the enormity of the act. Her face drained white, she broke the silence, flinging away the penknife and walking to him on the bed. She sat by him, laid her head on his shoulder and wept. "Can't you see?" she sobbed. "If I let you rape me, you will never love me."

She would have joined the long line of bondmaids, faceless, nameless to the men who called them up to their rooms and did not know or care if they ceased to appear because there were others to replace them. She would have joined that pool of bond-maids who were passed from bed to bed. Today's my turn. Tomorrow's yours.

Fourth Older Brother's sense of solidarity with the young master would have a new basis: we share the same woman.

"I love you so much," she said. "I will die if you leave me again." The simplicity of the utterance calmed him but did not lessen the stupefaction at the evening's strange unfolding. He continued to stare at her, watching her closely, following every shifting expression on her face, as she tended to the gash on his arm, cleaning it with a wet towel. Upon that face, tear-splattered but calm, were superimposed others that now came crowding upon him in a phantasmagoria of horror and wonder: that of the child-demon, sinking her teeth into adult flesh, of the exquisite little dancing, laughing girl who made his childhood happy, of the intense young girl who wept on a staircase because he was going away. For the first time, he became fully aware of her; for the first time, she stood in the center of this awareness and no longer on the shadowed fringes. He was bereft of speech, because he could not utter anything coherent. His silence was charged with a hundred perturbing thoughts which he could not begin to articulate, but one stood out in the strength of its clarity and certainty: this girl loves me truly. She would die for me. The thought elicited its own appropriate feeling: he was deeply moved and lowered his eyes to hide the feeling.

The long ensuing silence was only broken by her telling him, before she left his room: "If you want to know how much, you have only to meet me at the pond of the Forgetful Goddess."

XVI

A SLOW MOON ROSE. She had never seen the moon so beautiful before, or perhaps it was her tremulous joy that lent it beauty as it touched the clouds, trees and pond water with its silver.

The ugly little broken shrine was beyond the transforming power of moonlight, and the Forgetful Goddess, standing in its shadows, even more so. But it was in her power to provide adornments. From a little basket, she pulled some red silk ribbons to festoon the shrine and a small vase of artificial flowers for putting in the center. As for the goddess, the best was reserved for her. Han took out a small dish of red ink and began to paint a mouth on her, a smiling mouth, which together with the almond eyes, and a string of beads draped round her neck, presented a slightly coquettish appearance that was very pleasing. Then she took out the joss-sticks, a sizable bunch this time, lit them and began to pray to the newly cosmeticised goddess. She prayed fervently, holding the joss-sticks tightly in both hands and keeping her head bowed.

She did not need any rustling sound of moving bushes or twigs stepped upon or low cough to tell her of his presence. She knew he was already there, watching her.

After a while, he walked up to her and the realization by both, that the enormity of the evening's experience had no precedent nor ever would, caused them to seek a balancing calmness by resorting to almost banal opening talk: did you have difficulty finding this place? Have you had dinner? How long did you take to come here? See, there's a moon.

The vain goddess would urge herself upon his attention. He looked at the statue, turned to her and said, "Tell me about this forgetful Goddess," and she did, holding up the smiling deity to show him and telling him the stories she had heard about her. Sky God, it was said, was displeased with the little goddess once, for being presumptuous and taking it upon herself to grant a request which he himself had turned down and he punished her by taking away her hearing for one hundred years, so that she would hear no more requests.

"You were praying so fervently to her. Who were you praying for?"

The dead mother, Oldest Brother, Wind-in-the-Head, Wind-in-the-Head's husband, the kind clogs-maker, Popo, Popo's child—she was a self-appointed intercessor. He did not spoil the fragile magic of the evening's beginning by asking, "What about me?" just as she had not asked, "And why have you come?", to keep at bay, as long as possible, the direct expression of their love, in order to savor, as much as they could, the delight of its anticipation.

They sat together on the earth-seat under the tree, not touching, not even looking at each other, in emphatic manifestation of the tentativeness of young lovers, as if to wipe out the harshness of their earlier encounter in his room. They spoke quietly about what they remembered of their childhood experiences together, but warily, avoiding reference to anyone or anything that would intrude upon the purity of their feelings. Spitface could be mentioned, and *Sinseh* and the old *keo kia* woman, but not Choyin, and certainly not Li-Li. They talked and laughed, in complete ease.

217

"Do you remember the time we wanted to make Spitface swallow some baby mice?"

"Do you remember the time we danced in the rain? I was being punished and had to stand outside the house in the rain. Then you came and we danced together."

Do you remember. Do you remember.

Remembrance hushed talk into a gentle silence and both were quiet for a while, looking upon the lovely shimmer of light on the pond-water. The re-connection was perfect; all the pain of the past years was washed away. The evening's magic would move on to its next phase.

The goddess, ever helpful, helped once more. A flapping sound, as of a trapped bird, came from where she stood in the darkness of the shrine; the small glowing tips of the burning joss-sticks shed no light and told nothing. So they got off the earth-seat and went to have a look, and true enough, a small bird flew out, flapping its wings vigorously, throwing them together in a little start of surprise and delight. They stopped laughing and looked at each other, and came together in an embrace. She began to sob, for too much had happened, too much had been thought and felt for the tears to be held back much longer.

She thought, "I will never be this happy again," lifting her face to his, and he thought, kissing her with all the fervor of a charged heart, "I love this woman and will never leave her."

They returned to the earth-seat, sent back as newly professed lovers by the conniving goddess, and spoke no more, content to sit huddled against each other in the growing gloom and the sound of the wind rising. It came in a low wail and built up to an immense sobbing in the trees.

"It's getting cold," he said, holding her very close to him. "Would you like to go back now?"

"No," she said and laid her head on his shoulder. "We'll meet the storm."

The rain began to fall, in large drops but she would not relinquish her position beside him on the earth-seat. He looked at her anxiously but she remained totally calm, lifting her face to meet the large, cold drops of falling water.

Suddenly she got up. She walked to the edge of the pond and stood there, very still. He could see her dark form against the water's black shimmer. The rain poured down in sheets, a flash of lightning illumined her face, and a roar of thunder shook her body. She lifted both arms and began to turn her body slowly in the pelting water, turned it round and round in a slow dance of pure joy. He looked at her, his whole body shuddering to the joy of the gyre and ran down to join her. Slowly they danced in the rain, then moved their bodies to the quickening rhythm of their rising joy, shouting and laughing. They came together in the wet lunacy of their joy and desire and were on the ground, in the mud, while the storm continued to rage and the sheets of water, driven into the goddess's shrine, reduced the celebratory red ribbons to wet rags between the bricks and washed off the eyes and ears of the goddess.

PART THREE

Goddess

I

THE VISIT OF THE Blind Fortune-Teller was an event and warranted special preparations, such as eating dinner earlier to be in time to receive him at eight o'clock, and getting ready his longan tea, for he would drink no other.

None of the itinerant sellers of goods and services who came regularly to the great house was given this privileged treatment: not the *kuey* seller who came with the daintiest bean, yam and tapioca puddings, laid out in two large flat baskets strung on the ends of a long pole on his thin shoulders; not the peddler who carried on the back of his bicycle an immense metal chest of buttons, needles, brooches and hair ornaments, and certainly not the cheap pigeon man whose pigeons disgraced him by pulling out the wrong fortune cards and walking all over their own droppings on the cards. The bondmaids said they had at least got some amusement for their money.

The Blind Fortune-Teller was different. His wife who accompanied him on his rounds, carrying a large lantern and a long stick to beat off unfriendly dogs, said that many years ago, he had had a strange dream of Sky God from which he woke up completely blind. The gift of sight withdrawn, he was endowed with the far nobler gift of seeing into the future. His sightless eyes danced about in their sockets and saw deaths, accidents, suicides, a child dead in a bucket of water, an old man strung from a tree. Also a prosperous marriage, good health at last, a big win in a lottery. For a while, he went berserk, predicting the future of all and sundry. Since the predictions added up to more disasters than good fortunes, people began to fear and shun him and even, on one occasion, beat him up, convinced that he was the agent of an evil demon, rather than of Sky God, as he claimed.

He suffered severe injuries and during his recuperation, his wife helped tame his unruly gift into something like a finely selective and discriminatory talent: he foretold the fortunes of only certain persons, and he foretold no more deaths or loss of family property, but only minor misfortunes such as the birth of yet another female child or a period of family squabbling caused by an as yet unknown trouble-maker. Even these could be avoided if certain precautions were taken, such as drinking special blessed water or wearing special prayer paper, rolled up and put inside little metal cylinders or sewn up in small cloth bags.

The Blind Fortune-Teller's wife carried a covered basket containing a variety of these precautionary items which could be bought for a few dollars. It became a lucrative little business which expanded further into story-telling that cost much less, although the man spun the most dazzling tales anyone had ever heard, and still further into providing lucky lottery numbers for which the wife asked for no money but an *ang pow*, should the number strike.

Some people shook their heads and said that a greedy woman had ruined a divine gift. The man had surely been marked by Sky God for special work on earth. Sometimes, it was said, he broke free from his wife's manipulative power and reclaimed his gift in the most spectacular way, shouting out direful predictions against a background of thunder and lightning, his sightless eyes aglow with preternatural brilliance.

The longan tea ready and simmering in an earthen pot, the bondmaids awaited the visit, sitting on wooden stools in the kitchen and talking and giggling among themselves. Golden Fern whose sad years as Wind-in-the-Head were past and whose reclaimed name presaged prosperity and happiness in her new married life had come on a visit to be part of the enthusiastic clientele and to hear from the lips of the renowned fortune-teller himself confirmation of the good fortune. So had Popo who was combining a visit to her sister Peipei with the opportunity to ask the inspired man whether she was going to be a mother of more sons, being determined to single-handedly erase, on behalf of three sisters-in-law, their humiliation of a combined total of five daughters.

Choyin wanted the man to peek into the past as well as the future: what had happened to the money that she knew Chu had been saving? She said the dead Chu had started to appear to her in her dreams, always distraught, wringing her hands, and clearly asking for help.

At eight o'clock sharp, the Blind Fortune-Teller and his wife arrived, carrying a lit lantern. Both were as thin and dry as sticks, as if all fleshly substance had to be sacrificed to the consuming power of a unique gift. They were mere skin draped over bone: the lantern light threw into startling relief the white jagged stones of cheekbones, the dark sunken pits of eyes. Ageless, they would continue to roam the earth twenty, thirty years from hence, carrying their lantern and stick, stirring the pools of ancient fears and yearnings.

Once upon a time, said the Blind Fortune-Teller, as soon as his wife had settled him on a stool and given him the longan tea to drink. He liked to begin the evening's business with the plea- sure of his tales which tumbled out in a glittering cascade, borne upon his rich, quavering voice. The bondmaids crowded round to listen, enthralled.

There was a very poor man who made a living as sedan-chair bearer, bearing the weight of obese, silk-clad merchants and their wives along bridges and up hillsides, in blistering heat or bitter- est cold. One day he and his partner were carrying a man who was going home from a business transaction with a lot of money in a waist-pouch. The partner whispered to him, "Let us kill him, take the money and throw his body into a river." The man who had been honest all his life said No and the partner went ahead on his own, killing the rich businessman with a rock, taking his money and dumping his body into the river.

"This is your last chance to share the money," he said, but the honest man continued to shake his head and to say, "No! No!"

With the money, the wicked partner went into business and became very rich. Soon he was one of the richest men in the village, living in a huge mansion, while the honest man remained poor, continuing to live with his family in a miserable little hut.

Every day, during mealtimes his wife would wait for him to finish his bowl of rice and ask dutifully if he wanted a second helping. He would shake his head sadly and said, "*Bo tee! Bo tee!*" which meant "No second helping", as well as "No Sky God", many words having double meanings. For the man was making use of the opportunity, three times a day, to reproach the great god for having no eyes or ears, so that the wicked prospered and the good suffered. One day he heard that the rich man with his entire family had gone on a pleasure boat in a lake and drowned. At his next meal, he kept calling upon his puzzled wife to refill his rice-bowl. "*Oo tee! Oo tee!*" he nodded joyfully. For at last Sky God had opened his eyes and unwaxed his ears.

A wicked woman pampered her own daughter but ill-treated her step-daughter. One day she gave both girls maize seeds to plant in their plot of land but she had previously boiled the seeds given to the step-daughter so that they never grew, and the girl watched them shrivel away and herself died of a broken heart.

A young farmer loved his mother so much that every night he would take off his shirt and invite the mosquitoes to come and bite his body, so that, having had their fill, they would leave the mother alone and let her have a peaceful night's sleep.

A pregnant woman, craving a very rare fruit that grew in the emperor's garden, one day stole and ate it. She was killed for the outrage but the emperor was full of remorse later when the dead woman's child was pulled out of her body, alive and nibbling at the fruit.

226

The Blind Fortune-Teller became magical story-teller and would have gone on pulling out tales from the glittering treasure-chest of ancestral memory, if his wife had not tugged at his sleeve to remind him of the night's business.

The bondmaids saved up the stories for their own re-telling, often with ingenious embellishments to serve their own purposes, or mixed and matched selected elements from a wide range, to come up with highly original tales of negligent gods, erring humans, oppressed women.

The story-telling over, they settled down to the evening's serious business and requested the Blind Fortune-Teller to advise them about present actions needed to purify and sweeten the future. The New Year was coming and the strenuous, week-long spring cleaning, leaving no trace of dust or grime in each room but the air smelling fresh, ought to be carried out too in the little secret habitations of their hopes and fears.

The Blind Fortune-Teller obliged but persisted in talking in difficult metaphors, which had a sonorous gravity that the bondmaids did not dare demean with their mundane questions. Choyin would climb over three mountains and pass over four bodies of water. Popo must be careful of water but embrace wood and fire.

The very person who had no need to be told his future because he had none turned out to be the beneficiary of the single unequivocal prediction of the evening. It was the privilege of a divine appointee to be perverse, for as soon as Spitface came into the kitchen, the Blind Fortune Teller stopped talking and turned his sightless face to the grinning imbecile.

"You have come into much money," he said. The revelation was improbable enough for the bondmaids to convert it into a prediction which was still so improbable that they converted it further into a benign hint, that is, Spitface should not be ignored as the possible provider of lucky lottery numbers. Accordingly, amidst a great deal of excited chatter, they made Spitface pick out numbers from a heap of rolled up pieces of paper that they had originally intended for the Blind-Fortune Teller himself.

The blind man waited patiently, sipping his longan tea, while the drawing of numbers went on, with his wife eagerly participating. The man stiffened suddenly to a new presence.

"Goddess," he said as Han came into the kitchen. "A goddess who bleeds."

There was a momentary lull, as all looked up and tried to comprehend the meaning, but it was incomprehensible, like many of the things the man said when the madness descended on him. In the end, Han was drawn into the group and made to pull out some lucky numbers.

"How strange!" someone exclaimed, for the numbers matched Spitface's and for the rest of the evening, the imbecile and the young bondmaid were linked together by a divine quirk that appointed them the conduit for the divine munificence.

II

IN THE SILENCE OF their chamber, bride and groom awkwardly faced each other. The celebratory clink of glasses and voices raised in toasts, music from a hundred flutes, violins and cymbals, the screaming laughter of children quick to find one another in a crowd of a thousand adults, to form their own delighted enclaves—the noise had followed them to the door of the chamber, stopped there and beaten an understanding retreat. It was time for the bridal couple to be by themselves.

Among a lesser people there might be the rude throwing of pebbles at the bedroom window, or even a bold invasion of the marital bed itself, to help the bashful pair towards the consummation, but the union of the House of Wu and the House of Chang brooked no such crudity.

The large room adjacent to the bridal chamber, which was used for the display of the bride's dower, had hushed every one of its visitors into awed silence, for it laid before their eyes unending trays of necklaces, bracelets, bangles, brooches, rings and anklets. A bride whose endowment comprised no more than a pitiful clutch of small gold ornaments, some silk suits or a sewing-machine might come in for much ribaldry during the bride-teasing, might even be made to hear lewd verses or ditties. The brilliance of Miss Li-Li's diamonds dazzled the guests into respectful abstention from any coarse surmise about her sexual initiation. Even a highly inebriated cousin who had been a childhood playmate had merely held up his glass to wish the couple many sons; he had swayed and leered a little, then passed out and had to be carried away amidst much laughter.

This very cousin was responsible for the tremors that now ran through the bride's body as she sat on a chair, half-turned towards the groom, her little hands tightly clutching a handkerchief pressed on her lap, betraying the tremulousness. For his wedding gift to her was a jade ornament which, at first glance, suggested an exotic fruit or flower, but on closer inspection, showed a copulating pair ingeniously coiled around each other. This, together with a musical box which opened to another, equally enthusiastic copulating pair, was the sum total of Miss Li-Li's education in the raw actualities of the married state. She had blushed at the gift, uttered a little shriek and beat daintily at the wicked cousin with both fists.

In the privacy of her room, she had gazed at the figurines for a long time and had hurriedly put them away at the sound of approaching footsteps. As soon as she was alone, she brought out the intriguing gift again for further examination and also prospective application to her own married life which would begin very soon. She mentally disentangled the happy couple, then put them together again, like a child absorbed by a novel toy. In front of a mirror, she stared at her own naked beauties, blushed and suppressed a giggle. Curiosity worked upon a naturally lively disposition to produce an overwhelming sense of eager anticipation. In the last few visits just before the wedding, she had stolen sly glances at that handsome male body soon to lie naked beside hers on the marriage bed which was ready to receive them in the fullness of its satiny and silken splendor. She had thrilled to the accidental touch of his hand when she handed him a cup of tea, of his thigh when they were flung against each other during a delightfully bumpy car-ride.

The demands of dynasty superseded those of flesh. Her mother had drawn her aside a week before the wedding and told her that according to the family fortune-teller, the coupling should not begin till the second day, this being more auspicious for the production of a long line of sons. The House of Chang awaited a first grandson, the House of Wu a first great-grandson; nothing should come in the way of such momentous goals. Li-Li looked down and blushed. Her mother, looking anxiously at her, advised: "Say you are unwell. Rub Tiger Balm on your temples."

But the anxiety had been unnecessary. The bridegroom, on the first night, full of the good wine that his raucous guests had made him drink, fell into bed and slept soundly till morning. Her eyes watched his sleeping face closely, then traveled downwards, and once again, a little tremor of excitement exploded in her and sent a warm stream coursing through her body, as she stood giddily poised on the threshold of wifehood. He murmured something in his sleep and flung out an arm; she touched his open palm tenderly with her fingertips.

On this, the second evening, as they came together in their room after a grand dinner with the patriarch and matriarch and some relatives, the dynastic claims ought to combine with fleshly desire to draw them together and lead each other to the welcoming bed. But they continued to stand awkwardly apart, not looking at each other, not saying anything. The groom sat in a chair and began to pull out things from a pocket which he studied with elaborate attention; he went on to do a few more foolish, irrelevant things, looking more and more uncomfortable, the discomfort manifesting itself in a bright redness on the tips of both ears. The bride watched him from the corner of her eye.

At last he muttered something about having to check some stuff in the next room, got up from the chair and left in haste. By herself, the bride sat in her chair and looked gravely on the floor, biting her lip. At last she too got up, changed into her nightdress, turned off the lights and climbed into bed, the canopied richness of satin and velvet unmatched by the bleak little fear in her heart: what if after the second, third, seventh day, she had to tell her mother that her husband had not yet touched her? What if this led to the unkind speculation that he had found her unpristine, or not attractive enough? The fate of the bride whose in-laws unceremoniously despatched a roast pig to her family with its snout and ears hacked off would of course never be hers but she might suffer the sadder fate of nightly rejection on the marital bed.

Suddenly Li-Li felt very angry. She was his wife and he did not love or want her. Tears sprang into her eyes. She heard him returning to their room, felt the movement of the bed as he climbed on to it and settled himself beside her. She remained resolutely motionless, lying on her side, her back towards him. She was aware of every small movement coming from him, every small fiddling with pillow and blanket. It soon stopped, and there came the sound of deep breathing: he had fallen asleep. He had fallen asleep on the first and second nights of their marriage, while she lay awake, screaming inside with anger and desire. The silent weeping grew to loud sobbing. She felt him stir in the darkness, muttering something, then get up with a start and turn towards her.

"What's the matter?" he asked gently and, without waiting for an answer, said, "Don't cry" at the same time stretching out a hand to touch her. She moved away from his touch and burrowed deeper into the comforting darkness of her blanket and pillows, her body convulsed by a spasm of sobbing. He sat up, alarmed, and bent over, repeating solicitously, "Please don't cry." She felt the gentle pressure of his hand on her shoulder, the enveloping closeness of his presence. Women's tears unnerved him, he coaxed further, and she at last allowed herself to be turned around to face him and be drawn fully into his arms. The effect was to increase the intensity of the crying; for a while she surrendered herself to the full discharge of the evening's strange mix of anger, pain and longing, and bawled like a child, so that, even more alarmed at the prospect of her anxious parents appearing at the door, he held her tightly in his arms, stroked her hair and kept repeating, "Everything's all right, everything's all right," without exactly knowing what he meant.

Her sobbing subsided and she lay quietly in his arms, savoring the new sensation of the contact. It built up quickly into a feeling of pure pleasure; she felt and smelt his maleness and, greedy for more, pressed herself against him. Her body, suffused with a luxurious feline warmth and ease, stretched, then curled itself in sensuous fit into every curve of his body. The crying recommenced as a soft purring and took on a different quality, that of pure animal physicality, which communicated itself readily to him so that in a moment he had eased her gently down upon the pillow and come down upon her with a tremendous grunt of desire.

My husband, she thought with a glowing pride and joy all the while she was moving to the rhythm of his passion and felt a sharp pain that passed into the trenchancy of the pleasure: I am so happy. A loving woman, at the height of happiness, has the scent of danger in her nostrils. She smelt the peasant girl's earthiness in his face, mouth, loins. After it was over and they put on their robes and thought to drink a glass of wine together, she was almost impelled to ask, "Have you slept with that servant girl?" But the question now, as then, could not be asked, for it might provoke a reply which she could not bear to hear and which, once heard, would shatter her peace forever. She thought bitterly, as she poured her husband another glass of wine, coquettishly settled herself on his lap and felt his hands clasp her waist: "The peasant girl torments me on my own marriage bed."

It would not be so much longer. The birth of an heir would

change everything. For the gift of a son would link husband and wife together in the sacrosanct solidity of family continuity that no one, certainly not a servant girl, could hope to break.

The matriarch Chang watched her daughter's face every day for signs of that promise. Did she look paler? Did she crave salted plums? The signs might be speeded up by a whole regimen of healthful brews of ginseng, birdsnest and rare herbs, and regular offerings on temple and ancestral altars. Soliciting gods and deities on the one hand, the matriarch undertook, on her daughter's behalf, an active campaign of assiduous avoidance of evil spirits, on the other. She gave instructions that no nails were to be driven into walls, no mirrors hung up on doorways, no chickens slaughtered in the house. One morning, a servant reported, pale with fright, that the family cat which had just borne a litter of three kittens, had eaten all of them in the course of the night; only scraps of fur remained, scattered on the floor. The matriarch too turned pale with fear and a sense of terrible foreboding. She immediately consulted a temple medium who gave her a bottle of blessed water and a piece of paper to be burnt and its ashes to be mixed in the holy water for Li-Li to drink.

A pregnant woman saw a monkey in a cage and foolishly went near to look at it. The monkey screeched and made a face at the woman. She took fright. Her baby was born with perfect simian features, down to the low forehead and long, gangling arms. A woman gave birth to a horribly deformed child who was born with the entrails outside its body, because she had seen a dead chicken on the road in precisely that condition, as she was walking to market in the third month of her pregnancy. Yet a third brought home a cluster of live crabs and hacked off their claws with a cleaver; she too was pregnant and her baby was born with the last toe on each foot looking very much like a hacked off claw.

The matriarch Chang cleared her daughter's path of all unseemly-looking creatures and people. She gave instructions that the beggars, many of whom were misshapen or had grotesque features, were not to come up to the doorstep but were to be met half-way with the customary gift of money or bag of rice grains. She was against her daughter leaving the house at all, seeing dangers everywhere, but the young lady was adamant about accompanying her husband on every one of his visits home to his grandparents. He went back frequently, for he missed his grandfather badly, and would have preferred visiting alone, his wife's presence necessitating far more elaborate preparations among the bondmaids than he thought necessary.

The visit home together on the first day of the New Year to pay respects to his grandparents was obligatory. The adulatory fervor with which Choyin and the other bondmaids in the House of Wu welcomed each visit of Miss Li-Li was now doubled to match her new, enhanced position as the wife of the young master Wu. There had to be any number of visual reminders of this position, including a- change of hairstyle to the more sedate one of a single bun of hair at the back instead of the two side ones she had worn from childhood, as well as the presence of the matrimonial jewels on ear-lobes, neck, chest, wrists, fingers and ankles. The reminder Li-Li favored most of all was the simple one of standing as close as possible to her husband in full view of others. The small delicate arm gently tucked into his was unequivocal claim and warning: He's mine. Keep away.

That was her first action when they arrived in the House for their visit. Her arm securely entwined around his, her eyes searched the roomful of bondmaids and only stopped doing so when Choyin whispered, "She's in the yard hanging out the clothes. But she'll be here for the ceremony," the ceremony being the practice, during the New Year season, of the matriarch from the House of Chang or a female representative, formally presenting a New Year *ang pow* to each of the bondmaids. In her new status, Li-Li was entitled to this duty. She had looked forward to it, if only because it would mean that the peasant girl would come forward to her to receive the money, and in doing so, tacitly admit defeat: You are the wife of the young master Wu. I am only a bondmaid.

The young master left hurriedly to see his grandfather, always loath, like the old man, to be involved in the little mean-nesses of women, which he sensed each time he saw them whis-pering together.

"Here she is," thought Li-Li as Han entered the room to join the line of *ang pow*—receiving bondmaids. As always, the sense of triumph was mixed with the exasperation of necessarily demeaning herself through involvement with a servant girl. An aunt of hers had berated her husband, not for having a secondary wife for that was a prosperous man's entitlement, but for the secondary wife's connection with the riff-raff of the village: the girl's father was a rickshaw-puller and her mother a consumptive.

With queenly flair, Li-Li dispensed the *ang pows*, each accom-panied by two good luck oranges. Assisted by her bondmaid who handed to her the gift as each of the recipients moved up, she was maintaining the tradition of the House of Chang by which the Chang women regularly gave out food and money to the poor, to secure the gods' blessings for continuing prosperity.

"Thank you," said Han and moved on. Li-Li's eyes followed her for a while. I am going to have you watched, they said. And Choyin's eyes, following hers said, You will find mine competent. This girl is dangerous. She is worse than a demon. There came a start from Li-Li and a little shudder of aversion, as she looked at, then turned away from the person now entering the room. Spitface, always drawn to gatherings and crowds by a child's curiosity and hope for excitement, hobbled in, grinning, and pre-sumptuously took his place with the bondmaids, to have his share of whatever good stuff was being given out. Puzzled about Li-Li's exhibition of repugnance to Spitface when as a child she had been unaffected by the imbecile's presence and had, indeed, even played with him on a few occasions, Choyin looked again at Li-Li, now positively pale and pressing a handkerchief to her mouth, then at Spitface, as unkempt-looking as ever, his eyes grotesquely protuberant, his teeth horribly discolored.

Then she understood. Perhaps it was Li-Li's suddenly putting a dainty hand on her stomach, as if to protect any developing life inside from the shock of an encounter not less terrifying than that between the woman and the monkey in the cage, or the mutilated chicken on the road.

Choyin screamed at Spitface, "Get out! Get out of this room at once!" Totally happy where he was, Spitface grinned back.

"He wants an *ang pow*," said Peipei nervously, whereupon Choyin grabbed one from Li-Li's maid, shoved it in Spitface's hand, screamed again, "Get out! Get out now!" and began pushing him. Greatly puzzled, Spitface stopped smiling and looked around, murmuring.

A sudden sob from the terrified Li-Li coinciding with a surge of power in her thin arms, Choyin began to beat at the imbecile and scream even more furiously, "Get out of here! Can't you understand that, you idiot! Get out!"

Like a confused child, Spitface began to pucker up his face for a cry. He felt a pair of hands gently taking his arm, and heard a voice, as gentle as the hands, say, "Let's go," that made him smile again, so that in the course of a few seconds, his features had adjusted and re-adjusted with amazing rapidity, to accommodate the swing from joy to puzzlement and fear and back to joy again. For it was Han who had come up to him and touched him with kind hands.

"Let's go," she repeated and together they went out of the room.

There was no end to the stream of palliatives to relieve the stricken Li-Li: bondmaids ran in and out with hot water, hot tea, Tiger Balm. Li-Li gasped out a weak request: she wanted her husband. So somebody hurried to get the young master from his grandfather's room. By the time he appeared, looking worried, his wife had reached the stage of hysteria; she ran to him and began to sob. It took him a while to comprehend what had happened. When he did, the tautness of his face and voice showed the enormous restraint he was imposing on himself, as he struggled between the urge, on the one hand, to shout at a bunch of stupid women for working themselves up over a harmless imbecile who had been in their midst all these years, and the need, on the other, to maintain a public image of perfect marital amity. So he said quietly to his wife, "It's all right, everything will be alright," once again wondering at the meaning of a banality he was likely to be using for some time. Li-Li sniffled and blew into her handkerchief, the pathetic loving woman who will exploit every little *contretemps* to bring her man to her side, to force his indifference into a little public show of loving. She held her husband's arm tightly and was comforted to know everyone noticed he spoke lovingly to her. "The fool, the fool," said Choyin, shaking her head over the unspeakable possibility of Spitface being the cause of any harm to an heir of the Houses of Wu and Chang. She told Li-Li, "From now onwards, be assured that he will not be around when you visit."

The subject of the opprobrium was innocently sitting on a stool near the driveway, in front of the house. He had nodded with eager compliance when Han led him to the spot, carrying the stool, placing it carefully at a selected site and requiring him to sit there. Then she dug out from his pocket the *ang pow* from Li-Li, so reluctantly given, crushed it in her hands and flung it upon the driveway. Spitface gave a little cry of dismay and looked at her, puzzled, but he would sooner have stepped into a pit of live coals than gone to retrieve something that Han had thrown away so furiously. He watched her: she brought out of her pocket a wad of notes that she had gone to get from the cloth bundle in the hidden corner of his cupboard in the woodshed, as soon as she had led him out of the room and calmed him with a hot drink. She put the notes in his hand and showed him how he was to hold them; he was not only to hold them but play with them—fan them out, like a hand of cards, transfer them from one hand to the other, scatter them on the ground, then pick them up. She showed Spitface exactly how she wanted it done and he complied cheerfully, constantly looking up into her face for approval.

237

At the sound of voices and approaching footsteps, she stepped backwards and disappeared behind a pillar, indicating to Spitface that he was to continue with the activity. He did so, and so competently too, that when Li-Li and Choyin appeared, walking towards the waiting car in the driveway, both were astounded to see Spitface in the confident posture of one who had so much money that he could afford to throw away any not given willingly, which led their eyes to move from the handsome wad in his hand to the crumpled *ang pow*, on the ground, very near the car.

Startled, they looked at each other, and then their eyes moved to look at Han who had appeared and was standing beside Spitface. Spitface, the money in his hand, the repudiated *ang pow*, the defiant girl—all connected in another show of defiance that warned them against a demonic influence far too dangerous to ignore.

That threat was immediately confirmed. As Li-Li got into the car, followed by her husband, she saw him turning round quickly to look at the servant girl and saw the girl return the look with a knowing glance. Something like a little gasp escaped her and then was sucked back into the seething pool of her anger. She looked at her husband from the corner of her eye and saw that he was looking impassively ahead. She was quiet all the way home, her handkerchief pressed to her mouth.

III

SHE WADED INTO THE pond, close to the edge, not bothering to roll up her trousers; indeed, the idea was to wet them thoroughly, and the blouse as well. So she lowered herself slowly into the water, up to the neck, then rose, and without benefit of mirror, saw the fullness of her naked beauty outlined by the wetly clinging thin cotton blouse. She felt the firm contours of her breasts which she held forth proudly, with the same determination with which she had pulled them in and shrunk them in the searching gaze of hateful males in that huge house. She turned slowly to face the goddess in the shrine, the poor little goddess of the denuded eyes, ears and also breasts which one of these days, she vowed, she would restore to their full beauty. She said, "Thank you, dear goddess," and it was for many things, including the magnanimity of relieving oppressed hearts while her own remained saddened by the ill-treatment of Sky God. The god would ever reign in magnificent golden temples and throw his thunderbolts across the skies while she would be eternally confined to her pitiful little shrine and be punished by one-hundred year cycles of deafness.

Thank you for Golden Fern's male child. The birth of the baby boy had removed the last of the poor girl's anxieties; her pleased husband, the clogs-maker, gave her money for a gold chain, which made her weep. Unaware of the intercession to the goddess on her behalf, she had directed her gratitude to Sky God, and part of it to the Blind Fortune-Teller who had told her there would be many sons.

Thank you for Oldest Brother's prosperity. It was a prosperity she would not have a share of, but it made him very happy and improved his health vastly. He now flashed gold teeth. Thank you for Mother's release. For her mother had appeared to her in a dream, out of the gates of hell at last, having paid in full for her sin of selling children.

Thank you for—

The litany ended with her awareness of the approach of one person for whom she would shout out the most resounding Thank You. She immediately re-directed the joyful outpouring towards him and knew the goddess would smile in warm understanding. So she stood in the pond water and washed her face again and waited for him to come up to her, realizing with a smile, that the moon, far brighter than it was the last time they met, would enhance her gift of herself to him.

He saw. He did not think he had seen anything so beautiful—a woman, clothed and naked, rising like a water fairy in moonlight to meet him. The element of surprise created its own elements of surprise: instead of rushing down to her, as the rush of blood impelled, he amazed himself by staying where he was, nonchalantly rolling out a mat on the ground—a good-sized mat, for passion must still mind comfort—and sat and waited. As he watched her walk up to him—she obeisant water fairy, he detached powerful mortal—he smiled, thinking: How happy she makes me. He was in the mood for play, as he never was in either great house, curbed by the necessity of a hundred proprieties. This was a delightful game in which a beautiful, eager woman walked up to a man in her naked beauty and coaxed and wheedled him into accepting her gift. In the matrimonial chamber, male ardor did the wheedling and went through the due procedures of a systematic unlocking of shy female passion that would blush to do its own unlocking. The reversal of roles was titillating; part of a man's pleasure of dominance was to relinquish a small portion of the dominance, lie back and watch the little woman have her way. She fell into the role easily, as she had done in childhood, sensing each need, each whimsy and moving quickly to fit into it. So she took a sharp turn and walked back into the pond and was water goddess once more, on his account, not dancing to the moon, but moving slowly to allow the moon its teasing dance upon her body and pick out every beauty for the final gift-giving.

He ran down to the water's edge, pulled her out by the hand and dragged her, still running, to the mat.

Lovers at play, reclaiming the sporting innocence of children in wild, untrammeled territory, to erase the disquieting memory of that night of passion gone awry in a closed room.

The playfulness was not at an end. Prelude to passion, it bore none of the marks of passion. He carefully wiped her wet hair with a towel—pragmatic mat, pragmatic towel, brought in a little covered basket—like a concerned parent, not an eager lover.

Remembering the thoroughness of his bondmaid's towel upon his small boy's body each time he came out dripping from his bath, he wiped her eyes, her ears, the spaces inside her ears, while she remained still and docile, the good child submitting to the ministrations of towel, comb, brush.

More child's play and ploy. She brought out from her basket some rice cakes, victuals of love that gods and mortals fed each other. They put the rice cakes into each other's mouths. The reciprocity was precisely that of the newly wed pair at the banqueting table, where, before applauding guests, they pledged their love in food. The little proffered morsel of rice cake which he opened his mouth eagerly to receive canceled out the spoonful of rare sharksfin or birdsnest that must have been Li-Li's nuptial offering. The greater love-feast she was next leading him to, as she wiped his mouth with the wet towel, pushed away the rest of the food and gently went down upon him on the mat, would further cancel out the love on the silk and satin bed. The love could never have been offered anywhere but in her own territory, where in the gentle beneficence of trees and pond water, she could cast off the shackles of her bondage and rise in the fullness of her woman's beauty and power. A goddess no less than the one in stone she worshipped, she would commandeer all her resources to pluck this man whom she loved to distraction from his world and transport him into hers.

Once a month, he had said. He could meet up with her once a month. Love, measured out like the intervals of the moon's appearance in the sky, or of a woman's secret blood. They could only meet here, by the pond, for there was no other place. There was no need to go into the reasons: his wife and his wife's spy Choyin who probably knew, his grandparents who must never know. The strongest reasons remained himself and herself: he, the young master Wu, she the bondmaid Han. No greater gulf could roll between any two lovers. If he had been less and she more, they might have leapt to link in a proper union, and enjoyed a proper feast at love's table, not this pitiful helping of snatched hours.

What? A bondmaid for a secondary wife? No need to tarnish the name of Wu. Have the girl, have many like her if you wish. But a secondary wife? No need to demean the face of Wu.

So he came to her and said, Once a month, no more.

The loving woman has the fugitive's ferocious concentration of purpose. She thought, I will make his once a month with me so memorable he will despise his many times a month with her.

The determination with which as a child her ardent gifts of captured caterpillars and ants in boxes and improvised games had drawn him away from his rich toys, asserted itself once more to invest her every limb and muscle with energetic purpose directed towards his sole pleasure. But really, she had no need of a stratagem, for the immensity of her love, once he came into her presence and touch, overpowered all other impulses and bore them both along on a tide of pure joyous spontaneity. Her mind, her spirit, her body adjusted themselves to every nuance of thought, feeling and appetite in his; she lost herself in him.

He thought, with the same awe as he had thought that evening when she came into his room, fought him off with a knife and then clung to him with all the sobbing fervor of her simple, loyal heart: This woman loves me. She would die for me.

They came together in a tumultuous burst of their longing. Her thoughts could yet detach themselves, but only for a moment, from the power of the longing, to clothe themselves with sobering reality: This man loves me. But he would never die for me. There are too many other things for him to die for.

But they were thoughts to be banished quickly and relegated to those sleepless hours on the mattress on the floor at night; they were not for the present which had to be jealously conserved in the purity and strength of its ardor. On a mat, in a secluded spot, naked in her wet clothes, seeing and touching him after an unspeakably lonely stretch of days, she understood and wanted only the physicality of the passion, and thus unleashed upon him the full power of her longing. The gift of her body demanded the reciprocal gift of his. It amazed and delighted him. In the midst of the delightful violence of their love, one part of his mind wondered with some amusement, about the unsuspected eroticism in a woman's small demure limbs habituated to a regimen of tea-serving and back-knocking, and another part asked, with even greater amusement,-whether love on a mat in mosquito infested wilderness by a pond, could be superior to that on a satin and silken bed.

In the moonlight, he raised himself on an elbow to look upon the woman he loved, now lying still on the mat, but still gasping and panting, her hair spread in wet tendrils around her head. He thought again, I love her. I could not live without her. Passion passed into the quieter phase of ruminative sharing. They lay warm against each other and began to talk. Dreading the intrusion of any element that would mar the magic of the present, they assiduously avoided, by tacit agreement, any reference to the past or the future. Dreading the intrusion of Li-Li's name, they ended up avoiding all other names. They could only talk with ease about themselves. They talked about their first meeting by the pond, his first introduction to the goddess. The poor goddess, she said, was about to lose her head; she had noticed that there were cracks all around the neck, and one of these days, the head was going to drop off. He promised to repair her head the next time he came. He had no idea how to repair goddesses' heads, but she could depend on him. The goddess disposed of, they talked about themselves again, this time returning to their childhood from which once again they pulled out the most radiant memories and unabashedly altered or embellished them, for the past was only as good as it served the heart's needs of the present. So he never rejected the pathetic gift of the dead bird in the cage, he never stamped on her gift of a lantern and shouted at her, she never wept her heart out on the day he went away, they had never stopped loving each other from the time he saved her from death, and she saved him from the greater death of a lonely childhood.

They lay warm against each other on a mat on the ground

243

under a dark night sky, their universe shrunk to a joyful cosmology of two. And so the past evaporated, like the mist over the pond, like the joss-ash in the shrine from a previous visit, washed into the earth.

She wanted to give him something. She pulled out the bracelet with the jade image of Sky God and told him to stretch out his hand.

"No more gifts," he said. "You have given too much already."

She returned the bracelet to her wrist and said, "But I would still like to give it to you someday," adding slowly, "perhaps upon the birth of our son."

The defiance of the future was dangerous and broke the spell. She should not have said anything like that. For a long time, they lay still, saying nothing.

A woman, if she was suspected to have been with a man, could be weighed for proof, for she was said to become heavier after love. A man was tested for smell, not weight. His wife smelt infidelity in his hair and groins.

So he said, getting up: I have to go.

She thought, He is always having to go. He went away from me when I was thirteen and has been going away ever since. Even in my dreams, he stays only for a little while.

But they would meet again in a month's time.

IV

CHU BORE DOWN angrily upon her.

"Why did you give Spitface my money?" she demanded.

"But you gave it to me. I thought I could do as I liked with it," said Han. She wanted to add, "But you're dead. You hanged yourself, remember? How can you be talking to me like this?" She checked the impoliteness, both of the question and of the remark that almost escaped her lips, that it was very strange and improper of Chu to be wandering around with no slippers or sandals and her blouse opened, exposing both breasts.

"Thought! Thought!" grumbled Chu. She looked better than she did in life, appearing to have put on considerable weight, so that her breasts, which Han remembered to be flat and hard, were now rounded and full, as if ready to offer its nurturing goodness to a new-born child. "How can I explain this to Choyin? She's angry with me because she thinks the money should have gone to her. She pesters me day and night. Watch out. She's going after you. The Blind Fortune-Teller told her everything. We're both in trouble."

"Why should you care about Choyin now? You hated her very much," said Han, but Chu continued to ramble on, wringing her hands and saying, "She says we're to blame if Spitface comes to harm with the money. He's an imbecile. How could you have given my money to an imbecile? Did you know that the fool stood in the market place and started distributing *ang pows* to everyone who came along? He said he was the Monkey God who had come from Heaven with gifts for everybody."

"That's not true," said Han. "I can prove it." But Chu was no longer there.

She called loudly, "Chu!" and a woman appeared. It was not Chu but the old *keo kia* woman.

"Why are you still around?" she asked.

"Some of us walk the earth forever," said the old *keo kia* woman sadly.

"Why are you still wet?" said Han. "After all these years, one would have thought you would have dried your hair and clothes."

The old woman put a finger to her lips, as she often did when she thought people were getting impolite or unkind.

"Follow me," she said.

"The last time I did, you disappeared," said Han.

"Follow me," she repeated.

"Only if you lead me to Chu," said Han. "She's angry with

me. I have to explain everything to her. I don't like to see Chu so distressed."

"Alright," said the old *keo kia* woman.

"The last time you told me to follow you, you led me to a corpse hanging from the ceiling," said Han in a complaining tone. "I don't want that to happen again. I want to see Chu alive and well and happy."

"Alright," said the old *keo kia* woman.

Chu was alive but far from well and happy.

"Now I know why she had her blouse open," thought Han. For she saw Chu naked under the Old One on his bed and he was pulling at her breasts with his mouth, like a greedily feeding child. At the same time he was thrusting violently into her and making her cry. "See what he is doing to me?" she wept. "He's been hurting me these twenty years!"

The Old One pulled his mouth away from her breast to say: "Who's been hurting who these twenty years? You put bird shit in my food. You. You." Then he returned to his frenzied activity at her breasts, thighs, the soft spaces between her thighs, oblivious to their presence, a boar at its food trough, determinedly slobbering its way through.

"Save me!" cried Chu.

"We'll hang him!" said the old *keo kia* woman, and the next moment she and Chu were fastening the noose round the Old One's neck. He went limp as a plucked chicken hanging from its metal hook, ready to go into the cooking pot. His feet pointed downwards.

"That will teach you!" shrieked Chu and she made the obscene, finger-piston sign at him.

"You've hanged the wrong person!" screamed Han for the body had slowly turned round to face her; it was Spitface, not the Old One. Spitface's eyes were popping out grotesquely from his head; his tongue lolled out, thick and discolored.

Han ran up to his body, crying.

"It's all your fault," said Chu. "I told you you shouldn't have given him my money. The money was bad for him. The Blind Fortune-Teller warned you so many times!"

"Goddess, please help me," sobbed Han. "Please bring Spitface back. He's the only one who truly loves me. I was going to give him the gift of my bracelet, but now it's too late."

The goddess woke up from her sleep and said, "Why does everybody come to me for favors? So many of you, only one of me. I'm tired. Goddesses can get tired too, you know."

"Listen, Goddess, if you bring Spitface back to life, I promise—"

"Promises! Promises!" said the goddess. Han had never seen her so angry. "Please leave me alone for a while. I need to be alone."

V

BONDMAIDS' VISITORS WERE NEVER admitted, by the strict rules of propriety, through the front door of the great house; they entered by the back, into the kitchen, and were invited to sit down, not at the main kitchen table where the bondmaids had their meals but at a smaller side one. The humbler of the visitors refused even that honor, protesting, with elaborate deference, that their place was on the outside, where they stood in the sun talking in low voices and went away as soon as their business was done.

Oldest Brother, by virtue of the regularity of his visits, was allowed into the kitchen and sat comfortably by the side table. He made a great show of refusing any cup of tea or coffee that Han or Popo brought him but drank it all in one cheerful gulp. At first angry by Choyin's refusal to return his greeting, he soon got used to it and was even able to joke about it, deriving special comfort from the observation that Choyin, ugly, thin, dry as a stick, would have no place in the House of Flowers except as the cleaning woman whose job was to change the sheets in all the rooms and empty the spittoons.

Oldest Brother, flashing gold teeth and rings in his prosperity, laughed a great deal and visited often, bringing his gift boxes of rich cakes. He also brought a companion who waited for him outside, in the shade of a tree and would not go in even when Han came out and invited him in. He looked very young, a mere boy, with the petulant air of a girl, as he kept his eyes resolutely fixed on the ground and sullenly crushed leaves between his fingers, the whole quivering tautness of his body inviting Oldest Brother himself to come out and wheedle and cajole.

"You had better go out and get him in," said Han and watched as her brother went up to the boy and talked to him in a low murmur. The boy shook off his touch, like an angry child.

Oldest Brother, shaking his head and muttering, "He always behaves this way, let's not pay any more attention to him," came back into the house and sat down again. With a dismissive flourish of his hand, he stopped all questions or comments about his strange companion who, with powder on his face and an elaborate gold chain round his neck, was even stranger than the haughty, much made up woman of previous visits. Oldest Brother, making a sweep of the town's alleys to pluck out girls for eager waiting men, also picked up other desperately seeking people and unwisely let them latch on to him. He looked out at the boy under the tree, repeated, "Let's not mind him" and proceeded with the purpose of the visit.

It was again to persuade Han to go to work in the House of Flowers. To visit, said Oldest Brother delicately. To stay as long as she liked, in a room of her own. Few girls had this privilege. There was Old Cheng who came regularly and it would be a matter of time before one of the artful girls managed to insinuate herself into the old fool's favor and thence into his enormous wealth, comprising—here Oldest Brother picked his teeth and leaned towards his sister across the table—numerous rubber and coconut plantations in the country and elsewhere. Old

Cheng would set her up in undreamt of prosperity forever. None of the girls in the House of Flowers would have a ghost of a chance against her if she went there: she had exactly the looks, the gentle demeanor the old man wanted. Here Oldest Brother amused himself with a recounting of the coarseness of some of the girls, which marred their beauty, and put the men off.

Resigned to her brother's persistence on a matter that she thought she had successfully disposed of, she let him ramble on, to lead to a topic of overpowering interest. She could not have asked him directly: "Does the young master sometimes go to the House of Flowers?" But she did ask, "Does Fourth Older Brother continue to go to the House of Flowers?", in the hope that the second question would soon provoke a dilated rambling, as was Oldest Brother's wont, that would answer the first.

Oldest Brother slapped his thigh, gave a short, sharp bark of laughter and launched on an extended description of Fourth Older Brother's doings in the House of Flowers.

"Do you remember the woman who came with me on my first visit?" he asked. The woman who stole a flask and a bottle of Tiger Oil from a dead woman's bedside table and wrested a bracelet from the corpse. But Han said nothing and Oldest Brother went on to narrate, with great relish, what everyone in the House of Flowers was whispering about: the man was totally besotted, because the woman—her name was Orchid—had cast a spell on him. There was no other reason to explain why, out of the many beautiful young girls in the house, he chose the woman, ugly, coarse, bad-tempered, not even young anymore. She had used the magic of her secret blood on him, mixing it in his food and drink.

"She never thought it worth her while to use it on me," laughed Oldest Brother. He leaned over and said gravely, "Don't tell anybody this, but if you look closely at his eyes, you will see they are different—the eyes of a bewitched man." Bewitched men had glazed eyes, a certain pallor, a raging appetite for their bewitchers but shrank pitiably in the presence of other women.

She had not noticed Fourth Older Brother's eyes, but he was certainly behaving differently—he had stopped pestering her. There had been a brief period of intense animosity, when she expected him to come rushing out of his room to slap or kick her, for the humiliation of her spittle upon his face. Then he became indifferent, and finally, oblivious of her presence. For he had become involved with Orchid and the other women in the House of Flowers and retreated into a secret life of great roistering, sometimes coming home drunk and slipping a girl or two into his room. He had presumed too much on the patriarch's tolerance. The old man called him up one morning and told him testily that he was not to do such a thing again or—. The old man's health, of late, had been poor and had affected his naturally mild disposition so that between his fits of coughing, he rasped at errant members in his household and issued stern warnings. The warning hung in the air and Fourth Older Brother walked out of the room, looking dispirited, for he feared losing the bountifulness that had been his all these years. Once out of the room, he felt a resurgence of bad temper and wondered which of the bondmaids had been carrying tales. His suspicious were at first directed at Han, then settled on Choyin whom he disliked most of all.

He brought no more women into his room and began spending long hours in the House of Flowers, languishing in the indulgence of women and waking up one day to find that he had wandered into the domain of one of them and was powerless to get out. He was well and truly a captive of Orchid. The girls in the House of Flowers said they could smell her in his very hair. Between a compelling need for her and a resentment of her domination of him, he became thoroughly confused, and swung from wild elation to abject misery, when he became tearful like a child. A man possessed by the demon of a woman's secret blood. It was said the only cure for the malady was another woman's more powerful blood.

Oldest Brother grew very animated in the telling for he loved scurrilous tales. Shall I tell you of the time when she emptied his pockets. Of the time when he knelt before her and begged for mercy, and one of the girls had to come and remove the cleaver from her hand—.

Had Fourth Older Brother ever taken the young master to the House of Flowers? Impatience cut through the rich messy offering of gossip, like an extravagant, indigestible feast of food on an altar table, but sheathed itself in a quiet nonchalance. Oldest Brother said, "No", and went on to offer yet one more delicious tidbit: the servants from the House of Chang were saying the mistress Li-Li cried often because the master Wu was deficient on the bed. One servant heard her one night saying, "Is it water that flows through your veins?" Not all the matriarch Chang's preparations of special ginseng for him could correct the deficiency and secure that heir. Her poor daughter's womb remained unfilled.

"She ought to have come from our village," chortled Oldest Brother. "Look at Mother and all the other women who went *pok* every year, without benefit of ginseng or birdsnest! Sky God certainly has a sense of humor!" He wiped his eyes and went on, "Look at our father, he only had to look at a woman to impregnate her. But the great master Wu suffers from a lack with his own wife. How can he spare any in the House of Flowers?" Oldest Brother choked in his merriment. It was probably his pity of men and women in their unfulfilled lusts that brought on a thought that brought on a start of fright from his chair. He leapt up and gasped, looking out of the door, "Where's he gone?" for the sulky companion was no longer there. Oldest Brother muttered, "He's always doing this to me, I'd better be going," and was getting ready to leave when Peipei came in and nervously whispered something in Han's ear. The strange companion had wandered into the visitors' reception room and was even now touching the ornaments on the tables and hangings on the wall—they had better go and take him away before Choyin appeared. Oldest Brother gave a yelp and dashed to pull the perverse one back. The boy, a challenging smile on his smooth powdered face, was looking at a ceramic horse with studied insouciance. He looked up at Oldest Brother, and, still smiling, allowed himself to be led away. Oldest Brother whispered fiercely, "Why are you always trying to make me angry?" and the boy looked up calmly at him and knew he had won once more.

Han said, "Please don't bring him again or there'll be trouble," and later felt sorry for the indelicacy. There was no need for that; on his next visit, he brought no boy but a young woman— was there no end to the succession of surprise visitors?—who went up cheerfully to her and said, "Do you recognize me? I recognize you." Oldest Brother stood by grinning.

"Look again," said the high-spirited woman. Han looked again, but the woman who stood smiling before her, hair permed, blouse and trousers abandoned for alien frock with puffed sleeves, remained a stranger.

"I'm Older Sister," she said. "Don't you remember?"

The group of siblings she had waved goodbye to that morning, so many years ago, had faded into the mists of lost memory; only Oldest Brother remained to connect her with her past. This Older Sister, older by one or two years, must be part of those fragile fragments of memory that sometimes cobwebbed her dreams, yielding no more than tiny wisps of faces, faint whispers. Only Oldest Brother had a face, shape, voice. There were now three of them united in adulthood she a bondmaid, he a pimp and the third a—.

Her story tumbled out, eagerly supplied by both herself and Oldest Brother, in noisy, cheerful turn-taking. He had found her, quite by accident, working in an eating-house, shelling prawns all day, until all ten fingers were soft and raw and smelly as the prawns, and he had pulled her away from the meanness and squalor to work in the House of Flowers. She had just started work and she was happy. It was much easier work than shelling prawns and having both the owner of the eating-house, and his wife shouting at her all the time, and the money was much,

much better. Older Sister said she was aware that she did not have half the charms of the other girls but she could please. She had bought a large bottle of perfume and soaked her hands in it. The prawn smell was almost all gone. She touched her permed hair and handbag, then turned to Oldest Brother to remark that Han was too thin and pale. That appeared to be the cue for the next phase of the attack, for both now set upon her eagerly exhorting her to give up her present life—what was the use of staying condemned as a bondmaid?

"Let us be together, let us take care of each other," cried Older Sister enthusiastically. "Please come with us," said Oldest Brother with something of the brotherly protectiveness she remembered. She looked down, and kept her eyes fixed on her hands. "She is stubborn, our little Sister Han is very, very stubborn. Don't you remember the time she would rather suffer Mother's pinches than return a little spoon she stole from you?" The jocularity with which Oldest Brother often tried to defuse pain dropped futilely to the ground. "Please don't," he said anxiously, and Older Sister too said, "Please don't cry," for they peered into her face and saw two large tears forming in her eyes.

VI

"COME HERE."

Bondmaids were used to hearing the order, prelude to punishment, to dalliance. Their bodies would gather into tight knots of resistance but they had no choice. Go there. Go there to be scolded, pinched, caressed.

"Come here."

The Reverend, in the many years that he had issued the order to bondmaids, while sitting in his chair and enjoying a hot breakfast after the prayers in the ancestral room, had actually learnt to clothe the brutality with a silken softness. Peipei, like the bondmaids before her, reacted with the anxiety that was the residue of a whole host of jostling emotions—shock, fear, embarrassment—that had begun with the monk's unflinching stare.

Impatient for the girl to move towards him, the Reverend raised himself from his chair, leaned forward, pulled her by the hand and sat down again by the table. Fragrant tea, steaming rice buns, young girl were now ranged before him in a promising line-up of the morning's pleasures. The Reverend's impatience had to do with something he saw early that morning in the temple precincts, on his way to the great house for the ancestral prayers. The temple courtyard was already filling with worshippers who had come for the celebration of the feast of the Goddess of Mercy. The Reverend saw a young woman sitting on the temple steps, feeding her baby; beside her was a small pile of joss-sticks and flowers ready for offering to the goddess once the little chore was done. She was of nondescript appearance and wore peasant clothes, but the breast she was offering her baby was magnificent: the Reverend had a quick glimpse of its full engorged beauty before the blouse went down again and the baby's head blocked it completely from view. The Reverend lingered a little and experienced a most agreeable sensation when, at the moment of the woman's shifting her baby to the other breast, he caught a view of both, full, rich, creamy white, raw pink. It was but a momentary sight, for the woman was once more fully covered, quietly feeding her baby, unheeding of the noise and bustle around her, and certainly of the Reverend in his grey silk robe and holy beads. The monk walked on, but the vision stayed and inflamed desire, so that by the time he was ready for his breakfast, he had worked up his appetite to such a pitch that it would have precedence over the other: never mind if the tea or buns went cold.

He noticed, with much pleasure, that the maid Peipei, though not as pretty as her sister Popo, had a more developed body. He smiled at the girl. She smiled back nervously. He touched her hands gently and she went on with her work of laying the table. He put a hand up into her blouse. She stood very still and shook in her nervousness. The Reverend's fingers expertly undid the row of buttons on the bodice and then, as soon as the breasts burst out of their confines and assumed their full roundness, went into a frenzy of exploration of their beauty. They were still hidden from view by the blouse; such was the Reverend's eagerness to derive optimal pleasure from the activity that he had devised it in three stages, the second when he would lift the blouse and so see as well as feel, and the third and most satisfying of all, when the girl, in her nakedness, would be led to caress his, under his grey silk robe.

Each of the three stages was guarded by the caution that had always been the Reverend's hallmark in his secret pleasures: at the sound of approaching footsteps, the blouse could be lowered, the girl pushed away, the legs under the silk robe closed again, the eating of breakfast resumed.

So with great confidence, the Reverend went through each step in his scheme of enjoyment, thinking all the time, that of all the bondmaids in his experience, this one had the most beautiful breasts which invited the most thorough exploration of their beauty. He made her hold up her blouse, so that he could explore with both hands, as well as mouth. The girl's body was an endless territory for his pleasurable roaming: it was certainly a pity that he had to demarcate the boundary of his pleasure. Or had he? In the midst of a long drawn out sigh of satiety as he at last allowed the girl to remove her hand and indicated that she could go, a thought suddenly shaped itself into the beginnings of an intention: suppose he removed the boundary? It was after all one imposed by himself and could be as easily removed. The Reverend promised himself that he would think carefully about it and work out a new strategy of pleasure, if necessary. Meanwhile, he got ready to enjoy his tea and buns which, though they had gone a little cold, still made a very satisfying meal.

"He touched me. He made me do shameful things."

Actually, Peipei had not so much spoken about the incident as revealed it through tears, and much nodding or shaking of head to questions. She had, that evening, as she lay on her mattress, sniffled in the darkness. It was not secret sniffling but something clearly meant to alert a caring ear.

Han said, "Why are you crying? Is something the matter?" and the girl immediately broke into a sobbing.

"Don't cry," said Han and the girl moved to her mattress for solace. They whispered together in the darkness and gradually the girl's sobs subsided.

The Reverend, looking up, saw with much gratification that it was the same voluptuous maid who was coming in with his tea and buns: he saw, too, that she continued to look promisingly shy and nervous. A defiant look would have displeased and alerted him. He watched her as she poured his tea and tried to catch her eyes. The Reverend was not capable of a rakish wink but the sparkle in his small, narrow eyes as he finally compelled her to look at him wanted to tell her that the enjoyment ought to be on both sides, and that there was no need for any anxiety.

At the moment of her getting ready to go, he said, "Come here." She hesitated and he repeated, "Come here," with a slight show of impatience. She went to him. He merged the first two stages of his pleasure by doing something he had never done before, impelled by a new skittishness and the looseness of the blouse the maid was wearing that morning: he lifted the blouse and put his head inside, like a playful child, in a simultaneous exploring with hands and mouth. The maid's body stiffened. The monk gurgled, then suddenly stopped. There was a short, sharp, ominous pause before he pulled away his head from under the blouse, spluttering in fury. He lifted the blouse once again to stare closely at both breasts, stared at them in mute rage, not lust, in confirmation of the suspicion that had suddenly occurred to him when he closed his mouth on her beauty. For he looked upon breasts smeared with something—dirt, pigeon stool, whatever—that had been transferred to his plundering hands and, worse, mouth. The Reverend began to spit violently, reached for his tea, took a large gulp and spat it out in a cleansing. He did not know what to do with the smirched hands, which he held out, fingers splayed, well away from the soft purity of his silk robe. His rage rapidly blotched his face and neck, pushed out his eyes from their soft cushions and turned his voice into a squeak.

"You! You!" His voice returned, but he kept it low. He took a step towards the girl and she fell back, trembling. She was staring at him, white with terror, and it became clear that the author of this diabolical outrage was not herself.

"Come here."

The voice was charged with an authority that compelled the girl to move towards it. By now, she was trembling violently.

"Tell me who told you to do this."

She told him.

VII

THE HEAVY DOWNPOUR CHILLED the night air and drove the bondmaids deeper into the warmth of their blankets, curled against outside storms and terrors. Han uncurled, flung off her blanket and sat up on her mattress, rubbing her eyes with both fists to clear them of the heaviness that might detract from the task at hand. While the others slept soundly, she did a quick adjustment of hair and clothes, silently rolled up her mattress, stacked it in its place against the wall and walked out of the room.

Along the open corridors, she pulled her blouse tightly around herself against the wet and cold of the driving rain and resolutely walked on. She stopped outside the matriarch's room. The light was on: on rainy days, the matriarch's back ached so badly that she had to get up and sometimes rouse a bondmaid from sleep for the back-knocking. Han needed no summons.

With a devotion that smelt need a mile away, she was at its door in an instant. She knocked softly on the door and the matriarch opened it instantly, a heavy shawl on her shoulders. Her smile of immense relief combined with the rictus of distress to produce a most peculiar distortion of features, particularly of her delicately plucked eyebrows whose perfect moon arches now collapsed into a mess of little squiggles.

"You have come again; you are a good girl," she said and immediately went to sit on a chair for the back-knocking. "You ought to be wearing a warm coat in such weather," she said kindly. As soon as the back-knocking began, she launched upon a tirade against the useless Peipei, to balance the competence of one bondmaid with the ineffectualness of another.

Her own back-knocking skills were being put to the test, for the patriarch, confined to his bed by all sorts of ailments, complained of constantly aching shoulders and would have no one but his wife touch them. He was even more fastidious in his demands on her than she could ever be on a bondmaid. She had been in and out of his room the whole day. "And now this rain," she said, aggrieved that the conspiracy between her husband and the weather was robbing her of all rest.

The mournful cry of the wind took her thoughts in a different direction.

"He's started appearing," she said in a tone of gloomy confidentiality, referring to the Old One who had begun to appear in the patriarch's dreams. It was very odd indeed—not a single dream of him since his death, and then, suddenly all these regular appearances, coinciding with the many strange ailments. Such a thing had never happened before. It boded no good.

The matriarch gave a little sigh and said they might soon have to consult the Reverend from the White Light Temple. The talking eased the burden in her heart and smoothed away some of the lines on her face; the moon arches were arches once more.

She droned on; her voice had a somnolent effect which Han struggled against, fearing her eyes would close and her fists slacken, for she was determined to enable the old lady, at the end, to say, once again, "You are very good. I feel so much better. I don't know why I still have not got Choyin to agree to a change of duties for you."

The matriarch excited no special feelings of sympathy or aversion; she was simply there as someone to be respected and heeded because she was matriarch. But the respect and regard quickened into interest each time she was reminded of the old lady's special status: she was the young master's grandmother. By that connection alone, she merited special attention. Apart from the possibility of gleaning useful, new information about the grandson from the abundance of her garrulity, there was the simple diversion of trying to trace his features in hers, the quality of his voice, the mannerisms he must have picked up during the childhood years when she kept him so closely by her side. Everybody talked about how much the matriarch loved her grandson; she wondered, with a small smile as her fists did their expert sweep of the back, whether even the matriarch's love could match hers. Did the old woman, for instance, think of him every moment of her waking hours and wait for him in the dreaming hours of sleep? Would she consider her life a waste, unless lived for him alone?

The matriarch had been useful to her in her childhood; she remembered how her efforts to secure the old lady's approval had enabled her to stay beyond the reach of Choyin's punitive arm. The efforts must be redoubled now for the enemies had increased, both in number and malice. They surrounded her and would destroy her in an instant if they could. She needed all the help she could secure; the patriarch, reserved, irritable, was out of reach, but the matriarch, with a chronically aching back, was the kind goddess's answer to her prayers. Increasingly she was taking over the back-knocking work from Peipei, meriting gratitude there but provoking strong suspicion from Choyin who, she was sure, had already passed on the suspicion to Li-Li, for the two women conferred endlessly and made no secret of it.

"Since when did you become such an expert in back-knocking?"

"Peipei, you might as well learn to do other work. You are no longer needed for back-knocking!"

The girl, struggling to cope with the turbulence of feelings following the incident with the Reverend, broke down under the pain of a new mockery. Unable to talk to Han whom she felt she had shamefully betrayed, she requested an urgent visit from her sister Popo who came at once, carrying her baby. Peipei sobbed out her troubles; Popo immediately saw the danger, not of the monk's continuing attentions or Han's scheming, but the loss of a perfectly good position in the House of Wu. Accordingly, she set about removing the danger. She told her sister to disregard Han's advice from that day onwards and to carry on competently with her duties. The monk's playfulness was nothing and was part of man's nature that women had to endure; besides, he never went beyond breasts and respected a maid's pristineness.

"Look at me," said Popo. "Look at me and my good life with my family. If I had made a fuss and something bad had happened, would I be like this today?" And she held up her lucky male baby by way of reinforcing her point. Endurance. If women endured enough, a good life would eventually come to them.

"Don't listen to her," she advised. *Siau. Siau.* She told Peipei of Han's strange behavior from childhood. Peace-loving by nature, she continued to be amiable towards the strange girl, sometimes even bringing small gifts for her on her visits. She had switched sides irrevocably and, without being exactly aware of it, had become a spy for Choyin.

The spying intensified with each visit home by the young master Wu and Li-Li.

"There's no need to do any sweeping today." The sweeping of the corridors might allow Han to linger outside the room where the young master and his grandfather usually sat.

"Peipei will bring up the tea."

"No need to do any back-knocking for the matriarch today.

She says to tell you she won't need it today."

The hostility building up rapidly, Han could turn round sharply, flashing, lashing.

"Where's Spitface? Get him out of the way. Master and Mistress are coming."

"Where do you want him to go? Shall we tell him to go back to his rubbish dump? Why don't we just kill him? That would be much easier than getting him out of the way each time."

She would cast a quick, contemptuous glance at Choyin's tight face, before leading Spitface away and telling him to remain in his woodshed for the rest of the afternoon or go to the town and get something good to eat. She pointed to the little secret pile of money in the corner of his cupboard.

"All yours," she said. "She says it's not yours, but the dead say wrong things in dreams. Don't let anybody know. Now go and buy yourself a meal." She put some money in his hand and sent him off, knowing he would go straight to the food stalls in the market and help himself to his favorite duck or chicken noodles.

The hostility took on a new theme.

"Mistress Li-Li, don't be worried. We have got out of your way all that is unpleasant and harmful."

"Do be careful, Mistress Li-Li. You must take very good care of yourself. You cannot afford to take chances at such a time."

"Our congratulations, Mistress Li-Li. Master Wu must be so very happy."

She knew then that Li-Li was pregnant.

VIII

THE ONCE-A-MONTH FEAST, precious food in a vast desert of deprivation, was to be relished to the last morsel. Luckier women, dining sumptuously, could toss their surfeit to waiting dogs and beggars; she was a beggar who lived on Li-Li's surfeit and gratefully picked up the crumbs. An old, ragged beggar once came to the door and one of the bondmaids scooped up a cupful of rice grains from the large storage jar to put into his bag. She spilt a few grains, and the old man, with much effort, went down on the ground to retrieve them.

"Don't laugh, miss," he said reproachfully to the bondmaid who giggled to see him try to dig out two grains that had fallen into a crack in the floor, with his slow, bent fingers. "For people like myself, every single grain counts."

Even the few crumbs she had managed to pick up from Li-Li's table had to be guarded against being snatched away. As they lay together in the darkness after the act of love, and listened to the hum of the pond insects, she fought off the intrusion of the dark thoughts that would rob this moment of all its sweetness. The time after the act of love was the most dangerous, because spent love brought a return of reflection which brought a return of reality. The reality was a tiny child growing in a womb; no child of peace but of malevolent intent, it would emerge from its mother's body and taunt her: my mother was powerless against you, but you will see I have every power. My birth will be your death.

She saw him, powerful male baby, in rich silk clothes, adorned with gold rings and anklets, passed from arm to arm, in the tumultuous joy of the First Month celebrations when both the House of Wu and the House of Chang would send up the fragrant smoke of a thousand grateful joss-sticks to gods and ancestors. Asleep in his mother's arms and looked upon fondly by his father, the baby would say to her, more effectively than his mother ever could: Stay away, bondmaid. And his father would say: That was a foolish diversion of mine, my son. Yes, it was just that, a diversion, as you, my son, will lay claim to, in your time.

So, sleeping soundly in her arms, he stood immeasurably removed from her, in his glittering world of wealth and privilege and continuity. The mocking baby pulled him even further away; in a sudden spasm of fear, she tightened her hold on him and brought her lips upon his brow. He murmured something, shifted to a more comfortable position in the warm curve of arm and breast and murmured again before falling back once more into the rich ease of sleep after love. She listened to his deep breathing in the darkness and a thought flared, accompanied by a dangerously rising sob: This man sleeps, while I am in pain. This man comes to me once a month and returns to his world, while I perish in mine.

She could have gone on: This man has a future that stretches before him like a golden road; mine is a deep dark pond whose waters will close over my head. This man says he loves me but his love will retreat at the first sign of trouble.

The thoughts had to remain locked in her head; if they came out in a torrent of reproach upon her tongue, he might turn peevish and say, "What more do you expect me to do?" His gentleness forbade taunts but they would be just as hurtful, silent upon his dark brow and the cold taut corners of his mouth: I am the young master Wu. I have a hundred bondmaids at my disposal. I have chosen you and risk the anger of the House of Wu and the House of Chang in meeting you like this. What more can you ask?

She could be bold and say, A little more. What about giving me a regular place in your life where I could sometimes sit with you at table for a meal, get ready the bed for your coming to me, talk to you when I am happy or sad, tell you I am going to have your child?

And he would answer her question with another: How can you ever think that is possible? And then the atmosphere would become so unbearably charged with menace, that they would turn away from each other and sour the precious time together that would not come again for a while.

Why are you so foolish? Our poor, foolish little sister!

Oldest Brother and Older Sister had come to know about her

secret in a roundabout way. They had told her about Old Bao, who, despite taking a fourth wife, continued to haunt the House of Flowers. He was older than Old Cheng but bore better testimony to the revitalizing power of ginseng, snake's blood and crushed tiger's testicles. Also, he had a lot of money.

"Him!" said Han scornfully. "I know him." And then the story of his application to the matriarch for her came out.

"So why didn't you—" gasped Older Sister. "Do you know his Fourth wife—and she does not have half your beauty—wears gold buttons this big?" and she brought forefinger and thumb together in a circle to demonstrate the size.

"The young master Wu did not want me to marry anyone. He told his mother to turn down the offer."

The words which had been nursed in her heart as consolation came out through her lips as protest and surprised even herself. Oldest Brother and Older Sister turned to look at each other. "So," they said silently. "So this is the truth. Now we know why you are behaving so strangely and foolishly."

They berated her for her folly. "What do you get at the end of all this?" they demanded. They meant, "Get all you can from him while the going is good. Soon he will tire of you and find another young woman. They all do that. Don't fool yourself. Get all you can."

They told her the story of the young bondmaid, from another great house, who knew she could never rise to be secondary wife but who, over the years, systematically amassed a fortune in gold coins, so that when she was finally told to leave, she left a wealthy woman, adopted a daughter and lived the rest of her life in respectable prosperity. "A gold coin, if you please," she had said playfully, each time the old fool slipped into her room or pulled her up into his. He laughingly obliged, not at all minding this novel way of opening women's legs. She closed hers forever when his hoard of gold coins ran out. His wife discovered the loss and kicked up a row, screaming to have the wealth returned. But it was too late.

But you, look at you. The man robs you of your virginity. Who will want you now? And you are getting nothing at all? Why are you so foolish?

She could not have told them, for they would never have understood: I love this man. I have loved him ever since I was a little child. I would go to the ends of the earth to look for him.

She looked at him, sleeping in her arms, breathing gently. I could kill him, she thought. I could kill him and then myself; we could die together.

The little gift penknife would not do the work; anyway, she had thrown it away that evening in his room.

If we died now, we would become ghost-lovers. Ghost-lovers must be happiest of all, with only the rooster to mind. We would meet by the pond every day if we wished, and not just once a month.

Under the weight of so much melancholy musing, she fell asleep and woke to the touch and smell of a small white flower on a stalk gently brushing her cheek and eyelids. He was awake and smiling down upon her, in the mood for more love. He said, "Wait", got up and was gone somewhere. She heard the rustle of leaves and small plucking sounds, and saw him come back, in the darkness, with an armful of the tiny fragrant night flowers. He sat down beside her as she lay still on the mat and spread the blossoms on her breasts, perfuming them, combining sport and ritual. She wanted to tell him, "Not those. When we were children, we were told to avoid them and never to remark about their scent in the evening air. They are unlucky flowers," but desisted, letting him go on in his play of love.

"I love you," he said fervently when he went down on her again, crushing the blossoms, and she thought sadly, "You mean you will love me so long as your secret pleasure is not known."

The pond insects hummed louder. She lay in inner and outer darkness, while he continued in the laughing brightness of passion awakened once more. "I can't live without you," he murmured. She thought, "Tell me that again. Tell me that a thousand times, to chase away this sadness in my heart that will not go away, For I fear something is going to happen soon."

She heard a sound in a nearby bush, which could not be the wind nor bird nor insect, and thought, "It's happening already." And across the pond the little goddess in the shrine voiced her own uneasiness: Those flowers are not good. You shouldn't have let him pluck them and strew them on your body like that.

Their rich fragrance had an intoxicating power which inflamed his passion all the more, so that, if he could have had his way, he would have spent the whole night there with her, on the mat, beside the still waters of the pond.

I X

THIS IS STRANGE, she thought. I am sitting on a goddess' throne, and here are four golden urns of joss-sticks before me. Rice-cakes too. And look who's coming to make a request of me.

The goddess with no eyes or ears was the first supplicant. She was holding a lit joss-stick in her hand.

"You don't have to do that," said Han. "After all, you're the goddess. I'm only a bondmaid."

"You've got to help me," said the goddess and she looked very troubled.

"How can I do so? I've already told you. You are the goddess. You have all the power."

The goddess ignored her and went on, "You've got to help me. He gets worse and worse. He makes me deaf for one-hundred years. Then he beats me."

Sky God came up just then, looking for her. He looked far more ferocious in person than as a statue or effigy in his temple. His eyes were like burning coals. His mouth, rich, red and moist, opened to flash long, white teeth. His breath stirred the black pennants of his beard. The sunburst of gold spears on his back gleamed menacingly.

Sky God looked around and said, "Where's she?" When he saw her he said, "A-ah!" and aimed all ten fingers at her, sending forth a stream of energy that caught her and drew her towards him.

"Please help me," said the goddess, tearfully turning to Han.

"How can I? I'm only a—"

The goddess said impatiently, "How can you be so stupid? Look at your own wrist!"

She looked at her wrist and saw the thread bracelet with the jade image of Sky God. Foolish god, to allow himself to be graven in stone and gold and jade, and be at the mercy of women.

"Is it the right time of the month?" whispered the goddess.

"It is," cried Han joyfully "I can help you after all."

So she availed herself of her secret blood and brought down the jade image to the secret place.

Sky God screamed, "Not that! Please not that!" But the blood was already on his image. Sky God fell, still screaming, "Not that! Show mercy!"

"Did you show mercy when you made me deaf and trampled on me?" cried the goddess, advancing upon him. She laughed to see the golden spears collapse into a useless, tangled heap and the great god trapped in their midst.

"Where are your thunderbolts? Where is your lightning flash? Destroyed by the blood of woman!" She taunted. She turned to Han and said, "Give me your penknife."

The gift penknife hung around her neck, hidden in the folds of her blouse.

"No, no," cried Han, clutching it. "It was his gift to me. You cannot have it."

"A gift indeed," sneered the goddess. "That man is not capable of any giving. He is only making use of you. He says he loves you to keep you for his pleasure. But all the time he is secretly laughing at your folly. He laughs about you to his wife, you know."

"Yes! Yes!" agreed Older Sister who had appeared from nowhere. "He is the same as all men. The old fool made me shell prawns all day and shouted at me. One night he raped me. He pushed some money into my hand and told me not to tell anyone. I told his wife and she slapped me. How I hated them. I was so glad when Oldest Brother came to take me away."

"Nobody came to take me away!" cried Chu who came running up, "I suffered fifteen years."

"Give me the penknife," said the goddess. "I'll show him. I'll show all of them."

She wrested the knife off Han's neck, flicked it open and with one stroke, cut off Sky God's penis. She held it up triumphantly.

"Him, too, please!"

"And him! If he has ten penises, cut them all off!"

The dismembered god ran off howling, followed by the Old One and the Reverend, all clutching the bloodied emptinesses of their dismemberment.

Chu hopped up and down like a child, whooping for joy.

"He nourished it with ginseng," she shrieked. "I had to brew ginseng for hours to strengthen his lust. See where it is now. I'll pick it up and feed it to the ducks!"

"You think you are so clever?" said the old *keo kia* woman. Han had never seen her looking so stern. "You think you have changed anything? My advice is to endure."

"Quiet!" said Han. "I don't care if you are old. I'm going to say this to you. Stop coming and being a nuisance. You never help."

"I am the goddess and you listen to me," said the goddess and she surveyed everyone authoritatively. She had eyes and ears now, beautiful, well-shaped, alert. She handed the knife to Han.

"Your turn," she said. "He's treating you so shamefully. Your turn."

"No, please don't," cried Wu, but the goddess, assisted by Chu and Older Sister, were holding him down on the mat. He was stark naked, after their act of love.

"I love you," he said pleadingly to Han. "You can't do this to me."

"Come on, do it," urged the goddess. "This is your only chance."

"He says he loves me," cried Han. "How can I do this to him?"

"Foolish girl!" screamed Older Sister. "He's going back to his wife. Indeed, he's never left her. You are the one he's always leaving. She's going to give him a male child, and that's when he'll leave you and never come back!"

"Let us strike a bargain," said the goddess sternly. "If we let you go, will you make her your secondary wife?" She was standing over him.

"I can't! I can't!" he wailed. "I love her very much but I'm the young master Wu and she's only a bondmaid! Can't you see?"

"See what I told you?" said the goddess, turning triumphantly to Han. "Do you believe me now?"

"Alright," said Han. She took the penknife and lunged at Wu.

"It won't change anything, I tell you," said the old *keo kia* woman.

"Hey, you've only nicked his shoulder," cried Chu in dismay. "You're supposed to cut off his penis and fling it away where he can't find it."

"You have disgraced us all," said the goddess angrily. "How can you just nick his shoulder when you were supposed to cut off his penis? Give me back that knife!"

"Oh no!" cried Han. "I believe he loves me. He didn't want Old Bao to take me away."

"You! You!" screamed the goddess, really angry with Han now.

"Don't do that—" cried Han and she meant "Don't shake

your head so much. The cracks are still there. I told him to mend them but he forgot."

True enough, the shaking widened the cracks and the goddess's head suddenly fell off her shoulders and on to the ground.

"He did promise me he would mend your head, but forgot," said Han sorrowfully.

"Promises! Promises!" wept the headless goddess. And then suddenly there was pandemonium. They heard a loud clattering of spears and turned to see Sky God coming towards them, restored to his full strength and resplendence.

"So you thought you could destroy me?" he snarled. He pulled off his trousers and his penis sprang out in the fullness of its power. He proceeded to rape the helpless, headless goddess, thrusting into her most mercilessly. The others took the cue; the Old One pushed Chu to the ground and drove into her, the Reverend into Older Sister.

Wu came up to her and said, "Come." They were in a room. He slammed the door shut with his foot. He pushed her against the wall and lifted her blouse and ripped open her bodice. His mouth tore at her nipples.

"Go." He pushed her towards his bed and held her down, tearing off her trousers.

"Don't think you can use the knife on me anymore," he said, as he tore into her with a tremendous grunt. "I've thrown it away. It is lying at the bottom of the pond now."

"Be quick," said Li-Li from behind a screen. "Just get your lust over with and come home."

"Help me, goddess!" she begged.

"I can't even help myself," moaned the goddess and Han saw that she was still under the ferocious thrusting bulk of a naked Sky God with his sunburst of golden spears on his back. Blood flowed from her.

"This blood has no power over me!" laughed Sky God. "I broke it!"

"It's all your fault," said the goddess to Han. "You brought all this trouble on us."

"Help!" cried Han. She saw Spitface staring at them and yelled to him. "Help! Help me, Spitface!"

He came running up and pulled her off from underneath Wu. Sky God, still naked, still erect, pulled out a spear from behind his back and smote him dead.

"You can't do that!" shrieked Han. "He never hurt anybody in his life!"

"Run, everybody, run!" screamed the goddess. "There's no hope anymore. Run!"

"I told you but you wouldn't listen to me," said the old *keo kia* woman sadly.

X

"YOU ARE NOT DEAD," murmured Han thankfully when Spitface came into the kitchen for his morning mug of tea and biscuits. He sat by a side-table, deferentially hunched and ate cheerfully, grinning at her, his head very firmly on his shoulders, not detached from it in a raw mess impaled upon Sky God's golden spear. Bad dreams hung a weight of dark foreboding on tongue and limbs for the rest of the day; this one was the worst of all and laid a cold stone of fear on the heart. She went to a temple and bought a sachet of blessed flower petals. She put these in a bucket of water and washed her face with the water. The soft pink and red blossom-curls touched her skin with a sweet solace and dispersed the dread of the dream, but not of the reality, which hung over her, a dark cloud, distilled from the poison of baleful glares and secret whisperings aimed at her. In the great house, she moved alone, inwardly afraid, in silent spaces carved out by watchful suspicion and anger.

Choyin had even taken to spitting; within sight or sound of

her, the head bondmaid gathered the spittle to bring out in an energetic discharge in her direction. When no spittle could be collected in a dry mouth, the discharge was represented by its sound, a vehement explosion from tightly rounded lips—"P-p-poooii!" The Reverend met her once, along a corridor, and he stepped to one side, at the same time giving her a malevolent look that said, "Don't think you are so clever, Miss. Don't think you can get the better of everybody. Your day of reckoning is near."

The Reverend groped no more; he ate his buns and drank his tea in morose silence, his lust in abeyance, not flight, as he plotted a different strategy to deal with recalcitrant bondmaids.

Fourth Older Brother also met her once, also along a corridor. He steadied himself against a pillar, looked at her frowningly and struggled against the dense fogs of Orchid's magic which at last parted enough for memory to turn his look of perplexity into one of pure vitriol as he suddenly lunged at her and snarled, "You! You! You were the one who spat on me!" before they closed again, causing him to shake his head and blink stupidly and stumble into his room. Peipei stood on the edges of the raw anger, casting timid, startled glances at her and staying away as far away as possible; the washerwoman stopped talking to her and pulled away her little boy if he went up to look at her, his eyes wide with curiosity, being privy to whispered adult secrets.

So be it. Do what you will with me. I'm not afraid, she thought defiantly, but the cold weight of fear remained, connected with the secret rustling sound she had heard that night by the pond.

The washerwoman's little boy, seeing that his mother was not around, walked up to her and asked with round-eyed incredulity. "Is it true you have many demons in your body?" and she smiled and said, "Yes. You can tell them that I mean to keep my demons."

She needed help. She fled to the matriarch, her only hope of support in the great house, attaching her hope to that broad, ache-ridden back that would, thankfully, respond only to her fists. She had virtually replaced Peipei as back-knocker. She eased every ache and made the old lady smile. The smiles spun a protective cloak for her naked, shivering fears. She discovered, to her secret satisfaction, that the smiles could be further teased into the laughter of pure pleasure thus ensuring a cloak of greater protection. For the matriarch reveled in frivolous and scurrilous talk and was in the habit, after the back-knocking was over, to retain her for tale-telling. She responded eagerly, fitting the substance and the mode of the telling precisely into the quirks and twists of the old lady's penchant. She became both consummate back-knocker and inveterate gossiper. The old lady listened with the eagerness of a child, suddenly, in her old age, casting off the restraints of propriety and decorum she had imposed on herself in her youth. Having known opulence all her life, she liked to hear of the squalor of the poor, interrupting each narrative with a little incredulous "Is that so?" or "How could it be so?"

"I remember we were so hungry one day that we stole a packet of rice sticks from a shop. We sat under a tree and chewed the sticks. Once we stole from the gods. Our mother could not feed us because our father never gave her enough money. There was a piece of roasted duck on an altar table that a neighbor had put outside her house, in honor of the moon goddess. Oldest Brother took a stick, poked it down and when nobody was looking, ran up and picked it up. We spent some time cleaning the meat of sand and dust and then had a grand feast." Contemptuous of those who exposed their sordid family histories, she was prepared to unearth the most squalid story in her own, to humor an old powerful woman.

The old lady said that she had once seen a beggar child pick up something from a rubbish dump and put it in his mouth. She said, her eyes shining, "Bondmaids came into my house looking like skeletons and within months had good flesh on their bones!" She liked to say that the House of Wu was the only one of the great houses where bondmaids had unlimited access to the good things in her store.

"Have you ever heard of any house where bondmaids eat chicken and eggs and fish regularly?" she said smiling.

Having a husband who kept no concubine or secondary wife, she liked to hear of other men's rampancy and was able to contribute stories of her own father-in-law, the Old One of the barnyard habits.

"My brother knows of an old man who has four wives but who visits prostitutes frequently. He gets strength from drinking the blood of snakes and armadillos."

Too reserved and introspective to participate in the gossip of fellow bondmaids, she now dispensed prattle with practiced ease, to satisfy the prurience of an old, idle woman. The matriarch listened intently and said that when she was a little girl, she had an uncle who too drank snake's blood and ate bear's penis. The matriarch liked to hear stories of ghosts, but not the ghosts of those who had died in the great house itself. She asked briefly about the rumors concerning the old *keo kia* woman, the poor unhappy Chu, and the child with the harelip who had died so long ago, then said, with a little shudder, that she did not want to hear more.

Han adroitly moved on to the harmless tales of the Blind Fortune-Teller, which the matriarch decided she liked very much, and listened with the absorption of a child. "The Blind Fortune-Teller doesn't come anymore, which is a pity," she said, "for I would have loved to listen to his wonderful tales."

Han glanced up to see Choyin passing by and looking into the room, at precisely the wished for moment: the matriarch was saying something to her and laughing. The manifestation of the new camaraderie would be gall to the head bondmaid who would duly report it to Li-Li.

The young master may no longer be around to protect me but I have his grandmother. Now touch me if you dare.

She raised her small daily duties to a grand strategy of

cultivation—the meticulous, unstinting back-knocking, even during those hours of night when sleep weighed upon her eyes, the skillful story-telling, the hundred small gestures of concern and devotion that a vain, lonely old woman relished, even if they came from a bondmaid, such as searching the entire mansion for a lost favorite toothpick or ear-pick, gently drawing attention to a hairpin askew upon the bun of hair and carefully straightening it. Once, as she was rubbing some embrocation oil on the old lady's calves, she looked up and saw Li-Li passing by, and met the glare with a small smile.

Abuse me if you dare.

Choyin dared. The opportunity came when a stranger appeared at the kitchen door one day, asked for no one in particular, and began talking loudly about Spitface. The bondmaids stopped their work to listen. Choyin invited him in. It turned out he was the owner of the noodles stall that Spitface liked to frequent. The man had come to warn Spitface's friends in the House of Wu of impending trouble. A group of unruly hooligans ate with Spitface and made him pay for them. He obligingly pulled out notes from his shirt pocket. The hooligans ordered more than they could eat. The man said this had been going on for some time, and it made him feel very uneasy. He thought he should let Spitface's friends know. He left unsaid the main cause of his uneasiness: where was Spitface getting all that money from? Had the imbecile turned thief to feed a bunch of street idlers? The ungrateful poor, stealing from their benefactors, the magnanimous rich. Choyin thanked the man who went away much gratified by the satisfactory discharge of a responsibility that had been troubling his simple, honest mind for some time. Then she went in search of Spitface and dragged him into the kitchen where she subjected him to a loud interrogation.

"Money, money, you idiot!" she yelled, for he looked uncomprehendingly at her. She began searching his pockets and pulled out a fistful of small notes.

"Where did you get this from?" she demanded. "You usually

have only a few coins in your pocket. So where did you steal this from?"

The voice was raised to carry into the adjoining room where Han was doing the ironing. It brought her out immediately. She entered the kitchen, holding a half ironed shirt.

"Leave him alone," she said quietly. "He didn't steal anything. I gave him the money."

"Then you stole it!" cried Choyin. The accusation that she had wanted to make from the day she saw Spitface playing with a wad of notes for Li-Li to see, was now fully unleashed upon the torrent of her anger. "You stole if from Chu! You stole a dead woman's money!"

"Think as you like," said Han. "Spitface is no thief. Neither am I," and she returned to her ironing. Or rather, gave the appearance of it. For, once out of sight of those in the kitchen, she quickly slipped away to the matriarch's room. She walked up respectfully to the old lady who was as usual sitting in a chair. She said she had advice to seek from one who could only advise wisely. The matriarch said calmly, "What has happened?" and she told the story of how Chu had given her the money just before she hanged herself.

"She came to me with the money in a cloth bundle while I was asleep, shook me up and left it on my mattress. Then she went to hang herself. I didn't think to bother you with the sad tale and I didn't think to keep the money for myself, since I have all I need in the House of Wu. So I gave it to Spitface."

And now all this trouble with Spitface and the hooligans. What would the matriarch advise her to do?

She stood by patiently waiting, while the matriarch stopped fanning herself and reflected on the matter. At last she came up with the requested advice. The remaining money was to be taken from Spitface, so he would not get into any more trouble with bad people. It was to be used, firstly, to make a donation to the White Light Temple on Chu's behalf and secondly, to set up a small altar of remembrance to the poor woman whose soul must still be in torment. The Feast of the Hungry Ghosts was coming and Chu had nobody to pray for her and offer food to her.

Nodding in ready agreement to each suggestion in the course of the long speech, Han broke out, at its end, into a paean of warm praise for its wisdom, so that by the time Choyin came up to see the matriarch, in the later part of the day, to make the complaint she had been eagerly rehearsing, the matriarch was coldly dismissive: yes, she knew all about it; no, there was no need to do anything about it, because Han had already taken her advice to solve it quickly. The pre-emptive strike robbed Choyin of speech but not of action; she went in search of Spitface again, to punish him by a slap or a pinch or two. The imbecile could be depended on not to tell anybody.

It was Peipei who ran running to Han in fright.

"He's all beaten up!" she gasped. Spitface was standing in the yard outside the kitchen, whimpering. His face was badly bruised. One eye was horribly swollen, the lower lip was cut. When Han went out to bring him into the house, he rushed towards her and burst into tears, like a child. The memory of that other time, when she came to untie him from a chair, must have returned to accentuate the self-pity and need so that at the sight of her hurrying towards him with an anxious face, he let out a tremendous howl.

Spitface was incapable of answering questions but he could nod his head or shake it and demonstrate with fists and legs. The story slowly unfolded. He had been beaten up by a group of men in the marketplace. The noodles stallholder made a second appearance to fill intriguing gaps. He said the hooligans had as usual gathered to join Spitface for a meal; they were in very boisterous mood and ordered huge amounts of food in addition to beer from another stall. But when they found that Spitface had no money, not even to pay for his own meal, their mood turned ugly and they set upon him. They dragged him to a secluded part of the market, beat him and ran away. "My advice," said the stallholder gravely and with much humility, "is to keep him away from these bad people. Please don't give him any more money."

It would seem that money and Spitface were a fatal combination. He would be safer with just the small coins given by charity or earned from wood-chopping or latrine cleaning.

The injuries made Spitface ill. He lay on his bed in the wood-shed and received nourishing porridge cooked by Han.

"I'm sorry," said Han to the small photograph of Chu, flanked by two small urns of joss-sticks, two cups of tea and a plate holding a large pomelo. "But let me tell you that there is not a cent of your money with me or Spitface anymore, so I hope your soul will be at rest." She wanted to add, "Please don't come into my dreams anymore, because you always frighten or sadden me. I have enough fears and sadness without you." But that was not a respectful way to address a dead person, so she merely repeated, "May your soul find peace."

She looked at Spitface with his bruised face and said. "This is good," meaning that if the evil portent of the dream had already been fulfilled in the incident, Spitface had been let off very easily indeed by the gods. There was a man who had gone to the temple to thank the gods for having suffered a misfortune because it freed him from a greater.

Don't think you have been let off. Don't think I have not been watching and that others have not watched for me.

Choyin's malevolent silence screamed out the warning.

One of these others, in his furtive watching in bushes that night, was probably the delivery boy from the provisions shops, or the washerwoman's husband.

"The matriarch wants to see you."

Deliverer of messages, both innocent and direful, Choyin's mouth gathered in a tight smile of anticipatory victory. She knew, as she followed the head bondmaid to the matriarch's room, that the storm-clouds were about to break.

She entered the room, and shuddered to a hostility that crackled about her ears with screaming menace.

The matriarch was sitting in her chair, the smooth moon-arches of her eyebrows entangled in a frown of deepest displeasure. Li-Li was by her side, ubiquitous handkerchief of pain as usual pressed to her mouth. Her eyes were swollen with crying. Choyin took a bold position on the other side, no longer bond-maid but participant in an exercise of power and revenge that she had initiated in the first place. The matriarch of course had honor of first denunciation. She remained in her chair and her voice was surprisingly calm.

How could you. So well treated in the House of Wu from childhood. Such ingratitude. What would the patriarch say if he knew. How could you. After all the kindness. What would people say.

There were no tedious preliminary questions. Did you, or did you not?

On such and such a day. We have the evidence. We know everything.

The earlier efforts of cultivation and ingratiation had not been totally lost; they were clearly having the effect of somewhat toning down the old lady's anger. Under other circumstances, she would have risen from her chair and administered a slap or the famous pinches on the tenderest parts of thighs. She looked up now and then at Han and a softening in tone in parts of the tirade probably coincided with the thought that this strange young girl was not such a bad girl after all, being perfectly obedient and the perfect back-knocker, or with the thought, in a different direction, of the young spoilt grand-daughter-in-law who could not handle her own problems and came running to her elders and ruined their peace.

More annoying than the fact of this young bondmaid's seduction of her grandson—who was unfamiliar with such things, given man's ungovernable appetites?—was the fuss that the young mistress from the House of Chang was kicking up, instead of letting the man have his way and waiting for him to tire of the girl, as he must. But, thought the matriarch, with a weary sigh, it would always be-the lot of the old to bear with the ineptitude of the young.

How could you. You must not do such a thing to the House of Wu. We have been kind to you. You have been a good girl—

The discharge was losing its power; indeed, the old lady was visibly relaxing in her severity, as could be seen by a clearing of her brow. With angry energy, Li-Li took over. Removing her handkerchief from her mouth, she lashed out at Han in the fullness of her rage. Traitor. Prostitute. Scum. Ingrate. How long has this been going on? How can you be so shameless? How dare you, you a servant girl?

Her fury was the greater for its remaining unexpressed in the presence of her husband who, at this moment, was probably calmly reading his books in his study or enjoying a drink with his friends or taking a leisurely ride at the back of his car and chatting with the driver.

How long has this been going on? The loving woman, badly-injured, wants to know and be injured more.

Han remained silent in the midst of the tumult into which Choyin, at an appropriate moment, plunged with her own claims and accusations. Don't think I didn't suspect. Slipping away at strange hours in the evening. Coming back in the early hours. Don't think I didn't know.

The injured woman thought sorrowfully: Those must have been the nights of the lies. A man lies to his wife to steal out in the night to meet his mistress.

Choyin's anger intensified with the enlarging of the transgression: the girl had been causing trouble to everyone since she arrived at the House of Wu, fifteen years ago. A stream of invective flowed, bearing all the child's iniquities. And now this. Choyin flung out the *coup de grace*, with a flinging out of her thin, intense arms: the Blind Fortune-Teller had predicted that the girl, demon-possessed, would bring untold sorrow to the House of Wu. Li-Li screamed, "Get out! Get out this very instant, you scum, you whore, you devil."

The matriarch got up wearily from her chair and confirmed the decision that apparently they had been previously discussing: the girl had to go.

"You must leave," she said with a mixture of severity and tiredness. "I am an old woman who needs peace. The patriarch is unwell. We cannot have so much trouble in the House of Wu. You will leave. You will have enough money to take care of yourself until we find you employment."

The last gesture was purely hers; Choyin and Li-Li would have cast her upon the rubbish-heap.

She looked up. She looked up for the first time and said to the matriarch in a voice that trembled but was clear: "Do not trouble yourself about giving me money or finding me employment. I have myself found employment and will start today."

It gratified her to see Choyin and Li-Li look at her with a little start of surprise.

"Where are you going?" asked the matriarch and she replied, "The House of Flowers." The matriarch looked quizzically at Choyin and Li-Li. Li-Li stared, then gave a short sharp laugh of astonished derision. A gleam entered her eyes and made them sparkle.

"You are going to work in the House of Flowers? Where your oldest Brother is?" The tantalizing information needed confirmation.

"Yes."

Li-Li turned to the matriarch and whispered something to her. The old lady looked at Han and frowned. "You are going to work as a prostitute?"

"I am going to the House of Flowers. I will let my brother know immediately," and she turned and walked out of the room, in the full gratification of the thought that Li-Li, whose face was by now aglow with a most unexpected victory, was impatient to rush home and tell her husband: "I was right about that servant girl. She's a prostitute and will always be a prostitute. They all are."

XI

HAN DECLINED THE OFFER of assistance from Lotus and Rose—they all had flower names, and in time she too would be called Peony or Chrysanthemum or Jasmine, depending on what was left, or Lotus Number Two or Rose Number Three, depending on inclination—and proceeded to do the transformation herself. She stood before the mirror in the small upstairs room that Oldest Brother had assigned her and stared at herself. Men found her beautiful; she had kept her beauty for only one man but now it would be nurtured for the delectation of many. She looked at the boxes of powder and rouge, lipsticks, eyebrow pencils and tweezers, artful instruments of female enhancement for male pleasure, that the two girls had so generously lent her, and had an idea of what to do with them. She worked assiduously, rather enjoying the novelty of the experience and in less than an hour surveyed herself again in the mirror and smiled.

Nobody would have recognized her. The transforming effects of powder and paint were magical. She studied her enlarged eyes, her crimson bow of a mouth, her glowing cheeks. She had the face of a whore or a goddess, for even goddesses had need of the enhancing power of cosmetics, as the many temple statues and paper effigies demonstrated. The only difference lay in hairstyle. Her hair, severely and chastely pulled back into a bun at the back, was that of a pure deity. She chose whoredom and so loosed her hair and shook it into a rich shimmering cascade down her shoulders, completing the effect by pinning a saucy red flower at the side, above the right ear.

The riotous beauty being discordant with the comely, long-sleeved, high-collared blouse and loose cotton trousers that she had worn all her life, she now proceeded to cast them off. She picked up the dress, lent by either Lotus or Rose and studied it carefully. It was a long soft pink dress with coquettish ruffles at the collar and sleeves and an amazing number of buttons and hooks. Like the powder and lipstick, it challenged rather than daunted; she held it against herself in the mirror, then examined it again, turning it here and there, in and out, to master its intricacies. It was soon mastered. It encased her body perfectly which, like the transformed face, drew another gasp of astonishment: who would believe that this was the bondmaid who had left the House of Wu the day before? She gave a little chuckle of amusement.

The two helpful girls Lotus and Rose had hung giggling by the locked door, hoping to be the first to witness the transformation, but were called away. Oldest Brother walked in and smiled his approval. He said gallantly, "You look more beautiful than any of the girls here," and immediately relapsed into the morose state of the past few days. He began to confide his troubles: the boy companion was proving to be more difficult than ever and had even dared, the day before, to make a sudden appearance in the House of Flowers in defiance of all warning, causing deep displeasure to the lady who owned the establishment, whose favor Oldest Brother had been assiduously courting. He was anticipating a complaint from the House of Wu, for he had heard that they were blaming him for having introduced Orchid to Fourth Brother and therefore needed all the help he could get. Orchid had one night insisted on Fourth Older Brother taking her back to his room which, within minutes, she had stripped of everything valuable, including a clock belonging to the patriarch. Somebody later found a sachet of some strange stuff and an amulet hidden in a pillow. The couple had disappeared and nobody could find them.

Trouble upon trouble. Oldest Brother lifted his glum face from his hands and announced one more: Older Sister, ever unpredictable, had run off with a man she had known for only a week, taking money he had entrusted her with. Oldest Brother said it was borrowed money and let out a deep groan.

He looked at his youngest sister and saw hope. He saw hope because Old Cheng saw pleasure; indeed the old man who came always dressed in an impeccably tailored white silk suit and white topi and carried a gold-topped cane, had taken one look at Han and nodded approvingly. Old Cheng's nods of approval were pure gold.

"He wants to visit tomorrow," said Oldest Brother and went on to say, "He has vast rubber and coconut plantations."

"Alright," said Han.

Oldest Brother bestowed his own look of approval.

"Never mind," she said cheerfully, referring to his troubles.

Oldest Brother secretly marveled at the change. Within days, he had witnessed a startling metamorphosis of both appearance and behavior. He was reminded of the story of the Snake Woman who stepped in and out of her snakeskin, one moment an innocent maid and the other an evil enchantress. Having tried for a long time to get his sister to come to the House of Flowers and share his new life of prosperity, he ought to be glad, but felt uneasy; something was not quite right but he was not sure what it was. The woman who was standing in front of him in the soft, coquettish dress, with the crimson mouth and the siren's flower-adorned tresses was not his sister.

Old Cheng, with precisely this image of the beautiful newcomer in the House of Flowers imprinted in his eager mind, smiled and nodded when shown into the room, and softly closed the door. Old Cheng liked young beautiful bodies. He was long past even the effects of rare ginseng and snake's blood, but he had a robust enjoyment of simple pleasures such as watching a young girl comb her hair down her bare shoulders or bring him a cup of fragrant tea or massage his legs with oil.

The room was in semi-darkness, which he liked, and the newcomer was sitting in a corner, her back coyly turned to him, which he liked even better. She turned slowly to face him. He advanced with a little chuckle of delight, then stepped back with a start of surprise, for he was looking upon a wildly disheveled woman, not the glossily beautiful one the day before. The girl's hair was a wild tangle about her face and shoulders; some faded flowers hung limply in it. Was it the mere dishevelment of sleep?

Old Cheng stared. The girl came out of the pool of shadows and stood smiling in front of him. He said "Aar-gh" in fright and choked and spluttered, for he was looking upon a witch's face: it was besmirched with some frightful substance, the eyes were wide open and staring, the mouth was distended to reveal horribly blackened teeth. The clothes, moreover, were torn and dirty. The girl broke into a loud, coarse laugh, and he knew, for a certainty, that he was face to face with a mad woman in the House of Flowers. For some reason, the house of pleasure accommodated a lunatic and he had been shown into her room by mistake. Or was she a ghost? Had he entered some secret chamber in which a woman who had died years ago had come back to take her revenge?

The terrifying thoughts flew about in Old Cheng's head and made him recoil and utter little squeals of terror. He said "Oh no, oh no," when she advanced upon him, grinning, and backed towards the door. His old hands trembled violently but managed to turn the knob. He fled. She smiled. She could count on him keeping the secret to the end of his life. Rich old men were superstitious and an encounter such as this, charged with foreboding, would be sealed up forever. Old Cheng would never come to the House of Flowers again. Meanwhile, he would have recourse to cleansing baths prescribed by temple monks.

She laughed quietly to herself, thinking that in the course of less than a year she had, for the sake of one man, fended off three, in three different ways: she had dropped scalding tea on the first, spat on the second and frightened off the third. She pulled off the dead flowers from her hair, washed her face, cleaned her teeth, changed her clothes. Then she began again the whole laborious process of making herself up, to rival the consummate skill of Lotus and Rose who were clearly the favorites in the House of Flowers. She put on the pink dress and sat in a chair and waited. She knew she would not have to wait long.

True enough, just when she was beginning to feel a little sleepy and to nod, she heard the loud footsteps approaching: her heart thrilled to the angry purposefulness of the steps making directly for her door, of the voice that angrily called her name even before the eyes set sight on her.

"You!" roared Wu. She had never seen him so angry. She looked up silently at him.

"Get out of those clothes. Take that paint off your face. I'm taking you back."

He pulled her up from the chair. She continued looking at him, saying nothing. He glared at her, then looked around the room. His wrath continued to spend itself in the violence of sound and action.

"I said get out of those clothes!" he yelled. He tore off the red dahlia from her hair. "You whore!" He began to look for her clothes, saw the familiar blouse and trousers hanging on a peg, pulled them down and threw them at her. He saw her slippers under the bed, pulled them out and flung them at her head.

There had to be yet more action to contain the surging energy of his rage. He ran to a wall and began hitting it with his fists. He banged repeatedly, until his knuckles bled, then stopped and laid his face against the wall, panting. She watched him. He swung round to look at her, his eyes in a blazing fury. With a ferocious grunt, he pulled her towards him, shook her, then slapped her across the mouth, sending her reeling and falling upon the bed.

She lay there quietly, touching her lower lip which was beginning to bleed. They looked at each other. He was pale with shock at his violence. He sprang upon her and held her tightly in his arms, crying in the fullness of contrition, "Please forgive me, please forgive me, I didn't mean it. I swear I didn't mean it." She continued touching her lips. He brought her head down upon his shoulder and rocked her in his arms, in an agony of remorse and longing: "Please forgive me. I didn't mean to hurt you. I was just so angry that you had run to other men. I can't bear the thought of you being with other men, because I love you so much! Don't you see?"

It was the purest unburdening a man was capable of. She thought, her head still pressed on his shoulder, her lip still quivering with pain: This is the first time he has meant it. If a loving woman must first be struck to elicit the remorse to elicit the loving, so be it. She wanted to hear again the words of his loving, to pull them out of him, again and again, and save them, warm golden strands of memory, to touch and lay against her face, in a possible future time of chill sadness. She did not say, "Say that again," but made her own full-hearted declarations— "I have never stopped loving you", "There is no one I will love as much as you"—which took his responses to higher and higher levels of fervor, so that, clinging to each other on the bed like frightened, lost children, her lip still bleeding, his knuckles still hurting from their contact with the wall, they knew they had passed into that indefinable state of need and love for which there was no turning back.

What shall we do now?

Tenderness had to give way quickly to hard-headed thinking. Her hard-headedness dished out a hard demand: make me your secondary wife. Go to your grandfather and your grandmother and say, I am the young master Wu. I want Han the bondmaid to be my secondary wife. Go to your wife and say, I am your husband. I wish to have Han the bondmaid as my secondary wife. Then walk away without waiting to hear their answer because you are the master Wu.

He stared at her.

"What if I can't do it?" he said.

"Then I remain in the House of Flowers," she said. "There is no other life for me. I will never go away to live with Old Bao or Old Cheng. I will live and die here."

He continued staring at her.

"Don't you see?" she said, beginning to weep. "I need to be part of you. I cannot be the servant girl you meet secretly once a month and forget the rest of the time. I need to be with you on a proper bed, in a room, in a house. I need to know that when I

287

wait for you, sitting in darkness for hours, you will come. Most of all, I want to hold your arm in the presence of Choyin and the others and say to them, "He is my husband too. He will be the father of my children too.'"

There was a secondary wife who was allowed by the first wife to sleep with the husband only once a month. Even then, the woman managed to produce many children who were, however, taken away from her and brought up by the first wife. The secondary wife endured the pain for many years and after the first wife died suddenly of a strange illness, she had full possession of the husband and lived another twenty years with him in supreme fulfillment. If the gods were kind, cruel first wives perished first.

He could not stop staring at her.

She thought, "Weak! Weak! You say you love me, but it is a weak love."

He said, "I will do it. I am taking you home. Now put on your clothes."

XII

"I'M GOING TO TAKE you home."

Love's promise is always larger than the reality and has to be accordingly cut down to size.

"I'm going to leave you with someone trustworthy until I—" He left it unsaid, but both knew it meant the essential promise of making known his decision to his grandfather, his grandmother and his wife.

They decided that the most trustworthy and hospitable would be Golden Fern and her kind husband, the clogs-maker.

"Of course," said Golden Fern and she turned nervously to her husband for his assent, for even kind husbands should be consulted.

"Of course," said the clogs-maker who had once said he would rather be a simple clogs-maker living a simple, peaceful life than a wealthy man plagued by the intrigues of concubines and secondary wives.

"I'll get a room ready for you at once," said Golden Fern generously.

Later, in the quiet of night, husband and wife would discuss this strange development of events but only in whispers, so that their voices would not be heard through the thin, plank walls of the house. Now they were all effusive kindness; a bondmaid, half way to becoming the secondary wife of the young master Wu was suddenly elevated in their sight.

"Thank you," said Han gratefully.

"Only for a short while," she added, believing this to be the last transit in love's long, frightful journey.

XIII

THE HANDKERCHIEF WAS OF little use in assuaging the shock and pain, so Li-Li threw it away and instead pressed her knuckles into her mouth, biting deeply into them. The pain convulsed her small dainty body but she needed it to distract her from the larger pain. It was futile. She pulled her knuckles, white, bitten, out of her mouth and swung round to face her husband standing by the window. She said, "How can you do this to me?" How. What. Why. Women's hurt breaks through the sentence into the rhetorical question which breaks through into screaming invective: Get out! Get out of my life!

He waited for her sobbing to subside before repeating, simply and calmly, "I want to have Han as my secondary wife." He repeated also, "I love her," and hoped that the repetition would be sufficient to sustain wish against protest. Unsupported by any justification, the two assertions could only be strengthened by their own reiteration. So to every question that his wife hurled at him— "Why are you stooping so low?" "Is this my reward for being your devoted, loving wife?" "Do you want the House of Wu to be a laughing stock?" he could only say, "I need her," or "I love her," feeling foolish in the idiocy of unremitting repetition, and not surprised that it provoked another bout of screaming exasperation in his wife.

She screamed and whimpered abjectly by turns, veering uncertainly between the two extremes, neither of which seemed to have any effect on her husband. A thought shaped itself with startling clarity in the tumult of her anger: the demon-possessed bondmaid had turned demon-possessor and was making use of her new power to bewitch men. There was no other explanation for his attraction to her. No man had ever been saved from the sorcery of women simply by being made to face the fact: he would deny it with his last breath and be driven deeper into the sorceress's arms. But Li-Li was determined to fling the sordid truth into her husband's face, on the possibility that it might shock him out of the spell.

"Let me tell you this," she said. "You have been put under a spell by that demonic woman. She has used her secret blood on you. The next time she offers you food or drink, look carefully at it, sniff it for its smell." Her delicate sensibilities had not been fully protected from the raucous, squalid tales and gossip of the bondmaids; as a young girl, she had sat demurely on the edges of rough talk and listened, wide-eyed.

She continued, with no abatement of energy, "You are no longer yourself. Anyone can see that. I can even see it in your eyes. They are not the eyes of a normal man. Go and look at yourself in the mirror. The young master Wu bewitched by a common servant girl!"

She had exhausted the strategy of salting the wounds of a man's secret fears, and herself felt exhausted, falling back upon a mound of pillows on the bed, while he continued standing by the window, silent and unmoved. She said slowly and with great effort, "Go. Please leave the room this instant. I can't bear to look at you." He stayed where he was, feeling sorry for her and at the same time thinking, "My father and my grandfather would never have had to bear with women's shouting," and wondering, at the same time, about the wisdom of men marrying upwards.

"I told you to leave," she said wearily, flinging an arm across her eyes. But as soon as he started walking to the door, she sprang up and said, "Wait!" He stopped and turned to face her again.

"Tell me," she said. "Have you told your grandparents?"

"Not yet. But I'm going to," he said.

"Then go!" she said imperiously.

A woman in an agony of anger is in a greater agony of uncertainty. Get out, she says. Come back. Get out. Come back.

He was already at the doorway, when she once more lifted herself upon an elbow and called, "Wait!"

He stopped and waited. She became suddenly very quiet.

"I have to tell you something," she said in a small stricken voice. "I am with child."

He gave a start and made to go to her, but the hardness closed upon her again, and she began to scream and wave him away: "Go to her! Go to your whore! As if I cared!"

XIV

THE MATRIARCH SAT IN HER chair, her hands limply on her lap.

She said sadly, "You young people, you will be the death of me. Why is there so much trouble among you?"

There was no varying the mode or tone of the announcement of his decision and its reason: "I want Han the bondmaid to be my secondary wife. I love her."

The old lady sighed, shaking her head, "I thought the trouble was at an end when she went away. Now it has all started again."

She saw the matter purely in terms of its adverse outcome on her aching back, her poor ailing husband who was having those horrible dreams of the Old One again, the relationship with the House of Chang, which had never been good in the first place. She wanted her grandson to be happy, and to have a hundred bondmaids if he wished, but not if it caused trouble on this scale.

She continued, "I'm not as strong as before, you know. I cannot always take on the troubles of the young."

Better in the articulation of contrition than love, he knelt before his grandmother and begged her forgiveness, holding her hands in his. The old lady burst into tears and leaned against him. The tears had the marvelous effect of clearing away the irritations and annoyances that had been disrupting the even tenor of her existence and detracting from the small simple pleasures of gossip and new hairpins regularly brought in for her viewing by jewelers. Visibly cheered by the manifestation of her grandson's gentle caring, the old lady wiped her eyes and began to ask him about himself, whether he was eating well, what he was doing about the persistent rash on his foot, whether he liked the birdsnest she had got Choyin to send over. She complained, patting his arm affectionately, that since his marriage, he had never had the time to sit down with her for a nice long chat, as they used to do.

"My grandson," she said proudly, holding his arm. "My grandson, why do you have so little time for your old grandmother who used to call you her 'Precious Diamond' when you were a small child? Do you remember?" He remembered, with some embarrassment. She would announce loudly, before entering the house she was visiting, "My Precious Diamond is here too!" and show him off to a circle of admiring, giggling women.

He promised to visit her more often and gently explained that he had to spend the entire time of each previous visit home with his grandfather who was in poor health and was always cheered by his visit. The mention of the patriarch brought back the gravity on the matriarch's face. "Your grandfather must not be bothered by the troubles of you young people," she said, looking severely at him and speaking in a low, grave voice. "He is a very old man now and his last years must be peaceful. Oh, oh, why is this happening to me?" and the tranquil eyebrows once again broke into distressed squiggles.

"Grandmother, please don't cry. Everything will be alright."

He was suddenly aware that the untenability of his position had shrunk his communication to a few stock expressions, whether of love, denial or solace. Don't cry. Everything will be alright. Over the coming days, he thought, he would be using the same words to the crying women around him—his grandmother, his wife, his mistress, perhaps his mother-in-law, perhaps even the head bondmaid Choyin if she came weeping on his wife's behalf. Don't cry. As if the simple admonition could check women's tears or curses.

He felt tired. But he had passed the point of no return. He loved and wanted the bondmaid. He could not live without her. Against the solidity of this core of his need, everything else was a shifting penumbra.

"Please don't tell your grandfather," said the matriarch. She had an idea. By all means have the girl. But set her up in some place quietly, far away from either house, preferably in a different town. She knew of a man who had done this, very successfully. His wife came to know about it after a while but she feigned ignorance. Everything went on smoothly. Nobody was upset.

"Please don't tell your grandfather," she repeated earnestly. "The trouble is sure to distress him and make him worse."

"I will tell him, I have to," said Wu, meaning it was a promise he had to keep.

"Then wait for a few days," said the matriarch tearfully. "Can you not wait for a few days?"

"Alright, Grandmother," he said, comforting her for she had begun crying again.

XV

"My GRANDSON," said the patriarch in a weak voice. He made to rise from his bed, but Wu ran forward to forestall this gesture of affection with his own of filial concern: "No, no, Grandfather, you must not get up." He helped the old man lie back comfortably on his bed. The patriarch looked at him with tender affection; since his illness, his reserve had softened into great expansiveness and he now liked to have his wife or his grandson sit beside him and talk to him.

"This is very good news," said the patriarch. "I always knew I would not die before looking upon my great grandson. Now I will die happy."

Wu looked up and for the first time noticed Li-Li sitting quietly in a chair in a corner. So she had come on her own, to give the old man her news, to pre-empt his.

The patriarch turned his head in Li-Li's direction and asked her to come and sit closer to them.

"It is alright, Grandfather," she said, remaining in her place. She had neutralized the daring of a solo visit to the old man's room with the deference of retirement into a corner of the room the instant the purpose of the visit was accomplished and was now further demonstrating the deference by declining to intrude upon the intimacy of the two men.

The patriarch, pleased, repeated, "It is very good news," and went on to say that only the night before, he had had a dream of the Old One, but this dream was different for it calmed instead of troubled him. The Old One had actually smiled and said to him. "I lived to see a great grandson. You will have that blessing from Sky God too."

And now, said the old man, with gentle gratitude in his eyes, this confirming visit from Li-Li. In good health, he would have been irked to receive women's news from women themselves, even the supremely satisfying news of guaranteed continuity of his name, but illness had melted away the austerity so that even young grand daughters-in-law could approach without fear.

The patriarch, describing the dream in detail, was so moved by this manifestation of Sky God's benign power that a tear appeared in his eye. His voice quavered and Li-Li came up quickly and was in time to wipe, with her handkerchief, the large tear coursing slowly down his cheek.

The old man weeping in joy, his young grandson holding his hand, his young grandson's wife wiping away his tear and carrying within her the promise of a great grandson that would be the culmination of his hopes on this earth—nothing could be allowed to intrude upon the gentle sanctity of such a scene, certainly not any announcement of brutal intention. Indeed, the intention had for the time being receded far enough for Wu to enter fully into the patriarch's joy: the perpetuity of the House of Wu was ensured.

XVI

"SO?" SAID LI-LI that evening. It was question, challenge, warning. Into the little three-purposed word were distilled all the feelings that had been building up in her since that day when she caught the quick, furtive exchange of glances between her husband and the bondmaid Han.

So what are you going to do next? Do you still want to have anything to do with that servant girl? Do you want to kill your grandfather? Do you realize that you could be bringing the wrath of the whole House of Chang upon your head?

Wu was silent.

Li-Li stood facing him and said, "I know where she is. I want you to send a messenger to her with this message, 'I will not be seeing you anymore. I will have nothing more to do with you.'"

She looked at him with flashing defiance. Her eyes said, "Do it or I will go to your grandfather once again. The old man is on my side."

Generally indifferent to her, sometimes captivated by her coy sensuality on the bed, he found himself, to his surprise, hating her then. He wondered how it was possible to hate a woman and at the same time treasure her for the life she was nurturing in her. He recoiled from the piercing venom of her narrowed eyes, the bitter curl of her mouth, the sharpness of the laugh that cut the air, but he was drawn to that hidden part of her body which enfolded the growing life that would bear his name.

My son, he thought, my son. The Old One's great great-grandson, the patriarch's great grandson. The prodigious continuity of the House of Wu.

"Will you do it?" she asked again.

"No," he said.

"Then you have to bear the consequences."

XVII

CHOYIN WRUNG HER HANDS and shook her head. Li-Li had sent for her and she went hurrying from the House of Wu to the House of Chang. The large gestures of anxiety were both a manifestation of her concern for the young mistress in her plight, and of her need to demonstrate to the bondmaids in the House of Chang that, since her competence had been so openly acknowledged, she now had ascendancy over them. So she clucked her tongue, made agitated noises and ordered them about. Then she went to the young mistress's chamber, to comfort and serve.

For Li-Li had had a fall and started bleeding. A bondmaid had found her clinging to the staircase rails and weeping pitiably. A doctor had been urgently summoned. There was every fear that she would lose the child.

Now she lay in bed, pale and weak. Choyin helped her up to a sitting position and spooned nourishing black chicken soup into her mouth. Her mother sat beside her, looking anxiously at her and now and then nervously touching her head or cheek. The matriarch Chang would soon make another round of the temples and come back with blessed flowers and oil and the ashes of burnt prayer paper. The matriarch Wu had already consulted the Reverend who had said that there was an evil force determined to wreak havoc on the House of Wu. It had left, but was lurking around, waiting for the moment to strike. The matriarch gave orders for any number of ritual cleansings by the White Light Temple monks to fend off this evil influence. She shook her head and sighed, "No end of trouble! No end of trouble!"

Li-Li's eyes filled with tears and her lips trembled. The women came together around her in a solidarity of compassionate regard but dispersed the next moment, like disturbed moths, for the door had opened and Wu was walking towards the bed. Their deference carved out a large space for the expression of husbandly solicitousness. He sat down and looked anxiously at his wife. He asked, "What did the doctor say?" and she continued to weep silently.

"The child is safe," said the matriarch Chang, speaking for both doctor and temple medium.

"My son is safe."

Wu took his wife's hand and clasped it in his. The women quietly left the room.

XVIII

"THE MASTER WU SAYS he will not come to see you anymore."

The messenger was someone she recognized as one of the male servants in the House of Chang. She stared at him unbelievingly and he repeated the message dully, mechanically, his face devoid of all expression. The blankness belied the churning curiosity underneath, which would emerge, as soon as he returned, in endless noisy rills of gossip with fellow servants.

Golden Fern, standing nearby, heard, stifled a gasp and cast a startled, nervous glance at her, as she stood in the doorway, still staring at the messenger.

Who sent you? What exactly did he ask you to say? What else did he say? Was someone with him?

The questions broke through the staring stupor in a frenzy of urgency. The messenger turned and fled.

Han walked back slowly to her room. She lay on her bed all day.

"There's someone to see you."

Throughout her life, the message had jolted her body with hope and propelled it in eager haste to the visitor only to be beaten back by disappointment and pain. So she disregarded the message and flung an arm across her eyes.

"You'd better go in," whispered Golden Fern to the visitor. Oldest Brother sat by her bed and said, "I heard about your troubles. I'm here to help."

She said nothing. Her silence said, "What can you do?"

Oldest Brother said, "I am sorry all this is happening to you," and added with bitter gloom, "We are a doomed family. Sky God has put a curse on all of us! Look at Father. Look at Mother. Older Sister is a thief. She still cannot be found. She has run off with other people's money too. Everyone's looking for her." As for himself, he had troubles galore, and Oldest Brother began an outburst against the boy companion who had got him into serious debt and had moreover turned dangerous, assaulting him publicly. He turned to show deep scratches on one cheek that could only have been made by vicious fingernails determined to finish their work.

"He keeps asking for money," lamented Oldest Brother, by now so absorbed in his own problems that he was talking to himself. He was roused from his absorption by Golden Fern coming in timidly with a cup of tea.

Oldest Brother, looking at his sister lying still, with her arm across her eyes, was impelled to ask, with no small hint of sharp rebuke, "Why did you leave the House of Flowers? Old Cheng was all ready to favor you. See where your obstinacy has got you."

Han said, still keeping her arm over her eyes, "Get out. Get out this instant, or I'll sit up and spit on you."

Oldest Brother got up in alarm.

"Don't ever come here again."

"You are my only sister now—"

"I say get out."

Golden Fern later announced another visitor.

"Let him in," said Han. "He is the only one I will see."

Spitface came in, looking perplexed and troubled. When he saw Han, he rushed to her, spluttering in his agitation. He soon calmed down and sat by her bed, looking anxiously at her. She opened her eyes, looked at him and thought, "He is the only one who has ever loved me. He will do anything for me."

Golden Fern brought some coffee and biscuits and hurriedly left.

"I am with child," said Han sadly. "I was going to tell him, but he will never know now." Spitface, eating a biscuit, nodded eagerly. He was happy, sitting beside her.

XIX

"COME, LET ME TELL you a story."

Never a good story-teller, always preferring to listen instead, she was now eager to unload her story upon her audience of one. Spitface, ever alert to her beckoning sign, came to squat by her chair and look up at her. She sang her story:

The bird looks
The bee cries

The ants yearn
For my little flower
My little opening flower.

It was not a celebration of the flower's desirability, but a lament of its abandonment. He had come, taken away the opening beauty and gone on his way. He had left her emptied and despairing.

There was hope yet. If the flower could open a second time to expel his seed fully nurtured to his likeness, he would return. Men returned to claim sons, but turned away from daughters.

She touched the now visible swell under her blouse and said, "There is hope yet," and asked the imbecile sadly, "Do you think there is hope?" Hope for money had caused others to pull them both into frenetic little rituals for securing lucky lottery numbers. She was once made to put her hand into a jar and pick up sticks bearing numbers, and Spitface was once made to climb up a rambutan tree and throw down the small round fruit which were picked up and carefully counted. Virgins and imbeciles possessed special powers. Now hope again made her resort to sticks and stones and seeds. She made Spitface cast these repeatedly upon the ground and each time peered to see how they had fallen. They all indicated a male child. "Spitface, I will reward you," she said generously. She looked at the thread bracelet on her wrist, with the upturned face of Sky God. "I wanted to give this to him once, in promise of a son, but he would not accept my gift."

"Spitface," she said again, looking at him very gravely, "if it is a girl, you will know what to do, won't you?" A tray of ash would await the child about to be born. The first thing that the midwife did after pulling the child out was to look between its legs. For its sake, she hoped to see the tiny curl of promise, not the slit of shame.

"A girl," the midwife would say sadly and would be authorized to push the baby's face into the ash, to suffocate it before its next cry. Sometimes rags or a bucket of water did the job. Less than buffalo's dung or rice stalks that were saved, the new-born baby girl was cast upon the rubbish heap.

"Spitface, you will know what to do, won't you?" she repeated tearfully. Spitface with his uneven legs ran here and there on errands; he could lower himself into the sewer to retrieve other people's lost possessions, as indeed he was once made to do, when a bondmaid lost her gold ring. But instructions for the doing away of unwanted baby girls were beyond his ability to comprehend. He grinned happily. He had settled most contentedly into the daily routine of walking over to see her and spending long hours under the same roof as her. She chased away Oldest Brother who hung around sulkily, but welcomed Spitface.

Golden Fern who moved timidly around her guest with kind food and advice at the ready and stepped in at the first sound of a whimper, came in with her baby on her hips and said to Han, "You have not been eating well. You must eat well in your condition." Golden Fern's kindness was of the kind that was as inexhaustible as the pain eliciting it: she would trudge out to the village shop in pouring rain to get the Tiger Balm or salted plums craved by her guest tossing listlessly upon the bed. She woke up in the night to soothe a fevered brow or tame the wildness of dreams with a little prayer somebody had taught her, returning to calm her own husband, the kind clogs-maker whose kindness was not inexhaustible. "When will she leave?" he asked with restraint, not wanting to upset his wife too much.

"As soon as the baby is born," she said nervously and added, "Some money comes from the House of Wu," by way of reassuring him that the poor girl was not entirely dependent on them after all. Her brother came occasionally with small gifts of food and medicine, but not money, for, he said, he had fallen on hard times and would repay the kindness to his sister as soon as he was able.

Han asked Golden Fern to do her a favor. She raised herself

on an elbow on her bed, her belly now distinctly visible under her blouse, her face gaunt with anxiety, and said, "You must go to Auntie Hoo and ask her for her trousers so that I can wear them. Tell her to give me any old, torn pair she does not want." Auntie Hoo, mother of five sons, lent or gave away trousers to pregnant women who hoped that part of her great good luck would be imparted with the trousers. Auntie Hoo was obliging; back came a pair of worn grey cotton trousers which Han immediately put on, grateful for its touch against the skin of her smooth round belly. A very rich matriarch secured for her pregnant daughter an antique bed on which a woman had borne six sons, another a magnificent jade bangle worn by another woman with similarly selective fecundity. The poor resorted to used clothing but the method was said to be no less effective.

There were more requests. The child must not only be male but healthy. Great was the grief of the woman who had a male child at last but lost the poor puny undernourished baby within a month. So Han asked Golden Fern to cook more food. She ladled an immense mound of rice into her bowl, finished it quickly, then held out the bowl for more. She ate the second helping just as voraciously. Li-Li would have no need to hold out bowl or plate; a spoon would always be at the ready, at her mouth, held by a conscientious bondmaid, and it would hold, not plain rice, but rare ginseng or black chicken or finest pork.

"Our rice jar gets empty very quickly," said Golden Fern's husband, his kindness almost all gone.

"Her brother is coming today with a bag of rice," said his wife and even she wished for the birth of the child to take place soon, for Han to be gone.

"Is she losing her mind?" he grumbled. "Does she bathe at all?" For Han wore Auntie Hoo's trousers continuously and was beginning to smell.

"Shall I cut your hair and fingernails for you?" said Golden Fern anxiously but Han shook her head. Her hair hung in limp strands around her face. She allowed Golden Fern to comb it and tie it in a tail at the back. There was an intensity in her eyes that was frightening to look at.

"I have come again. It has been a long time."

Huge with the coming child, she stood before the goddess in her shrine. Neglected for months, both shrine and goddess were pitiful. With her fingernails, she dug out a small shred of red ribbon hidden between the two stones, remnant of a lost happiness, and stared at it. Then she stared at the goddess, headless, breastless, denuded of all her features, and began to weep.

"Forgive me my ingratitude," she wept. "You gave me hope when all hope was gone, and I never came to thank you. Now I come, and I am ashamed to say it is to ask for another favor. I come to ask that the hope will not be a false one."

Dear Goddess, she said, with an urgency so great she bled inwardly. Let not the child be female, like you or me.

"As if I would let you down like that!"

She saw the goddess before her, intact, beautiful, smiling.

"Dear, dear goddess," she said. "I am so glad to see you whole and happy once again." She gazed at the goddess and marveled at her beauty, then turned, startled, to see Li-Li walking towards them. She whispered to the goddess, "See who comes, and see the shape of her belly." For Li-Li was very big with child now, with a belly like a perfectly shaped round melon, promise of a son.

"I have come to tell you," said Li-Li with a curl of her fine, red mouth, "that when my son is born, my husband will cease to have anything whatsoever to do with you. Right now, he sends money to you. Don't think I don't know. I have spies everywhere. But my hope is in my son. He will destroy you, once and for all!"

Han thought, "Her belly is perfectly round, whereas mine is a little pointed." She whispered desperately to the goddess, "Goddess, she's right. She'll have a son and I'll have a daughter! He will go to her and cast me off forever. All hope is gone for me!"

"You have so little faith in me," said the goddess reproachfully. "I have been watching over you and taking care of you since you were a child and you still have so little faith in me."

Han and Li-Li lay on the ground, side by side, about to give birth, presided over by the goddess.

"Are there to be no midwives?" cried Li-Li.

"There will be no need for midwives," said the goddess. "Now lie still and be patient. The births will take place shortly."

Li-Li was the first to feel the expulsion of the child from her body. It came out in a rush of water and blood from between her raised legs.

"No! No!" shrieked Li-Li, for it was a girl. The pitiful little flatness between the baby's legs, with its small faint slit, was the first thing they saw.

Then it was her turn.

"No! No!" shrieked Li-Li again, for it was a boy child who kicked his legs wide apart to proudly announce the little wrinkle of maleness between. Li-Li, abandoning her girl-child, tried to wrench the boy-child from her, but she fought her off and held her son tightly in her arms, sobbing for joy. He had saved her.

"What did I tell you?" said the goddess, clucking her tongue and shaking her head. "I hope you will now have more faith in me."

XX

THE MIDWIFE WAS READY, with the basin of hot water and towels. She whispered to Golden Fern, "It will not be an easy birth. She's in great pain already."

Golden Fern sent Spitface home, saying, "Go home. Don't come again till much later, Han's very ill. Do you understand?" She told Oldest Brother who was standing outside the house, "The midwife says it will not be an easy birth."

She lit two joss-sticks to Sky God and prayed for a safe delivery.

From behind the closed door she heard low moans, which rose in a crescendo of screams that rent the air. She remembered the child Han biting off the ears of a rag doll or the corners of pillows and once repeatedly knocking her head against the wall to silence pain with pain. Not the pain of childbirth alone but the greater pain of a fearful outcome must have wrecked that small body and driven scream after relieving scream from it.

At last there was silence and Golden Fern tiptoed into the room to see the girl sunk back upon the pillows, gasping, her eyes closed, her face and hair wet with exertion and terror.

The midwife said, "It's a boy."

Golden Fern bent over Han and repeated, "It's a boy." Han slowly opened her eyes. "A boy," she repeated. She needed the confirming evidence before the cold stone of fear could be fully lifted off her chest. The midwife brought the child, bloodied and squalling, its little legs open to offer the indisputable evidence, to show her. She pulled herself up from bed with a gasp and grabbed the child. She held it tightly in her arms, sobbing in her joy.

Golden Fern could not resist imparting the second joy. She glanced at the midwife who was washing her hands in a basin of water at the other end of the room, and then bent and whispered to Han, "It's a girl for her. Just two hours ago. I heard it from someone who was told by one of her bondmaids. She's crying. She does not want the master to know."

"Thank you, Goddess," said Han. She touched her newborn's hair, eyes, nose, cheeks and finally the small bud of a penis and laughed at the thought of the enemy looking upon an ignominious cleft.

"I want Spitface," she said suddenly to Golden Fern.

"I sent him home," said Golden Fern in alarm.

"Please look for him," said Han.

Golden Fern went out of the room, wringing her hands, but

was back in a moment with Spitface. The imbecile had never left but stayed, like a loyal, devoted child, through all the screams of anguish. He now hurried towards Han on the bed, looking extremely worried. He looked with deep perplexity at the baby. Han removed the bracelet from her wrist and gave it to him.

"Take this to the master Wu," she said. "Please go quickly."

She felt faint. The room spun round her. She felt the child being gently taken off her and then herself being sucked gently, sighingly, into a long, dark easefulness.

XXI

"NO," SHE SAID, with rising terror, but no sound came out. "No, you are my enemy, and I don't trust you near my precious son." For in the darkness, she discerned the shape of Choyin and recognized the voice, though it was a mere fragment of a whisper.

"You told me you never wanted to see me again, but I have come once more," said the old *keo kia* woman. "It will be my last time. I want to warn you against your enemies. They will seek to destroy you and your son."

"Stop them! Somebody, please stop them!" she screamed and she meant both the midwife who was picking up her baby and Choyin whose arms were stretched out to receive it. She saw Choyin gently rocking the child, wrapped in a thick towel.

"Don't worry, Little Sister, I'm here to take care of you," said Oldest Brother and he gently wiped the perspiration from her forehead with a handkerchief. "Rest, Little Sister. Go back to sleep."

She wanted to ask, "What are you and Choyin doing here? Don't you know I don't want to see either of you again? Get out!" but her words were like trapped birds, futilely banging against the hard cage of her throat.

She felt a restraining hand on her arm and heard Oldest Brother's soothing voice again: "Little Sister, don't exert yourself. You are not well. I will always take good care of you."

She struggled to break free of his hands and leap out of bed for she saw Choyin leaving the room with her baby.

"Stop her, please stop her!"

"I will stop her! I have the power!"

To her tremendous relief, she saw the goddess once again. Tears welled up in her eyes. "Dear, dear goddess," she said. "I will always have faith in you. Please bring my baby back."

Somebody laid the soft bundle back in her arms.

"She deserves it."

She saw Choyin strung from the ceiling rafter, looking more ghastly than Chu; unlike Chu, she still had her slippers on. The slippers never dropped off, even though her feet pointed downwards and moved with the body.

"She can hang herself a hundred times for all I care!" Han said, cuddling her son.

"Safe and sound," said Oldest Brother. "You must not excite yourself any more, Little Sister. You need a lot of rest, you know."

She heard muffled voices, moving feet, the sound of a door closing.

"Thank you, Goddess."

A heavy drowsiness settled on her and laying her face against the child wrapped in a warm towel in her warm arms, she fell asleep again.

XXII

THE MIDWIFE AND Oldest Brother quietly watched her and cast uneasy glances at each other, in the manner of those witnessing madness and choosing wisely to let the madness run its course. She screamed, ran at them, beat her fists upon their chests, then returned to look upon the child on the bed, its towel thrown open to reveal, not the proud little curl of male flesh, but the apologetic slit of female shame. She shrieked relentlessly, and continued to appeal to them, alternately hitting them with her fists and kneeling before them with clasped hands, to help explain the unspeakable horror of that tiny female presence on her bed.

"I gave birth to a son," she finally sobbed in an abatement of the insane rage, crumbling to the floor in a heap. "I did not give birth to a daughter."

The midwife and Oldest Brother came forward and helped her up gently. They led her to the bed and made her lie down. The midwife wrapped the baby again with the towel, picked it up and gently rocked it in her arms. Oldest Brother said brightly, "Drink this. It will be good for you. The best ginseng. It cost a lot of money." She whimpered, repeating, "I gave birth to a son. I saw him. I touched him." She turned to the midwife and said sharply, "You delivered my child. You delivered a boy, didn't you? Quick, tell me!"

The midwife cast another uneasy glance at Oldest Brother who said soothingly, "Little Sister, you are unwell. You were in a delirium throughout the birth. You were shouting and screaming."

"Are you saying I am mad?" she shrieked in the manner of a mad woman, rising from the bed to flail at them again. "I know I gave birth to a boy." They began again the whole tedious process of composing the wildly swinging arms, calming the contorted visage, checking the torrent of abuse.

Oldest Brother said, "You are not well. You need much rest. Let me take care of you." He went on to say he had brought ginseng and birdsnest, which the midwife would brew for her, to coax back her strength after the arduous childbirth.

A sudden gleam came into her eyes and she shot up from the bed again. "Get Golden Fern! She will be my witness. She was here when the baby was born."

"Golden Fern has gone away with her husband. She will not be back for a while. It was some important family matter. We will take care of you while she is away."

So much information, delivered in a calm, even flow, could only have been rehearsed; the midwife, when she finished, looked to Oldest Brother for endorsement, but he only said, "Yes," feebly, in a retreat of eagerness.

"I will give you a ginseng drink afterwards," said the midwife. "You need nourishment to feed your baby," adding, "whether male or female."

XXIII

"GODDESS," SHE PLEADED. "Please help me. I'm very confused. Indeed, I think I'm going mad."

Her voice became threatening. "If you don't help me, I will lose faith in you forever. I will never have anything more to do with you."

The goddess said sulkily, "What do you want this time?"

"Tell me what happened," she said tearfully. "I gave birth to a son. Why do I now hold a daughter in my arms?"

"Simple-minded girl!" said the goddess with some scorn. "When you were a child, your mind was sharper. You heard sweet words and searched for the poison hidden in them. You saw a smile and waited for the mask to drop off to expose the hate. You picked up one tiny dropped word here, another there, and you knew where the trap was and how to avoid it. Whatever's happened to that sharpness?"

As in a puppet-show, Choyin, the midwife, Oldest Brother were ranged in a villainous row of dark shadows, and behind them was the darker shadow of Li-Li, howling over her new-born and promising great gain to any who would change her sorrow to joy. More shadows: Oldest Brother's companion, the powdered boy, goading Oldest Brother on, saying: "This is your last chance. Do it for me, or I leave you forever," and Golden Fern's husband dismissing her protests, saying, "What's wrong? She owes us money, anyway. See how many times we had to fill the rice jar on her account." Her little new-born baby boy was their gain; he was made of gold and they came shrieking to claim their share.

"Goddess, thank you," she said humbly. She thought, "There is hope yet." She was thinking, not of the goddess whose capriciousness sometimes marred her kindness, but of Spitface.

XXIV

WU STARED AT THE thread bracelet that Spitface had just given him.

"My son," he said and was too moved to say anything more.

XXV

"IT WILL NOT stop me."

The huge raindrops fell heavily on her head, nose and arms which were holding the child tightly, wrapped in a towel. The child began to cry, not from the wet, but hunger, for she had never troubled to feed it.

"I'm going to return you, as you are not mine," she said. "If they don't want you back, I will leave you on their doorstep. But they must give me back my son. I want my son back."

The rain began to fall in angry torrents. One part of her mind detached itself from the pain and terror to connect the driving sheets of water and rising howl of wind with a memory of joyful

dance and union, but it was a transient detachment only, returning quickly to the present fearful prospect of a long walk in
blinding rain and wind with a fever rising and a new-born baby
protected only by a towel.

"But I must," she said, trembling all over. "I must. This is my
last hope."

She saw a blinding flash in the sky, which sent her reeling
backwards, and heard a tremendous boom which threw her to
the ground. She lay sprawled in the mud, and felt a sharp pain
in her legs creeping rapidly up her body, but all the time, she
held the baby tightly. She lay still for a while, submitting to the
angrily pelting water, then saw a massing of shapes around her
and heard a chorus of urgent voices.

"Quick, get her up."

"Get the baby"

She felt the baby being taken from her arms and herself being
pulled up by the armpits. She struggled frantically, crying, "No!
No! You have done enough to me. Don't stop me! I want my son
back!", heard Oldest Brother say, "Somebody help me carry her,"
heard Choyin say, "The child's alive," and struck somebody's
shoulder with a feeble fist before all became dark and silent
around her.

XXVI

VOICES. ALWAYS VOICES around her, which she was helpless
to answer.

"We know you're the best person to help her."

"We are deeply grateful."

The voices were Choyin's and Oldest Brother's. With a
tremendous effort, she managed to open her eyes, and saw she
was right; she discerned their unmistakable forms by a doorway,
an unfamiliar doorway. There was a third person, facing them

and talking to them, and not so unfamiliar, for she would recognize his bald pate and robed corpulence anywhere.

The Reverend said, "I will see what I can do. Some demons are more difficult to drive out than others. Hers will be the most difficult of all."

She heard Oldest Brother whine, "You must help my sister! She is the only one I have left in the world!"

She heard Choyin say tersely, "You must trust the Reverend. Your sister has been giving endless trouble. We hope this is the end of the trouble." Seeing Oldest Brother come to take a last look at her, she closed her eyes again and lay very still.

"Goodbye, Little Sister," he said tearfully, touching her forehead. He added, even more tearfully, "Forgive me," and then left hurriedly with Choyin.

The Reverend came to where she lay on the bed, rigid and white as a corpse. Her eyes were closed, but she could see the contortions of pure hatred on his face as she heard him whisper, into her ear: "Let's see how clever you are now, Miss. Don't think I'd forgotten. I've never had a peaceful night's sleep since that day. From tonight I will sleep well "

From the moment the girl was delivered to him in the White Light Temple for the demons to be expelled, once and for all, from her body, the Reverend had decided on a scheme of exquisite revenge and pleasure, which he elaborated by the minute, with self-congratulatory fervor If fifteen years ago, her body had convulsed to the ritual of the expulsion, this time, it would be broken to achieve a breaking of that spirit that had been allowed to go unchastised for too long. The proud girl would be brought whimpering to her knees. Revenge was the first and clearest part of the plan; the rest was less clear but no less invigorating. Unwanted by anyone, including her own spineless, whining brother who would sell her again for half the amount, she could be made a permanent helper and resident in the White Light Temple, with all the exciting possibilities that such an eventuality suggested. The Reverend smiled and allowed his imagination a delightful little frolic. He watched the girl, pale, motionless, Lying on the mattress on the floor, and liked his plan very much. She stirred, calling out deliriously, "Goddess! Goddess! Please come! Please help me! "

He thought, "Only I can help you, my girl." She went on calling with mounting anxiety, "Goddess! Goddess!" and he finally shouted, "Quiet!" before going out of the room and leaving her to her delirium.

His absence immediately caused the weight of heaviness to fall off her eyelids, her limbs, her whole body so that she sat up on the mattress and looked in wild-eyed terror around her.

"I heard you," said the goddess, but it was only her voice; she remained absent.

"Oh, help me, Goddess !" she cried. "Please come to me. They've got me again. Please help me."

"No, you come to me," said the goddess. "That's the only way you can save yourself. Come to me."

"Alright, Goddess."

She found, to her surprise, that she had the strength to stand up. She tottered a few steps, steadied herself and felt the strength return to her legs.

"I'm coming, Goddess," she said.

XXVII

"WHERE IS SHE?" cried Wu. His lips were white, with the running and the fear. Spitface was with him, gasping and panting.

"I don't know," shrugged the Reverend. "Choyin and her brother left her on the mattress here. She was sleeping." He added that the ceremony of expulsion was for the following morning.

"Where is she?"

The roar of frenzied anger took the Reverend by surprise.

He looked coldly at the young master Wu and said, "I don't know. She was delirious. She kept calling on some goddess."

XXVIII

HAN SAW SKY GOD by the shrine, harassing the goddess. "Hey!" she shouted at him. "You have no right to be here!" She had thought this was one spot on earth where his power could not intrude.

"I can be anywhere I like," laughed Sky God, and continued to torment the goddess, using one of his golden spears to prod her here or poke her there, so that she skipped about helplessly, like a much bullied child.

"Goddess, why are you allowing him to do this to you?" shouted Han. "Why aren't you fighting back?"

"I can't!" wailed the goddess. "It is not the right time of the month."

Once a month, she had dominance over the god, frightening him with the potent discharge from between her legs. Even goddesses benefited from the power of woman's biology.

"I can help you, Goddess!" cried Han, and she moved quickly towards Sky God. True enough, he began to show fear and cry out, "No, no, stay away from me! Please stay away!" For a woman's parturitive power was many times greater; the opened womb, discharging child and blood, frightened men into staying away.

"I will save you, Goddess!" said Han triumphantly, advancing upon Sky God who trembled like a coward. But it was too late, for the god, before he fled howling, picked up the goddess and hurled her into the pond. She fell with a big splash and the dark waters closed over her. "Don't be afraid, I will save you," said Han and she ran to the pond and waded into the water.

She walked deeper in and felt a tremendous chill grip her entire body, but still, she moved forward resolutely to save the goddess. She felt the water come up to her chin, her nose, her eyes, and she looked down and saw the goddess Lying at the bottom of the pond, looking up and smiling at her. It was a beautiful, whole face, with eyes and ears. The goddess said, "I will never lose them again."

"Goddess, I want to thank you for everything," murmured Han. "I've never really bothered to thank you properly."

"Go back," said the goddess. "Go back. He calls." For across the water, there came the call of her name.

"What about you?" said Han, and felt the water washing over her head and gently caressing her limbs.

"Let me be," said the goddess. "My work is finished. Yours is about to begin. Go back."

"I hear him," Han murmured, for her name came over the water, shrill with urgency. She felt powerless to turn back and move towards him, being pulled down by the water, gently but determinedly.

She thought, "I once dreamt of us at the bottom of the sea, with the warm sea—waves washing over us, safe and happy together, hiding from the rooster's cry," before she felt herself being pulled up.

She thought, "This is strange. I'm always falling down and being pulled up, always falling into darkness and being dragged up into the light."

She thought, "It's him. I can't see clearly, but I know it's him. He's come for me at last."

With a deep sigh, she surrendered herself to the sensation of being carried with enormous difficulty, like an unbearably heavy burden, and then laid on the ground.

"You are still alive."

Relief and terror choked him as he knelt and held her tightly in his arms, by the edge of the pond, relief to see her opening her eyes to look at him, terror at the certain prospect of an unspeakably brief period before those eyes would close again. He was frantic with the need to fill that period with all his love and longing that had stayed in shadows all those years, afraid to emerge to meet the bold radiance of hers. He wanted to tell her his love now, but spluttered horribly in his grief, pressing her to himself with savage intensity and in the end managing only to say, "Don't die. Please don't die."

The bold radiance refused to die.

"I gave you a son," she said smiling triumphantly. "I knew I could do it." He pressed the bracelet, with its cool piece of jade, against her cheek, for her eyes were no longer seeing.

"Yes, I saw and I came," he sobbed.

"A beautiful, healthy boy," she said.

He wanted to say, his heart ready to break, "Don't talk to me of sons! Don't talk to me of anyone or anything but ourselves, for we have so little time together," but it was a choking grief that allowed no words, so he kissed her forehead, her hair, her eyes, her lips.

He snarled, "Go away!" to the imbecile who came crying, wanting also to see and touch for the last time, for he was jealous of the time left and wanted all of it for himself. He and the imbecile who had come together to this sad spot would later weep together, but now nobody was allowed near.

From the darkening sky, there fell large drops of rain.

"A storm's coming," he said. "Let me carry you away."

"No," she said. "We'll meet the storm."

The rain began to fall on them. She smiled and he knew she was thinking of the many storms of their joy and love, their wet union in mud and laughter by the pond. He tightened his hold on her, as much to fend off the intrusion of Spitface who was throwing himself upon them in howling sorrow, as to conserve that last bit of life ebbing out of her. He held her for a long time afterwards and heard their love reverberate in the splendor of storm.

EPILOGUE

SOME YEARS AFTER the death of the bondmaid Han, stories began to spread off a goddess residing in the pond, who worked miracles. One woman claimed she was cured of a horrible skin disease by drinking the pond water. Another said that a drink made from the bark of a tree growing near the pond gave her a male child after five female children. A shrine was erected to the goddess who was called Goddess with Eyes and Ears, because she always saw and heard with compassion. Women came to pray and leave offerings of joss-sticks, flowers, food and money. When the crowds grew bigger, the Reverend from the White Light Temple appointed himself the shrine priest, conducting ceremonies and benefiting from the cash offerings. But suddenly and mysteriously, he disappeared. Some said he was struck by a strange disease and was ashamed to show himself, others that he had become mad and had to be confined to a little room in the temple. The Reverend was apparently not the only victim of the goddess who could be as vindictive as she was generous. Within a year, two children in the House of Wu died, a little three-year-old boy who was said to be the young master Wu's son by the bondmaid, and a little girl who was the child by his wife Li-Li, from the House of Chang. The boy had been suddenly taken ill

317

one day with a severe fever and died, and the girl who was the same age, also died shortly from the same mysterious fever. It was said that Li-Li almost went insane with grief. The patriarch died peacefully in his bed, attended by the matriarch who had grown silent with all the sorrows. The imbecile Spitface who had been with the family for almost the entire span of his life, one morning died in bed in his woodshed, apparently of natural causes. But by that time both the House of Wu and the House of Chang were ready to attribute every death to the malignant power of the goddess. It was seen at its most terrifying in the case of the young master Wu. People said it would have been better if he had died. His hair went white overnight and he became reclusive, keeping to himself and behaving like a madman, often stealing out at night to go to the pond. There was one other person who went to the pond. He was the bondmaid's oldest brother who felt great grief at her death and for a while, underwent a period of self-chastisement in a temple. He left his work as a procurer in the brothel known as the House of Flowers, and after some time, disappeared, some said, to a foreign country.

The Houses of Wu and Chang consulted fortune tellers, geomancers and temple mediums who told them that the curse of the bondmaid was a powerful one that would be borne by generations to come. It would only disappear when the waters of the pond dried up. For a while; the two houses considered the strategy of actually draining the pond. But the project was abandoned halfway because, it was said, the wrath of the goddess re-doubled and manifested itself in a string of misfortunes on the two families. They had no choice but to resort to the last escape from a curse, that is, to cross a large body of water and settle in another country, as curses do not travel over water. So the two families uprooted themselves from Singapore and sailed to settle in China where their ancestors had come from. Only the young master Wu remained behind. He insisted on taking care of the shrine of the goddess. He said she would come eventually for him and he would wait for her. The pond dried up after a time and the shrine fell into decay, but he remained where he was, living in a little ramshackle hut that he had built near the pond, unaware of the passing of the years, and believing, right to the end, that the goddess would one day come for him, and that they would be united, not in water and storm, but the splendor of fire.